I0699752

TWO SUMMERS AGO

ANDREA JORDAN

Cover design by nskvsky

Copy edited by Christie at Maple House Editing

ISBNs: 979-8-9915720-0-2 (hardcover), 979-8-9915720-1-9 (paperback)

Library of Congress Control Number: 2024918783

Published by Andrea Jordan

Printed in the United States of America

...

TWO SUMMERS AGO,
THE WORLD WENT TO SHIT

TWO SUMMERS AGO, I visited my brother who lived in fucking Oklahoma, of all places.

I initially wasn't going to go. I'd applied to several medical facilities over the course of a month, looking for a job that I'd hoped could occupy my mind and my time. Unfortunately, I was not given a position by any of the facilities. So, as a Hail Mary, I sent in one more application and put off my decision about either going to Oklahoma or staying in New York until I'd exhausted all my options. My bags were packed, but I still thought there was a small chance I'd get a job in the city.

I lived in the heart of New York City, and I know what you're thinking—it has a bad reputation; there are huge rats, rude people, and smelly subways—but I promise, it wasn't all that bad. I mean, I'm sure it is now, with all the dead people walking around, but to be fair, everywhere in the world is bad right now.

How the world was versus how it is now … God, I don't even know where to begin. I went from being an easy-going, motivated woman to becoming a ghost of who I once was. It was like my entire personality was altered—interests, connections, and communications were totally changed.

Of course, the last two years have been a chaotic, heartbreaking mess, but that's to be expected when you have a storm cloud over your head, following your every move.

That, and the help of an apocalypse.

Some days, I felt cursed.

Needless to say, I didn't get the job I waited for that summer. For my own sanity, I knew it was best to go see my brother rather than being unemployed, sulking on a couch for a couple of months until I went back to college for graduate school. So, I ventured off to Oklahoma to spend the hot months of June and July with my brother, who had been begging me to visit.

Here's how that went.

TWO
SUMMERS
AGO

THE WORLD WENT TO SHIT

1

DOOMED FROM THE GET-GO

WHEN I WOKE UP that morning, the first thing I did was check my email. I'd sent in one final application in hopes that I would be able to stay in New York before fall semester started.

I opened the mail app on my phone and nervously waited for my new emails to load. After a couple of seconds, one new email appeared at the top of the list. It was from Regional Medical, the facility I'd been anxiously waiting to hear from.

I glanced at the subject line, which read, "Thank you for your interest…" and immediately knew it was going to disappoint me. I swallowed the lump in my throat and quietly sighed, then I opened the rest of the message.

We regret to inform you that we have moved forward with the hiring process, and your application was not selected. Thank you for your interest in the position here at Regional Medical.

I archived the email and threw my phone back down onto the end of the bed. I knew that email meant I needed to get ready to head south, so that's what I was going to do.

I slung the blankets to the right side of my lonely, queen-sized bed, sat up on the edge, and looked over at a picture propped up on my vanity. It was me and my brother, Caleb, the night of my college graduation.

He had his arm around my shoulders, dressed in a button-down shirt and khakis with the biggest smile on his face. A smile that showcased his belief in me.

I smiled slightly at the memory of that night. Truth be told, I missed my brother. I missed him a lot, actually. Maybe seeing him would make Oklahoma bearable.

Eventually, I forced myself to get up. The wood floor was like ice on the bottoms of my feet, but I knew with summer approaching the temperature would be nice, despite my day already being ruined by one single email. I rubbed my eyes with my cold hands as I internally screamed at the failure of my bachelor's degree. But, as my brother would gracefully say, *life goes on*.

I exited the bedroom and headed to the kitchen to fix a bowl of cereal. I opened the stainless-steel refrigerator door and grabbed the milk that sat alone on the second shelf. I unscrewed the cap and, because I had trust issues, sniffed the milk. The stench made my nose crinkle in disgust. The fucking milk was spoiled.

I looked down at the expiration date, which showed a date well over a week ago. "Shit."

Disappointed, I poured the half-gallon of milk down the drain, followed by cold water from the faucet. Then, I turned and threw the jug into the trash can. Except I miscalculated my throw and the jug hit the rim. It ricocheted off the tile floor, making a thudding sound—once, twice. I sighed loudly as I walked back over to pick it up and aggressively put it into the trash can.

I'd already packed my car with enough luggage to last me the entire summer because subconsciously I lacked the ability to think anything would work out the way it should in my life. And look, I was right.

I was pretty much set for Oklahoma; I just needed to shower and get dressed. So, after the disappointing cereal encounter, I walked back upstairs to my bathroom. I undressed in the chilling breeze coming from the air vent positioned above my head. I don't know why I never adjusted the thermostat—I was always cold.

I shivered and turned the shower faucet on, giving it time to warm up before I stepped in. I was in there for what felt like forever, enduring the hot water running down my body.

Then I heard my phone ring from the bed. I assumed it was Caleb calling to check in on the status of my summer plans.

Sigh. He'd been calling and texting me every day, wondering if I'd found anything. I'd spent the entire week in my lonely apartment, staring blankly at the four walls of my bedroom, thinking about life and school and work. Caleb, while well-meaning, was just adding to the stress.

My apartment hadn't always been this lonely. I used to share the space with my ex-best friend, Taylor.

Taylor and I met during college where we were both studying nursing. She was a lousy friend most of the time and there was always a fifty-fifty chance that she'd bail anytime we made plans. I liked her company when I could get access to it, but it had to be convenient for her. If one of her other friends reached out, she'd conveniently have to cancel because of some crisis or emergency.

Somehow, despite her flaws, she eventually moved in with me so the two of us could save on expenses, and our relationship grew stronger for a little while.

I'd also had a long-term boyfriend, Reece, that lived in the area and worked as an attorney for a massive firm. He had a narcissistic personality and was self-absorbed beyond belief. I stayed with him because his finances were a nice perk in our otherwise toxic relationship, and I hated the thought of starting over with someone new.

He treated me badly for the duration of our four-year relationship, but my last straw was when I walked in on him and Taylor having theatrical, porn-like sex on the brand new linen sectional sofa she and I had bought together.

I stood in the entryway of the living room for a solid ten seconds before they even realized I was there. They were so loud that they hadn't even heard me walk in. Taylor was dressed in some role-play maid outfit with her blonde hair tied up in a ponytail. I hadn't known Reece was into that kind of thing, but then again, we rarely had sex at this point.

In a sense, I was actually relieved to witness the two of them, because it was the motivation I'd needed to finally remove them both from my life without feeling guilty.

Reece was a terrible boyfriend, but he was also a master manipulator. When I'd tried to break up with him previously, he'd cry like a little fucking girl. It made me feel like the bad guy even though I was the victim of his cheating and abusive behavior.

After that incident, I broke up with Reece and kicked Taylor out. Her name was never officially on the lease which made it much easier.

And that's when the apartment became quiet, lonely, and detrimental to my mental health. I used school to keep my mind occupied, but after graduating, I didn't have any more classes until the master's program started in August. Getting a job was my only other choice for keeping my summer busy and my mind clear, but since that hadn't worked out, going to Oklahoma was the best decision for me. I thrived off human interaction, and staying here would only damage the progress I'd made.

I finished my shower and pulled the curtain aside. The metal grommets clanked against the rod as I did so, exposing me to the cool air conditioning that filled my apartment. I stepped out onto the soft, black rug, grabbed a towel and patted myself dry. Then, wrapping it snuggly around my body, I walked into my bedroom.

I made my way over to the bed and picked up my phone to see who had called while I was in the shower. It was Caleb. I decided not to call him back to tell him the news. I wanted to show up and surprise him with my shortcomings.

Yay me.

After toweling off and getting dressed, I quickly blow dried my hair and threw it into a ponytail. I didn't feel the need to fix my hair or makeup because the drive from New York City to Pocola was nearly twenty hours long on the fastest route, and that would be draining enough. I had an Airbnb booked in Nashville to give myself a break from driving, since I figured trying to squeeze twenty hours of driving into one day would be nearly impossible.

Then I did some last-minute checks, making sure there was no laundry in the washing machine, no perishables in the cabinets and refrigerator, and that I had left nothing important behind.

I looked around, reminding myself of what I had to come back to. I was planning on returning in August right before classes started, so this apartment and I would be reunited before I even knew it.

It had taken me nearly a year and half to land this apartment after initially being placed on the waitlist, so I had decided to keep paying the rent for it over the summer. I didn't want to come back to the struggle of finding a place to live, so dishing out the expensive rent of a New York apartment for two months was a sacrifice I was willing to make.

I bet you're wondering how I was able to afford an apartment in New York as an unemployed graduate student. Well, depressingly enough, Caleb and I received a decent inheritance after our parents died in a car accident a couple of years ago. He and I didn't talk about it much, but it brought us closer together for sure. Caleb was my only sibling, and even with the huge distance between us, we called each other almost every day and visited when we had the chance. He had become my best friend, and I could talk to him about anything.

That said, not getting the job—or any job, for that matter—was embarrassing. Bruising, even. I couldn't bring myself to talk to him about that right now. I knew he'd be encouraging and supportive, but I couldn't help but feel like I'd failed our parents and disappointed him. That was a heavy weight on my shoulders.

Grabbing my bags, I gently pulled my apartment door shut and locked it behind me. I walked down the narrow hallway and exited out to the parking garage—a rarity in New York and another reason I didn't want to lose this apartment. Most people here walked, grabbed a taxi, or took the subway, but that wasn't how I liked to get from here to there. I preferred the comfort of my own vehicle in my own company, without worrying about the opinions of others.

I settled into the driver's seat of my car and programmed my Airbnb's address into my maps app. Then I began the long, boring car ride. I listened to the same few songs over and over, filled up with gas, and ate some almost out of date snacks from the convenience store.

The drive to Nashville was anticlimactic, but the night in Nashville, that's a whole other story…

2

ROAD TRIP WORTH REMEMBERING

AFTER ALMOST THIRTEEN HOURS, I finally made it to the house that I would be staying in. Caleb tried to call me probably fifteen times, but I didn't answer because I still wasn't in the mindset to talk about the situation yet.

The house sat in an area surrounded by other properties that seemed to be set up specifically for bachelorette parties. There were so many cars lined down the side of the street that I barely found a place to park. It required me to parallel park, and luckily no one was around to witness that struggle. I didn't even have to parallel park on my driver's test—*thank God.* I'd probably still be retaking the test if that were the case.

The owner of the Airbnb messaged me the code to unlock the door about an hour before I'd arrived. So I exited the car—leaving most of my luggage inside except for my shower supplies and a change of clothes—and walked up the steps of the porch to the front door. I found the keypad, and after typing in the code, the door unlocked.

It was such a cute house, decorated in multiple shades of pink, lots of records, and Dolly Parton memorabilia. There was no doubt that I was in Nashville—the heart of country music. It was a shame I'd only be here for the night.

After a quick tour I plopped onto the white couch, tilted my head back against the cushion, and closed my eyes. Nashville was on Central Standard Time, so it was an hour behind New York City. It was nine o'clock at night here, but to me, it was ten o'clock, and I was exhausted. Driving could be simultaneously a mind-numbing and draining experience.

As I lay on the couch, I heard a commotion of cheerful, screaming girls coming from outside. I walked to the front door and opened it so I could peek out. There were about ten girls trailing into the neighboring house with feather boas, lots of sparkles, thigh high boots, and booze.

As I began to close the door, one of the girls noticed me and signaled for me to wait. She was the only one wearing white, so I assumed that she was the bride amid a bachelorette party. The other girls went into the house, and the bride branched off toward me.

"Hey! Do you live here? I'm sorry if we're making too much noise. I'll tell the girls to lay off," she said apologetically.

I stepped out onto the porch. "Oh, no; I'm just here for the night. I wanted to see the fun of a bachelorette party," I admitted with a smile.

"Why don't you join us? We're going to a bar before we head out in the morning."

"I would, but I didn't pack anything except T-shirts and lounge clothes. I don't think that's bar attire," I said.

She lit up instantly. "Girl, grab your stuff and come over. We have just about everything you could imagine!"

I smiled and considered her offer. Why not? This could be what I needed to reconnect with myself and absorb the social interaction my body longed for.

"Okay. I'll be back in just a second," I said sweetly, stepping back inside to grab my purse and phone. I noticed a new missed call from Caleb.

Sigh.

The bride was waiting for me at the bottom of the steps when I came back outside. She gave me a friendly smile, and I followed behind her as we walked the short distance to the house next door. It was decorated similarly to mine, only bigger and even more over the top. There was a faux grass wall with a pink neon sign that said *Last Rodeo*. As expected, it was very chaotic, with luggage thrown all over the floor and girls everywhere.

"What's your name?" she asked over the many ongoing conversations around us.

"Sammi."

"I'm Blair," she said before looking around the room. She whistled flawlessly and the house grew quiet and attentive almost immediately. "This is Sammi. I invited her to go out with us tonight, so I need y'all to help her glam up and find something to wear!"

All the girls swarmed either to me or their suitcases to dig through what they had. I was honestly thrilled, because a night out would be the perfect remedy to take my mind off everything. Blair had made this such a welcoming experience that I thought I might have made a new friend for life.

A blonde girl grabbed my arm and pulled me toward a bedroom which had been set up as a hair and makeup room, with a ring light positioned in front of a chair. "Okay, Sammi, I'm going to fix your hair while the girls find you an outfit. Is that cool with you?"

"Absolutely, thank you!"

She motioned for me to sit down in the chair, then plugged in a curling iron and waited for it to heat up. She began brushing through my hair, then sprayed a quick spritz of heat protector onto it and began wrapping my hair around the barrel in perfect sections, one after the other. It didn't take long to put waves or curls in my hair because my hair was naturally wavy on a good day—though more often than not it became a mess of awkward frizz by the end of the day.

While she was working on my hair, another girl entered the room with a massive makeup bag. She sat it down on a table and studied my face for a second before selecting a foundation that matched my skin tone and getting to work. Luckily, she kept my makeup natural, which was what I was most comfortable with.

When they were done with my hair and makeup, one of them handed me a mirror to see the results. I studied myself in the reflection for the first time in a while. I had wavy, dark brown hair with a middle part, and my eyes were a mixture of brown and a golden color. I had faint freckles across my cheeks and a slightly upturned nose. I'd never been self-conscious, but I also didn't think I was anything special. The makeup was simple but made me feel pretty, and my hair looked soft, the frizz completely tamed. I gave the mirror back with a confident smile on my face.

As I stood up from the chair, the bride entered with a silver sequined mini skirt, a pale pink tube top, and a beige denim jacket with bedazzled tassels and fringe around the back and down the sleeves. She handed the pile of clothes to me. "Try these on and see what you think," she said sweetly.

I took the clothes from her hands, and the room cleared out as I undressed. Every girl here, including me, was about the same size, so I was sure the clothes would fit.

I put the outfit on and looked into the floor-length mirror that sat across the room. I turned to the side and straightened out the skirt. I noticed a new glowing confidence in myself just from the gestures of these girls and all they'd done for me in such a short period of time. I felt like this was where I was meant to be.

Blair knocked right before she entered the room, pausing in the doorway to assess my outfit. "Oh my God, you look stunning! What size shoes do you wear? I think I have the perfect boots."

"I'm usually an eight."

"BRB," she said excitedly as she hurried down the hallway. She returned seconds later with sparkly silver knee-high boots. I slipped them on, zipping them up.

"Perfect! Are you ready to have fun?" she asked, grinning from ear to ear.

I nodded and grabbed the purse and phone from my lap.

All the girls gathered together and headed out of the door, toward a hot pink limousine parked outside. We piled in and squished next to each other on the leather seat that stretched around the perimeter of the vehicle. After we were all inside, the driver took off toward the bar. Music was blaring at an almost unreasonable volume and we chaotically shouted over the music, repeating ourselves over and over again.

"Thanks for inviting me. I'm glad I got the chance to meet everyone," I said at what felt like a yell.

"No problem! We're going to have so much fun tonight," Blair said excitedly.

We all drank a glass of champagne en route to the bar, and soon enough we arrived, all jumping out of the limo. From the outside, the bar looked huge. I felt like it would take no time at all to lose all of the girls in the crowd. Our IDs were checked, and we were released into the bar.

The girls headed for the dance floor, and I followed behind them. They started dancing, some of them alone, together, or up against a random guy. I had never been bold enough to just approach a guy I didn't know and dance up against them, so I hovered awkwardly for a second. But as I twirled around, I saw a man watching me from across the room.

He was wearing a pair of brown boots with dark khaki pants and a blue denim button-down shirt that was unbuttoned just the right amount, revealing a hint of his chest. He had a beard, and his hair was dark brown, short, neatly groomed, and covered with a cowboy hat. He held a bottle of beer in his left hand as he and a group of friends stood right beside the dance floor.

Blair moved over to me and spoke into my ear as quietly as she could, considering the music in the background. "That guy wants you. Get him to dance with you," she said encouragingly, nodding her head toward the man I'd been drooling over.

"I don't know…" I said nervously.

"He's been looking at you since you walked in the door. There's no way he's going to have a problem with you dancing up against him."

I blushed and looked back over at him. He took a casual sip of his beer, his eyes piercing through me.

"Good luck," she said before walking back to a group of her friends.

I took a deep breath before mustering up the courage to approach him in front of his friends. It was all so unlike me.

"Hi," I said as I reached him, trying to come off as confident.

He smirked. "Hey."

"Why aren't you dancing?" I asked flirtatiously.

"I was waiting on you to ask me," he said, looking at me up and down.

He was with a couple of his friends that looked a little rough around the edges. One of them was heavier with a cowboy hat that covered his dark hair. He had a beard that was a little longer than the man I was about to dance with. The other friend was skinny, tall, bald, and smelt like cigarettes. They seemed nice, but I was only interested in their hot friend. They were giving him looks of approval as if they'd been talking about this already.

"Well, are you coming?" I asked, reaching my hand out to him.

He took a last sip of his beer and handed it to one of his friends, then grabbed my hand. We squeezed our way through the crowd of people, and just as we found a spot on the dance floor, a voice began talking over the music.

"Okay everybody, if you're from Nashville you already know what time it is. If this is your first time at the Honky Tonk Tavern, you're in for a treat! Get out on that dance floor and get ready to do some line dancing," they said enthusiastically.

I panicked, my eyes widening for a brief second. I was far from a country girl. I'd been living in the city for a few years, and I had definitely never line danced before. I had just got the confidence to ask him to dance, and then I was going to embarrass myself by not actually knowing how to! What had I gotten myself into?

He saw the look on my face and chuckled to himself. "You don't know how to line dance do you?"

"Not at all," I said, trying to seem playful but probably coming off as anxious. A swarm of people were beginning to line up in rows across the dance floor.

"Come on, I'll show you. Just follow my lead," he said, grabbing my hand and pulling me toward the very back row.

They started playing a Luke Bryan song, and he began showing me some steps at a slower pace than the people in front of us. "Step out with your right foot, then step behind your right leg with your left foot."

He continued going through the steps as I watched and mimicked his moves as closely as I could. I stumbled a few times, which caused him to laugh, but by the end of the song I pretty much had it down pat. We exchanged laughter and smiles just about the entire time we were dancing—it was invigorating.

Soon the song finished and the line dancing broke up. I was trying to catch my breath, and he and I walked to the edge of the dance floor to talk.

"You're not from around here, are you?"

"I'm from New York. I'm just passing through on my way to Oklahoma to see my brother for the summer," I said.

"I never thought I'd be teaching a city girl how to line dance," he said with a chuckle.

"I never thought I'd be line dancing with a country boy," I retorted, smiling.

He grabbed my waist and pulled me closer to him. I could feel my heartbeat getting harder and faster as he looked down at me with his big blue eyes. He smiled at me while brushing my hair behind my ear. "You're really beautiful, you know?"

"You're really handsome," I said back, our faces only inches apart.

"It's too bad you're not from Nashville."

"Why?" I asked.

"I think I could fall in love with you pretty fast," he admitted.

I looked at him with a hint of confusion, unsure if it was just a line.

"I've only known you for a little while, but dancing with you was the most fun I've had in a long time. It was real and raw, and I have never felt that way with anyone down here. I come to this bar every weekend, and I've never seen a girl that caught my eye the way you did tonight."

I blushed. "Thank you. I've had a lot of fun tonight too. I wish I wasn't leaving in the morning."

"I guess that means we just need to make this night as memorable as possible," he said seductively. He leaned over and cupped my face, kissing me gently.

A million butterflies took flight in my stomach and I returned the kiss with desire—a desire I'd never felt before. We began kissing more passionately for a minute before I pulled back, looking into his eyes. I was a little startled to realize we were still standing in the middle of the bar.

"So, I think I should probably tell you my name now," he said with a cocky grin on his face.

"Why's that?" I asked flirtatiously.

"Because you're going to be calling it out in a few minutes."

I raised my eyebrows in shock and couldn't help but bark out a laugh at his audacity. I grabbed his arm and pulled him behind me as we headed toward the back bathroom. It was dimly lit throughout the inside of the building, and it was open like a big barn, allowing an easy escape to somewhere private with this beautiful man. I pushed through the bathroom door, pleased to find it empty, then turned the lock.

He pushed me up against the wall, placing his right palm flat against the wallpaper behind me. His warm breath hugged my neck while he pulled the jacket off me. He placed it carefully on the countertop before he kissed from my neck to right above my breasts.

I trembled, closing my eyes and breathing heavily. I craved his lips on mine.

He rubbed his palms against my thighs until his hands were underneath my skirt, teasing me while he looked into my eyes. Before I knew it, he was taking my skirt and everything else off me.

My heart was pounding so hard from the excitement and thrill I felt in his company. I wanted this man so bad I was aching—and I got him.

It was *so* worth it.

After I caught my breath and put my clothes back on, he looked over at me, smiling as he said, "Bailey."

"It's a little late for that," I replied, giggling.

He smirked. "Sorry, I got sidetracked."

"I'm Sammi," I said as I turned to the mirror and tried to fix my hair with my fingers. I knew it would be apparent to everyone in the bar that I'd just had sloppy bathroom sex, but I honestly didn't care. I was on cloud nine.

I continued to mess with my hair, but it was not budging. Bailey laughed again as he watched me struggle. He took off his cowboy hat and sat it on my head, covering up the bumps and tangles that resulted from our exhilarating time in this bathroom.

He stood behind me as I looked in the mirror and gave me a soft look that seemed like it was filled with love. I knew it couldn't be—we'd just met, after all—but if you'd seen that look, you'd say the same.

I wished this night would never end.

He leaned in to kiss me once more before we headed back over to the door to unlock it. As we walked out, there were a couple of girls waiting outside who gave us scandalous looks as we giggled and hurried by them like school children.

Bailey took my hand and guided me through the bar toward the door we had entered through. From here, the sound of the music was dampened and we could feel the relief of the cooler air from outside floating in.

"So Sammi, do you think you might come back to Nashville anytime soon?"

"I think I could fit that into my summer schedule," I said, smiling.

"You know, we could make this work, me and you," he said, hope in his expression.

"You really think so?" I asked.

"Yeah. I mean, could you ever give up city life?"

I considered his question. "It's not completely out of the question," I said eventually.

"You probably think I'm crazy," he scoffed, looking away.

"No, I don't."

"I don't normally meet girls at the bar, and I definitely don't hook up with them in the bathroom," he joked. "But there's something intoxicating about you. Just looking at you, touching you, smelling you … it does something to me."

I blushed, locking eyes with him once more before gazing around the bar again. It was still as lively as it had been when we first arrived. Just watching the crowd dancing and laughing made me feel tired. I couldn't stop myself from yawning, and Bailey looked like he knew I was exhausted.

"Can I give you a ride home?" he offered.

I looked back at Blair and the other girls who were still dancing and drinking. I knew they wouldn't be leaving anytime soon, so I took him up on his offer.

He grabbed my hand and guided me out to the parking lot. He took us over to a white Toyota Tacoma and opened the passenger-side door for me.

Chivalry is not dead, I thought as he held my hand to make sure I got in okay. I buckled in as he went around to the driver's side.

When he got in, he started texting on his phone. "I'm just letting my friends know that I'm leaving," he explained. After he sent the text, he handed me his phone, which had the "new contact" screen pulled up, and gave me a sweet grin. "Do you think I could have your number?"

I smiled as I typed my number in and sent myself a text from his phone. I handed it back to him, and he cranked the truck up.

I looked at my phone for the first time since I'd gotten to the bar, and I had a text message from Caleb.

Caleb: *Hey, little sis. Is everything okay? I haven't heard back from you, and I'm starting to worry. Please call me.*

"Everything okay?" Bailey asked after seeing my expression change.

"Yeah, my brother's just been calling and texting all day. I didn't exactly tell him I was coming to see him."

"Why not?" he asked as we pulled out onto the road. The highway was very quiet this late into the night. We occasionally passed another car, but it almost felt like we were alone out here.

I paused, unsure how much I wanted to share about my disaster of a life.

"I know we just met, but you know you can tell me anything right?" he said after a moment.

I half-smiled. "I don't want to scare you away before you get the chance to fall in love with me."

"That's unlikely, but I understand," he said sweetly.

He didn't press the issue. I just gave him directions to the house, and we sat in silence for the remainder of the ride.

After a few minutes, we arrived at my Airbnb. There wasn't a free parking spot, so Bailey parked in the center of the road as we said our goodbyes.

"I wish you didn't have to leave tomorrow," he said calmly.

I leaned over to kiss him. "I'll call you and text you every day. I promise. We'll meet up again soon," I said an inch from his lips.

I took off his cowboy hat, but he refused to take it. "Keep it. That way you'll always remember the guy you hooked up with in the bathroom in Nashville."

I playfully hit his shoulder and we shared a laugh.

"It was pretty great, wasn't it?" I teased.

"Yeah, it was," he said, biting his lip.

"Goodnight, Bailey," I said as I stepped out of the car.

"Goodnight, Sammi."

I smiled like an idiot as I walked up to the front door, his hat in my hand. I got goosebumps from the cool night breeze of the city.

I went to type in the code to the door, but once my fingers pressed the first number, the door eased open. I froze for a second, thinking back to when I left with Blair. I closed the door, but I didn't remember locking it.

I turned back to see if Bailey was still parked in the street, but he had already started driving back toward town. I could see his taillights in the distance.

I set the cowboy hat on top of my head to free my hands, unzipped my purse, and quietly pulled out my gun from the holster it had been sitting in. I took gentle steps, but my boots didn't allow me to be totally inconspicuous.

I flipped on the light switch to the entryway and walked into the kitchen, my gun pointed straight ahead. As I rounded the cabinets on the left side of the kitchen, I saw the figure of a man turning toward me.

3

ADRENALINE RUSHED

"**Jesus Christ, Caleb**; I could've fucking killed you!" I said frantically.

"Damn, Sammi, put the gun down! It's just me," he said, laughing anxiously, his eyes wide and hands raised in defense. "Nice hat."

I lowered the gun and stuck it back down into the holster that I kept in my purse, then took off the hat and placed it on the counter. "You didn't think you should let me know you were here before I came home at one o'clock in the morning to an unlocked Airbnb?" I exclaimed, my hands flailing in frustration.

"You weren't responding to my calls or texts; what was I supposed to do, Sammi? You could've been buried in the woods somewhere," he said, only half-joking.

I rolled my eyes and he walked over, hugging me tightly.

"I swear to God, I'm going to stop sharing my location with you," I mumbled into his shoulder.

"I'm glad to know you can take care of yourself." Then, more softly, "I just worry about my baby sister."

Once he let go, I sat down at the kitchen island. The metal barstool was like ice beneath my bare legs. I sighed, placing my face into my hands.

"What's wrong? Where did you go tonight?" he asked, clearly curious about the way I was dressed—especially since I wouldn't usually be caught dead in sparkles.

Me and Caleb were very close, so I felt comfortable telling him just about everything going on in my life. We'd been through so much together. Even after he moved to Oklahoma, he called me every single day. We still annoyed the hell out of each other, but we were all we had.

I paused for a second, then explained, "It's a long story, but the house next door was having a bachelorette party. They invited me to go out with them, so we all went to a bar downtown."

"Did you have fun? Did you meet anyone?" he asked, glancing at the hat.

I hesitated, then couldn't help but smile like an idiot. "I met this guy named Bailey. He taught me how to line dance, we talked … we just had so much fun," I said, looking off in a daze as I recalled tonight's events.

"Is that where you got the hat?"

"Yes," I admitted, blushing.

"Is that all that happened? You're smiling like you married the guy. You didn't elope, did you?" he asked jokingly.

"No, but there might have been a brief session of scandalous bathroom sex," I said with a giggle.

Just as I said this, the front door shut again and I turned around in a panic to see who had overheard my embarrassing confession. To my horror, it was Jackson, Caleb's best friend.

"Scandalous bathroom sex, huh?" Jackson teased as he walked into the kitchen, pausing behind my stool.

"Oh my God, you didn't tell me you brought Jackson!" I said, my cheeks flushing.

Caleb shrugged, clearly finding the situation humorous. "You know we do everything together." He and Caleb had first met when they were assigned to the same company for their internship during college, and they'd practically been joined at the hip ever since.

"Ugh," I groaned.

I could feel my cheeks burning. I hadn't seen Jackson since last Christmas, when Caleb hosted a party with all of our friends. Jackson had brought his long-term girlfriend, Sophie, as his date, and I'd brought Reece because we were still together at that point. Jackson hated Reece, so much so that it made me wonder if it was due to a sense of protection, or if he wanted me to finally become available for him.

There had always been this weird tension between us ever since we first met when he came with Caleb to my high school graduation party. I was never sure if it was a brotherly kind of love or something more. There were definitely moments we'd shared that pointed toward something more, but he had never made his feelings clear. He was terrible at that—but then again, so was I.

Plus, Caleb had always told me to stay away from his friends in high school, and I assumed that still applied, even though we were older now.

I'd always hated Sophie because she made everything about her, and she treated Jackson so badly. He'd show up with daisies, and she'd criticize them for not being roses. He'd buy her a necklace, and she'd cry that she wanted earrings. I never understood why he kept tolerating her. He was hardworking, kind, handsome, and reliable. She was just … not. She was the typical mean girl from every high school movie.

Jackson and I had never kissed or anything, but we flirted almost every time we saw each other. It was usually innocent and playful compliments or dirty jokes, but he'd always use Sophie as an excuse to keep the conversation from progressing to something he'd feel guilty about later. Even with their on and off relationship, he just couldn't shake Sophie long enough to see me as anything more than a friend, so I didn't try to pursue anything with him. I wanted to respect that he was in a relationship, but damn, I wish it was with someone who deserved his loyalty.

Even though Jackson and I had never been anything more than occasional flirty friends, I still felt guilty or weird with him hearing about my boyfriends or hookups. It almost felt like I was cheating on him, even though we weren't even remotely together.

I was humiliated that he had walked in on my conversation about the sex I'd had in the bar. I felt icky, almost as if I were damaged goods.

I stood up from the stool and headed toward the bedroom to hide from the two of them. I laid down on the bed, still clothed in the itchy sequins. The fabric smelled of Bailey's cologne, and the scent gave me a sense of comfort and safety. Knowing I would still have his hat after removing the other reminders of tonight gave me a feeling of peace I didn't know I needed. It was like a prize I'd won at the fair—so special and exciting.

I rolled over onto my right side, facing the doorway as my phone vibrated on the nightstand.

Bailey was calling me.

My face lit up like a Christmas tree, and I picked up my phone, pressing the green circle on the screen to answer it. "Hello?"

"Hey, it's Bailey," he said sweetly.

"Who?" I teased.

"The guy that taught you how to line dance and then rocked your world in the bathroom," he responded, mock-offended.

I giggled. Thank God he couldn't see me right now because I was blushing so bad; I could feel it. "Oh, *that* Bailey."

"I know it's late and you're exhausted, but I have a few minutes before I get home. I just wanted to get to know a little bit more about you," he said.

"Okay, what do you want to know?"

"How old are you?"

"I'm twenty-six. How about you?" I asked curiously.

"I'm twenty-seven."

"Perfect," I said. He laughed, and I imagined feeling his breath on my neck. I closed my eyes and refocused. "So, you live in Nashville?"

"Yes, I have a construction company down here. That's where my buddies and I spend most of our time," he said in his adorable country accent.

"That's so cool," I replied enthusiastically.

"It has its perks." He paused. "So, what do you do?"

"Well, I just graduated nursing school, but I couldn't seem to get hired anywhere for the summer," I admitted. "That's why I decided to visit my brother in Oklahoma."

"They're missing out," he said, and I smiled silently on the other end of the phone. "You know … I bet there are plenty of nursing jobs around Nashville. There's a hospital right down the road from my company," he said persuasively.

"That's tempting," I replied, a small smile playing on my face.

"Well, I'm pulling into my garage, and I know you've had a long night. I'll text you when I wake up in the morning, okay?"

"Sounds good. Goodnight, Bailey," I said sweetly.

"Goodnight, beautiful."

I hung up the phone and let out a deep breath, then sat up and moved to the edge of the bed. I stared down at the bright screen of my phone. Behind my apps was a picture of Caleb and Jackson with their arms around me as we all smiled at the camera. It was taken at a Christmas party before my parents died.

Despite everything with Bailey, I couldn't help but think about Jackson. Part of me hoped he was jealous over what he overheard in the kitchen, but maybe I was just manifesting a connection between us that only existed in my head. If Jackson wanted me, wouldn't he have said something sooner? He'd had so many opportunities in the past.

I locked my phone and sat it down on the bed beside me. I inhaled deeply before unzipping the boots, kicking them onto the floor before standing up. I had my back to the door as I slowly began undressing. I'd left the bedroom lights off after coming to lie down, so it was dark in the room, but the door was slightly cracked, which allowed a little light to filter in from the hall.

Suddenly the bedroom eased open behind me as more light from the hallway crept in.

"Sammi?" Jackson whispered.

On instinct, I turned to face him, almost completely naked.

"What?" I asked as he hesitated in the doorway.

After a few moments of contemplation, he moved into the room and shut the door behind him, taking careful steps over to me. I could feel the presence of his body now only inches away from me. I felt vulnerable, but safe at the same time.

He sighed deeply, clearly struggling to fight off his temptations. I don't think he expected me to be undressed when he came to my room, but he wasn't exactly trying to hide the body language that showcased his lustful feelings. His eyes wandered from my legs up to my eyes before they locked with mine, intense desire obvious in both of our gazes.

"What do you want, Jackson?" I whispered seductively.

You don't know me that well yet, but I was unhinged. I was in a reckless state of mind during this time, so most of the decisions I made were the wrong ones. This could've been one of them; it came so close. It was at my freaking fingertips.

I moved closer, my gaze fixed to his lips. They were right there. But then, he pulled away.

"I-I'm sorry. I shouldn't do this with you," he said quietly before stepping back and looking away. He quickly slipped out of the room, leaving me to try and make sense of the encounter.

What just happened?

I was out of breath from the adrenaline and desire I'd been bottling up whenever I thought about what it would feel like to be with him. My heart palpitated nervously as I wondered what made him resist. Every insecurity flooded my mind while I stood frozen like a statue from humiliation. Maybe I had been right earlier—I was damaged goods.

Suddenly, I was overwhelmed with this feeling of being exposed and guilty. I couldn't bear the cool air of the room anymore, so I walked over to grab a tee and a pair of pajama pants from one of my bags. I felt icky being naked, as if I'd done something horrible. Had I?

I lay down on top of the bed, staring up at the ceiling. At this point, I wasn't sure if I wanted Jackson or Bailey. I'd seemingly been rejected by Jackson, but that almost made me want him more. Then again, I got butterflies whenever I thought about my time with Bailey.

I just knew that I was off my medicine, and I'd be starting a shit show soon if I didn't get back on it. It was bound to happen. I felt it coming.

Several minutes passed before a knock came at my door.

"Hey, the girl from next door is here," Caleb said softly as he eased into my room.

I stood up from the bed and gathered the clothing scattered on the floor. I knew I was carrying a look of defeat, but I didn't want Caleb to think something was wrong, so I tried to give him a hint of a smile as I walked over to him, my arms full of items to return to Blair. He looked at me suspiciously but didn't question my demeanor.

"Would you mind giving her this for me? Tell her I had an amazing time, and I am so grateful she brought me along," I said.

"Of course," he replied, taking the handful of clothing and finding his way back to the front door.

I shut the door gently behind him before dragging myself back to my bed. I tried falling asleep, tossing and turning and finally burying myself under the covers instead of on top of them. I turned to one side, then the other, and then to my back, but I couldn't sleep. I forced my eyes closed, but it felt like they would inevitably open back up, like stage curtains obscuring an actress trying to hide from flying tomatoes. I was a prisoner to this bed.

I thought about taking a shower, but I didn't want to draw attention to myself at this time of day. It was almost sunrise, which was well past the time I should've been asleep.

I finally got up from the bed, planning to head to the kitchen to pour myself a glass of water. Caleb was sleeping on the couch in the living room, so I assumed Jackson was given the spare bedroom.

Caleb and Jackson had always had such a close, meaningful friendship. They were both playful yet protective of each other. I admired them both so much. They'd always been so good to me. I was willing to bet that they'd fought over who was going to sleep on the couch because they were just those kinds of guys. They put others' comfort and wants above their own. Always.

Before going into the kitchen, I tiptoed to the spare bedroom and peeped inside to see if Jackson was asleep. He wasn't. I saw the light from his phone screen shining on his face as he looked over to see me standing in his doorway.

I turned to head back to my room, but he whispered out for me. "Sammi, wait. Come back."

I closed my eyes, wincing at the thought of him witnessing my hopeless gaze into his room. I bit my lip and slowly walked into the bedroom. He was tucked away under the comforter, his head propped up on a pillow. He locked his phone and used his arm to hold his head up as he watched me intently.

"I'm sorry; I couldn't sleep," I said apologetically.

"Me either," he said softly.

I folded my arms across my chest and leaned against the door frame. My heart felt heavy. There were a multitude of emotions rushing through my body. For a second, I'd forgotten everything about tonight, even Bailey, who'd been so good to me. I wanted nothing more than to lie down beside Jackson and feel his warm hands holding me. I knew that's where I would feel safest, at ease.

I stared at him from across the room for a few seconds before he spoke.

"I'm sorry about earlier," he said quietly.

"It's okay," I responded, frowning.

There was silence again.

"I just felt like, in that moment, you wanted me," I admitted.

"I-I don't know. You were right there…"

I looked down at the floor, embarrassed by how desperate I was for his attention. I wanted to tell him how I felt, and really I just wanted to be wrapped up in his arms, but I couldn't find the words to say to him.

"I'm having a hard time falling asleep. Do you think I could sleep in here with you tonight?" I asked.

He paused, hesitant. I knew what he was about to say, and I immediately regretted coming to his room at all.

I'd heard that pause before. It was late last summer at one of Caleb's friend's houses. Everyone had been drinking and having a good time, but as the sun set and the warm air grew cooler, most of the crowd dispersed for the night. I stayed outside, alone in the swimming pool while Caleb helped his friend clean up inside.

I'd been sitting on an inner tube when Jackson walked outside. He saw me in the pool and decided to run and cannonball off the diving board right beside where I was floating. His big splash knocked me off the inner tube and into the water. He came up out of the water, flipped his wet hair back, and swam over to me, grabbing me by the waist while we bobbed in the water.

"Jackson, you know I hate getting my hair wet," I said, laughing as I locked eyes with him.

"What are you going to do about it?" he teased, biting his bottom lip.

I went in for a kiss, but he stopped me and admitted that he and Sophie were back together after another breakup.

That night in the pool, I too had been in a relationship with my terrible significant other. The only difference between Jackson and I was that I wasn't afraid to be as horrible as the person I was with. I was ready; Jackson just didn't have the heart to do that to someone. I admired it, but I also despised it.

So, I recognized Jackson's infamous pause as I stood in the doorway, right before he confirmed my suspicion. "Me and Sophie are back together. I should've never come into your room in the first place. I—"

I didn't wait for him to finish. I darted out of his room and back to mine. I was so embarrassed. I'd just assumed his actions earlier were because he was single or wanted to pursue something with me. I felt like such an idiot.

Damn Jackson and his faithfulness to Sophie.

I laid back down in my own bed and tried to erase the incidents with Jackson from my mind. I reminded myself of the great time I'd had at the bar with Bailey. I smiled at the memory of us dancing, laughing, and having a fun night. I just wasn't sure if I could make it work with the distance, even though I wanted to.

My thoughts were so conflicted. Did I want Bailey or Jackson or no one? I was a mess. I had issues, and they would become clear sooner or later.

I started to cry at the chaos roaming freely in my mind. I finally fell asleep under the warmth of more accompanying tears.

~

When morning came, we all took showers, got dressed, and prepared to head to Oklahoma. Caleb was loading his and Jackson's belongings into the back of Jackson's black Jeep that he had moved closer to the house now that some of the cars had cleared out. It was so packed along the street last night that they'd had to park toward the end of the road. I lamented that if I had seen Jackson's Jeep, I could've mentally prepared for their surprise visit.

My eyes were red and puffy—evidence of me crying last night. I hoped it wasn't obvious, but I knew it was.

I walked into the kitchen for a glass of water and found Jackson leaning up against the counter, sipping on a mug of coffee. I turned around quickly, walking toward the front door to avoid him.

"Sammi, are you okay?" he asked, clanking the mug down on the granite countertop.

I paused and faced him, still feeling a bit embarrassed. "No," I said emptily, shaking my head. I dismissed myself and headed out of the door. He remained inside until he finished his coffee.

Once the cars were finally loaded, I sat in the driver's seat of my car as Jackson and Caleb piled into the Jeep. I was prepared for a lonely car ride while I trailed behind them—only Bailey's cowboy hat accompanying me in the passenger seat.

Bailey had sent me a good morning text message, but I hadn't responded because I wasn't in the mood to continue a conversation knowing I'd be driving. So I played music from my *Sad Song* playlist for the entire trip.

About seven and a half hours later, we arrived at Caleb's house.

Once we had parked, I looked down at my phone for the first time in a couple of hours, and Reece had texted me, begging for my love yet again. He said he had really messed up and wanted a second chance.

More like eighty-second, I thought, chuckling to myself. The guy was a weasel. I literally wouldn't piss on him if he was on fire.

I unbuckled my seatbelt and locked my phone before stepping out onto the driveway. I looked around. There were only a few houses on this road, all a reasonable distance away. This was a quiet, calm location for cleansing the mind and relaxing, which was exactly what I needed.

Caleb and Jackson exited the Jeep, walking toward me with heavy steps on the graveled drive.

"Nothing like New York City," Caleb said proudly.

I smiled half-heartedly. I really did miss the city already. New York had been my home for the past few years, while Oklahoma had become Caleb's.

Caleb and I went in two completely different directions when we graduated high school. He was three years older than me, so he left first and moved down here to follow his dreams, I guess. At least that's what he told me over the phone when I'd asked him what the hell was in Oklahoma. Our parents were alive when he graduated high school, and they supported him one hundred percent throughout his journey to college and finding himself. I was never sure what his dreams entailed or what Oklahoma had to do with it, but he was happy.

He'd originally moved to Oklahoma for college with no plans of making it permanent. But the longer he stayed and after meeting Jackson, he decided this was where he wanted to settle down and call home, especially after our parents died, when he found it too hard to come back home to visit.

Schoharie, New York had been home for most of our lives. I didn't stray far when I went off to college or when I eventually found an apartment. I remained hopeful that one day Caleb would move back to the city, but just standing outside his house in this moment, hearing the birds and the breeze, made me begin to understand what there was to love about Oklahoma.

Caleb walked through the open garage doorway toward the side door and unlocked it, swinging it open wide. He tucked the keys down into his pocket and prepared to unload the luggage.

I popped the trunk of my car and had begun unloading the suitcases when Jackson hurried over. "I got it," he said, taking one from my hands.

I let go and headed toward the inside of the house, ignoring unnecessary conversation and eye contact.

Caleb looked over at both of us in question as I brushed past him. They eventually followed behind me with my belongings, setting things down in various spots.

"The guest room is to the left, right down that hallway," Caleb said warmly, heading back to grab the last items from the car.

I slowly walked in the direction of my room, observing the pictures he had hanging on the walls. One of the pictures was of Caleb holding his college acceptance letter before he moved out. It seemed like just yesterday I was begging him not to go.

He'd lived in Oklahoma for about eleven years now. He stayed in his college dorm originally before moving into an apartment, then to a few rental homes until he purchased this property about a year ago. This was my first time seeing the new house in person.

I peeped into my room and scanned through the rest of the house, admiring each detail. I was very impressed. The house sat on a large plot of land with a big front porch that had an immaculate view of the mountains and land surrounding it. The house itself was well organized and squeaky clean; it looked almost as if no one lived here.

The guest room I was staying in was painted a shade of blue so light it was almost white. The bed was neatly made with lots of space for me to unload my luggage. I was amazed with the presentation of this house. I could tell he took pride in his hard work that made this home possible.

I didn't bother unpacking; I just headed into the living room where I joined them on the big sectional sofa. I sat in the middle section where it curved. Caleb was at the end to my left, and Jackson was a cushion down on my right. We all sat in silence, preoccupied with our phones.

"Have you heard from Reece lately?" my brother asked, probably already knowing the answer.

"Um, well, he actually texted me a few hours ago expressing his undying love for me," I said sarcastically, propping my feet up on the ottoman in front of the sofa.

"Would you ever get back together with him?" Jackson asked.

"No," I said, irritably.

My brother peered over at Jackson and I, clearly suspecting that something was going on between the two of us.

"Okay, what's up with you guys? Y'all have been acting weird since we left Nashville," he said sternly.

I remained silent, but Jackson said, "She's jealous."

"Am not!" I scoffed and stood up in protest as Caleb raised an eyebrow. "When are you going home, Jackson?" I asked, annoyed.

"Oh, this is home; I live here," he said playfully.

I covered my face with my hands and groaned. Then I stormed down the hallway, shouting, "You're the one who's jealous!" behind me.

I went to my room and plopped onto the queen-sized bed, staring up at the ceiling, watching the blades of the fan spin around, over and over again. I held my phone out in front of me as I thought about responding to Reece with a hateful message, but I didn't. I just ignored him. Instead, I navigated to the Instagram app and typed in Jackson's username. I wanted to see if he'd posted with Sophie. Were they serious this time?

I scrolled down his feed and saw only a handful of pictures featuring him with Sophie. Most of his photos were of adventures like hiking or kayaking, but none of them ever included her. That's why I was always so surprised they would get back together all the time. They barely had anything in common.

He'd always told me that she was the one who initiated the breakups because she "needed time to think," but even I knew that was code for "I want to sleep with someone else without feeling guilty about it."

Not to mention, she was always rude to me. I never understood her beef directed at me; I hardly even talked to the girl! I think in the few years I had known of Sophie we'd maybe said four sentences to each other. Admittedly, one of those sentences was me telling her that she was a bitch because she told Jackson he didn't make enough money to support her, and that some guy named Grant made twice as much as him. I don't know how I didn't punch her in the face that day, but if I saw her again, I might.

Now I was in Oklahoma: home of the bitch.

4

STRANGER THINGS HAVEN'T HAPPENED

FOR A COUPLE OF weeks everything was fine and dandy at my brother's house, even with Jackson here with us. Jackson and I didn't really talk unless we had to, and I avoided him like the plague most of the time to save myself from any more embarrassment. We'd hit a wall that night, and I thought about it a lot more than I should've. But it was difficult for me, even now some time had passed.

I didn't think he'd said anything to Caleb, and I didn't feel that I could talk to my brother about it because if it affected their friendship in any way, I would feel terrible. There was a reason he never wanted me to date his friends when we were in school, and that's because I ruined everything I touched. I really hoped I hadn't ruined this for him too.

However Caleb knew something was up; he always did. He hadn't said anything because Jackson was doing a great job of acting perfectly normal, as if nothing had transpired between us. I'm sure to Caleb it just looked like I was grumpy because I was homesick or something. It looked one sided for sure.

I'd become very close with the four walls of my bedroom, and to be honest, I was going stir crazy. I craved human interaction, but I wasn't going to get that here unless I accepted that Jackson would be a part of it.

Distancing myself over the last couple of weeks had taken a toll on me. I went through a patch of lows, but now I was feeling a high creeping up on me. I had some self-confidence for the first time in a while, and I was determined to make the most of it. So tonight I decided I was going to go out. I was tired of being cooped up in this house, and I wanted to go do something … maybe someone.

Feeling reckless was a trend when I was on a high. I think the doctor called it a "manic episode," but that was a bit dramatic, if you ask me.

These episodes typically lasted about four days, but half of the time I couldn't tell anything was different. The manic episodes were like a switch had flipped in my personality, mood, and decisions. It wasn't a gradual difference in who I was; it was very evident to everyone except me. I was just blind to it because that's how the disorder typically affected me. After the episodes were over though, guilt would hit me like a freight train—always.

Everyone could tell something was going on when I was off my medication, but I was often unaware of the choices I was making until it was too late. At this point, I'd been on this euphoric high for about three days already, so I wanted to keep up the feeling and do something that'd be problematic and exciting. It was kind of like day-drinking to keep the buzz or prolong the effects of a lasting hangover. It was exhilarating to act on those temptations and feelings.

I began to get ready to go out. I wore my hair down and put on light makeup. Then I threw on a short, black mini dress with a pair of feathery heels. My plan was to go to a nightclub in the city that I had Googled a few hours earlier.

I looked into the full-length mirror in the corner of the room, straightening the dress out with my hands. I felt very scandalous and sexy in this outfit, and my confidence was sky high.

I snatched my keys from the dresser and headed out of my room. My heels clacked loudly on the tile floor as I approached the island in the kitchen. Caleb and Jackson were sitting on the couch, and they both turned around to see what I was doing. I ignored them, smiling from ear to ear as I grabbed my purse and headed outside to my car.

This was enough to catch the attention of Caleb, who quickly hurried after me.

"Sammi, where are you going?" he asked with concern in his voice.

"Out," I said, giggling.

"Out where?"

"Oh my *God*, Caleb, relax. I'm going to the Poplar Pub Point," I said, pressing the unlock button on my car's key fob.

"That place is bad news," he said worriedly.

I turned to look up at him before I got into the car. Jackson was now standing beside him in the doorway.

"Have you been taking your medicine?" Caleb asked sternly, crossing his arms.

"Have you been taking your medicine," I mocked in a condescending voice.

Jackson gave me a hopeless look, and I just rolled my eyes at them. "Screw you, Caleb. I'm going out."

I climbed in my car, started the engine, and began driving. Barely a minute passed before Caleb and Jackson started taking turns calling my cell phone. By the eighth call I was so annoyed that I decided to turn my phone off and leave it in the car to avoid the stress of the two of them ruining my night.

I should have never told Caleb about my diagnosis, I thought as I threw the phone onto the floorboard and kept on driving. Now, in Caleb's mind, every time I'm happy or enthusiastic it means I'm having an episode.

I had never told Jackson about my diagnosis, only Caleb, but I wasn't shocked that he'd shared about it with his friend. The thought made me angry, and I stomped my foot on the gas pedal.

Streetlights and neon signs illuminated the road as I drove into the city. The place I was going to was situated on a hill overlooking the busy downtown businesses that made this area thrive at this time of night.

The vibe of this club was a little bit different than the bar in Nashville. It had a darker color scheme, dimmer lighting, multicolored strobe lights, and techno style music.

Once parked, I left my phone behind, only grabbing my purse. As I entered the unfamiliar building, I looked around in every direction until I spotted the bar. Once it was in my sights, I walked over and started the night off by ordering a shot of tequila. I almost had to yell for the bartender to hear me over the music. Why was it so loud?

I took the first shot, then ordered another, leaning up against the edge of the bar and watching the crowd of people dance to the music. After the bartender returned with my second shot, I quickly took it and clanked the glass onto the bar before heading out onto the dance floor.

It didn't take me long to find a group of guys to dance with now that I'd had a sudden change to an outgoing personality. I typically didn't approach men to dance—except when I'd met Bailey—but of course now I was "manic," so I wasn't afraid to dance with anyone. I was on a high; I had so much energy that I could have danced all night. Time didn't feel the same when I was like this.

The guys I was dancing with looked to be a little bit younger than I was. I would say they were probably about twenty-one or twenty-two, college age for sure, and barely old enough to drink. They looked innocent. Harmless, really.

One of them had blonde hair and brown eyes. He was dressed in jeans and a black collared shirt. The second guy was tall with black hair and green eyes, and he was wearing black skinny jeans with a band tee. I could tell they were the sidekicks to the third guy.

The third guy had brown hair and dark eyes, almost black. There were light freckles across his cheeks that made him look innocent and rebellious at the same time. He was the cutest out of the three of them, and he held himself with a confidence the other two guys lacked, which was another thing that made me attracted to him. He was wearing jeans with a white button-down shirt, and he didn't try to hide the fact that he was checking me out as I turned with the beat of the music.

For a while we all just danced to the music playing loudly around us. I gradually eased closer to the cute brunette guy, dancing right up against him. I didn't really have intentions of going home with anyone or having anymore bathroom sex. I'd had every intention to do just that when I came here tonight; I thought I could just pick a guy and have guiltless, shameless sex, but the more I manifested it, the worse I felt.

Despite my subconscious mind whispering rights and wrongs, like an angel and a devil on each shoulder, I did want to have a good time and get drunk—I just didn't want to sexually involve myself with anyone else. Part of me was still holding on to the idea of Bailey or Jackson. Even though I was in this reckless state of mind, I did still care about Bailey and—as painful as it was to admit—Jackson, too. But I wasn't going to let that stop me from getting wasted, at least.

The four of us were out on the dance floor for at least an hour. It could've been longer, but I'd lost track of time without my phone. I'd made several trips back to the bar to get more shots, and I still didn't feel like I was buzzed. Okay, maybe I did, a little. Still, I felt like I should've been a lot more drunk than I was.

Eventually, the brunette made a trip of his own to the bar to retrieve some drinks for himself and his friends. Before asking them what they wanted, he asked if he could buy me a drink. I nodded happily while his friends asked him to grab them a beer.

As he headed for the bar, I stayed behind with the other guys as he spoke with the bartender. I turned around to look at him, and he smiled back at me with a nod, the bartender side-eyeing me suspiciously. It looked like they'd exchanged some words discretely. Maybe they knew each other.

"Are you having fun?" the black-haired guy asked while we continued to listen to the loud music, dancing with less energy while we waited for their friend to return.

"Oh yeah," I said, nodding happily as he gave me a smile back.

A few minutes later the brunette returned, carrying drinks in both hands.

"Sorry, the bartender was a little backed up," he said apologetically, handing each of us our drink.

I took my glass from the Brunette and swallowed the entire drink in just a few gulps. His friends smiled devilishly at him when I sat the glass down on a nearby table, wiping the remaining drops from my lips. They'd each been taking small, careful sips of their beers, watching as I gradually began acting differently.

The vibe had changed between the three of them. It felt strange. I didn't know why, but it did. I tried to ignore it, insisting that I allow myself to have fun. I blinked several times, trying to clear up my suddenly blurred vision, and eventually I could see straight again.

They seemed like they could sense something was going on, but oddly enough they didn't mention anything about it, as if they expected it. I thought the odd sensations were related to the excess alcohol I'd consumed, but this was unlike any time I'd been drunk before.

There were several short periods between these episodes where I was fine. I tried to make the most of that time, initiating conversation amid the loud music.

"So, what's your name?" I asked the brunette loudly over the music.

"Uh, Walker. What's yours?" he said hesitantly, looking back at his friends.

"It's Sammi with an *I*," I said, smiling flirtatiously.

I suddenly felt a pain in the front of my head. It was like a migraine, pulsating uncomfortably. Then there was an evident decline in the way I felt. I was dizzy, fatigued, and disoriented, so I decided I should take a timeout. I felt bad enough that I contemplated calling Caleb to come pick me up, but I wanted to avoid that.

I grabbed my forehead and winced as the sharp pain persisted. "I think I'm going to sit down for a minute."

"Are you okay?" Walker asked, seeming to be genuinely concerned now.

"I'm fine. I think I just need to take a break," I explained, placing a hand over my forehead as it throbbed in pain. I was uncomfortable and beginning to regret the last couple of drinks I'd had. I half expected it to run its course after several minutes, but it only got worse. I couldn't imagine staying here until it wore off, but I knew I couldn't drive home in this state. I was in no condition to be out on the road.

I took a seat on a small sofa close to where we'd been dancing, and Walker joined me.

"Do you want to go to our apartment across the street? You can crash there while the drinks wear off. I can call someone to come pick you up," he offered generously.

"No, no, it's okay. I'll call an Uber," I said.

"That's not necessary. We don't mind, I promise," he insisted.

"Are you sure? I don't want to bother you guys."

"It's no problem; it's a short walk from here. It's in that building right across the street," he said, his voice so friendly.

I nodded as I prepared to get up from where I was sitting. I was able to stand up, taking slow, careful steps until I was beside Walker. He signaled to his friends who were close by, and they began following behind us. I grabbed onto one of Walker's arms as he helped guide me out of the night club and onto the street, and we made our way over the crosswalk that led to the brick apartment complex where they lived.

I looked back toward the parking lot that my car was sitting in. I remembered that my phone was still on the floorboard somewhere, and I would need it to get in touch with Caleb or Jackson.

"Can we grab my phone out of my car? I think I should call my brother," I said, my eyelids growing heavy.

"We'll go back for it after we get you settled in," he said, his friends nodding agreeably.

I concurred and let Walker and the two other guys lead me to the elevator inside the simple but clean apartment building. The blonde quickly pressed the up arrow and the elevator doors slid apart. He turned and nervously looked into the corner where a camera was mounted, aimed in our direction, then we all stepped into the elevator.

The blonde guy pressed the button with the number three on it and the doors shut. I was still wrapped tightly around Walker's arm as we made it up to the third floor. The dark-haired guy pulled out a key and unlocked the door just a few steps from the elevator.

Once he pushed the big metal door open, I felt the air-conditioned breeze sweep across my face, tiny strands of hair tickling my cheeks. They took me into a bedroom and laid me down on a freshly made bed. I closed my eyes and hoped I could fall asleep. It felt like every muscle in my body was relaxed. Still, I wasn't sure what I was getting myself into. This seemed too convenient, too planned. I slowly opened and closed my eyes a few times, trying to clear the fogginess in my head.

"Are y'all going to get my phone?" I asked as Walker stepped into the room. My speech was slow and slurred.

"What does your car look like?" Walker asked, crossing his arms.

"Uh, it's, um … a blue Bronco," I said, my eyelids now heavier than ever.

He walked back into the hallway and began speaking to the other two guys. "I need y'all to go get her car and move it to the apartments on the south end of the street. If her brother comes looking for her, he may go sniffing around the bar, and someone is bound to have seen us leaving with her. It needs to look like she went home with someone, just not us," Walker said, as if he'd done this before. "Go get her keys out of her purse. And if you see her phone, toss it," he instructed.

Somewhere in the foggy recesses of my brain, panic flashed through me, but I couldn't find the energy to do anything about it. My limbs were heavy, and I fought to keep my eyes open.

The blonde guy entered the room and unzipped my purse before digging through it for my car keys. As he did so, he found my handgun. Unable to move, I watched as he stared at it for a second before going to show Walker. "Dude, she had a gun in her purse," he said, almost in a whisper.

"Give me that, you idiot. Just go move her car. I'll stay here with her."

"Just make sure I get a turn this time," the blonde guy said.

I heard the two guys leave the apartment to go do some more illegal shit, and I knew now without a doubt that I'd been roofied. I wondered how long it would take before I was completely unconscious.

~

I groaned as I came to consciousness. I wasn't sure exactly how much time had passed or even what day it was. One thing I did know was that I was in my room at Caleb's house.

I blinked and rubbed my eyes. My whole body hurt and my head pounded. What had happened last night? I remembered driving to the bar, refusing to answer Caleb and Jackson's calls, then dancing with a group of guys. After that? Nothing. How did I get home?

I could hear Jackson and Caleb talking in the hallway.

"Do you know what's had her locked up in her room for the last little while she's been here? Something happened, and I think that's what caused her to spiral," Caleb said.

I held my breath as I waited for Jackson's reply, but none came.

"What did you do? What happened, Jackson?" Caleb prompted, suspicious.

He hesitated for a second before speaking. "Sammi and I ... we had a moment or something, I don't know. I kind of shook her off because I was with Sophie, but the way I acted, it came off like I wasn't with her. I think Sammi wanted something to happen, and honestly, I kind of did too. I didn't want to say anything, but—"

"You and Sammi? How long has this been going on?" Caleb interrupted, a hint of anger and confusion clear.

"Nothing has happened between us besides talking and this tension we have. I didn't expect it to affect her like this. I would've never done anything intentionally to cause her to be reckless and put herself in danger. Please believe that," he said painfully.

"I know that," Caleb acquiesced. "But do you want to be with her or is this just some phase? You know she's got a lot of baggage. She means well, and she's a great person, but I don't know about this bipolar disorder shit, man. I don't care if you want to be with her; just know she's a lot sometimes. This is just a glimpse of how her nights typically turn out while she's having an episode."

My brother's words hurt me, but I couldn't exactly argue with their truth.

"I don't know how to take care of her," Caleb admitted.

I rubbed my eyes and got up from the bed, then pulled off my dress and threw on a tee with pajama shorts. Still groggy, I opened the door to my bedroom and stumbled into the kitchen, interrupting Jackson and Caleb's conversation as I did so.

"God my head hurts," I complained, my voice tired. "What happened last night?"

Caleb sighed and explained that after I drove off last night, he was suspicious that I'd stopped taking my medicine. After confiding his worries in Jackson, they had been through my room and discovered the nearly full bottle of medication hiding in my bedside table.

While I was gone, they tried to find a reasonable solution for bringing me back home before something happened, but I think Caleb was trying not to be overbearing and push me away with his suffocating protective tendencies. They tried giving me time to come home, but after I ignored their texts and calls, they figured they should come get me.

They arrived at the bar to find two guys breaking into my car. This triggered a vague memory of being in the guys' apartment—I think one of them was called Walker or something—and the blonde guy going through my purse to get my car keys.

My brother explained how they forced the two guys to admit where I was, then ran to the apartment to find me roofied and unconscious, lying on a bed in only my underwear. Luckily they arrived before Walker and his gross friends could assault me.

Jackson is silent, his arms crossed over his chest, as Caleb tells me how Jackson held him back from attacking Walker, then carried me out of the apartment safely, wrapping his jacket around my body to keep me warm.

Tears of fear and guilt spring to my eyes as he finishes telling me what happened last night. Then he gets back on the subject of my medication, and I feel a flash of annoyance instead.

"Sammi, I counted your pills, and you've been off your meds for a while. This prescription should've needed a refill weeks ago. What were you thinking?"

"Give me a break," I replied, annoyed.

Caleb slammed the amber pill bottle on top of the counter, the remaining pills rattling against the sides. "What is wrong with you?"

"I think the doctor called it bipolar II," I snapped, rolling my eyes. I walked over to the refrigerator to grab something to drink, Jackson watching me but not speaking.

"I'm taking you to the doctor," Caleb said sternly.

"Why? I'm fine!" I yelled, slamming the refrigerator door shut.

"Sammi, you nearly got raped last night!"

I remained silent for several seconds. When I spoke again, I was a little calmer. "I'm not going to the doctor," I said simply, storming off toward my bedroom.

I slammed my door shut behind me and sat down on the bed, my back against the headboard and pillows. I pulled my knees up to my chest and closed my eyes. Seconds later, Jackson entered the room.

"Well, well, look who it is," I sneered, eyes glassy.

He sighed and sat down on the edge of my bed. "Sammi, I'm sorry. I never meant to hurt you."

"Well, you did," I replied, my voice shaking. My tough, hard ass attitude was wearing off and the guilt was trickling in.

"I broke up with Sophie," he admitted.

"You mean she broke up with you? Again."

"No, I broke up with her."

"Why?" I asked, staring at him, an emptiness behind my eyes.

"Because I want you. You're the only girl I've wanted for a while, but then you go and do reckless shit like skipping your meds, leaving a club with a bunch of strangers, and nearly getting yourself raped. I just can't do that with you, Sammi," he said with pure frustration.

I remained quiet.

"Why did you stop taking your medicine? Caleb said you had been doing so good this past year."

"I stopped taking them after I found out I didn't get the job. I knew I should get back on them, but then you happened. I wanted to be with you that night and you rejected me. You always reject me! Even when I feel like you want me like I want you, it's always Sophie. It always has been, and it always will be," I said, tears streaming down my face.

I hated hearing all these things coming from his mouth. It pained me; stirring up emotions I did not want to feel. He looked at me, a similar pain in his eyes. We were never both emotionally and physically available for each other, and it was a terrible feeling.

"You did this to me," I cried out, burying my face in my pillow.

He stood up and exited the room. It was a bad place to leave things—and me. I felt so ashamed of everything I'd done and for what I'd put the two of them through last night. I couldn't bear to face them, not right now, or for a long time.

～

For the next few days, I locked myself in my room, afraid to step back into the lion's den.

Caleb would bring my meals to me, breakfast time always accompanied by my pill. He'd stay in the room long enough to watch me swallow it, inspecting my mouth before exiting the room again.

I felt like I was in a mental institution. This was driving me insane. So much pain, regret, and shame swarmed my mind. When depression hit me, it hit hard. It forced a wall between me and those I cared about. I was afraid my actions had finally run Jackson away for good.

I was still in contact with Bailey, but it was hard to maintain feelings and interest for someone who wasn't physically with me. Jackson was here; I could see him, touch him, smell him, and I had somewhat of a history with him. Bailey was the perfect guy for me, but Jackson had always had a hold over me.

I wasn't sure if I should keep trying with Bailey or Jackson, but for now, I had bruised whatever me and Jackson had going on. I just didn't know if it was beyond repair.

5

GOOD NEWS AND BAD NEWS

AS THE DAYS WENT by and I waited for my medicine to make me feel normal again, I had time to wallow in self-pity and think about the many ways I could apologize for my behavior and my reckless decisions. I'm not going to lie, I struggled with it for a while. There were nights I thought about screaming, crying, running—I even thought about taking my own life. At the time, it seemed easier than living the way I'd been living.

Believe it or not, I wasn't always like this. I was happy. I didn't need pills to fix my brain chemistry, and I certainly didn't need a man to make me feel worthy of living.

How did I get here? That's a question I'd asked myself so many times lately. I couldn't escape this, any of it. I just had to find a way to push forward, so I did.

About a month after starting my medication again, things were back to normal with my mental health, at least for now. Though I was contributing absolutely nothing to society—or to my brother's household. I knew Caleb probably wished I would clean or cook or something, but I felt like I needed to isolate myself until I was fixed.

I was ashamed. I had this degree that made me equipped to help people, but how was I supposed to help people when I couldn't help myself?

This illness had taken so much from me. It took me so much longer to get through nursing school compared to other people my age because mental illness created a lot of barriers in life. Education, love, friends, employment … I could keep going, but I won't. My focus was constantly hindered, and at times, I was hospitalized for my outbursts and manic episodes.

I knew Caleb was beginning to feel guilty for moving so far away now he'd seen me so reckless and unaware of the consequences of my disorder. He was finally seeing it up close and personal, not just hearing stories from the doctors whenever they called him (my emergency contact) every time I was committed.

The truth of the matter was that no one was going to hire a bipolar nurse; call it discrimination, call it an unfortunate circumstance, I don't know. I thought about withholding that information on the "voluntary" equal employment opportunity page on applications because, despite them saying they would welcome anyone regardless of their diagnosis and disability, that was a big fat lie. Every time I checked a mark by "bipolar disorder," I knew they wouldn't be moving forward with my application. It put a big red flag that said "liability" over my head.

I held out hope that a company would be willing to work with me and understand the accommodations that could make the job more maintainable. I didn't want special treatment, just a chance, you know?

So since I was finally feeling better, I thought I would try my hand at the small community hospital close to Caleb's house. I needed to take back control of my life and give myself a purpose—something to keep me and my mind busy. That'd been my plan for coming to Oklahoma in the first place. I had not had a manic episode since the night at the bar, but I suppose that's to be expected when you're medicated. At least, that's the goal.

In the time I'd been avoiding Caleb and Jackson, I'd been talking to Bailey, because he was the only other person I had. We were slowly getting closer again after I'd disappeared for short periods of time here and there for reasons unknown to him. I trusted and cared for him, despite my mixed feelings about our distance.

It also helped that Bailey didn't know about my disorder, so he was the only person who couldn't judge me and didn't know what I'd done.

He'd call or text me every morning and every night, and we were making plans to meet halfway between Pocola and Nashville toward the end of my summer stay. I couldn't wait to see him again.

Bailey was the person that encouraged me to apply for a job down here. I hadn't told him much about my time here in Oklahoma, but he knew I wanted to get a nursing job more than anything. He told me to hold my head high and take control of my life. So, I took his advice and woke up this morning hopeful and anxious to start this journey.

I didn't have an interview scheduled for the hospital I was going to, but I was hoping they'd give me one while I was there. I wanted to look professional to leave a good impression, so after taking a shower, I dressed in a navy pantsuit with a pair of black heels. I curled my hair into big, loose waves and did my makeup simply yet elegantly.

Once ready, I grabbed my purse from my nightstand and clunked down the hallway into the living room. Heading toward Caleb's computer desk that was tucked away into the left corner, I grabbed the resume I'd printed earlier.

Beside his computer, I had a box of my belongings that I had brought from New York with me, all organized meticulously and neatly. Inside was a blue folder that held my important documents like my birth certificate and social security card. It made it convenient for preparing for things like job interviews. I peeped into the box, spotted the folder, and pulled it out to take with me. I flipped it open to stick the resume down into the right pocket.

"Where are you going?" my brother asked from where he sat carelessly on the couch, a bag of chips in his right hand, remote in the left.

We hadn't had a real conversation in weeks, and the last time he asked me where I was going, I created so many problems for him. But this time his tone was different. It was like he trusted my intentions, which encouraged me, whether he knew it or not.

"I'm going to apply for a job," I said semi-confidently, now standing to the side of the television screen.

"That's great, Sammi," Jackson said as he entered the living room.

I half-heartedly smiled, still carrying the weight of my guilt and embarrassment. I looked down at the ground and walked away, grabbing my keys and paperwork, ready to conquer rejection. I knew I was a qualified nurse, despite my actions during my episodes, but I would be committed to my own health more passionately if I had patients' health to be responsible for as well. Plus, I was intelligent. They don't just let anyone pass the NCLEX these days, that's for sure.

I went into nursing because healthcare had been interesting to me for a long time. Being someone with a mental illness, I thought I could help advocate for others and be more compassionate toward patients like me, who were struggling.

I originally wanted to become a psychiatric nurse, but during my clinical training, I'd done a pediatric/obstetrics rotation. The nurses I worked with let me stand in on a woman giving birth and showed me the beauty of bringing a child into the world. From that moment on, I'd fallen in love with that area of nursing.

A few weeks later, I'd assisted a nurse in taking care of a sick child in the pediatric unit. It was a young girl who was in remission from leukemia, but she was vomiting and severely dehydrated. I worked with her for a few days before she was ready to be discharged.

Watching a child overcome sickness and witnessing a newborn baby see the world for the first time was a wonderful experience, one I wanted to be a part of throughout my entire nursing career.

I exited the house and climbed into my car. Then I set my phone's GPS to help direct me to the hospital, and about twenty minutes later, I arrived. It was a relatively small, quaint building. The luxuries were limited, but they seemed to be in dire need of nursing staff, based on the advertisement they'd posted online.

I parked my car, grabbed my folder, and walked into the entrance of the building, my heels making my presence known. Automatic glass doors parted ways, two ferns sitting on either side.

"Hello! Can I help you find something?" the elderly front desk clerk asked sweetly. She had glasses, gray hair, and was dressed in a white blouse with navy pants.

"I'm looking for Human Resources," I said politely, clutching the blue folder.

"That will be to your left, down the hallway, Room 107."

"Thank you," I said before heading in that direction.

I turned to the left and studied each room number until I approached a wooden door with room number 107 beside it. I gently turned the knob and pushed through. Inside the room were two wooden desks lined against the wall, the kind you'd see in a school. Only one was occupied—by a young woman with black, shoulder length hair. Her bright white teeth were visible when she smiled over at me and asked, "Hey, how can I help you?"

"I saw that you guys were hiring a registered nurse on the OB and pediatric unit, so I wanted to come by and put in an application," I said nervously.

"Okay, great! If you want to grab an application form from the top bin on the wall, you can take a seat at that desk and complete it. And if you have all of your documents with you, I can start scanning in and checking everything," she added, looking down at the folder in my hand.

I flipped it open and handed her the paperwork. We sat in almost complete silence as I worked on the application, only her typing away on the computer and the scanner running in the background making any noise.

"NYU School of Nursing, that's quite the journey to here. What brought you to Oklahoma?" she asked as she looked at my degree.

"Oh, I have family here," I said.

"Well, we're glad to have you here," she replied politely.

I returned a smile before I continued carefully reviewing each question on the paperwork in front of me. After I completed the front page, I flipped it over and saw those haunting questions about illnesses and disabilities. I studied each checkbox for a few seconds. Autism, ADHD, bipolar disorder, the list went on. I looked back up at the word "voluntary" and courageously checked the box that said I'd prefer not to say, because in all honesty, I did prefer not to say, and that was better than lying and just marking N/A.

When I was finished, I handed her the application as she looked over each question briefly. For about thirty minutes she asked me the typical interview questions regarding my experience, education, strengths, weaknesses, and all that fun stuff.

She didn't ask me about the disorders page; I was pretty sure it was illegal to ask an applicant any questions in that regard, unless they disclosed the information openly.

I answered all her questions confidently, and eventually she said, "What day would you be able to start?"

The question took me by surprise because I'd had an immense amount of self-doubt recently. This gave me the boost I desperately needed.

"I can start tomorrow?" I said hopefully.

"Okay, great! The obstetrics and pediatrics unit is located on the third floor of the hospital. The dress code is any shade of pink scrubs. You'll be on the clock at 7:00 a.m. and get off at 7:00 p.m. every Monday, Tuesday, and Wednesday, which should fit in perfectly with the availability you gave on your application. Here is a key card that allows you access to the supply rooms, medicine rooms, and all the other restricted areas. Do you have any questions for me?" she asked professionally.

"I don't think I do," I said, smiling.

"Okay, if you want to sit in front of my camera lens, I can snap a picture for your name badge."

I stood up from the desk and walked over to the chair that sat in front of a white wall. I looked into the camera lens and smiled as she clicked the button, the flash blinding me temporarily. Seconds later, a badge was printed out, and she handed it over to me.

"If you think of any questions after you leave, just give me a call," she said as she laid her business card down on top of my paperwork. "We'll see you bright and early, Miss Peters."

I grabbed the paperwork and business card and stuck it back into my folder, then thanked her and left the room.

As I walked back into the hallway, it took everything inside of me to contain my excitement. For once, I felt accomplished, like everything I'd done up until this point served a purpose. I couldn't wait to tell Caleb; I knew, despite everything, that he'd be happy for me.

I waved to the front desk clerk as I left the building and walked to my car. I started the ignition, buckled up, and backed out of the parking spot.

Driving toward the exit that led back to the main road, I noticed a dark green Mustang parked on the other end of the lot. Its headlights lit up as the driver started the vehicle.

During my drive home, I decided to make a pit stop by one of the local convenience stores to buy a few snacks, since my brother relied heavily on ramen and salad as his means of survival.

But as I stepped out of the vehicle, I felt very uneasy. I looked around at the almost empty parking lot. It was still early in the day, but I didn't feel safe, similarly to how I'd felt that night I met Walker.

I chose not to dwell on it because I needed good vibes. I'd just gotten a job—this was a good day! Great, even.

I locked my keys in the car like I always did, so that I could just punch in my code on the outside of the door to unlock it. Then, I walked across the concrete parking lot to the store. The bell above the glass door rang as I entered the mostly empty store.

To ease my anxiety, I knew I wouldn't linger; I'd be in and out. I walked up and down a couple of aisles while I decided what to buy. After a few minutes, I grabbed a handful of snacks and approached the counter.

The cashier was a short blonde with ratty hair, premature wrinkles, and the scent of a heavy smoker. She wore a company polo shirt with black pants and had a name badge pinned to the left side of her shirt that said "Penny."

"How are you doing today?" she asked nicely.

"I'm good, how are you?"

"I'm doing just fine, darling," she said as she grabbed each item, pulling them across the counter, the plastic wrappers rustling as they moved. She scanned the barcodes and told me the total of the items, and I paid with my debit card. Penny handed me the receipt and my bag of snacks, then I was on my way.

"Have a good one," she said.

"You too," I said politely, smiling back at her.

I pushed open the door to the store and walked toward my car. When I got to the end of the sidewalk, I noticed the green Mustang was now parked directly beside me. They were backed in a space, so their driver's side door was right across from mine.

I approached my car, trying to act like I hadn't recognized the vehicle. I avoided eye contact with the driver, who was almost a shadow behind the heavily tinted windows. I kept my head down and pulled the handle, so anxious that I forgot to unlock it first. Realizing my mistake, I nervously began pressing the code to unlock my car but pressed the wrong numbers and had to restart the process.

At this point, I was fidgeting and fumbling, paranoid that something was about to go down. I would have felt better if my gun was in my possession, but for the sake of this snack run I'd taken only my debit card with me to save the trouble of carrying my entire purse.

For someone who was typically hyper-vigilant, I sure did fail to meet my own personal safety standards. I wouldn't make that mistake again.

I was finally able to unlock my car. I grabbed the handle, barely opening the door before the Mustang's driver door opened. A man stepped out and, before I could process what was happening, he lunged at me from behind. He slammed my head into the driver's side window repeatedly, forcing the door shut.

I kicked my leg back and tried elbowing him, but I seemed to miss with every hit and kick. He held me up against the car while simultaneously throwing punches to any part of my body he could reach.

When he spun me around, my face was covered in blood, and my eyes were burning and blurry from the trauma and blood rolling down into my sockets. I was crying from fear and confusion as to what I had done to deserve this. I didn't understand.

I was thrown to the ground and kicked repeatedly in the stomach. He stomped on my legs and feet, and it felt like he crushed every bone in my left foot as he pinned it to the ground and smashed it.

Then, as quickly as it had started, the man got back into the Mustang and sped off, his tires squealing. I laid on the concrete, blood pouring out of various parts of my body, unable to move and wondering if someone would find me.

Luckily, not a minute went by before the cashier stepped out of the store, preparing to take a smoke break. She lit her cigarette right before dropping it to the ground when she saw me. She rushed over in a panic.

"Oh my God! Oh my God! I'm calling 911, baby girl. You're going to be okay," she said soothingly as she dialed the three numbers on her old prepaid flip phone. Then she spoke into the phone, "Um, yes, I just found a girl beat up really bad in the parking lot of Pump Pub on Highway Twenty-four. She's in pretty bad shape, y'all need to hurry," she said in a raspy, country accent.

I don't remember much of what happened next. I know Penny held my hand and tried to comfort me as we waited. Then, I heard distinct sirens from the ambulance and police cars. I was placed onto a stretcher and transported to the hospital that I'd just left after my interview.

Somewhere between blacking out and regaining consciousness, they'd gotten in contact with my brother to alert him of what'd happened through the emergency contacts display on my lock screen.

I couldn't help but feel guilty that I'd put my brother through so much stress since I'd arrived in Oklahoma. I had to be driving him insane.

~

Sometime later, I woke up to find that I was lying in a hospital bed with monitors and wires hooked up in every direction. One of the machines was beeping, and I started blinking repeatedly, trying to focus my view. I laid there, confused, sore, and worried.

The door to my room opened and Caleb and Jackson entered, intense fear in their eyes.

"Sammi, hey, you're awake. I'm so glad you're okay. I was so worried," Caleb said, stepping to my bedside as I looked over at him. "The paramedics told us you were attacked at the gas station. I'm so sorry this happened to you."

I was in too much pain to talk, but I tried to smile to reassure my brother. He and Jackson moved to sit in the chairs that were pushed into the corner of the room.

It felt like my eyes were bulging out of my head from the swelling, my body ached all over, and I was anxious, not knowing who'd done this to me or if they'd ever be caught. Was I just an easy target, or did I already have enemies in Oklahoma?

There was a knock at the door and a doctor entered. He was a middle-aged man with graying brown hair and glasses, wearing all black with a white coat on top. He seemed like he felt sorry for me, much like everyone else lately.

"Hello, I'm Dr. Williams. I've been taking care of Miss Peters."

Caleb sat up straight in his chair, giving the doctor his full attention.

"When Miss Peters arrived at the emergency room, we checked for lots of different things, considering the severity of her condition. We did X-rays and ultrasounds to check for any broken bones, internal bleeding, and a few other things," he began, speaking mostly to Caleb and Jackson.

I closed my eyes because it hurt more to keep them open, but I was carefully listening to every word he said. I was alert but let the doctor relay the information to them while I replayed the traumatic incident in my head, wondering what I could have done differently to protect myself.

Likewise, Caleb and Jackson listened to each word. I opened my eyes a few times to see what was going on and could barely see Jackson glance over at me every so often; I could tell he was anxious and concerned about me.

"Based on the results from the exams we performed, I've diagnosed her with TBI which is what we refer to as a traumatic brain injury. Once she is fully alert, I can determine the severity of it, but she may have trouble concentrating, remembering certain things, or have some confusion."

Caleb covered his mouth with his hand as he whispered, "Oh my God."

Jackson placed his hand on Caleb's back to try and comfort him.

"Her left foot is broken in several places, so we have that casted," he continued. "She's got several broken ribs, but the good news is even after the trauma to her abdominal area, the baby is still in great health."

The room fell silent. You could've heard a pin drop.

What did he just say? I felt my heart sink. I couldn't be pregnant! I was not fit to be a mother.

Jackson and Caleb looked at each other, then back at the doctor with furrowed eyebrows.

"I'm sorry, the baby?" Caleb asked, confused.

"You weren't aware that she was pregnant?" he asked, genuinely surprised.

"Not at all," Jackson said, his voice shallow like he was thinking heavily, unsure how to react. It sounded like there was a lump in his throat.

"She's about eight weeks pregnant," the doctor added as he looked over at me. When no one said anything, he added, "I'll give you guys some time to take all of this in. I'll be back in a little while to check on her and put together a care plan for getting her back to full strength."

The doctor exited the room while we all began to process everything he'd just told us. My mind wandered back to the night of the bachelorette outing.

Fuck.

How was I going to tell Bailey? There was no way he and I could make it work long-distance. And would he even want a child with me, or would he tell me to hit the road?

Had I officially run off both guys I could actually see myself being happy with? Because I knew this would be the icing on the cake for Jackson. Why would he want to be with me after finding out I was carrying another man's child?

6

INTO THE WILD

I WAS APPARENTLY TWO months pregnant, and I hadn't even had a clue. It seemed like life was continuously full of surprises, and I was ready for some kind of normalcy in my life, because *damn*.

I had been hospitalized for over a week, a tiny baby growing inside of me. I stayed in a room on the second floor of the hospital because I wasn't far enough along to need to be monitored by the labor and delivery unit.

I was still mentally unstable and bruised, with two black eyes, and they had many different things going on to help me recover. Most of the time I was heavily sedated, though they came in from time to time to check my cognitive functioning and to see how I was feeling. We hadn't accomplished much, considering I still hadn't said a word to anyone. I don't know what I was waiting for. Maybe I was afraid.

Despite the progress I had and hadn't made, I couldn't stay in this hospital forever. I knew the only way I'd get out was by participating in the therapy and speaking when the doctor came in.

Caleb and Jackson had briefly stepped out to get breakfast in the hospital cafeteria like they had every day since I'd been here. While they were gone, the doctor stopped in, and I decided to make an effort to speak and see where I was at with my traumatic brain injury.

As he knocked and entered, he found me lying in the bed, buried beneath about five hospital blankets. I was so cold that my body was shaking, and it felt like I was in an ice bath.

Dr. Williams looked up at me, a warm smile on his face. "Hey, Sammi. How are you feeling?"

"Not good," I choked out, and his eyes lit up at my speaking. He walked over and took a handheld thermometer from his white coat, scanning the surface of my forehead as it beeped.

"102.1. You're running a pretty high fever. Can you look straight ahead for me?" he asked as he clicked on the light in his hand. "Follow the light for me."

I followed the light with my eyes as he moved it from left to right.

At this point, Caleb and Jackson returned from their breakfast run, easing into the room. The two of them took their seats in the corner and gave their attention to Dr. Williams.

"Now I'm going to show you several pictures of some items, and I want you to say what they are. Can you do that?"

I nodded.

He grabbed a small stack of cards from his pocket and held the first one out to me. I could sense Caleb and Jackson anxiously waiting to see my responses. "Can you tell me what this is?"

"A bird."

"That's good. And what about this one?" he asked as he put the first card at the back of the stack.

"A-a…" I said, stumbling as I tried to describe the image.

"It's okay. Take your time."

I closed my eyes and moaned in frustration. I knew what the picture was, but I couldn't get my brain to relay the information to my mouth.

"Sammi, you know what that is," Caleb said supportively as he looked over at the image.

"Can we skip this one?" I asked as I opened my eyes.

"Of course," the doctor said, revealing the next image.

"An apple," I said quickly and confidently.

Everyone in the room looked slightly concerned by my response.

"What?" I asked, confused.

"It's normal to get similar items mixed up during these practices. We made good progress, and that's the outcome we want," he said encouragingly, looking over at my brother.

Caleb pursed his lips and half-heartedly smiled at me when I gave him a sad look.

"Sammi has a fever which can be normal for patients with a TBI, but I'm going to rule out an infection before I determine when she can be discharged."

"Okay, thanks," he said as Dr. Williams exited the room.

I rolled over, my back to them, shivering under the blankets.

"It's okay, Sammi. It'll be okay," Caleb reassured me, but I didn't know if either of us believed his words.

I didn't know what I had intended to accomplish with the doctor today. I guess I was just ready to go home to Caleb's house, but my mind and body had other plans.

～

Several more days had passed, and the staff here had done all they could in making sure that I was on the right track to healing. I was finally getting discharged today. Although I hadn't really spoken to them, Caleb and Jackson hadn't left my side the entire time I'd been here.

The whole time, all I could think about was whether I even wanted this child. I was a bipolar mess—what kid would benefit from me as a mother? My life was a disaster. And one day the child would ask me the romantic story of how I met their father. What a story that would be to tell.

I didn't even know if Bailey would want any part of this child's life. I kept playing scenarios in my head of how he would react when I told him. He hadn't asked for this. And when he inevitably decided he didn't want me or the baby, I would be a single mother, bumming off my brother and Jackson.

Oh, and Jackson—he'd probably never want to be with me now. I was carrying another man's child, a result of my reckless behavior. Why would he want me? Why would either of them want me? I was damaged goods, like I'd thought all along.

And that's what had gone through my mind every single day since I'd found out I was pregnant. I was a nurse who lived for childbirth and children thriving in the world, but I didn't particularly want that for me yet. I wasn't ready.

"Sammi, we signed your discharge papers. Caleb has got all your stuff and is pulling the car around to the front. I'm going to wheel you out," Jackson said, parking a wheelchair beside my bed.

I sat up, wincing from the pain of my broken ribs and avoiding eye contact with him. I was anxious, scared, embarrassed, and hopeless. I managed to scoot to the side of the bed, balancing my weight on my good foot. It was secured into a boot so that I could hopefully begin to walk on it without relying on crutches. Then I plopped into the wheelchair.

Jackson wheeled me out of the room and toward the elevator. He pressed the down arrow and the doors quickly slid open. It was empty, so once the doors slid closed, we were alone. He pressed the button for the first floor, and I felt a jolt as it moved down. We waited in awkward, heavy silence as it descended.

"I love you," Jackson blurted as the elevator came to a rest on the first floor.

"What?" I gasped. It was the first time I had spoken to him since the assault.

Before he could respond, the doors opened and Caleb was waiting there, his car parked right outside of the entrance. Acting as if nothing happened, Jackson wheeled me toward the double doors. As we passed the front desk, the woman who interviewed me walked by, doing a double take as she passed.

"Sammi! Are you okay?" she asked, concerned.

Jackson gently stopped the wheelchair to allow me to speak to the woman he probably didn't recognize.

"I'm sorry I didn't show on my first day. I was in an accident after the interview, and I've been admitted since then. I understand if you need to find someone else for the position," I said, almost ashamed.

"No, no, I was just worried after you missed your first shift. I called to see what was going on, and your brother answered. He told me a little bit about the incident. I am so sorry that happened to you. You just worry about getting better, and your job will be here when you're ready to come back."

I smiled, relieved. "Thank you."

She sweetly patted my shoulder, then Jackson continued to take me out to the pickup area.

Caleb greeted us, and they both helped me into the car. Then we were on our way, driving on the boring Oklahoma country roads. I looked out of the back seat window the entire ride home, just staring into the fields we passed by.

Everything seemed normal until I noticed what looked like a man staggering and limping very heavily in the middle of a tall grass field. He was moving almost like he was injured.

"Caleb, do you see that man?" I asked.

He slowed the car down just enough to be able to look more closely. "He looks hurt. I wonder if he needs help?"

Though I'd been the one to point him out, dread settled in my stomach at the idea of stopping to speak to this stranger. "I've had my fair share of danger lately. I don't think we should risk investigating what this guy is up to," I said, a slight shakiness in my voice.

Caleb shrugged in agreement and I watched the man grow smaller in the distance as we drove further away. For some reason, I couldn't shake the feeling that there was something odd about him. I'd never seen anyone walk that way before, even when injured. It was an eerie sight, but it wasn't our business to become involved in. Hopefully the man was okay. I just wasn't willing to stick around and find out.

We continued our ride home in silence, all inside our own heads, I guess.

~

A couple of weeks passed, and I was now nearly three months pregnant. Life was still awkward, weird, and I was going stir crazy sitting in this house with Caleb and Jackson. I had not been to work yet, but I was planning on going in two to three weeks, as soon as I got this boot off.

I didn't exactly plan for my visit here to go like this, but I should've expected it from fucking Oklahoma. This place was probably going to be my downfall. I wasn't optimistic that's for sure, and it was hard for me to even be excited about my new job when dramatic situations kept happening to me. It was like I had a monkey on my back.

After everything that had happened and now that I was pregnant, I had decided that it was best for me to not go back home to New York or start another semester of college. I was going to extend my trip here to properly recover both mentally and physically and to spend time with my brother, since I hadn't really done that either.

Despite everything I'd gone through, I was currently in a healthier frame of mind. I was slowly making decisions about my future and finding something to hold on to.

Of course, I was still struggling with pregnancy and relationships, especially after Jackson had told me he loved me. I hadn't gotten the chance to talk to him about it, but it had weighed heavily on my mind since leaving the hospital that day. I decided that today was the day I was going to talk to him about it.

Caleb had gone out on a grocery run while Jackson stayed around the house to straighten up a bit. I hobbled into the kitchen to grab a bottle of water and found him sweeping around the kitchen island. He was wearing blue jeans with his cowboy boots—literally my weakness—and a tan Carhartt tee.

As I walked past him, my boot clunking against the floor with each step, I smelled the scent of his cologne and it affected me more than it should have. My heart fluttered, and I closed my eyes, silently inhaling his scent.

Jackson stopped sweeping and watched me closely as I stood a few feet away from him. We made eye contact, but he still didn't say anything; he just stood there, holding the broom tightly as he leaned against the counter.

"Did you mean it?" I asked before realizing I'd said it.

"What do you mean?" he asked.

"In the elevator, when you said you loved me. Did you mean it?"

"Of course, I did."

I stepped closer. He was much taller than me, and it always felt so perfect when I was standing next to him. He propped the broom up against the wall and looked down at me, his deep blue gaze finding mine. He brushed my cheek with his warm hand and slowly leaned in.

For the first time, Jackson and I shared a kiss. It started off gentle, but soon the kiss deepened and our tongues danced. Suddenly he pulled away and swiped everything off the island, then held me around the waist and picked me up, sitting me on top of it.

"Is this okay?" he asked, his breathing heavy.

"Yeah," I whispered, our lips meeting again.

His hands roamed up and down my back, waist, and legs. I wanted him so bad, even more than I'd wanted Bailey that night at the bar.

I had just started unbuttoning his pants when the kitchen door opened. It was Caleb.

"Oh God, my eyes!" he cried dramatically as he slapped a hand across his face, half-joking but also a little horrified.

I carefully eased down from the counter, blushing. "We were just…"

"Changing the, uh, lightbulb," Jackson lied, fastening his pants.

"The lightbulb that's clearly not blown? Yeah, sure," Caleb said, raising his eyebrows and smirking.

Embarrassed, I went to my room and hid for the remainder of the day, laying in bed and thinking about Jackson and our kiss. I also thought a lot about Bailey and decided that today would be the day that I called to tell him about the baby. I hadn't talked to him since the assault. I felt horrible about it, but I just hadn't been up for talking to anyone.

Caleb informed me that he and Jackson had made plans to go to the gun range for target practice. They were both avid hunters and enjoyed perfecting their aim and skills. I assured them that I would be fine alone at the house, deciding it would be the perfect opportunity to call Bailey. Then, as a reward for facing up to the call, I'd order pizza for us all, since I was starving.

The sun was beginning to hide behind the beautifully colored clouds in the sky, and I was trying to find the words to say to Bailey in this phone call. After what had happened earlier with Jackson, I didn't know how I wanted Bailey to react. A part of me hoped he'd call things off, so that I could be with Jackson without feeling guilty. The other part of me still longed for Bailey; I wanted to see what life might be like with him.

After pondering what to say for several minutes, I finally decided to just click "call" on his name and find the words once he answered.

It rang for a while, and I was about to hang up when he answered. "Hello?"

"Hey," I said anxiously.

"Sammi! I haven't heard from you in a while. Is everything okay?"

I started to tear up, overwhelmed by everything that had happened since we last spoke. I kept trying to tell myself that he was such a gentle, caring soul. He'd understand. Then, I'd ask myself, *What if he doesn't?*

My silence carried through the phone, and he prompted, "Sammi?"

"I'm sorry. There's so much I need to tell you."

"You're worrying me. Do I need to come to Oklahoma? You can tell me anything."

"I was roofied at a bar during one of my manic episodes. Caleb and Jackson had to get me from some guys' apartment," I began.

"Manic episodes?"

"I have bipolar disorder. I stopped taking my medicine when I was having a hard time at the beginning of summer. I get reckless," I admitted.

"Are you okay? They didn't hurt you at the apartment, did they?"

"No." I paused. "I mean, I don't think they did. But after I got back on my meds and was feeling better, I went to apply for a job. On my way home, I got attacked by some man at the gas station."

"Oh my God, Sammi! You need to get out of Oklahoma. Come to Tennessee and live with me for a while."

"I don't think you'll want that after I tell you this next part," I said, tears streaming down my face.

"What is it?"

"When they took me to the hospital, they told me I had broken ribs, TBI, a broken foot, and they … they told me I was pregnant, Bailey."

He remained silent for a second, then asked, "Is… Is it Jackson's?"

He asked this because I'd been transparent with Bailey about the ups and downs that I'd had with the two of them. He'd known I was caught in the middle this entire time, so he was right in asking if it could be Jackson's. However, I had never had sex with Jackson, despite what might have happened earlier in the kitchen if Caleb hadn't come home when he did. There was no doubt that this was Bailey's child.

"Bailey, I've never slept with Jackson. This baby is yours," I said.

I heard him breathe out a sigh of relief, and I could almost feel him smiling through the phone. "I'm coming to Pocola tonight. I want to see you. I *need* to see you."

"Are you sure? I just threw a lot at you. Is this what you want?"

"I've been down bad for you since I first laid eyes on you, Sammi. I can't see myself with anyone but you, and I'm getting to the age where I want to settle down and start a family. Trust me, I want this."

I smiled like an idiot, but the thought of Jackson lingered in the back of my mind, and that made me panic. We'd come extremely close to being intimate today, and I honestly didn't know what to do.

Who do I choose? How do I choose?

"Text me the address, and I'll see you tonight," he said sweetly.

"Okay, I will. Bye."

After hanging up with Bailey, I texted Caleb to ask when he would be home, then laid my phone down on the kitchen island and moved over to the refrigerator to look for a snack.

Suddenly, I began to hear gunshots. A *lot* of gunshots.

I slowly hobbled to the door, my boot helping me move. The garage door was raised, so I walked out into the open space until I could see the neighbor's house down the street.

A huge military truck was parked in the road and a group of men in uniform had an entire family lined up outside, shooting them one by one.

My eyes widened, and I gasped, hurrying back inside to grab my phone. I tried to call 911 and Caleb, but there was no service. How was there no service? I'd literally just called Bailey, and now nothing—no signal.

I put my tennis shoe on my right foot and walked as quickly as I could to the side door, my body still in tremendous pain from too much movement. I opened the door, but couldn't see anywhere safe for me to escape to or hide. The backyard was an open field and downward slope leading to a forest of trees and the distant Ouachita Mountains. I knew I couldn't manage it with a broken foot. The soldiers were wandering up and down the road and some were in the grass; I knew they would see me and shoot me down in a heartbeat.

Suddenly, there was a knock on the front door, followed by a man's voice.

Silence, and then a loud banging noise. They were trying to kick the door in.

I could see the woods in the distance, but I had no idea how I would get there without being seen. I was running out of time, and I didn't know where I could hide in this house.

I hurried to the furthest room, which was Jackson's, rounding the corner right as the front door swung open. I quietly maneuvered into his closet and carefully slid the door closed behind me, trying not to make a sound, though his hangers rattled as I hit them with my shoulders. I quickly stopped their movements with my hands and tucked myself away into the corner.

The closet was small and shallow and wouldn't work as a hiding place for long. I closed my eyes and inhaled the comforting scent of Jackson's clothing as I waited for the soldiers to find me.

I was shaking; fear was taking over my body like it had the day I was attacked. My gun was in my purse out in my car, so that was out of the question, and I had no idea what the code to their safe was.

Heavy, frantic footsteps pounded on the living room floor. I tried hiding behind the clothing, but if they were to open the door, I'd be seen in an instant. But I'd had no other options at such short notice, and I refused to be dragged from underneath the bed. I heard doors being opened and slammed, items being knocked into the floor and stepped on, and men speaking angrily.

"I know there's someone in here," one of the soldiers said in an accented voice.

"We've checked almost the entire house. It's empty," another man said.

"I want every inch of the house searched. The television is still on; someone is here."

"Fine, but go ahead and check the neighbor's house; we've got this."

The first soldier left and two remained, flipping the house upside down. Jackson's room was on the far end of the house right past Caleb's, but I knew they were making their way to find me.

The footsteps grew louder as each minute passed. I kept my eyes shut and braced myself for whatever was about to happen. I was fully convinced this was how I was going to die.

Seconds later, the closet door swung open. I was face to face with a tall man in a uniform pointing a gun at my face.

"Please don't shoot me," I begged as he stepped in and yanked my arm until I stood.

He was tall, muscular, and had a dark complexion with a thick black mustache resting above his lips. He grabbed a syringe from his pocket and ordered me to take my long-sleeved shirt off.

This man was about to inject me with something and then kill me.

I chose not to fight as I was already injured and couldn't take another beating. If this was my fate, I was just going to accept it. I pulled my shirt over my head, right as a gunshot sounded in the front part of the house.

He turned around and called out to his partner. "Perez, is everything okay in there?"

And then, a second gunshot, this time to the head of the soldier in front of me.

As his body collapsed, I turned to find Jackson at the entrance of the bedroom, holding a gun. I stood in the same spot, shirtless and frozen as my eyes widened in shock. The world around us was collapsing, people were being murdered, but thankfully, my life had been spared. For now, at least.

Jackson ran over to me, Caleb close behind. I slowly reached for my shirt, and simultaneously they asked, "Are you okay?"

I silently nodded and slipped the shirt back on.

"Sammi, we've got to go. They're going to notice when their soldiers don't come out after hearing gunshots," Caleb said.

I stepped over the dead body and wiped at the blood spatters of this stranger that were painted across the surface of my skin. We headed toward the back door as quickly as we could. I wasn't sure if we'd ever be able to return to this house to retrieve any of our belongings, but I knew I needed to get my medication. I'd end up dead for sure if I went into a manic episode while the world went to shit.

"Caleb, my medicine," I began.

My brother bolted into the kitchen, slinging the cabinet door open to grab the pill bottle. He stuck it into his pocket, still carrying a gun that was attached to a sling over his shoulder.

"Perez, what's taking so long in there?" a voice echoed from the walkie talkie belonging to the first dead man.

I followed close behind the two of them as Caleb cracked the side door open. The back door led to the porch that had steps which would take too long to go down, so the side door that led straight to the grassy downhill yard was the obvious choice.

My adrenaline was rushing, but I was so thankful Caleb and Jackson had found me when they did. What had been in that syringe?

Footsteps approached the front door, clearly coming to investigate the commotion and sudden lack of communication from their companions.

"They're heading for the front door. We need to go, now!" Jackson cried. He gave his gun to Caleb and grabbed me, carrying me because that would be faster than my attempt at a run. We bolted for the woods, hoping we wouldn't be seen. I didn't look back; I just closed my eyes as Jackson heroically carried me.

Who were these people? They were clearly not American soldiers; they were from somewhere else. Germany, maybe? It was like we were suddenly in the middle of some kind of war, a war no one was prepared for.

I could tell Jackson was getting tired, but he kept pushing with each stride as we worked toward the woods. In the distance, I heard the shout of a soldier in a language I was unfamiliar with, but I knew that meant we had been spotted. I was sure they would not be happy to find two of their men dead within the house either.

The soldiers began shooting bullets in our direction right as we reached the deep, wooded area which luckily offered more protection than the open field. I could hear the wind behind the bullets flying around us.

Caleb slowed on his running to catch his breath, and Jackson placed me onto the ground. He grabbed his gun back from Caleb, and the two of them took position behind some trees, looking through the scopes of their rifles and taking shots at the three soldiers running down the hill after us.

I saw them all fall to the ground, one, two, three.

I took my first deep breath in a while. For now, we were in the clear, but that would only be until the other soldiers in the area took notice and figured out there were armed threats to them hiding in this forested area. We needed to move.

We began walking through the woods, not sure where we were going, but hopefully away from these foreign soldiers. The woods were dense, filled with many trees full of leaves from the hot summer weather. Pine straw, rocks, and dirt filled the ground beneath us.

I kept looking around in fear that there was someone hiding out, waiting to shoot one of us down. I was the only one unarmed and injured, slowing the two of them down. I felt like I was going to be the cause of all of us dying. I began crying at the chaos of everything that was happening.

Jackson looked over at me, and I longed for his touch. He eased over beside me before looking into my eyes and hugging me, still careful not to hurt my healing ribs. His nose brushed over my neck, and I instantly felt safe. I wanted to be in his arms. I wanted to be anywhere but here.

Caleb smiled, sensing the connection between the two of us. Once we released our hug, he grabbed my hand, and the three of us continued walking through the trees until we could find a car or an abandoned house to hide or drive away in.

For the next couple of hours, there was no sign of any more soldiers, but they were around; there was no doubt about that. The gunshots in the distance were proof enough. We were still in a wooded area, skirting the edge of civilization, avoiding open areas and streets.

Caleb looked down at his watch before saying, "We've walked four miles. The sun is starting to go down, and we need to find somewhere to go before it gets dark. I don't want to be out here blindly with these soldiers. They probably have night vision gear, and we don't."

"Do you know where we are? Is there anything close by?" I asked.

"I think the public library is another mile ahead. Going into a populated area is risky, but we need somewhere to shelter for the night and if we keep going straight, we should come out close to the entrance," he said confidently.

I nodded, and we continued to walk. My body ached with each step I took, but I knew I didn't have a choice but to fight through. We needed to find shelter, and I needed to make sure we got there without slowing down.

"Are you good to keep going?" Caleb asked.

"I'm fine," I said, wincing. "Just keep walking."

We only walked a few feet before we heard a rustle in the leaves not too far from where we were. Caleb and Jackson guarded me, both facing opposite directions with their guns pointed straight ahead. We soon spotted a body creeping down from the side Caleb was facing. They looked injured, and the sight reminded me of the man we'd passed by on the way home from the hospital a couple of weeks ago.

"Are you hurt? Put your hands up so we know you're not armed," he called out.

They didn't raise their hands; they just kept slowly creeping toward us. It was an eerie feeling. They were getting closer, and I could see they were now visibly in bad health. I wasn't sure how he was still walking given the condition he was in. In fact, the man looked … dead.

Caleb ran in the man's direction to try and help, but as he approached, the man lunged and Caleb was suddenly wrestling with a seemingly possessed body. The sounds of the man's groans sent chills throughout my body.

As I looked on in horror, Caleb's feet started to slide down the slope he was standing on, and I could tell he was beginning to panic.

"Jackson, help!" he called out, trying to push away the flailing body.

Jackson ran toward the two of them, lifted his gun, and shot the man in the head. The body collapsed lifelessly onto the ground.

I had a bad feeling about this, so I moved closer to investigate the encounter. As I looked down at the cold, discolored body, I realized that Jackson hadn't killed him. He'd been dead all along.

My eyes widened. "Holy shit! That's a zombie."

7

WHAT LIES AHEAD

THREE OF US STOOD around the body in silence, hardly able to process what had just happened.

The body looked dead before we'd killed it. The man had lost the pink to his skin, making him a pale gray color. His eyes were sort of glossed over, and his fingernails had dirt underneath the edges, as if he'd started his journey by lying on the ground, projecting himself up once the virus had spread throughout his body.

I bent down to touch his skin, and he was cooler than most but still fairly warm. Based on that, he hadn't been dead long at all.

When I'd thought of zombies before, I associated them with rising from their graves after centuries, their frail fingers clawing at the surface of layered dirt and grass. But this was different. The people six feet underground were still down there; these people—zombies, corpses—were like us a week ago, but they were less fortunate in escaping the epidemic that was, at the very least, spreading through Oklahoma.

Oklahoma. Oh fuck. My heart dropped as I remembered Bailey and his cowboy hat that I'd left behind in the house. Bailey was headed to that house; the house where we dodged literal bullets. Before, I was anxious about how we would cope with having a baby together. Now my bigger concern was about him arriving to a trap—or worse, a war zone. I was terrified that he was going to be executed upon arrival, and I had no way to warn him about the dangers here.

Had they made it to Tennessee, too?

I was sure these people, this army, had been all over the United States at this point. After all, why would they start in Oklahoma? But how would we find survivors? Surely there would be other survivors, right? And hopefully Bailey would be one of them.

This attempt to wipe out the living population was frightening. Something I knew I would have nightmares about for years to come. The unknowns were still unknown. I mean, what would happen if its nails tore through our skin? What if it bit, coughed, or sneezed on us? Would we become infected? Anything was possible, and if this really was some kind of virus, its means of spreading could be endless.

In nursing school, I was so intrigued by microbiology, bacteria, pathogens, and microorganisms that determined a vast portion of our lives. I'd read about influenza, coronavirus, HIV, and others—some of which made perfect sense and others that I felt drawn to because of their unknowns. I can't say that any of those ever scared me, but this? This did. I did not want to die this way, and I did not want to see anyone I loved die this way.

I just didn't understand how the world could change in one quick flash. We didn't know how to live in a world like this. We didn't know how to survive, how to fight.

As we continued walking through the woods, Jackson looked over at me. He gave me a hint of a smile before asking me about the incident at the house. I think he was trying to make sense of everything too.

"Sammi, what was that man trying to do to you in the house? Why did he make you take your shirt off?" he asked.

"When the soldiers found me in the house, they wanted to inject something into my arm. They're injecting people with some kind of virus or something and then killing them," I said. My mind was flooded with thoughts and emotions, trying to figure out what exactly they had drawn up in that syringe.

The two of them stood with a blank expression on their faces as we stopped walking. Jackson eased closer to me and grabbed my hand, squeezing it gently, his palms sweaty.

"I think whatever they're injecting people with is what causes them to turn into zombies. They're trying to create a man-made apocalypse," I said.

"Let's get to the library before we start speculating about the possibility of a zombie apocalypse. I don't even know what to say to any of this," Caleb said with a chuckle and a strong suggestion of dark humor. He'd always had his own way of coping with difficult situations. He was one of those people who talked with his hands, using them to back up his internal feelings with expressive, dramatic gestures.

We continued walking the remaining distance to the library. I slowly hobbled through nature's summer debris, feeling more tired than in pain. After about thirty minutes, we reached the edge of the woods, several yards from the road. There was no sign of anyone, which was both a concern and a relief.

The library appeared to be old, or historic, if you want to be more politically correct. It stood alone off to the side of the road. It was built with dark red and faded tan bricks that had a little bit of mold in the parts shaded from the sun. There were small shrubs around parts of the building, and it seemed like it had been a part of this community for a while. I could imagine the traffic it once had slowly dissipating in the world we live in now, where you could download eBooks or Google anything on your phone in seconds. Still, there was a charm to a public library that always seemed to keep them alive, no matter how advanced society got.

Caleb and Jackson cautiously surveyed the area to see if there were any soldiers nearby, but everything appeared to be clear.

"Okay, let's check the inside of the library. Sammi, stay between me and Jackson."

I nodded as we began walking up the slight hill beside the road and onto the warm asphalt. Jackson locked his arm around mine to help boost me up the small slope.

Caleb led the way to the entrance, gun ready for use. He grabbed the handle of the glass door and pulled it toward himself. It creaked slightly, the hinges straining, and I winced at the noise. I didn't want to draw attention, but it was too late. The growls of a half dozen zombies echoed throughout the library, the sounds growing louder as they followed the noise they'd heard from the front entrance.

Did they still have enough cognitive functioning to associate that noise with a door that they were familiar with? Or were they following the scent of us that they were alerted to by the sound?

My brain was like a light surrounded by bugs continually flying into it—recognizing a chorus of buzzes but unable to locate the single source that started the initial onslaught. I was having a hard time sorting my thoughts, but I managed to pull out the most urgent one.

"Caleb, if you shoot them, the soldiers will hear us. They'll come looking. What are we going to do?" I asked worriedly as I backed away from the door that he was still holding open.

"Shit. Shit, shit, shit!" he said quietly, frustrated. "Do you have a knife on you?" he asked, turning to Jackson. The faces of zombies were now in view.

"Just one," he said, pulling it from his pocket.

"Come back me up," he requested as they walked into the library entrance.

Using the end of his gun, Caleb hit the glass casing on the wall that housed a fire extinguisher and axe. The glass shattered, and he grabbed the axe from the hooks as Jackson followed him. They walked further into the library's large entrance hall, greeting the dead corpses coming for them. I slowly entered behind them but stayed pressed up against the door.

Caleb was now face to face with three zombies, while another group came from the far end of the hall, working to slowly catch up with their accomplices.

Jackson began stabbing the leftmost body in the chest over and over as he used his arms to fight off the rabid dead man. I could tell he was beginning to panic.

I cringed at the sound of their rotting teeth clanking together as they drooled over the thought of tearing our bodies apart, limb from limb. The stab wounds inflicted to the zombie did not seem to have much, if any, effect on it.

Caleb swung the axe in one fluid motion over the head of a younger, female zombie. It cut right down the middle of her parietal skull bones and into her brain. Blood gushed out as he tugged hard at the axe to remove it from her head. The body collapsed to the floor in front of the third zombie, an elderly woman. She moved at a slower pace than the others, but she was now facing my brother. She had to have been the librarian because she was wearing a name tag and wore modest vintage-looking clothing.

I felt sad for these people. You wake up, go to the library to work or check out a book on something mundane like bird watching, only to be ambushed by foreign soldiers wielding a mysterious concoction that turns you into a walking corpse. Talk about a bad day. They couldn't have imagined this would be their life when they went to bed last night.

I thought back to the zombie we'd killed in the woods. A gunshot through the head is what severed the connection between movement and activity.

"The brain, Jackson! Stab him in the brain," I said, my voice loud and shaky.

He pulled his knife back up again as he plunged the blade into the frontal lobe of the zombie. His body promptly fell onto the floor. The other three zombies were now right behind the remaining corpse of the librarian as they crept up from the back of the building. Caleb hit the librarian in the head with the axe, and he and Jackson prepared to execute three more.

I watched as they turned the dead bodies back into dead bodies, the two of them coated in blood splatters. We all sighed a short breath of relief after they'd killed all six of them. But our moment of recovery was short-lived. I'd been carefully standing away from the battle, leaning against the wall, but suddenly a growl emanated from a small hallway tucked away to the right of where I stood.

Before we knew what was happening, a zombie snuck up behind me, almost grabbing me as I turned and fell to the ground. I scooted away from it as Jackson and Caleb quickly ran to me. I backed up against a table, feeling around for anything I could use as a weapon. I grabbed a candlestick from the surface and forcefully shoved it into one of the eyes of the zombie as it tried to bite me.

Jackson and Caleb watched as it collapsed beside me as I struggled to catch my breath. I shut my eyes, taking deep breaths in and out.

Jackson stuck his arm out for me to grab hold of while he lifted me off the ground and back onto my feet.

"Are you okay?" he asked worriedly.

"Yeah, I'm just great," I said with sarcasm.

I looked down at my clothes and body, thinking of the virus. The chances of the virus being spread from the zombies' blood touching the skin was unlikely, unless maybe there was an open wound or it entered the body through the eyes or mouth, but still, I didn't exactly feel like taking chances.

Whoever created this injectable thing was brilliant, insane, and wanted the population to drop significantly and maybe completely wipe out the country—but why? Who were we at war with?

Caleb looked at Jackson and then over to me. I could almost feel his chest rising and falling with each heavy breath he took. I was tired for them. He scanned the hallway once more before planning our next move. "Let's double check all of the offices and rooms before we get too comfortable," my brother said.

I stayed back while the two of them spent a few minutes checking the entirety of the library for more zombies. I felt paranoid being alone, injured, and weaponless. I'd dodged my fate once—actually twice, if you count the zombie I just killed—but I didn't think I'd be so fortunate again.

Luck just didn't work like that for me. Once I saw their faces again and they gave me the all-clear, I felt relieved.

I stepped over the bodies as Caleb guided us through the entrance hall. Now the commotion was over, I had a chance to actually take in the room. It had dusty, busy wallpaper plastered over every wall, with dark brown furniture scattered around. I studied each detail, hoping this wouldn't be the last place I ever stepped foot in.

We passed several small rooms and alcoves tucked away into the walls, and eventually under a big archway to enter the library proper, which held thousands of books I bet no one had read in years.

Caleb confidently walked us through the main area. "Fun fact, this library was built in the twenties, back when wars were between groups of people—not people and the dead. They built a panic room-slash-bomb shelter bunker underground. When I was working on a bridge last spring, one of the crew members told me a story about one of his distant relatives that'd helped put it all together."

I felt like I was on one of those tours where you learn about all the historical facts of older buildings. The kind of tour I'd never voluntarily sign up for.

You could tell that this room had housed most of the zombies, because books had been pushed into the floor and stepped on, chairs were knocked over, and debris blocked several aisles. There were also blood stains seeping into the floor, likely from when they'd been killed by the soldiers. It looked as if the bodies had just walked in circles, crashing into objects until something grabbed their attention. They were like windup toys with no real destination in mind.

"Is that where we're going?" I asked Caleb.

"I think that's our best option until we can figure out a game plan," he said.

We slowly made our way to a back room that looked like it had archives and documents filed away in it. A dusty armchair sat in the corner on top of a big, patterned rug, and Caleb bent down and pulled up the left corner of the rug. Assessing the newly revealed floor, he grabbed the top seam of the wooden piece that was a slightly different color than the surrounding planks and pulled it up.

My mouth dropped open as it moved to reveal a staircase. So this was the hidden entryway to the basement bunker that Caleb had told us about. I was glad to know the story he'd been told wasn't a myth.

The staircase was dark, dusty, and had a vague mildew smell, like water had soaked into the old carpet, staying for years. Caleb's gun had an attachment with a laser and flashlight on it, so he used that to shine a light down the staircase while Jackson went down first, holding my hand while I eased to each step behind him.

Caleb looked around upstairs once more before grabbing the inner handle of the wooden piece and pulling it down. He reached his arm through the space between the floorboards to grab the edge of the rug and was able to flip the corner back over, so that when he shut it, the rug would fall back into place, covering our secret hideout.

We reached the end of the staircase and entered a space that clearly hadn't been used in quite some time. Jackson released my hand as he panned the room for the light switch, finding it to the left side of the staircase. The light hesitantly flickered on.

Once the room was lit, I scanned the room and was shocked to find a child hidden in the corner, sitting with their knees raised to their chest. He was quietly sobbing, visibly distraught.

"Please don't kill me," the young boy begged.

"We're not here to hurt you, I promise. We're hiding, just like you," I said softly while slowly closing the gap between us. I sat down on the floor next to him and he scooted away just an inch as he tried to understand our true intentions.

"Are you with someone?" I asked.

"I came here with my mom. She wanted to get some books for me to read at school. It was my first day back after summer break, but then the bad guys got here."

I looked over at the backpack beside him. "Where is your mom now?"

"They killed her. Then the librarian brought me down here before they saw me," he said, sniffling.

"I'm so sorry," I said. I gently wrapped my arms around his shoulders, hugging him as he mourned the death of his mother at such a young age, an age where he could barely comprehend such heinous acts. "You're safe now."

Several hours passed as we all sat huddled on the floor. I laid my head on Jackson's shoulder while the young boy lay across my lap. He seemed to have taken a liking to me as I comforted him while he attempted to get some rest. I gently rubbed his hair to try to make him feel safe. I couldn't imagine what he'd gone through, watching his own mother be slaughtered for no reason.

I wasn't sure what time it was at this point, but it had to be close to nightfall. None of us had really said anything since coming down here; we all just took in the quiet, calming atmosphere of not having to worry about zombies and soldiers.

As the time continued to pass by, I began to feel soft rumbles inside of my belly from not eating lunch or dinner. I looked over at Jackson and Caleb, who were just sitting with their heads against the wall. I placed my hands on my stomach, hoping I didn't wake the boy with the noises.

"What's wrong?" Jackson asked worriedly as he saw me look down at my stomach.

"I'm just hungry," I said.

"I'm sorry. I've been trying to think about where we could go next or where we could get some food," Caleb said, despair in his voice.

The boy lifted from my lap, rubbing his eyes with his fists. He turned to his side and grabbed his backpack, then unzipped the big pocket and pulled out a metal Spider-Man lunch box. "I have a sandwich and some snacks," he offered sweetly.

"I can't eat your food; you eat it," I said, smiling at his generosity.

"What if I split it into four pieces?"

I looked over at Caleb and Jackson who both nodded in approval. "Okay," I said kindly.

He opened the lunchbox and took out a Ziplock bag that held the sandwich. He used his tiny fingers to tear the bread into almost equal fourths.

"This one is a little bit bigger. Who should get the biggest piece?" he asked calmly.

"Sammi, you're pregnant, you eat that one," Jackson suggested.

The boy looked down at my belly that wasn't yet at the stage where it was showing much evidence of a baby, then stuck out the bigger piece to me. "You have a baby in your belly?" he asked as I grabbed the piece from his hand.

I smiled. "I do." I began eating as he passed the other two pieces to Caleb and Jackson. "What's your name?" I asked the boy as he swallowed a bite of the remaining square of sandwich.

"Greyson."

"Hey, Greyson. I'm Sammi, that's my brother Caleb, and that's Jackson," I said, pointing.

"Is Jackson your brother too?"

"Um, no. He's…"

"I'm her boyfriend," Jackson said confidently.

Greyson smiled and Caleb looked over at me, cocking his head slightly while smirking. I fake smiled as my stomach dropped. Hours ago, I was getting ready to play house with Bailey and potentially become something more, and hours before that, I'd almost slept with Jackson. Jackson said he loved me, and he meant it. And by now, I wasn't sure if Bailey was even alive any longer. I did have feelings for Jackson—strong feelings—so I was willing to see where we could go as a couple, even during a zombie apocalypse.

"Is it a boy or a girl?" Greyson asked.

"Um, I'm not sure," I admitted.

"I always wanted a little sister. Maybe it will be a girl, so I can be friends with her," he said innocently.

I smiled, my heart breaking for this sweet little boy.

Jackson was gazing at me from where he was sitting, and I felt butterflies in my stomach. I could tell I was blushing, but I just had to embrace it at this point. Looking back at him, all I could think about was if he was imagining a life with me. Was he thinking about how our life could look, raising a baby together, growing old together? I know I was.

Greyson pulled out a bag of chips, a bottle of water, an apple, and a candy bar from his lunchbox. He handed me the bottle, and I untwisted the cap, taking a few sips before passing the bottle to Jackson. We all took a drink before passing it back to Greyson.

Caleb had been in deep thought for a while. I knew this was a lot to take in for anyone, but he was a leader and a protector. I knew he was thinking of every possible way he could bring us to a safe place, and I had no doubt that he would. Eventually Caleb seemed like he'd come to a decision about where we would go next. He ran his fingers through his hair as he inhaled deeply. Jackson straightened up, and we all looked to Caleb to tell us the plan.

"Greyson, have you ever read any comic books?" Caleb asked.

I furrowed my eyebrows in confusion as Greyson cheerfully said, "Yes, my mom would buy me them all of the time."

"Did you ever read any about zombies?"

"Yeah, they eat your brains," he said.

"That's right. They're scary, and you don't want to get near them," he began.

I looked over at Greyson and grabbed his hand. I could tell where my brother was going, and picked up on the thread. "Greyson, we're going to have to find somewhere else to go when the sun comes up. I need you to be prepared for what's out there, okay?"

He nodded.

"The bad guys could still be looking for people, and we cannot let them find us," I continued. I tried to think of how I could explain to him what was going on, but could a child process the concept of a real-life zombie? More complex than a comic zombie for sure. "The bad guys are killing people, but then they are coming back to life as zombies," I explained.

"So, the bad guys are making zombies?" he asked.

"Yes. We cannot let them get near us. So, when we get ready to go back outside, I need you to be brave and stay close by. Can you do that?"

He nodded once more.

It was seemingly nighttime, as we all grew sleepy. Caleb turned the light off, and I think we were all able to sleep throughout the night, for the most part. Once we were awake, Caleb gave us the rundown of today's plan.

I was anxious about leaving the bunker to face the world again. I could never be fully prepared for this life. Or maybe I could? Had everything I'd been through prepared me for this?

We all sat around the perimeter of the room, like we had the night before. Caleb looked over at me as I anxiously picked at the skin on my fingers. I could tell he was silently judging my nervous habits. He'd always hated it when I pulled the skin from around my nails; he said it made him hurt just watching me. It was more of a compulsion now—just wanting to keep picking until my fingers were smooth, even if that meant causing them to bleed. Just another thing on a long list of bad habits.

Caleb reached down into his pocket to reveal the amber-colored prescription bottle that held my medication in it. He unfastened the white cap, dumping out one pill into his hand. He looked down at the inside of the bottle, frowned, and screwed the cap back on, shoving the bottle back into his pocket. "There's only four left," he said worriedly.

I half-heartedly smiled. "Yeah."

"Well, I have a plan for today, so hopefully we can find you more medication along the way," he said and leaned over to hand me the pill. Greyson gave me the bottle of water that still held a couple of sips. I hated the way a pill felt sitting on my tongue in a dry mouth, so I'd always take a sip of my drink first, stick the pill into my full mouth, and then swallow it.

After the pill went down, Caleb stood up, stretching before taking a deep breath. I was trying to prepare for how we would move forward today, but I knew we'd be taking many risks for our survival.

Onward and upward.

8

WHAT'S IN STORE

I TRIED TO BE hopeful for today. I thought maybe the soldiers would clear out and move on to their next town, or maybe they'd go back to wherever the fuck they came from. I needed stability, comfort, and security, but that wasn't in the picture right now. And with Greyson in the equation, along with my unborn baby, things were a little bit more high-stakes. I couldn't be selfish, risky, or careless anymore; he didn't deserve that and nor did this baby.

Before the world went to shit, I didn't even know if I wanted to have a baby. I didn't consider myself fit to be a mother. But now that Jackson had declared that we were a couple, I wasn't sure what that meant for me and my pregnancy. We hadn't exactly had the chance to talk about any of this. Did this mean that he wanted to father another man's child? A man I wasn't sure would ever be in the picture again, considering the current state of the world. Then again, abortion wasn't really an option anymore, I guess, considering everyone was likely dead. And the same for adoption.

But the thought of having this baby without the assistance of doctors, nurses, and medications scared the literal shit out of me. I wasn't built for a natural birth. The only thing I had going for me was that I was an obstetrics/pediatric nurse, but I couldn't exactly perform my own birth. I guess I would have to work with the guys and prepare them for what was coming. That would be my best bet.

"So, what's the plan?" I asked Caleb. Greyson sat beside me, playing with an action figure from his backpack.

I watched Caleb's expression. He seemed uncertain. "We're sitting ducks in this bunker, and the dead zombies upstairs are proof that we were here. We just need to go somewhere further away, more secluded, at least until we know the soldiers are done reincarnating people into zombies."

"So, we need a car, right?" Jackson asked. He pointedly looked over at Greyson, hinting that the boy might be able to help us.

Caleb nodded and cleared his throat. "Greyson, I know this is hard for you, buddy, but we need a car to get out of here. Do you remember what your mom might have done with her keys?" Caleb asked hopefully, squatting down in front of him.

"She always put them in her purse," he said sadly, looking down at the ground.

"Do you remember what your mom was wearing?"

"She had on a pink sweater," he said, fidgeting with his toy, clicking its arms around nervously.

I thought back to the six zombies Caleb and Jackson had killed when we first arrived and remembered the younger woman wearing a baby pink sweater. She couldn't have been much older than me, and her life was over, just like that. I couldn't imagine a normal day ending up the way hers did. It just wasn't fair.

Caleb stood back up, sighing deeply. "Okay. Let's try to find a way out of here. You two stay behind me and Jackson," he said.

We quietly gathered what few items we had and accepted our fate, no matter what awaited us upstairs or outside. Caleb led the way up the steps, pushing up on the wooden piece and then propping it open. He climbed out right before Jackson, who reached down to help me and Greyson out. I grabbed Greyson's hand and turned to whisper into Jackson's ear.

"Can you and Caleb move his mom's body? He shouldn't see that."

He nodded and he and Caleb walked back toward the entrance where his mother laid, her skull split open from the impact of being hit with an axe.

Greyson and I stood back while I looked around the empty space for a quiet minute, then peered down at Greyson. He had jet black hair, blue eyes, and fair skin. He had been wearing jean shorts—I didn't know those were even still a thing, but they were cute nonetheless—with a green tee. His backpack from downstairs was now securely resting on his back. It was the same Spider-Man design that matched his lunchbox and his black tennis shoes.

He was precious.

"How old are you?" I asked him as we waited alone.

"Six. And a half," he added.

I smiled at him. "That's awesome!"

"Yeah. I'll be seven at the end of February," he informed me.

"No way! That's my birthday month," I said excitedly.

He looked so impressed, and we both giggled quietly.

We waited for a few minutes while Jackson and Caleb worked in the entrance, doing what they could to keep Greyson from seeing his dead mother. When they moved back through to where we were, their hands were painted in blood from moving the mutilated bodies.

"I think we're ready," Caleb said, a pair of keys jingling in his hand. He must have found Greyson's mom's purse somewhere.

We followed behind them through the same area we'd entered yesterday. There were no longer six bodies lying on the floor, but the bloody evidence remained soaked into the abstract printed carpet.

We made it to the door, but Caleb halted suddenly, and Jackson put an arm out, stopping mine and Greyson's progress.

"Is everything okay?" I asked, confused. I thought this was supposed to be a quick getaway. But then I looked up and realized why we'd stopped.

Outside was a seemingly lost and frazzled soldier—dressed in a green camouflage uniform with tan boots—stumbling around. He was holding his right hand over his left arm, and blood covered several parts of his body. It seemed like he'd been separated from his group, and he looked confused, desperate to find help.

Caleb backed us all up against the wall to hide from the soldier's sight, in fear that he was a threat. But, after studying the soldier circling the parking lot for a minute, it was clear he was only a straggler. There was no sign of anyone else.

"Should we go outside?" Jackson asked after a few minutes.

"No, let him figure it out," Caleb said as they watched the soldier cross the parking lot. "There are four zombies going after him. He won't make it," he said, noticing a group of zombies approaching the soldier.

"Shit, he's headed for the door," Jackson said, running to turn the deadbolt over, locking the door.

The soldier ran as fast as he could, despite being injured. He reached the glass, his bloody hands smudging it as he pressed against the door. He pulled on the handle, only to discover we'd locked him out, then banged his bloody fists against the glass, begging for us to let him in. "Please, open the door! Let me in," he yelled in a strong accent.

I pulled Greyson against me and covered his ears with my hands to shield him from the sight as we remained silent, watching as the corpses surrounded him, beginning to rip him apart. I looked away in disgust, holding back the urge to vomit. The sight of dead people eating the flesh from bones was hard to stomach.

Eventually, the cries of the man were muted and only small parts of him remained.

Once the man was dead, Caleb turned to me, using his arm to wipe the sweat from his forehead. "Jackson and I are going to go out there and get rid of the zombies. You stay here with Greyson. Go back into the main hall so he doesn't see."

I hated the idea of my brother and Jackson willfully walking into a horde of zombies, but knew it was necessary if we were going to escape. So

I took Greyson's hand and led him to the children's section of the library, trying to keep him distracted while they fought off the zombies.

Fortunately, as they explained later, the four zombies were preoccupied by picking the remaining meat off the soldiers' bones, so they were able to take them out fairly quickly and easily. They dragged those bodies away—as well as what was left of the soldier—before returning to the room we'd been hanging out in.

"Okay, we're ready to go," Caleb said. They were now even more covered in blood and guts.

Once again, we headed back out to the library's entrance, Greyson holding onto my hand as we made our way out into the parking lot. There were only a few cars nearby, and Caleb looked around, trying to determine which ride our set of keys belonged to.

After a second, Greyson pointed toward a beat-up brown sedan. It had rust in several places, a small dent on the back, and a busted taillight. I could picture Greyson's mother as a single parent who worked long hours to make ends meet; that's the story this car and Greyson's personality told me. This car that'd once been a symbol of his education, his mother, his life was now a symbol of escape, survival, and danger.

We entered the car and Caleb took the driver's seat, Jackson took the front passenger side, and me and Greyson took the back seat. I helped him into his booster seat, thinking to myself, *What's the point?* I tried to quit thinking negatively, but sometimes intrusive thoughts swarmed my mind. I had to act like everything was okay so that Greyson wouldn't fear what was happening around us. I fastened him in so some part of all of this would seem familiar.

Caleb pulled the gun strap over his head and handed it to Jackson, along with the bloody axe. Jackson laid them both in his lap, next to his gun. Then Caleb stuck the key into the ignition, and the car started up. We pulled out of the parking lot and headed toward the nearby Walmart. I looked back at the gloomy library parking lot, still occupied by abandoned vehicles and a pile of corpses.

We didn't really have a plan other than driving to the store. We hadn't thought up any strategy or escape plan, just going off good faith at this point and hoping nothing went wrong. I knew this wouldn't be a quick, in-and-out run, but my brother seemed optimistic that this would be an easy task.

Throughout the ride, I continuously looked out of the window to make sure we weren't going to encounter any soldiers. So far, it was a ghost town. It was so strange seeing the roads like this. It was so quiet and lonely, which was something I'd never encountered up north. I don't think I'd ever seen a road this empty while living in New York.

I was amazed at how a country with millions of people could turn into this nearly vacant version of itself. There wasn't a single person in sight, only a few abandoned cars along the highway that we maneuvered around. This had never been a heavily populated area to begin with, so the roads weren't blocked off by lines of cars. I was sure the interstates and major highways were impassable due to the number of people trying to escape. I figured it would be difficult to find a route toward a city or another state that wasn't packed full of cars along the main roads. I guess we'd cross that bridge when it came to it.

We soon arrived at a big Walmart right outside of Pocola. Without traffic or law enforcement watching for running stop signs, you could get from place to place pretty quickly. It was a little more populated here— likely with people who were probably dead and walking in circles by now. The parking lot was still nearly halfway filled with cars, and this made me wonder just how many corpses we'd have to wrestle with inside.

I could already see the silhouette of a zombie in the distance as it limped closer from across the lot. These fuckers were faster than the comics made them out to be.

I'd observed at the library that the elderly woman moved slower, and the younger woman moved more effortlessly. It seemed as if, once they died, they kept the capabilities, stamina, and functioning of their previous self.

This little discovery scared me. I couldn't outrun a fast zombie with this boot on—especially not one who had been fit and athletic in life. I mean, technically they didn't run, but they didn't drag along either. I didn't think they cognitively knew what the difference between running and walking was, so their instinct was just a typical walk. It was like muscle memory.

We drove up and down several aisles of the parking lot before Caleb pulled into a nearby spot, relatively close to the front entrance but still a safe distance away in case the store was overrun by zombies and we needed a quick escape.

"Are y'all ready?" he asked, looking out of the windshield.

I sighed. "I'd just feel better if I had my gun. I'm in no position to race a zombie today," I said thinking about the one I typically carried prior to this new shit show society.

"My mom keeps one in here," Greyson said as he reached forward to put his hand on the center console.

I lit up when Jackson opened it up and pulled out a handgun. But my glee was short-lived when he checked to see how many bullets were inside of it and there was only one in the chamber. Still, I guess that was better than nothing.

He handed it to me, and we exited the vehicle like some badass gang, though looking slightly less cool than I would have liked. Jackson gave Caleb his gun and left the axe behind in the seat.

We chose to ignore the straggler zombie that was a safe distance away to save our energy for what was inside, but then it yelled.

"Help, please!" the man said as he continued walking in our direction. He wasn't a zombie; he was just injured, limping with his left leg.

We weren't as on edge as I thought we should be, but we were armed; we at least had that going for us. The man would be stupid to try anything, so I felt confident that he was genuine in seeking help. We all remained beside the car while the man approached us, wincing from the pain he was experiencing. I looked down at his leg, but I couldn't tell much through his cargo pants.

We turned to face him, looking at his pained expression in silence for what seemed like several minutes.

"What happened to you?" I eventually asked, since no one else thought to address the situation.

"My leg," he choked out.

"Can I look at it? I'm a nurse," I offered, half hoping he'd decline. But instead, he nodded.

I squatted down to pull up his pants leg. I folded it up toward his thigh to uncover a wound on the side of his leg. It was most definitely a bite mark, one I assumed came from no other than a zombie. The skin around the area of the bite was inflamed, red, and it looked as if he was losing circulation to that section of his leg. What did this mean though? I was curious to see the consequences of this wound. As cruel as it sounded, I kind of wanted to keep him around to observe him. Like a science experiment.

"You got bit," I said dryly.

Jackson stepped over to see for himself, and the man looked down too. "I-I guess so. I was inside the store hiding from those things when the shelving beside me collapsed onto my leg from a big group of them piling up against it. I was panicked and in pain; I never considered that I could've been bitten while the fuckers were grabbing at me from every direction," he said.

I pursed my lips as I continued to observe the wound. If a single zombie bite affected his ability to walk this bad, there had been something transmitted into his body, and from the appearance and changes to his leg, my suspicions were probably correct.

I gazed back up at the man, feeling sad that he would probably die soon from this infection. He had to be only in his late thirties, not even halfway through his life. He had short, stubby facial hair with a bald head, and he was dressed in camouflage cargo pants, a dirty tee, and muddy boots. He reeked of cigarettes, and his voice was a little raspy; it reminded me of Penny from the gas station, almost like a comfort I didn't know I needed.

Jackson and I stepped back again as we all processed the meaning of a zombie bite.

"What do you think? Am I going to be alright?" he asked me worriedly.

"We should try to clean up the wound. Then maybe it won't get infected," I said, not really believing that the bite would heal but attempting to ease his anxiety.

He nodded.

"I'll need to get some supplies from inside," I said, looking over at Caleb.

"So, you've been inside of the store?" Caleb asked the man.

"Yes. There's about forty of 'em near the toy aisle. Some girl bumped into a toy that started talking and playing music, and those dead ones went straight for it. I was hiding in the garden center, but when they got to the toy aisle, I think they could smell me because no matter how still and quiet I was, they found me. A swarm of them surrounded me, and that's when the shelves collapsed on top of me. I managed to crawl out before I took off out of that entrance in the outdoor garden center," he said, pointing to the furthest entry.

We all looked over at the fenced in area filled with plants and bicycles, before looking at each other.

"Did the girl make it out too?" I asked curiously.

"No. I think she's still in there, but I don't believe she's worth saving. She was going to let them kill me to save herself," he said angrily.

"Well, we need to go inside. We'll try to get some first aid stuff for your leg, but it just depends on what it's like inside."

"I'll go with you. I can help you find your way around," he offered as he bent over to fix his pants leg.

"Are you sure?" Jackson asked.

He nodded.

"Okay, let's go in through the grocery side, farthest from the toys to avoid that group hanging around. We need food and water no matter what, but if we can, we need to find first aid kits, camping supplies,

Sammi's medicine, antibiotics, and anything else from the pharmacy worth grabbing. We don't know when the next opportunity to get supplies will be," Caleb said sternly.

I stepped behind Greyson, unzipping his backpack. Then, I opened the back door of the car to sit his belongings down onto the floorboard. "We might need to put some things into your backpack, okay?" I said gently.

He nodded sweetly as I brushed his hair with my hand. Then I reached to the front passenger seat to retrieve the axe and handed it to the man. I wanted him to at least stand a chance.

We all followed Caleb as he took off walking toward the grocery side entrance. The automatic doors continued to work because access to power hadn't yet become an issue, but I knew it would probably be gone soon enough.

The inside was no different than any other day besides some items being knocked over and buggies full of random items from people who'd left when trouble started brewing. The lights were on throughout the entire store, the coolers were still running, and the sound of a singing toy echoed in the distance. The longer I listened, the more I realized it wasn't just a toy making all that noise, but it was the growls of dozens of zombies adding to the music. We looked around, and it was clear that the zombies were all still gathered on the opposite end of this huge store, mesmerized by the music.

As ridiculous as it seemed, when I saw the sign for the restrooms, I felt so relieved. I had been avoiding the urge to use the bathroom, but I couldn't hold back for much longer. I was not built to pee in the woods. Well, not yet anyways. So, I took this opportunity. "I'm going to the restroom," I said.

"Well, let us check it out first. There could be a zombie in there," Caleb said, his voice still low.

"I'm capable," I said, waving the hand that held the gun and raising my eyebrows in annoyance.

"You have one bullet, Sammi," Jackson chimed in.

I rolled my eyes before saying, "I'm aware."

"Fine, but yell if you need us. We'll keep an eye on Greyson," Caleb said, patting the boy gently on the shoulder.

The four of them branched off to various aisles to gather food and water while I walked toward the restroom. Jackson took Greyson with him, and I smiled to myself as I watched the two of them together. It gave me a glimpse of what could be our future, if we were lucky enough to have one.

I pushed through the door of the restroom and looked around cautiously before entering the center stall. I sat the gun down on the metal bin attached to the side divider. Then, I locked the door—out of habit, not because I thought someone would walk in on me. I did my business and tried to appreciate the luxury of a clean working toilet.

As I stood up and pressed the handle to flush, a growl echoed in the bathroom. I panicked, unsure of where the noise was coming from. I looked down, and there was a zombie crawling toward me from under the handicap stall. It managed to grab my leg and instinctively, I screamed. Loud.

It was scary having dead people coming at you; I hadn't yet accepted that this was my new reality.

The zombie held on to my leg while tugging and pulling with force, just like a human could. On a normal day, I'd probably be able to yank my leg away, but it had me by my right leg, and my left leg being in a boot really affected my balance once my good foot was temporarily out of commission. I tried yanking it, but I failed. I collapsed to the floor, hitting my hip on the tile and attempting to grab the gun, but it was out of reach.

The zombie was a young girl with red hair, green eyes, and freckles. She was lying flat on her stomach, arms stretched wide with my leg in her possession. She was growling and salivating over the anticipation of chewing into my flesh, but my movements were preventing her from holding me steady long enough to get a bite in. I kicked, screamed, and stretched my arms as close to the gun as I could.

Eventually I wriggled around enough to the point that both of my legs were under the stall. I forcefully kicked the girl in the face with my boot, so that I could free my right leg. She went for the other leg, grabbing it tightly. Then, she bit down into my boot. She tried multiple times to bite through the thick material surrounding my injured leg and foot, growing angry when it was unsuccessful.

While the zombie was preoccupied with biting into my boot, I managed to get my hands under the stall and quickly unfastened and painfully slid my foot out of the boot. I managed to scoot myself back after releasing my leg from its grip, grabbing the gun. I unlocked the stall door and inched away just as the zombie realized the boot wasn't going to satisfy its cravings. Once her face reappeared under the stall, I pulled the trigger, shooting her right between the eyes.

I laid my head down in defeat as the door swung open.

"Sammi, are you okay?" Jackson asked, out of breath from his sprint into the restroom.

Caleb ran in right behind him. "Sammi!" he yelled.

"I'm fine," I said, closing my eyes, tears streaming down my face.

Greyson and the man from the parking lot were not far behind. Now everyone had gathered in the restroom to see the zombie that had caused all of the commotion. Jackson moved into the stall, knelt down, and gently rubbed my cheek as he tried to comfort me.

"Are you hurt?" he asked as he examined my body.

I sat up, sniffling and wiping the tears from beneath my eyes. "I'm fine. It grabbed me from under the stall and I fell and hit my hip," I explained, rubbing my sore side.

Caleb walked over to the stall to retrieve my boot, and the man from the parking lot followed, gazing at the zombie. "That's the girl," he said.

Caleb handed Jackson the boot and he helped me put it back on before grabbing my hand and pulling me to my feet. I hobbled toward the handicap stall where the zombie had been to see for myself. I approached the girl's still body and examined her skin and limbs before discovering that she, too, had been bitten. The bite was on her right arm. It looked similar to the man's, and I noticed that right above the bite was a dry speckle of blood, like she'd been injected sometime recently.

I looked over at the man and his face dropped once he saw that she had possibly died—or turned, whatever—from a bite.

That quickly left our focus when we heard a chorus of zombies marching through the store. My eyes widened in fear. From the chants of zombie growls getting louder and louder, I knew we were about to be surrounded and trapped. We were in trouble.

"The gunshot! They heard the gunshot. Get the door! It won't lock without a key, and they'll be able to push through! We have to hold it shut," I yelled.

I hurried over and grabbed Greyson, pulling him toward me. "I need you to go into that last stall, lock the door, and stand on the toilet. They're smart; they'll see your feet. The zombie in there is dead. It won't hurt you, okay?" I said worriedly.

He ran and did just that as I hurried to the door where Caleb, Jackson, and the man were now standing, their backs against the door, trying to keep it shut while forty-some zombies pounded against the outside. I joined in on the efforts to keep them out, but there were only four of us against their small army. Our feet were slipping further away from the threshold.

"We can't hold them," the guy said painfully as he used every ounce of energy in his efforts to hold the door.

"Go get in the stall," Caleb said sternly.

"What? No! I'm helping."

"Sammi, go," Jackson said angrily.

I gave them a look of despair and brokenness as I feared what would happen if the door gave way. I hesitated, hoping this was all a bad dream and that I'd wake up any minute. But it wasn't.

"I love you," Jackson said as I looked up at him hopelessly.

We'd been moving back and forth with the door, and the opening between us and them was getting bigger as we gradually lost energy. I released my hold and hurried over to the stalls as quickly as I could.

"Greyson, let me in," I called.

He opened the creaky door with silent tears streaming down his face. I grabbed him and sat down to the side of the toilet seat, sitting him in my lap. I rested my feet on the divider of the stall and held Greyson up against my chest, brushing his hair with my hands in an attempt to comfort him as gunshots unloaded over and over and over again. It was painfully loud, and the echoes of each bullet shook the walls.

This went on for a minute or two until I heard an empty *click, click, click*. One of the guns had run out of bullets.

There seemed to be far less growls now, but there were definitely still a few of them left. I could hear the cracks of their skulls from the man swinging the axe. One of the guys yelled in agony, and it sounded as if they were being torn apart by multiple zombies. I could hear skin being ripped and bones snapping.

I closed my eyes and held Greyson closer as I thought about Caleb or Jackson being eviscerated by zombies. Being unable to see anything that was going on was killing me inside. I could not do this without them. They had to be okay.

They *had* to be.

9

MONTHS OF MOTEL

A COUPLE MORE GUNSHOTS fired, and then … silence.

There were no longer growls coming from numerous zombies, just the heavy breathing of the two guys left outside of the stall. I cried with Greyson in my arms as I feared whose body had been mutilated feet away from us.

Eventually, I knew it was time to face the truth. I let Greyson down and walked over to the stall door. I hesitantly unlocked it, preparing for the worst. Easing the door open, I saw the man from the parking lot ripped into pieces and blood pooled over the floor.

I sighed deeply, and Jackson walked over to me for a hug.

"What is wrong with you?" I balled up both fists and angrily beat them against his chest repeatedly. I sobbed, and my hits gradually became weaker. I sunk my face into his shirt, letting out a mild wail.

"It's okay. We're okay," he said, wrapping his arms around me.

Caleb walked over to me, and I pulled away from Jackson to hug him. "I can't lose you two," I said as my brother comforted me.

"You won't," he reassured me, rubbing my back.

From what we could tell, the store was no longer occupied by the dead—only the four of us. We'd managed to load up the car with as many items as we could fit in the trunk and around me and Greyson in the backseat.

We weren't in the clear, but we would be okay for a little bit longer.

It was strange to think that there were no longer responsibilities like bills and work; from now on, our lives were just about surviving. In some ways, learning to survive was what I'd been trying to do my entire life, but now surviving had a different meaning. It meant I had to live for more than just myself. I had Caleb, Jackson, Greyson, and this baby, all relying on me to survive.

After we pulled out of the store, we just started driving. And driving. And driving. I lost track of how long we'd been on the road, between dwelling on my near-death experience and what the world was now. I wasn't sure where we were headed or if we even knew.

There was still no cell service, and I think that had something to do with the military invasion. Their plan was probably to cut off our access and communication with the world. No one could help us. And no one would want to risk it after millions of people had been turned into walking corpses. We were a dead country. Lost causes. No one was coming to save us.

As the day gradually passed by, I continued looking out of the window to watch our surroundings. The clock in the car at least gave us the normality of time; one thing that would never change, even when the world did.

We were only in the first couple of days of life in an apocalypse, but it was taking a toll on all of us. With no contact with others or the outside world, our hope was deteriorating, and the car ride was so quiet I felt like I could hear my own heartbeat.

I sat up and leaned toward the front seats as I said, "Turn on the radio."

"Why?" Caleb asked.

"Just turn it on," I said with a hint of irritability. I was curious to see if the car could pick up any working radio stations.

He pressed the media power button, but only the sound of static filled the car. White noise on each channel he clicked through. I frowned, disappointed. Then Jackson reached over and played around with the AM and FM, and to our surprise, there was a voice fumbling around behind the static. After a couple of adjustments, the voice became audible.

"If anyone is out there, we have a safe haven in Oklahoma City. Come to Omni Hotel; we welcome all survivors. I repeat, if anyone is out there…" the message continued, repeating the same words.

We all eagerly perked up, but Caleb quickly turned the radio off. "It's a trap," he said pessimistically.

"What do you mean? We need to go there," I said.

"There's probably an army of soldiers waiting on everyone desperate enough to fall for this. We're not even a week into this; how would they already have enough resources to welcome survivors?"

"Jackson," I said, hoping for backup.

"I don't know. It sounds too good to be true, Sammi. I don't think we should take risks like that when we're not in a terrible position. We've got food, water, a car… I don't know," he repeated.

"We need somewhere safe to go. I need security," I pleaded, looking out of the window as a handful of zombies marched around the fields, intrigued by the movement of our car.

"I'm sorry, Sammi, but it's a death sentence. We're not going there. They sound too solid, calm, like they just have unlimited supplies to hand out. The odds of that being legit are not good," Caleb said.

I pouted for the next hour until we arrived at a small, rundown motel. The neon light was buzzing outside as the sun began to set. We'd had a long day between the grocery store and driving, and although I'd much rather have been at the hotel from the radio, the guys had outvoted me. A part of me wanted to keep pestering them about it, hoping they'd change their minds, but I knew better than to get my hopes up.

Greyson was slumped over in his seat, having been sound asleep almost the entire ride here. I smiled as I watched him take subtle breaths while he dreamed. I was going to wake him up soon, but I wanted to let him rest just a minute longer before returning to reality.

We pulled into the almost vacant lot, the gravel crunching underneath our tires. I could see from the car that the front window clerk was a walking corpse, pounding on the glass while we parked.

Greyson woke up as we hit a small pothole that rocked the car. He rubbed his eyes and looked curiously at the outside of the building.

We all got out of the car and Caleb turned to me apologetically, giving me sad eyes. "I'm sorry. This isn't the Omni Hotel, but it's our best option right now. I think this will be a pretty decent stay," he said, observing the outside of the motel.

I pursed my lips and nodded.

Jackson didn't speak; he just followed Caleb to the window where the clerk fumbled around; a useless dead body locked in a tiny room. I could hear her growl through the window as papers blew around on the desk from the wind sweeping through the small hole that met the counter.

She looked like she'd been dead a little bit longer than any of the other zombies we'd encountered. It seemed like they'd been to this city at least a week before hitting Pocola. It amazed me how different she looked to the fresher zombies we'd encountered, with her dry, wrinkled skin, empty eyes, and rotting teeth. It was becoming evident that time played a huge role in their appearance and agility. It would one day be in our favor, but for now, it was too early in the decomposition stage for their stamina and elasticity to be affected.

The two of them opened the side door that led to her office, and Jackson held her still while Caleb stabbed a knife through her skull. Her body fell like literal dead weight onto the floor, and they retrieved a couple sets of room keys that were hanging on various hooks stuck into a peg board.

We hadn't grabbed any of our things from the car yet because we weren't quite sure what we were getting ourselves into. We decided to scope out the rooms before wrestling zombies with our hands full.

Caleb led the way down the left side of the tiny motel. The two rooms they'd gotten keys to were at the very end of the strip, 101 and 102. Jackson took the first room, and Caleb took the second, both with weapons in hand to protect themselves against any zombies.

I was sure the keys that were left with the clerk belonged to vacant rooms, but for peace of mind, we knew it'd be safest to scan for unwanted guests. It was hard to imagine that there could be dead bodies filling each of the rooms here. From the looks of this place, I don't think they got much business anyways.

Greyson and I hung back on the sidewalk right outside the doors until they were finished. The streetlights kicked on with a soft buzz; that's the only sound I could hear. The world was so quiet without traffic and interaction. It was an eerie feeling, especially with the sky growing darker.

Luckily, both rooms turned up empty.

"Okay, the rooms are untouched and ready to go," Caleb confirmed, meeting me and Greyson where we stood on the concrete, underneath the faded awning.

"How should we split up the two rooms? One has a king bed, and the other has two queen beds," Jackson said.

"I was thinking me and my new pal Greyson could bunk together in the room with the two queen beds, and you and Sammi can take the king," Caleb said, winking at Greyson.

He smiled in admiration of Caleb. Every time he protected us, it was clear Greyson grew more hopeful of what our future held. I could tell just by the look in his eyes when he watched Caleb and Jackson that they were like superheroes to him.

Caleb sat his hand on Greyson's shoulder as the two of them walked toward their room. When they got to the door, Caleb turned around and said, "Let's try to get a good night's sleep. Yell if you need us."

Jackson nodded and walked in the direction of our room. I followed closely and almost nervously behind Jackson as he opened the door. Everything had changed so suddenly that I forgot how to interact alone with him. It was like we were meeting for the first time, the awkward stage forcing its way back into our relationship. I'd never pictured myself dating Jackson; it was always just a silly flirting game for most of our friendship. Now that we were boyfriend-girlfriend, things seemed so unfamiliar to me.

I walked into the room after him, locking the door behind us. I scanned the room before taking slow, hesitant steps toward the edge of the bed, letting out a sigh once I'd sat down.

I looked around the dim motel room. It had dirty, dark red carpet, the older style of paneling on the walls, a window that looked out into the surrounding trees, and a mini fridge that sat on top of a wooden desk with missing paint spots.

Jackson plopped down beside me, so carefree, as if we'd been together forever. I think this was the closest we'd been to each other since we almost had sex on the kitchen island. That felt like years ago. But now, in this run-down motel room, there was finally a moment of relief from the dangers of the outside world. It was just me, Jackson, and my thoughts.

"What's on your mind?" he asked, always knowing when I was inside of my own head.

I turned to look at him, and he stared back at me. "We just haven't really gotten the chance to talk about anything. I don't know how you feel about a lot of stuff, and I'm worried that things are going to change," I admitted.

"What do you mean? How I feel about what, Sammi?"

"Me, us, this baby—all of it," I said as I turned away.

"I love you, Sammi. I know what I'm signing up for."

My heart fluttered in simultaneous fear and excitement, but the more I thought about it, the more I really wanted to make sure he knew what he was getting into. I turned back to face him, noticing that he'd never looked away.

"Are you prepared to be a father to a child that isn't yours? Or be with someone who has bipolar disorder in the middle of a fucking zombie apocalypse? Or to take on the responsibility of a six-year-old boy like he's your own?" I asked, my tone stern.

He placed his warm hand on my face, gently moving his thumb across my cheek. "I want everything that comes with you. Can you trust that?"

I sighed and gave him the slightest smile as he kissed my forehead. "Yes, I trust you with my life," I admitted.

"Good," he said, wrapping his arm around my shoulder and pulling me closer to him.

I wanted to tell him about Bailey driving down to be with me and this baby before everything went down. I just didn't have the heart to tell him while we were having a moment. I was happy with him, but I knew I could've been happy with Bailey too. I felt guilty about being torn between the two of them, but Bailey crossed my mind on a regular basis. On one hand, I just kept thinking about the possibility of Bailey being out there looking for me, and on the other hand I wanted to enjoy and appreciate the here and now, the physical presence of Jackson.

Since we'd been in the room, it had grown darker outside and the moon was shining behind thick, gray clouds. We crawled into the king-sized bed that was made up with a fluffy, vintage-patterned comforter. While the stitching was a bit itchy, it definitely beat the floor of the panic room basement at the library. We fell asleep in each other's arms in no time.

~

Morning came, and I was the first to wake up. I found myself kneeling in front of the toilet, vomiting up what little food I'd eaten the day before. I took deep breaths in between puking episodes. I had the bathroom door shut, trying to block out the noise to avoid waking Jackson, but it apparently didn't work because he rushed to my side minutes later. He held my hair back and gently rubbed my back until it passed.

Once I was confident I was done puking, he helped me onto my feet and left the room. I leaned over and turned on the shower faucet, running my fingers through the water as it gradually got warmer. The motel room was stocked with complimentary tiny bottles of toiletries, so I decided to take advantage of a shower while I had the opportunity.

The bathroom was tiled in mostly tan colors with some occasional red and green tiles mixed in. There was a single sink on a countertop and a gold framed mirror directly above it. The tile was cold on the bottom of my feet, but it made me feel like I was back at my apartment in New York.

I unfastened my boot and sat it to the side, then undressed and stepped into the shower. For a while, I just stood underneath the water, letting the warm drops hit my face and back. I closed my eyes, trying to relax, but I became distracted by my own thoughts.

Suddenly I heard the bathroom door open, and I rubbed the water from my face and opened my eyes to find Jackson behind the foggy glass.

"Mind if I join you?" he asked in a flirty tone.

"Uh…" I was hesitant but couldn't articulate why.

"What's wrong?" he asked.

"I don't feel confident right now," I admitted.

"What? Why? Sammi, you're beautiful."

I continued to let the water pour down my back as I watched the silhouette of his body behind the glass door of the shower.

"I'm pregnant."

"Okay? You don't look any different," he said.

"I just don't want to ruin your attraction to me," I admitted, embarrassed.

"Nothing could ruin my attraction to you. You look just as beautiful as you did when I first met you. But I'll respect your decision," he promised.

There was silence for a few seconds, then he turned to leave.

"Wait," I said, and he swiveled back around. "Come in."

He quickly undressed before joining me.

I wasn't far enough along to physically show much—or any—evidence of a baby, but mentally it made me feel insecure and as if I was less attractive. The appeal of me would disintegrate, I thought. I was nervous for him to see me fully undressed. He'd seen a lot of me when he came into my room that night in Nashville, but that was the extent of our encounter.

He was finally going to be inches away from me as I was completely naked and vulnerable—and then I realized I'd never seen him this way either.

The shower door slid open, and he stepped in. His body was perfectly sculpted, his hair catching a few drops from the shower head. He looked down at me as if he'd been waiting forever for this moment. His hands rubbed over every inch of my skin, and I felt completely wanted, adored, and appreciated.

He was gentle but firm as we kissed underneath the stream of water above us. Then he turned me around, my hands holding me up against the glass of the shower screen.

I gasped as he entered me for the first time. There were so many factors that would've, under normal circumstances, made this no different than a one-night stand, however Jackson made every second special. He'd seen all of my baggage—the entire truckload—and still accepted me and loved me for me. I could feel that when I was with him. Our connection was authentic.

I wasn't sure how long we were up in the shower together, but it was long enough to use up all the hot water from the tank. We laughed while in each other's arms under the now cold water before turning the faucet off and scrambling for towels to dry off with. The bathroom floor was soaked as we searched the cabinets for towels. After we'd found them, we wrapped them around ourselves before heading into the bedroom, still giggling.

As we lay on the bed, not caring that it was getting wet, we turned to face each other and smiled like school children. It was so rejuvenating being this carefree. For a second, I forgot about everything else in the world. There were no zombies or soldiers, just me and Jackson in this room together.

Eventually, Jackson and I got dressed in the same clothes we'd been wearing, and once Caleb and Greyson had their own showers, they joined us in our room for an early lunch. Last night, Caleb had stashed what perishables we had got from Walmart into the mini fridge, and from that we were able to eat bologna sandwiches and chips.

Boredom soon began to set in, and I found a magazine in the bedside table which kept me occupied for a few hours. Then Greyson and I played basketball with the wadded-up magazine pages I ripped out after I finished reading it cover-to-cover for the third time.

Our day had passed by so slowly that it felt like watching paint dry. But boredom was preferable to zombies, and we knew this was the safest and most stable place for us right now.

And that was our life for four whole months.

10

WHAT'S NOT TO LOVE ABOUT LUCY?

THE MAJOR DIFFERENCE BETWEEN the first couple of days and these last few months was that the power was now gone. Without the support of humans, we'd known it was only a matter of time. It was now winter, so without the production of electricity, we had no source of heat unless we started a fire. Our water supply had run out too, as well as gas supplied from the cities and other places. Our water lasted a little bit longer than the electricity, but the pressure got weaker and weaker as each day passed until it was just a drop.

During our first week at the motel, Caleb and Jackson had cleared every single room that was occupied by the dead. Occasionally, we'd get a couple zombies in the parking lot, but it wasn't anything we couldn't handle.

The supplies we'd stuffed in the car from Walmart disappeared after about a month, but I was fortunate enough to have two Boy Scouts with me who were able to start fires and scavenge for minor things.

Not even a mile down the road there was a Dollar General and an old gas station that we had been using as our go-to supply shop and gas station. When we first found it, the store had quite a few cases of water to keep us hydrated, batteries and flashlights to give us some light when the sun was gone, and blankets to add to our beds in these cold months.

Jackson and Caleb worked hard to keep the store cleared out, and it'd stayed relatively empty from zombies all this time.

We'd gotten a one hundred count stock bottle of my medication, along with an almost empty opened bottle, in the run to Walmart that first go around, but I was now down to the last handful of pills. We had also now pretty much wiped out the Dollar General of water and other necessities, so we were making plans to go to another store a little bit further out to restock on supplies.

I was also finally out of that fucking boot, but I only had one shoe, so that was on my shopping list, too. It'd been put on the back burner for a while because Dollar General didn't have a shoe selection, and I hadn't really left the motel anyways.

I was a few days shy of being seven months pregnant. By now I was carrying a round belly that did not fit into the shirt I'd been wearing like a crop top since my belly had grown. So maternity clothes were also on the list. But with the current state of the world, I just wanted to make sure we had food, water, and shelter above anything else. I'd worry about the little things later. For now, I was focusing on this baby and my relationship with Jackson as we prepared to become parents.

Jackson had been very involved with me during this pregnancy; he often rubbed my belly and talked to the baby like one of those gushy dads. I thought it was adorable, and I'd felt so happy and content during most of our time at the motel.

However with each new day that passed, we seemed to be drifting a little further apart. Greyson had been begging to sleep in the bed with us every other night, so we obviously gave him our attention instead of each other. And now that I was in my third trimester, sex and romance just weren't in the cards for us. I was physically exhausted most days, and I just didn't feel confident in myself. It was always hard to know what Jackson was thinking, and I feared that he no longer found me attractive.

I spoke to Caleb about it occasionally, our sibling relationship still as pure and strong as it had always been. I told him that I was going to continue to go through the motions with Jackson and try to keep our spark going, but that he seemed distant and preoccupied most days. It felt as if I was slowly losing him.

I had obviously not heard from Bailey, but he was never a forgotten memory to me. I was beginning to come to terms with the reality that he was probably dead. I just hated knowing that I wasn't prepared for what became our last conversation, and I especially hated that he'd never get to meet his child. I think he would've made a wonderful father.

I sometimes thought about a world where Bailey was alive and wondered if I'd ever be able to find him. It was hard to lose technology and the ability to socialize that created a much different world prior to the apocalypse. We were essentially living the same day over and over again. Wake up, eat, lay in bed, repeat. We didn't get out much past the extent of the motel parking lot, not unless we had to. It just seemed too risky. It took a toll on us mentally, but while we'd had our fair share of struggles the past few months, we were surviving.

Then one day, we met Lucy.

The four of us were getting ready to load up and head toward a store to find maternity clothing and other things for me and the baby. We'd finally gotten around to doing it, and I was so happy to have the chance to leave the motel. I felt like I was going stir crazy, staring at the same surroundings day after day.

But then a girl pulled up in a bright red Chevy Cruze, as if the world remained the same as it had been.

She was in her early twenties, not much younger than me, and she was stunning. She had straight, blonde hair and blue eyes. And even in the midst of a zombie apocalypse, she had a glowing, radiant face. It was a particularly cold day, and snow flurries were beginning to fall from the sky, so she was dressed in a winter jacket, white gloves, boots, and black yoga pants that showed just how perfect her toned body was.

She stepped out of the car and we paused to assess the situation, hesitantly easing in the direction of the car in case we needed to have an escape plan. These days you didn't just casually run into other people. We actually hadn't seen anyone since the Walmart incident, so for someone to be out and about driving made me wonder if she was a soldier, or just another survivor.

She smiled, flashing a set of beautiful white teeth. "Hello. I'm sorry to just show up like this, but I'm Lucy. I'm part of a bigger group. We have a camp, refugee site, whatever you want to call it, about eight miles down the road," she said cautiously, as if she sensed our uncertainty.

She'd placed her gloved hands into her coat pockets as the wind blew a cool gust past us. I was particularly cold because we left Pocola in our summer clothing, and we hadn't geared up on sweaters or pants yet. I knew to her we probably seemed like we were struggling, but I was perfectly content in our motel.

"How did you know we were here?" I asked skeptically.

Caleb and Jackson didn't seem to be wondering the same thing. They were just gawking at her like they hadn't seen a woman in years.

"I've seen you guys when you've gone out into town. You're tough. You know how to handle the dead, and we need people like that," she said persuasively.

"So, you've been watching us," I said, my tone sharp.

"Yes. We had to make sure you were good people. We can't risk bringing anyone dangerous into our camp," she responded.

"Why should we trust you?" I asked, shivering from the cold air.

"I wouldn't if I were you, but I promise it makes a difference being around more people. And we have warmer clothes, solar panels, and everything you could need for childbirth," she said as she looked down at my belly.

I narrowed my eyes at her before rubbing my stomach, but Caleb perked up as she said that. He turned to Jackson, who gave him a look, before responding almost immediately without even considering my feelings. "Okay, let's do it."

"Caleb!" I said aggressively.

He looked at me as if he were surprised that I was opposed to this proposition.

"Give us a minute," I said to her, irritation clear.

She gave a hint of a nod before gazing in Jackson's direction with a smile.

"What are you doing?" I whispered angrily as I grabbed Caleb's arm and pulled him to the side.

Greyson and Jackson joined in the huddle.

"Finding somewhere better for us to live," he said defensively.

"The radio broadcast, Caleb! Remember when you told me it sounded too good to be true? This! This sounds too good to be true."

"She could've killed us already if she wanted to. She's been watching us, so if she wanted us dead, we'd be dead," he said, crossing his arms. "Face it, we're running low on everything. It's winter, so we need heat, and they have heat. They have food, water, clothing, and stuff you need for the baby. Isn't that what you've wanted?" he added.

"So just because it's a pretty girl saying these things you'll go at the drop of a hat? Yet, when it was a message on the radio from a man, you didn't trust it. Screw you. I'm not going. We're safe here," I said, storming off toward the motel.

I walked into our room, embarrassed for so many reasons. Embarrassed that she looked like that, when I'd been wearing the same clothes since the start of the apocalypse. I was wearing shorts in winter, for fucks sake, and my shirt didn't even cover my belly anymore.

Embarrassed that I only had one shoe, so even when I tried to storm off, I was stepping on painful gravel with my cold, shoeless foot, like an idiot.

Embarrassed that I was seven months pregnant and not in shape or toned like she was.

And then for my brother and my boyfriend to be starstruck by her … that genuinely hurt my feelings. I couldn't bear to witness the interaction any longer, and I was hurt that no one had come after me.

Except Greyson. My sweet, sweet Greyson.

I was sitting on the edge of the bed when the door creaked open, Greyson appearing in the entryway. He shut the door behind him and joined me on the bed.

I always felt a sense of comfort when I had Greyson near me. I considered him my son now, and we'd gotten very close during our four months at this motel, playing games, cuddling, talking, and just being with each other. He and I had a birthday coming up, so I'd been thinking of ways to celebrate and considering what gifts I could get him from the store today.

Greyson didn't speak; he just hugged me from the side as I began to cry. Pregnancy hormones and whatnot. All I wanted was to protect him and keep him safe.

Jackson and Caleb remained outside with Lucy for nearly half an hour. Eventually I heard a car door shut and move over the gravel, as if leaving the motel. Moments later, Jackson and Caleb came into the room. I sniffled and wiped under my eyes, trying to disguise my current state of mind, but it was obvious I was upset.

They stood beside each other, arms crossed. "Sammi, we need to go to this camp," Caleb insisted.

"I'm perfectly content with my life in this motel," I said.

"They have a doctor, one that can help you when you get ready to give birth. They have the medicine that you need. They have enough food to last for a while. I don't know what else you could want."

"You two can go if you want, but me and Greyson are staying here. We can take care of ourselves."

"Sammi, you're being ridiculous," Jackson said in an annoyed tone.

Greyson tugged at my sleeve and quietly said, "Mama, I think we should go."

My heart sank the moment he called me mama. I loved this little boy. I loved him more than I loved myself or anything else in this world. He'd become my best friend over the past four months, and I didn't want to ignore his feelings. I also didn't want to deny him the opportunity to think for himself and to have a normal life. I owed him that. He had a say in this life we were living, and for that reason I decided we would go.

And it was the worst decision I made in my entire life.

11

OPFER TEMPLE

I FELT LIKE GOING to this new community of people would change my life, and not for the better. I was negative toward every gesture and conversation about it, and I was dismissive toward the guys being overly nice to me while we packed up our belongings. I knew that they believed they were doing the right thing, but it just felt so hypocritical considering they had shot me down with the radio broadcast all those months ago. It just seemed … weird. It was like she had hypnotized them. She painted such a great picture of this place—there was no way it was legit.

We packed up the car in silence before saying goodbye to the motel we'd called home pretty much since the start of it all. Greyson held onto my hand while I took one last look outside. I frowned, and the four of us got into the car and out of the cold winter air.

Caleb drove us, following the directions Lucy had given them, until we reached a gate. There was a black metal fence, not too tall, surrounding what looked like a nursing home or assisted living type facility. Every surface was covered in a layer of snow, now much heavier than the flurries we'd been getting over the last few days.

Caleb eased up toward the gate code panel and Jackson sat up straighter in the front passenger seat, as if he was a kid seeing Disney

World for the first time. I wanted to get a good look around, but I was protesting right now and didn't want to give them the slightest feeling that I was happy or into this idea. I held my head against the back passenger door, staring straight ahead.

The windows in our car didn't roll up or down, so Caleb had to open the door and reach his arm around to the panel. He pressed the metal buttons that corresponded with whatever code Lucy had given them.

Greyson was in the backseat next to me, cuddled up under a blanket for extra warmth. He'd given up his booster seat on all of his recent car rides because he said he wanted to be big and strong just like Caleb and Jackson. I thought it was sweet that he looked up to them, and I think that influenced his decision in wanting to make this change. I didn't resent him for it, but I wish I had done more to help him make the decision.

I could tell Greyson was excited, but I think he was holding back because of me. I felt guilty, I really did. If this really was some great new start, I would come around. But I'd always been hyper-vigilant, especially when I was in the right state of mind. I just had this gut feeling, and my gut was always right. Always.

A few seconds after my brother pressed the last digit, the gate slowly opened ahead of the car. He shut the door and drove straight down a long paved road that was becoming less visible as the snowflakes came down thicker onto the ground.

We approached the front of the building and continued driving past it toward the first row of parking spots.

The building was amazing. It was huge and looked like a lodge you'd stay at on vacation in the mountains. The exterior was stone, dark, and neutral colored with wooden details. It had a drop-off circle around the entrance and a sign out front that said "Opfer Temple Assisted Living and Long Term Care Facility," with a cross on the far right. The word *Opfer* had been added on with what appeared to be hand carved wooden letters. It seemed like the people here had made this place their own. I wondered what the hell the word meant.

The parking lot was packed with cars. I wasn't sure if all of the vehicles belonged to the current residents here, but if that was the case, they had quite a lot of people living here.

Looking at the selection of cars, they all appeared to be new and clean, as if they'd been used recently. Like seriously, every single car we passed looked brand new. Our car was pathetic in comparison. It struck me as stuck up and selfish to worry so much about having a fancy car when people were hungry, cold, and dying out here in this mess of a world.

This place seemed stable, and I was sure it would definitely be an upgrade from the motel facility-wise. I just couldn't help but think about what it would've been like at the Omni Hotel. It probably operated similarly to this—providing rooms, food, and other supplies—but I just couldn't understand why this was any different, safer, or more legit than the radio broadcast.

Eventually, we were able to find a parking spot between a black Cadillac SUV and a red Audi sedan in the row of spots furthest from the building. Caleb left the car running, and I remained silent. I was inside of my head again, picturing how our future would be now that we were here. Would we feel normal again?

From the coded gate to the nice cars to Lucy and her perfect everything, I was feeling more and more self-conscious. I knew I wouldn't feel like I belonged here. I mean, I'd been sponge bathing for weeks because bottled water only went so far, especially when you needed to save some for drinking.

We hadn't exactly been putting ourselves out there either. We went scavenging when we had to, and we could no doubt hold our own and protect ourselves, but we didn't like to go out more than we had to. With me being pregnant and Greyson being so little, we had more to lose, and it wasn't worth the risk of running into a crowd of zombies or leaving the two of us at the motel alone when there were still so many unknowns—at least that's what Caleb and Jackson would use as their excuse.

Yet, the first sign of Lucy and they're ready to risk it all. Call it jealousy, call it skepticism or hyper-vigilance, but usually when your gut was trying to tell you something, you needed to listen to it.

"Sammi, please say something. You've been quiet since the motel," Caleb said sadly.

"I just want to be alone," I said as I grabbed the door handle. I threw the blanket off of my legs and stepped out into the icy wind. I walked to the trunk of the car to retrieve the small bag of my belongings.

Greyson scooted over and jumped out of the back of the car behind me. He was holding onto the blanket we'd been cuddled up under as he dragged it across the asphalt. I wanted to lash out and tell him to leave me alone and quit following me, but I reminded myself that I wasn't mad at him. He didn't deserve for me to take it out on him.

He hurried over to me and I frowned, taking the blanket from his hands and wrapping it around his back as protection from the cold. I grabbed the backpack full of his toys, threw it over my shoulder, and grabbed my own bag.

I could see Jackson and Caleb talking through the window, most likely about me. "She's going to spiral," they were probably saying.

Goosebumps covered my body as my bare legs were hit with the chilling breeze. The toes on my foot with no shoe were numb as it rested against the ice-glazed parking lot. Snowflakes gathered on the surface of my hair while I studied the outside of the building. I was miserable.

After a second, I began walking toward the entrance, waddling like a homeless redneck penguin, Greyson trailing behind me. Eventually, the guys joined not too far behind. It was a decent distance from our car to the front doors of the massive building.

When I reached the double doors, I grabbed the right handle and pulled it toward me. Inside the entryway was a clean wooden floor with minimalist white and neutral-colored walls.

The aroma inside was that of some type of soup. My stomach had been growling all day because we'd eaten the last candy bar last night and there were no other snacks left. I hadn't had a real meal in such a long time, so I'd be lying if I said I wasn't excited about that. I was literally salivating over the smell.

The scent took me back to one night when the three of us had homemade vegetable soup at the house in Pocola. What I would have given to go back to those days.

We slowly walked toward the end of the hallway, studying each aspect of the interior of the facility. Then, Lucy appeared in the archway straight ahead. She perked up when she saw Caleb and Jackson following behind me. Her blonde hair flowed gracefully in the breeze from her purposeful walk as she moved toward us.

I avoided eye contact and instead just continued looking around. From the cross on the sign out front and the scriptures distributed in various places, I knew that this had been a religion-centered assisted living facility with the weird, adapted name of Opfer Temple. It had to be Latin or something.

I'd never been a religious person; I just didn't see the appeal of waking up every Sunday to sit for an hour and be preached at about something you could do on your own and in private. Religion just always seemed so shady and negative in the media, protesting outside of Planned Parenthoods or telling you that you were damned for hell if you were lustful or homosexual. And the general feel of this place definitely gave me cult vibes. What did I know, though?

"I'm so glad you guys decided to come live with us. You made the right decision," Lucy said happily as she reached us. She was still dressed in her expensive-looking clothing.

She didn't make eye contact with me; it was always directed toward the guys, and that didn't sit right with me. It was like I was a ghost—completely invisible. It was like she had wanted them to come, but she didn't necessarily seem thrilled about me or Greyson coming as a package deal.

I turned back to Caleb and Jackson, who both smiled ear to ear at her. I felt threatened by her in regard to Jackson; I'm not going to lie. I felt like she was attracted to him, and I could tell he was attracted to her, which hurt me way more than it should've. I probably wouldn't have felt as bad if he and I were on better terms, but I didn't know where his mind was. This move made me worry about the future of our relationship.

Greyson grabbed my hand and comforted me as we faced this new environment together. I could tell he was nervous, and I sensed that he felt guilty for wanting to come when he knew I'd felt so strongly against it.

I was glad he wasn't immediately comfortable like Jackson and Caleb seemed to be. I needed someone to be a little on edge with me, because my boyfriend and brother were making me feel shameful or wrong for feeling this way, and that hurt me. They always swore they had my best interest at heart, but no one had my best interest at heart more than I did.

Lucy excitedly began giving us the rundown. "I'll show you to your rooms, and then you can join us for dinner. Mrs. Becky made Brunswick stew," she said cheerfully.

She took a turn to the right side of the hallway where the rooms began. At the end of that hall, there was a door that led to a stairway. Even the quiet stairwell was beautiful, with handcrafted detailing on the railing and art hung on the walls. Lucy looked back to make sure we were still close behind while she held onto the railing with each step.

We took the stairway up to the third floor of the building, where our rooms awaited. She opened three doors, and I looked at her in confusion. That meant she was either separating all the adults or putting Greyson in a room alone, neither of which should've been happening.

I looked at Jackson and Caleb, who seemed not to take issue with this, so I made a point to question it. "Why are there three rooms?" I asked.

"Oh, are you married?" she asked in a condescending manner, finally looking at me.

I narrowed my eyes at her. "No?"

"Well, we don't believe in fornication or living with someone if you're not married."

I laughed humorlessly. "You're not serious, are you?"

"If you want to stay here, you have to follow our rules. We still have our religious beliefs that all our guests abide by. We're not forcing you to stay here, so you're free to leave," she said dryly.

As I opened my mouth to say something, Caleb spoke up. "Three rooms will be great, thanks," he said, carrying his bags into the third room.

I took the second room for the sake of getting away from her, and Greyson came in behind me. Jackson took the first room after he and Lucy stood in the hallway talking about laundry, clothing, toiletries, and instructions for where we would go for dinner.

I pushed closed the door to our room and sat down on the sofa pushed against the far wall to take everything in. The rooms were originally designed for assisted living residents pre-apocalypse, so they were like tiny apartments. They had restrooms, closets, beds, couches, mini fridges, and so much more.

I wanted to hate it here, but it was already better than the motel, except for their stupid ass rules. It was ridiculous that you couldn't stay in a room with your significant other if you weren't married. I mean, it was a zombie apocalypse, for fuck's sake—were we actually still worried about sins and following Lucy's religion's elementary societal norms?

I was anxious to hear about the other rules they had here.

As I continued to ponder my thoughts on the couch, there was a knock on our door.

"Greyson, can you see who's at the door?"

"Yes, mama," he said, running from the far side of the room.

Behind the door, Caleb was standing patiently. Greyson let him in, and he took calm, quiet steps inside, shutting the door behind him.

"Hey, are you okay?" he asked.

"You know the answer to that, Caleb," I said, staring up at the ceiling.

"It's a lot, I know. But—"

"Do you know any of the fine print that comes with this place? Do you know all of their stupid rules?" I asked angrily.

He finally took a seat beside me on the sofa as I sat up to face him. Greyson explored each drawer and door in the room while we talked.

"I don't. I think they're going to tell us after dinner," he said.

"I don't want to go. I just want to stay in here," I said, my stomach vibrating beneath my shirt from the baby's kicks.

"Sammi, I know you didn't want this, but you're about to have a baby in less than two months. We need you to have a doctor, medicine, food, and shelter for yourself, your recovery, and this baby. That motel can't offer you those things indefinitely, and I'm not equipped to protect you if something goes wrong when you have this baby. I don't want anything to happen to you. Besides Jackson, you and Greyson are all I have."

"Omni Hotel," I said dryly.

"What?"

"Omni Hotel," I repeated.

He stared back at me with a blank expression.

"That was probably just as good as this place. We could've gone months ago, but you two made me out to be overly optimistic and gullible to the idea of a utopia in all of this. I think you want to like the idea of this place just as much as you want to get to know Lucy," I said, rolling my eyes.

He ignored my dig about Lucy. "It was too new. There was no way someone managed to staff and operate a safe place during an apocalypse not even a week into it. It was too risky. This place has rules implemented to keep us human and give us some normalcy. We needed to wait for real people to establish places like this. We had to wait it out," he said, frowning.

I said nothing, looking away as he stood back up. "If you want to shower before we eat, I'll wait for you," he said. "I know it's intimidating meeting new people and feeling like the odd man out, but you're not alone in this. You don't have to be."

I looked down at my dirty, shrunken shirt and shoeless foot in embarrassment.

"Lucy told Jackson that there was a room on the first floor set up like a thrift store with clean clothes and shoes for everyone to share and use.

Do you want to go look around at what they've got? It might make you feel better," he suggested.

I nodded.

"Greyson, do you want to go with me and Sammi? We're going to get some clothes to change into."

"Yeah," he said happily, hurrying to join us from the bathroom, where he'd been exploring.

The three of us went back to the stairway and headed down to the first floor in search of clothing. It was located in a big room that looked like it could've been where the assisted living residents once did activities or played games. It was huge. There were labeled sections of racks with baby, child, and adult-sized clothing, and everything was organized and neatly hung up according to size and color. I was ecstatic at the prospect of finally getting clean and well-fitted clothing.

I found the little boys section and looked at the tag inside of the shirt Greyson had been wearing since we found him in the library. It was no longer a bright green, pressed tee; it was slightly faded, wrinkled, and showed signs of dirt from our many play dates in the motel lot.

I slid the hangers across as I scanned through each item, trying to find his size. I came across a red tee, and when I pulled it off the rack, I saw a big Spider-Man graphic on the front and immediately knew this was perfect for him.

I turned it around to show Greyson, and his face immediately showed the beautiful excitement that I loved. It was perfect.

"Spider-Man! Can I wear it now?" he asked enthusiastically.

"After I get you a bath, okay? We wanna be clean when we put our new clothes on."

He smiled and nodded.

I also grabbed him a pair of black sweatpants to keep him warm during this icy winter and a black jacket to go with his short-sleeve shirt for if we were to go outside again.

Caleb found a change of clothes for himself and met me and Greyson over at the maternity section. I found myself a black pair of leggings and a blue long-sleeve sweater top with slits on the sides. I grabbed Greyson a pair of sneakers and got myself some black flats and then got us some undergarments and socks to wear. I think I was most excited to finally have two shoes.

"Did you get everything you needed?" Caleb asked, giving me a genuine smile. I think he sensed that I seemed a little happier.

"I think so," I said as we headed back out toward the stairwell, and Caleb patted me on the back gently, trying to comfort me in this transition.

We went back up to our rooms so we could get bathed and join our new community of people for dinner. I wanted to look presentable and make a good impression because these were the people we'd be living with for potentially a long time, and as stupid as it sounds, I wanted Jackson to notice me again.

As much as I disliked Lucy, I was hoping the others would be friendly and make this experience enjoyable. I wanted to make friends and hopefully find other children that Greyson could play with. I really had no idea what to expect going into this, but I was opening up to at least being optimistic.

I gave myself and Greyson a bath after returning to our room. Then we got changed into our new clothes, both of us looking and feeling better than we had in months. I kept my hair down, brushing through the subtle waves with the hairbrush left in the bathroom.

As we exited our room, I calmly asked Greyson. "Can you go into Uncle Caleb's room for a minute? I'm going to go see Jackson before dinner."

He nodded and ran over to knock on Caleb's door. The door opened, and he went inside while I knocked on Jackson's door. A few seconds later, the door opened to his beautiful face.

"Hey, you," I said happily, walking inside.

"Hey. You seem to be in better spirits," he said hopefully.

"Somewhat. I still think it's stupid we can't stay in the same room."

"I know. She didn't mention that at the motel," he said, frowning.

"Let's see what happens at dinner," I said, raising my eyebrows and leaning up to kiss him on the lips.

We walked back into the hallway, where we found Lucy. She stood with her arms crossed, looking at me with disappointment. "When we say you can't stay in the room with someone you're not married to, that means you can't go into their room at all. No closed doors. Nothing," she scolded.

We didn't say anything; we just stood in shock like we were in the principal's office. Luckily, Greyson and Caleb stepped out into the hallway, creating a diversion from her lecturing. She gave me one last irritated look before she began walking back toward the stairway.

We all followed her downstairs to a large cafeteria-looking room. There were many long tables with seats distributed evenly on both sides. Buffet tables were lined up on the right side of the room with workers standing behind them, serving portions of the Brunswick stew Lucy had mentioned.

We took almost everyone's attention upon entering. It was apparent we were late.

"Well, just grab a tray and a plate and get in line. The workers will serve your plates for you; just tell them if there's anything you do not want. You can sit anywhere you'd like, and after everyone is finished, we will meet in the chapel to discuss all the rules with you all," Lucy said, pointing to each relevant spot within the room, then disappearing amongst the tables of people.

We took our spot at the end of a short line. Caleb grabbed a stack of trays and plates and passed them back to each of us. The women serving food were both middle-aged with gray hair pulled up neatly under their hairnets and wearing white aprons over their clothing. They smiled at each of us as they gave us a cup of soup, a slice of cornbread, corn, and shredded cheese. Bottles of water were sitting on the last table, so we each took one of those as well.

The room was full of different conversations and laughter from people who had been living safe, somewhat normal lives. I was starting to feel confident in the decision to come here, despite being distanced from

Jackson. I was happy that they were happy, and that was enough for me at this moment.

I scanned the room for a place to sit. In the far corner I could see a man sitting alone, his back toward everyone else, looking both physically and mentally isolated. It seemed strange that even with all the luxuries and people here, someone felt the need to sit alone. I decided to see if it was okay to sit beside him, wanting to try to make someone's night a little less lonely.

Greyson followed closely as we brushed our way through the cafeteria until we reached the man. When I was a couple of feet away, I spoke.

"Is it okay if we join you?" I asked politely.

As the man turned around, I dropped the tray of food onto the floor, certain I'd seen a ghost.

It was fucking Bailey.

12

GO WITH YOUR GUT

BAILEY'S EYES WERE ALMOST as wide as mine as the cafeteria grew quiet and everyone stared at me. I'd apparently caused quite the commotion. He jumped to his feet as we both got down on the floor to try to clean up the mess I'd made. We were inches apart, and I looked up at him, a little confused that he hadn't said anything. I expected an excited reaction, but he was acting strange, like he didn't recognize me.

"Bailey—" I began, but he immediately interrupted me, a sense of urgency in his voice.

"Sammi, you have no idea how happy I am to see you. I had been hoping I'd see you again, but you cannot act like you know me. This place… it's not what it seems. Do you understand?" he said quietly, tone stern.

Before I could respond, Jackson and Caleb hurried over to my side. They sat their trays down at the table and began looking around for napkins to wipe up the mess on the floor. Jackson grabbed a wad of napkins from a table close by while Caleb kneeled down beside me. The two of them had never met Bailey, so they had no idea who he was.

"Are you okay? What happened?" Caleb asked worriedly as he started to clean up the food.

"I'm fine; I just lost my grip on the tray," I said, easing back up from the floor. I put my hand on my back as it ached from carrying a baby inside of me.

Bailey stood back up as I did, looking down at my belly with a warm look in his eyes. I could tell he wanted to smile, but for whatever reason, we couldn't act like we knew each other. I wasn't sure what he meant by what he said, but I trusted him. I would do anything he told me to do.

"I'll get you another tray," Jackson offered, making his way back to the line.

Bailey sat down beside Greyson, trying to act like he had been helping and nothing more. I walked around to the seat facing him. Everyone else had finally gone back to their conversations by the time Jackson placed my new tray in front of me and he and Caleb sat on either side of me. We all ate in silence.

I was internally thrilled to see Bailey; it was like being reunited with the love of my life. All these months I'd thought he was dead or gone forever, but the whole time he'd been eight miles away from the motel. I kept catching myself staring at him, but I had to remind myself to act normal, no matter how hard it was. He looked good. Great, actually. But he didn't look happy. I assumed it had something to do with what he'd just told me.

This place isn't what it seems.

What did he mean by that? How could I talk to him in private without someone seeing us or catching on to our history? I had to figure out what he was talking about.

"Have you been here long?" Jackson asked Bailey.

I took small bites of food as I listened to their conversation.

"I've been here a while. I've kind of lost track," he said dryly. "What about you?"

"Oh, we've been staying at a motel a few miles down the road for several months."

"The four of you?" Bailey asked.

"Yes. This is my girlfriend, Sammi. That's my best friend, Caleb, he's Sammi's brother. And that's Greyson—he's like our adopted apocalyptic son," he said jokingly.

Bailey's expression grew empty, like his heart had dropped. I had been planning to keep my relationship with Jackson on the down low because I didn't want him to see that I'd moved on—because clearly, he hadn't. But I guess that had gone out of the window now. I wanted to remind him that I'd chosen him; he was on his way to me before this all happened. How was I supposed to admit to him that I thought he was dead?

In a perfect world, Bailey would've made it to me, and all of us would have escaped together. Jackson could have remained a good friend while I was with the father of my child. But when people were being murdered or eaten alive by the dead, I needed a companion, someone who could take care of me and this baby. I didn't want to be alone, and I did love Jackson, so much.

What was I supposed to do now? Confess to Jackson that we'd been sitting with Bailey at dinner, and that I wanted to be with him? Or sneak around with Bailey to figure out what he even wanted now that he knew I'd moved on? Or was I just supposed to ignore the fact that this baby's father was here, alive, even though we couldn't even be alone in the same room because we weren't married?

It was all so much to think about. I wanted to stay with Jackson, but I also wanted Bailey. I knew I'd need to make a decision now that they were both here. I just didn't know how to make the right one.

I put the spoon back down on my plate, my appetite gone. I knew Caleb could sense that there was more going on inside my head that contributed to that tray dropping incident earlier. We had always had silent conversations just by looking at each other; it was like our superpower. I could tell it was bothering him, but he chose not to dwell on it at that moment.

After the short conversation shared between my two love interests, we finished our meals in silence. Bailey remained seated while the rest of us stood up and took our trays to the counter for clean-up. Jackson and Greyson walked out into the hallway ahead of us while Caleb gently grabbed my arm to get my attention, pulling me back from following.

"Sammi, what's going on?" he asked, brow furrowed.

"What do you mean?" I tried to seem oblivious.

"What happened for you to drop that tray? You looked—I don't know. You just seemed shocked or surprised," he said, trying to catch my eye.

I remained silent. I was trying to think of a lie to tell him, but I couldn't figure out what to say. He could always tell when I was lying anyways.

"That was Bailey, wasn't it?"

I pursed my lips before confirming. "Yes."

"What does that mean for you?"

"I don't know. Please, just don't tell Jackson. I have some stuff to think about, and I want to be the one to tell him," I said, finally looking at him.

He nodded and patted my shoulder as we headed out to where Greyson and Jackson were.

As we waited for Lucy to meet us to take us to the chapel for our "entrance counseling," I watched the cafeteria clear out as people went back to their rooms. A couple of men and women began wiping down the vacant tables, sweeping the floors, and emptying the garbage cans.

It seemed like they'd given jobs to some of the people here. I guess someone had to take on tasks like cooking and cleaning, and a place with this many people needed structure. But it made me wonder if they'd be giving us jobs, too. I was sure we'd have to earn our keep somehow. A place like this had to be going through supplies fairly quickly, so contributions surely needed to be made to keep it running.

I had been observing every aspect of this place, how it operated, and what the people were like. The cleaners seemed to be content with their roles. In fact, everyone was suspiciously easygoing and happy, except Bailey. I wanted to uncover the truth behind his insinuation, but I didn't even know where to begin. He'd been here for a long time, and he'd never lied to me before, so I trusted his judgment and opinion of this place.

Lucy's approach shook me out of my thoughts. "Follow me, and I'll take you to the chapel where Brother Gabe will go over all of the rules. He's the leader of everything here, and he ultimately makes the decisions," she said as she began walking.

She took us back toward the front entrance of the building, swaying her hips and making a special effort to bring attention to her leggings with each step she took ahead of us.

To the left of the double doors we'd come through earlier, there was a short hallway that led to the chapel. Lucy carefully pushed through the door, which creaked loudly. We followed her inside and found a man standing at the altar.

The chapel had brown carpeted flooring with wooden, cushioned pews in three columns across the room. There was an American flag behind him with a beautiful glass-stained mosaic in the center.

"Brother Gabe" had dark hair with hints of gray distributed throughout the strands. He was dressed in all black with a haunting look on his face, and he looked to be around fifty years old.

We all hesitantly took a seat in the front middle pew as he acknowledged us. "Welcome. I'm Gabe, and this is Opfer Temple. This meeting means that you have decided to come live here. We're glad you have joined us. In joining us, we ask that you follow our rules at all times."

I exchanged looks with Caleb and Jackson before turning back to Gabe.

"We are a faith-based facility. There is no cussing, killing of those alive or dead, weapons, fornication, or being in a room alone with the opposite sex unless you're married. We also ask that you abide by our curfew of ten o'clock, and we ask that you do not go out into the back courtyard as that is where some of our members go to pray in private or to mourn those who have died. We like to know where every member is throughout the night, so that we are sure you're safe, and we want everyone to be respectful to those who have gotten permission to go into the courtyard."

"You don't allow killing the zombies or using weapons?" Caleb asked in a concerned manner.

"Thou shalt not murder. They are still people, and weapons make our members feel uncomfortable and unsafe. We've confiscated the ones you've brought with you for everyone's safety," he said sternly.

I glanced over at Caleb and raised my eyebrows as Gabe continued with his speech. "If you're here, that means you have access to our facilities like water, power, food, and clothing. In a democracy, those things are paid for. Here, those things still have a price to be paid. Each person is assigned a job to help contribute to the smooth operations here. You two men will help with scavenging trips for keeping up our stock of supplies. Sammi, since you are pregnant, I will not be giving you a job yet. That means these two will have to work extra to pick up the slack. Any questions so far?"

"What do the children do during the day?" I asked quietly.

"We have a nice playground around the side of the facility that we just finished putting up a couple of weeks ago. They have access to that, and there are also several classes that our teachers hold throughout the day. We have a library beside the clothing room if you ever get bored, too."

I nodded, and Greyson smiled in excitement.

"Jobs start at eight o'clock every morning, starting tomorrow. You report to this chapel to meet the others that will be working with you. We also have several members that do checks throughout the facility to make sure everyone is where they should be and following our rules."

"What happens if we break a rule?" I asked.

"I wouldn't break the rules," he warned.

I nodded, suspicious.

"We also have two doctors here that can check you out during your pregnancy if you'd like," he added.

"Sammi also takes medication. She's almost out, and Lucy mentioned that you guys had a medicine supply that would have what she needs," Caleb said. I looked away, feeling a little uncomfortable.

"Ah yes, I think I remember her telling me that." He grabbed a small notepad and pen and walked over to hand it to me. "Write down the name and strength, and I will get Lucy to bring it by your room tomorrow."

I scribbled the name down and gave it back to him. After this, he dismissed us for the night and we headed back to our rooms.

It took me several hours to fall asleep. Despite being in this seemingly secure environment away from the zombies, I somehow felt more unsafe than I had in a while. I was starting to dissect every single thing I noticed here to figure out what they were hiding. I was quickly becoming obsessed with it.

~

The following morning, Lucy came by my room with an orange prescription bottle of pills. I peeped inside and noticed they were a different color and had a different imprint on the tablet than usual. I asked her what the medication was, because it didn't match the medicine I'd been used to taking.

"The doctor here said we didn't have the same manufacturer in our stock. That's the same exact medication, it's just made by a different company, so it looks a little different," she replied.

I didn't trust her, but she didn't hesitate to answer, which made me think she wasn't lying. I nodded and didn't question it any further.

While she was here, she took Greyson to the classes they had for the children. He'd hardly been able to sleep because he was thrilled to finally be around other children again. It was no surprise that he was up bright and early, filled with pure joy. He couldn't wait to make friends and go to the playground. It was all he talked about while we laid in bed last night.

I hadn't had much time with Caleb or Jackson, but I knew they would be busy jumping back into helping out and working the jobs they'd been assigned. Since I'd have most of the day to myself, I decided that I'd go by the library to find some books to read while Greyson was gone.

As I walked down the first set of stairs to the second floor, I could hear people talking. I took the first steps quietly as it became clear that Lucy was in the stairwell talking to Jackson and Caleb, smiling and looking so beautiful. I could see them down at the bottom of the railing, hanging on to her every word.

I was a little too far away to hear exactly what they were saying, but she started laughing at something and placed her hand on Caleb's shoulder. A look of disappointment crossed Jackson's face, as if he was jealous. I could tell he liked her. I could tell both of them did, and I wished it didn't bother me as much as it did.

This thought clouded my brain and occupied my mind in a way that affected my ability to think clearly. I was flustered and so distracted as I took the next step down that I completely missed it, tumbling down the rest of the steps that ended right before the set that Caleb, Jackson, and Lucy were standing by.

As I landed, I hit my head on the floor so hard that it started throbbing. I touched my fingers to my head, finding a warm, wet wound that was dripping blood.

The three of them looked up the staircase, confused, and immediately rushed over.

"Oh my God. Sammi, are you okay?" Caleb asked, panicking.

"I'm fine; I just wasn't watching where I was going," I said.

"Let me take you to the doctor. It looks like you may need stitches," Lucy suggested as I looked down at my bloody fingers.

"I'm fine, seriously," I insisted, wincing in pain as I moved. I was beginning to feel lightheaded thinking about the blood leaving my body. Even being a nurse didn't help with my ability to tolerate blood and injury. I could tell I'd done a number on myself with this fall, but seeming this weak and vulnerable in front of Lucy wouldn't help my case at all. It would only prove that I constantly needed saving, and that Jackson and Caleb were better off without me here to burden them.

I sat up between the sets of stairs, the room spinning just a little bit faster. My whole body ached, and I was afraid that something was wrong with the baby. My eyes teared up from the pain and embarrassment I was feeling.

Jackson grabbed my hand to comfort me. "You need to get checked out by the doctor, Sammi," he said.

I took a shallow breath and closed my eyes as a tear ran down my cheek.

"Did you hit your stomach?" Jackson asked.

"I don't know. I-I don't think so."

"You two go on, I'll take her to the doctor. You don't want to be late for your first day of work," she said.

"I'll check on you in a bit, okay?" Jackson said sweetly before standing up.

I half-smiled as Lucy turned to Caleb. "There's a wheelchair in a closet close to the entrance if you want to grab that for me."

He nodded and hurried out of the stairwell and toward the front entrance as Lucy and Jackson helped me to my feet and down the last of the stairs. Lucy opened the door that led out into the main hallway and Caleb quickly returned with a maroon leather wheelchair that squeaked with each rotation of the wheels. I sat down and gently placed my hands on my belly before I exhaled deeply.

"Take care of her, okay?" Caleb said to Lucy while half-smiling.

"I will," she said in a flirtatious manner.

If my head hadn't been spinning, I would've rolled my eyes, but I didn't have the energy. I was just ready to get my visit with the doctor over with so I could get back to my room and lay down.

We parted ways and Lucy wheeled me to a room set up as a doctor's office. She parked the wheelchair in a small waiting area before going into an adjoining room to talk with the doctor.

I looked around the room that was painted a calming light bluish green color. There were a couple of chairs and a small table with a stack of magazines in the corner. For a moment, things felt normal, like this was a typical appointment before shit hit the fan.

I waited for a few short minutes before Lucy returned and told me that they'd come out shortly to check on me. She left the room, and I sat alone in silence while I waited.

Eventually the door opened, revealing a friendly brunette man wearing khakis, a polo, and a white lab coat. He looked at me with a smile, and I instantly felt comfortable and safe. I don't know how to explain it, but I could tell he was a good person.

I sat up, returning the smile as he walked over to me.

"Hey, Lucy told me you took a fall. Do you want to stay in the wheelchair, or do you want to try and walk?" he asked calmly.

"I think I can walk," I said. I stood up from the chair, pausing for a moment in hopes that the dizziness would clear up.

"Are you sure?" he asked, noticing my hesitation.

"Yeah, yeah; I'm good," I insisted as my vision became clear again.

I followed closely behind him as we walked into an examination room. I sat down on the bed, the paper crinkling underneath me, and anxiously picked at the skin around my fingernails as I waited for the assessment to begin.

"So, what's your name?" he asked as he put on a pair of gloves.

"Sammi," I said.

"I'm Ryan," he introduced himself. "How far along are you?" he asked, taking several steps toward me to take a closer look at the laceration on my head.

"Um, I'm about seven months, I think," I said, looking down at my belly.

He paused. "Sammi…" he repeated quietly, as if thinking intently. "Oh shit."

I blinked. Wasn't cussing against the rules? Oh well, who was I to judge? I cussed like a sailor.

"You're Bailey's Sammi," he realized, stepping back and looking at me.

"Uh," I said, worried that I'd already caused trouble for myself and Bailey.

"It's okay, I know it's supposed to be a secret. He's my best friend here, so we tell each other everything, including the infamous Sammi that he fell in love with instantly in Nashville."

I tried to hide my urge to smile, but hearing this made me so happy. Finally, someone else was in the circle of secrets.

"To find him in the midst of this, in a world filled with the dead, gives me hope. I didn't think I'd ever see him again. I didn't think he'd ever get to meet his child," I said sadly, looking down at the tile floor.

"I bet his mind is racing right now."

I frowned. "How is he?"

"He's tired, mentally. This place ... it's draining," he said in a roundabout way.

"So, I'm assuming you know what he meant when he told me that this place wasn't what it seemed?" I questioned.

His expression darkened. "People go missing, Sammi. They just vanish. We don't know what happens to them, but one day, another person is just gone. We ask questions, and people lie to us. They finally got mad that we cared so much, so we had to back off, turn a blind eye to avoid being next."

"Where do you think they go?"

"Honestly, I think they take them off somewhere and kill them."

I swallowed the lump in my throat, about to ask another question when the sound of the clinic door shutting startled us both. Ryan quickly grabbed some supplies and began cleaning the gash on my head. Seconds later, Gabe entered the exam room, not knocking or anything. He crossed his arms and meticulously watched the two of us, as if he suspected something.

I was extremely anxious. Had Gabe been eavesdropping? Had he heard us?

"I heard about what happened and just wanted to make sure you were alright," Gabe said.

"I'm fine, I just fell down the stairs," I said, wincing as Ryan touched the wound.

Gabe nodded and remained in the room until everything was finished, almost like he was supervising us. I definitely got the feeling that he wanted to ensure that Ryan didn't say anything to me about this place. It was an eerie feeling. I felt like my safety had been compromised.

Ryan took care of the laceration on my head and checked on the baby, who seemed as healthy as ever.

Once he'd finished, I decided to go back to my room for the remainder of the day and try to figure out what to do. What could I tell Caleb and Jackson to get them to want to leave? I suspected they wouldn't be on board with the idea, at least until I had evidence. And how could I get some time alone with Bailey to discuss what Ryan had told me? I needed to get all of us out of here, but I didn't even know where to start.

While I was being examined, Caleb and Jackson went out into the big scary world for their new assigned jobs. I couldn't help but fear for their lives. We didn't know these people. We didn't know if they'd protect us like they'd protect themselves.

And they weren't allowed to carry weapons or to kill the zombies, which was just delusional. Did they think it was possible to just, what, walk around them? The bastards could damn near run if they wanted to. What if they were trapped in a bathroom like before? Were they just supposed to accept their fate? Were they all just sacrifices? Was all of this worth it?

These questions crossed my mind continuously throughout the day, until they finally returned that afternoon.

As we ate dinner, Caleb and Jackson chatted about their day. Caleb said the zombies looked like they were decomposing, and the smell of them was horrible, way worse than before.

One of their members was bitten, and the leader of the group told them that he had to be left behind. This scared me more than anything, because what if it had been them? I wouldn't have even gotten the chance to say goodbye.

I continued to keep Bailey a secret, as well as my new friendship with Ryan. I kept details of my doctor's visit very vague, leaving out most of the particulars even though I wanted nothing more than to confide in them about this weight I was carrying around. I was worried they were beginning to adapt to the ideals and rules we were being taught. I think they honestly wanted to do everything they could to make this work and to comply with every aspect. If I took that little hope from them, I was afraid they would resent me.

I think Greyson was probably the only one of us that had had a good day. He told us the many activities he'd done and the friends he'd made while we ate. I was happy he'd had that opportunity, honestly. He hadn't been able to be a kid for a while, so allowing him to learn and play reopened a door into normalcy again.

After dinner, we returned to our rooms and prepared for the next day.

And then the next day.

And the next.

13

GERMAN GUESS

DURING THE MONTH AND a half we'd been at Opfer Temple, I'd tried to be respectful of their extreme rules, and I worked very hard not to break any of them, including being alone with Jackson or Bailey. I did everything just as I was supposed to so I could avoid any consequences.

But it wasn't enough. And it never would be. Something felt off about this place, and I'd tried everything I could to investigate what Bailey and the doctor had mentioned without raising any red flags. There was some shady stuff going on here, and it gave me a bad vibe. And for Ryan to say that people frequently went missing just didn't sit right with me. I needed to know what they were hiding.

I tried to make a mental note of every person here, and it didn't take long before I began to notice several of our members disappearing sporadically, just like Ryan had mentioned. It seemed like every few days, I'd expect to see people sitting in the same seats at mealtimes, but they were just not there anymore.

No one seemed to notice or acknowledge this, other than me, Bailey, and Ryan. I couldn't tell Caleb and Jackson what they had told me, though I occasionally mentioned the empty seats and missing members to Caleb and Jackson. But as always, they thought I was overanalyzing the situation.

Caleb would just say, "People move on, Sammi. They don't stay here forever. It's normal."

But then again, he was dating Lucy now. Can you believe that? So, what even was "normal"?

It was almost immediately after we got settled in that they decided to start dating each other, and the two of them had been all giggly and flirty for the last month.

I guess when these are the only people you see every single day, it's better to be with someone than no one. It could easily get lonely. I would know, because Jackson had been distant again. He worked all the time, but Lucy and Caleb somehow always managed to have free time with each other. And when Jackson and I did have a little time together, it didn't feel the same. I wondered if he'd found out about Bailey, but I couldn't be sure and I didn't think he'd ever tell me if he had.

I'd been taking the medication that Lucy brought me, but I felt myself slipping. I was drifting into a manic episode, my thoughts and desires becoming erratic and reckless, and it was going to be too late to stop it soon.

I was almost certain Lucy had been giving me something other than my bipolar medication; I just wasn't sure what it was and I didn't know what to do about it. I thought about going back to Ryan and asking him, but Gabe kept a close eye on me.

I told Jackson and Caleb that I'd felt off lately, but they were almost dismissive of my concerns. It seemed like the only way I could be sure was to slip into that part of me I'd avoided for so long. I don't know how else to explain it other than like an addict relapsing. The feeling of being manic was exhilarating. In the past, it had made adherence to my medication nonexistent. But I was afraid Jackson and Caleb would accuse me of not taking my medications since I'd been guilty of that before too. I was worried about whose side they were going to take, fearing that it wouldn't be mine.

I'd been following the rules of this cult-y place for the past month and a half, and I was getting fed up with it, which didn't help my growing desire for chaos. It seemed like every other day Lucy was scolding me for a small thing like going to my room a couple of minutes after our strict ten o'clock curfew, or holding Jackson's hand in the hallway.

So today, I was planning on really breaking some of their dumb rules. I was going to go to Jackson's room after hours because I needed to kiss him, hug him, and just be in his presence longer than at the cafeteria table. I wanted to salvage our relationship that was diminishing more each day.

So, once it was finally past curfew, I waited on Greyson to fall asleep before tiptoeing out into the hallway. It was dimly lit at this time of night, and there was usually no one roaming the halls for rule breakers until about midnight.

I went to quietly knock on Jackson's door, but it was already cracked open. Curious, I eased it open further, and you wouldn't fucking believe who was standing, naked, in Jackson's room.

My heart sank as I watched Jackson gawking at Lucy's body as he sat in his boxers on the edge of his bed. She turned to look at me, her expression a mix of smugness and disgust, before I ran back to my room in shock.

I shut the door, locking it behind me, then ran into the bathroom and began to sob. I didn't want to wake Greyson, but I was losing myself more and more.

I guess I was half expecting Jackson to come after me and give me some kind of explanation of what the hell was going on, but he never came.

This whole time she'd lectured us about rules that she was breaking herself. Adultery, fornication, all that shit. Caleb's heart would be broken too when I told him—his girlfriend and best friend stabbing him in the back. It was an awful feeling.

Eventually, I sat down on the white tiled floor with my back against the door until I cried myself to sleep.

~

Once morning came, Greyson went to class while I stayed in the room alone. My eyes were puffy and red, swollen from the hundreds of tears I'd cried and the feeling of betrayal from one of the men I trusted most in my life.

Caleb and Jackson had gone to work before I'd gotten the chance to speak to them, but I wasn't planning on talking to Jackson anyways. My heart was shattered—I wasn't sure if I could get past this. Part of me considered staying in the bathroom indefinitely while hiding from everything crumbling around me, but I couldn't do that.

Not today, anyways.

I'd been keeping up with the date after finding a calendar in the desk by my bed. In doing this, I knew today was Greyson's birthday. I wanted to do something special for him, like maybe find some Spider-Man toys or a cupcake to eat.

But although I wanted to make this a happy day for him, I couldn't help feeling wound up about what I'd witnessed last night. I wanted to get to the bottom of this place once and for all. *Opfer* had to mean something, and today would be the day I discovered what.

So, I went down to the library and found the Latin dictionary. I searched cover to cover for anything pointing to the word, but it didn't make sense. I couldn't find anything. Was it a name, perhaps related to Gabe in some way, since he was the founder of this place?

I went back up to my room and laid in the bed all day, thinking and thinking. Once early evening hit and the sun began to set, a thought crossed my mind.

What accent did the soldiers have? It had to have been German or something.

Shit, maybe it's in the German dictionary.

I hurried back down to the library, scrambling for a book on German words. I flipped through page after page until I found it in the Os: *Opfergabe.*

And it stood for sacrifice.

I slammed the book shut as my heart began to race. The people disappearing, they were being sacrificed. But why? Was it because someone had broken a rule? Was it part of some religion?

I had to find Greyson and the guys. I had to tell them.

I went to the room where the children usually waited for their parents to pick them up in the afternoons, but I didn't see Greyson. Immediately the panic set in, and I had to find someone I could trust.

I ran down to the doctor's office. The clinic was empty, so I burst through the door to the examination room. Thankfully, Bailey and Ryan were both there. I felt immediate relief, and I knew I could confide in them.

"Sammi, what's wrong?" Bailey asked worriedly.

I was almost hyperventilating at this point. I hadn't really gotten to talk to Bailey at all, so for this to be the opening to our first actual conversation felt bizarre. I knew he'd have no trouble believing me, but could he help me? Did he know where they might've taken Greyson?

I tried to catch my breath before telling the two of them what I'd discovered. "Opfergabe—it means sacrifice. I think they're sacrificing people, and Greyson is missing. He's missing! I can't find him," I said, sobbing hysterically.

"Wait, slow down. You think they did something to Greyson?"

"I know they did; I can feel it in my heart. I've got to find him before they do something to him," I cried.

He opened a cabinet, revealing a gun, but before he could reach for it, I snatched it and took off out the door. Bailey called out for me, but I was headed for the field outside where I'd seen Gabe and a group of others congregate in the past. He'd told us it was exclusively for members praying or mourning, so I had been referring to it as the forbidden courtyard. I thought that might be where they took their victims, since they completely blocked it from anyone not in the inner circle.

As I ran down the main hallway, I came across Jackson and Caleb, who had just gotten back from their scavenging trip and were standing talking to Lucy.

I caught a flash of worry on her face as I stopped to address her.

"Where is he?" I yelled angrily as tears continued to pour from my eyes.

Jackson and Caleb looked concerned and confused. "Where is who, Sammi? What's going on?" Caleb asked, trying to calm me down.

"He's in the courtyard, isn't he?" I said, knowing I probably sounded crazy and erratic.

"Sammi, I don't know what you're talking about," Lucy said defensively.

Caleb was genuinely concerned, but he wasn't entirely sure what the hell was going on. I just knew I couldn't waste any more time. I quickly brushed past them and headed straight toward the door that led out into the courtyard—the courtyard that Lucy protected from people like me.

As I opened the door to the cool outside air, I became flooded with anger. A part of me thought I was having a mental breakdown. What if Greyson wasn't missing and this was all part of a manic episode?

"Where is he?" I yelled angrily, charging toward the group of people in the distance.

Lucy ran out after me, followed by my brother and Jackson, then Bailey and Ryan. I walked toward the group of men and women dressed in black, noticing Gabe amongst them. His eyes widened at the sight of me.

"Lucy, get them inside, now," he ordered angrily.

"Sammi, what's going on?" Caleb repeated, concerned.

"Greyson is missing! He's—" I cut off on a choked sob as I looked over and found him, lying lifelessly in a circle, surrounded by Gabe and the others.

I screamed painfully with the knowledge that Greyson had been murdered during some sacrificial ritual. I could feel the ground crumbling all around me, but before I could be swallowed by anguish, a switch flipped inside me. Without hesitation, I reached down and grabbed the gun from my waistband before pointing it at Gabe and pulling the trigger.

The bullet shot straight through his head, and he fell to the ground.

Then another gunshot sounded. Only this one was aimed at me.

I looked over at Lucy as she pointed the gun toward me, right before I collapsed to the ground, crashing like the world around me.

Happy birthday, Greyson.

14

A WAR AMONGST PEOPLE

MY SWEET, SWEET GREYSON was gone.

I'd failed him; I hadn't protected him like I should have. The irony was, I came here for him. I wanted to do right by him and give him a safe place to live, but this ended up being the worst decision of my life. To everyone else, it had seemed like Opfer Temple was our saving grace, but I knew in my heart from the first time I saw Lucy that something wasn't right. I just never thought this would be the end result.

Today was meant to be a celebration for his birthday. But instead of celebrating his life, I was mourning his death. He'd become my son, my moon, and my stars. I'd lost it all, and I was sure this was my "punishment" for breaking Opfer Temple's rules.

And I couldn't even run over to his body to hold him one last time, because now I was the one struggling to live.

Gabe's followers had scattered as the gunshots sounded and Lucy sent a bullet through my body—and then another, and a third. Caleb immediately went after her, knocking her to the ground and grabbing the gun from her possession as the members of Opfer Temple made their way outside to see what was going on.

Everything was hazy; my body was in pain, but slowly going numb, and I couldn't tell exactly where I'd been hit. I couldn't help but think, *I'm dying, aren't I?*

This was it for me. I just knew it. Tears pricked my eyes as I wondered what would happen to my baby.

People pooled out into the forbidden courtyard. Everyone was in a panic and scrambling as they didn't know where to go or what to do since their leader was now dead. I'd killed him. Screams of fear and despair filled the air around us as the innocent, unaware residents scattered in every direction.

Jackson ran over to me, tears trailing down his cheeks, unsure what to do to save me. He tried holding pressure on my wounds to stem the bleeding, but it was impossible to do with three gaping holes and only two hands.

Somewhere amongst the chaos, Bailey and Ryan came to my side to assess the situation. Jackson's hands were now covered in my blood as I looked up at him from the ground. I could see something change in him as he realized what was happening. He was distraught, begging for me to stay alive, his hand resting over my bump. I knew he didn't want to leave my side, but Bailey and Ryan took over, trying to keep me alive.

Jackson stood up, looking down at his hands and back over to me. Then his eyes searched the crowd, trying to find Caleb. My gaze followed his, trying to keep alert, and I eventually spotted Lucy wrestling with Caleb, ordering him to let her go.

I felt sympathy for my brother. Up until this moment, they'd been a couple. He'd had to quickly react as his girlfriend shot his sister, and all the secrets of this place had reached the surface. They'd murdered Greyson, they'd nearly murdered me, and now he was somewhere between saving me and stopping her.

I mean, what did you do in this situation? You couldn't just lock her up; it was an assisted living facility, not a prison. He couldn't bring himself to kill her either. It'd be different than killing a solider. And after you killed someone, everything about you altered—you never went back to who you were before.

Trust me.

I couldn't tell exactly where I'd been shot, I just knew I was in pain all over my body. I was in and out of consciousness and I was losing so much blood. I needed to stay alert for so many reasons pertinent to the situation at hand, but I was quickly withering away.

I felt a prick of despair as I realized I hadn't had a chance to tell Caleb and Jackson what I'd discovered about this place. They were probably so confused. But we were in enemy territory. Those words *Opfer* and *Gabe* were German for sacrifice. The soldiers that had attacked us at the start had an accent that I now know was German. The people here were working with or for the German soldiers that were injecting the population with something before killing them.

I tried to get out the words to warn Bailey, who was tending to my wounds, but I found myself losing consciousness instead.

Was this it? Was I dying?

~

I tried to find the strength to peel my eyelids open against the bright light beaming in through a window to my right. It took me a second to adjust to the sun; it had been a while since I'd seen it, even before I was shot.

I was shot!

I blinked probably ten times to finally get a clear picture of the room. Initially, it felt unfamiliar, but after looking at each corner, I did start to recognize this place. It was the hospital I'd been in a couple of times now, during my job interview and after the parking lot attack.

I was confused. How'd I get all the way back here?

I knew I'd been shot, but I couldn't piece together what exactly had happened before that. I tried to think back to the last thing I could remember, and once I put the pieces together, a tsunami of pain flooded my mind. The image of Greyson lying lifelessly on the ground felt like a sharp dagger piercing through my heart and my lungs.

I struggled to breathe, the heartbreak so intense. My sweet Greyson was gone.

I slammed my eyes closed, forcing myself under control, before opening my eyes again and focusing on my surroundings rather than the cause of my hospital stay.

There was no one in the room with me, which didn't feel right. Where were Caleb and Jackson? Bailey? I didn't remember them getting hurt back at Opfer Temple, but had something happened after I lost consciousness? Had my actions gotten them hurt too?

I thought back to the gunshots that entered my body from the pistol Lucy had pointed at me from across the courtyard. Now I was no longer surrounded by chaos, I could sense where I'd been shot. One bullet went through my arm, one through my leg, and the other through my...

I gasped as I realized where the third bullet had hit.

My stomach.

I cautiously looked down and rubbed my belly. It was no longer round, bloated, and hard like it had been when I was a growing baby. Had the bullet Lucy sent through my stomach killed my baby? The thought was painful. I'd already lost Greyson, and now my unborn baby.

I almost wished I'd never woken.

I looked around the room once again. All of this felt wrong. Had I hallucinated the last few months of my life? Was I just waking up from being beaten in the parking lot?

I knew I was sending myself into a spiral. I was going to make myself crazy unless I found someone to tell me what was going on. Something was up; I was sure of it. My heart rate was beating rapidly, my palms were sweaty, and my breathing was heavy—suffocating, almost. I had to figure out what was going on.

I sat myself up the best I could, throwing the covers off my legs. I had just thrown one leg over the side of the bed when the door opened.

It was Bailey.

Immediately, I felt safe and at ease. With him being here, I felt like things might be okay after the war amongst people, living and dead, back at

Opfer Temple. I had no idea how long I'd been here, but Bailey looked the happiest I'd seen him since the night at the bar when we danced together. He was dressed in blue jeans, boots, and a black tee. His facial hair was a little longer now than when I'd last seen him.

He rushed over to my side, sitting on the edge of the bed, and I swung my leg back over into the bed and repositioned the pillow behind my head. I smiled softly at him as he placed his hand on mine. It was like feeling the sun for the first time.

"Hey! You're awake," he said happily. The light in his eyes was pure and bright, like a million stars in the sky. I could look into those eyes forever.

He brushed a strand of hair from my warm cheek before staring at me, almost like he wasn't sure what to say or where to start. Scenarios of what was going on played in my mind, and I needed to figure out what had happened at the temple to determine the events that led to me being here. I took it upon myself to ask the questions I almost didn't want the answers to.

"How did we get here?" I asked worriedly, my voice still groggy. "I have so many questions."

"I know you do, baby. I have a lot to tell you, I'm just worried that you won't be able to handle it all right now. You've been out of it for nearly a week. I was afraid you wouldn't wake up." He frowned. "You lost so much blood from the gunshots that I thought you were going to bleed out before we could get you somewhere safe. That was the worst feeling I've ever had in my life," he admitted, visibly upset. "I felt so defeated and helpless."

"Tell me what happened. I want to know everything," I said, trying to brace myself for what was to come.

He swallowed hard, hesitating to speak.

"I can handle it," I said, even though I wasn't sure if I really could.

He sighed. "Sammi, after you collapsed, shit hit the fan. I swear almost a hundred zombies made their way through the gated fencing in the courtyard. They'd followed the sound of the gunshots and within minutes we were swarmed. People were scrambling everywhere, and we were just trying to get you somewhere safe."

I could imagine it vividly: An army of zombies leaning on the fence, putting their weight against the old, rusted bars. After a second, it would crash to the ground, and they would pour in. Screams of women, men, and children echoing inside and out, only attracting more zombies. Mass chaos overrunning a seemingly happy, perfect place. People being bitten or chewed apart, limb by limb, by the starving corpses. Caleb and Jackson probably tried to wrestle Lucy into a room, but as zombies approached their unarmed bodies, they would have had to flee and find keys to a vehicle or safe room.

I bet so many people died that day, and I was solely to blame for sending that first gunshot that killed Gabe.

But who kills an innocent young boy on their birthday for the sins of their mother?

My heart literally broke all over again at the thought of Greyson's death. He was probably so scared, wondering where I was and why I hadn't protected him. I wish I'd had one last chance to tell him I loved him and that everything was going to be okay.

Bailey's voice breaks me from my imagined reenactment of the day.

"Ryan and I lifted you up and ran you around to the ambulance truck that we kept on the side of the building. We loaded you up, and when we went back to help Caleb and Jackson with Lucy, we couldn't find them anywhere. I promise, Sammi, I looked everywhere, but everyone that was still alive had escaped—or tried to. Zombies were everywhere. I had to save you. If I stayed and looked any longer, you would have died," he said, regret filling his words.

"So, Caleb and Jackson, are they…" I began.

"I'm confident that they escaped. I didn't see their bodies amongst the dead. They're smart and strong. I'm sure they—"

I interrupted. "We have to go find them." I abruptly sat up, wincing in pain.

"Sammi…" Bailey warned.

I opened my mouth to say something, but then my heart sank once again as I looked down and remembered I'd been missing something.

My baby, that I'd been carrying around for months, was no longer a part of me.

It was in this exact hospital that I'd first found out that I was pregnant. I'd been so terrified that Jackson would hate me or resent me, but he was so supportive. I kept it from Bailey for a while, but I think he was excited—I could tell from his voice when I'd called him that day that he wanted this. It was his baby, after all.

Though I'd had two men fighting over a role in mine and my child's life, I'd made a decision that day everything first went down—I was ready to honor that life with Bailey. But now I couldn't do that without knowing if Jackson was okay. It wouldn't be right to carry on and live a life with Bailey if he was out there looking for me. Despite what he'd done with Lucy—whatever I'd walked in on the night before I'd been shot—I know he loved me and cared for me.

And Caleb … he was all I had left of my family. He was my best friend. I could never stomach anything happening to him, especially at my expense.

Even though Opfer was mostly Jackson and Caleb's decision, I agreed to go after thinking about what would be the best living situation for Greyson and my baby. I'm sure we all felt guilty in a way, and I just wish I'd had the chance to mourn alongside my brother and Jackson before we were forced apart to fight for our lives.

This was all so confusing and overwhelming. A zombie apocalypse? Really, universe?

I felt my empty stomach. I was struggling with the new world we were living in. Greyson and the thought of raising a baby of my own were the main factors in keeping my mind healthy throughout this transition. If both of those things were gone, I wasn't sure how I could outrun or ignore this dark shadow following behind me.

"I lost the baby, didn't I?" I asked as my eyes glassed over with unshed tears.

He looked down, and I began to cry, reading his silence as confirmation. I dropped my head in defeat, picking at the skin around my fingernails.

It seemed like Bailey was trying to find the words within our shared silence, and after a few seconds he found them. "I didn't know what you wanted to name her," he began.

Our eyes reconnected and he grabbed my shaking, cold hands to stop me from picking my fingernails. They had begun bleeding from my nervous habit.

I tilted my head to the side, and asked, "It was a girl?"

"She *is* a girl."

Suddenly, my world started spinning again. My eyes lit up as I let out a giddy laugh, crying happily as Bailey smiled with glassy eyes.

"She's hanging on for now, but we have limited energy available for some of the resources she needs. Ryan has been working tirelessly to keep her comfortable. We just have to hope her tiny body is strong enough to handle everything. But we have a daughter, Sammi—and she's just as beautiful as you."

This was what I needed right now. Hope. I needed something to convince me that everything in my life at this point wasn't useless or depressing or gone.

Caleb and Jackson had lost us during the attack, but I was hopeful that we'd find each other again soon. They were intelligent, and they knew how to think in times like these. It almost seemed like they were made for this. They were the main reason that I had survived this long, but I hoped for my sake that they weren't the only reason, since I'd have to live without them for however long it took to be reunited.

I was positive they would dedicate their lives to finding me and I would do the same for them. The urgency I had to be reunited with them was unmatched, but if I were to run into a crowd of zombies, I'd die almost instantly in the condition I was in. It was a death wish, and they'd agree with that. I needed to heal before facing the world again, or it would all be for nothing.

I hadn't been around Bailey enough to know the extent of his knowledge and experience about zombies and how to properly kill them. We'd need to be on the same page, so that our first mission into this world would be successful.

But for now, all I wanted was to see my daughter. I almost felt like this was a dream, and seeing her in person would discredit the negative doubts that she was actually alive.

"Can I see her?" I asked.

Bailey sighed. "I don't think that's a good idea right now. I think you both need to take it easy."

"Please," I gently begged.

"Maybe tomorrow, okay? She needs a little more strength. The first time you see her doesn't need to be while she's hooked up to a bunch of machines," he said calmly.

I nodded, accepting his suggestion. I took a closer look around the room, noticing we had power and fully-stocked cabinets. It seemed almost untouched from before. Either that, or it had been kept up with by new residents. I was afraid of it being the latter scenario, based on what had happened at Opfer.

I furrowed my brows before asking Bailey, "Was there a community of people here when you arrived or is it just the four of us?"

"Surprisingly, the hospital was nearly untouched. There were hardly any zombies, and so far, we haven't seen anyone that's alive."

"I just hope we haven't intruded on someone else's space," I said.

"Ryan and I haven't had much time to check out the other floors or rooms here, but I think we would've bumped into someone by now if they were living here," he said.

"Yeah, that's a good point. We're lucky we came here. It seems like it saved our lives."

He smiled and leaned over to kiss my cheek gently. "I don't know what I would've done if I'd lost you and..." he paused as he looked over at me.

"Grace," I said, almost in a whisper. "That's our daughter's name."

There was pure love behind every muscle that created his smile. He leaned down, gently cupped my face, and kissed my lips.

I'd never really given much thought to what I'd name the baby, mainly because I didn't know if it was a boy or girl. But as I laid here in this bed, it felt so right to name my daughter Grace to honor Greyson. I knew he would've been the best brother to her. It killed me to know he'd never get that chance, and she'd never get to know him.

~

For the remainder of the day, Bailey brought me the correct medication for my bipolar disorder, along with medications to assist my pain and other issues Ryan was treating. Fortunately, the pharmacy in the hospital was stocked on mostly everything.

I laid in bed, thinking and thinking, as that was all there really was to do here. No cell phones, no television, and no video games to keep you occupied in your free time. It was so boring. I never realized how much I took my prior life for granted.

As the sun began to set, Bailey returned to my room, walking over to the window that looked out into the front parking lot. "I know you have a lot going on right now, Sammi, but I never really got the chance to get closure on things back at Opfer. Seeing you after all that time when I'd thought I'd lost you, it was everything. I wanted to talk to you more, but it was so hard to do that with everyone watching our every move."

I frowned at the memory of being so happy to see him but unable to act on it.

He continued, "That first day I heard your voice behind me in the cafeteria, my heart immediately started pounding. I couldn't believe we'd found each other. Part of me thought we'd pick up where we left off, even if we had to hide it from Gabe and Lucy, but then to hear about you and Jackson…"

I shut my eyes, knowing where this was going. I owed him honesty, and I did want to explain everything that had happened after he and I had gotten off the phone that day. The day the world changed.

"Jackson and I were together for a while during, you know, all of this. You knew I had feelings for him; I was transparent about that. But that day, I'd chosen you. Not because we were having a baby together, but because being with you was never complicated like it was with Jackson. It was refreshing," I began.

Bailey looked down at the ground, and I was unable to tell what he was thinking.

"I thought about you every single day, but I didn't know if you'd survived. I saw what they were doing to people, and it was by pure luck that Caleb and Jackson showed up when they did to save me. I didn't want to think they'd gotten to you, but dead people were walking around eating people. I knew nothing was impossible," I said, shutting my eyes for a moment. "I needed someone, and he was there for me. For months he, Caleb, and Greyson were all I had. I love him, but I'm in love with you. I chose you. In all those months I lived without you, there was a void inside me. I care about him, you know that, but we were meant for each other. I really believe that."

He gave me a small smile. "I've been in love with you since I laid eyes on you; I think you've figured that out. Believe it or not, I tried to find you every day. I tried to go out with the scavenging crew to look for anything that pointed to you, but the others caught on to my side mission. They told Gabe, and Gabe put me on lockdown. He said I was risking the lives of others, and he never allowed me the opportunity to leave again. I was essentially a prisoner there, despite how easy it may have seemed to escape. They allowed people to leave if they chose to, but I saw Gabe send men after them to kill them not long after they left. I knew he'd do the same to me. They were not what they wanted people to think they were."

I remained silent as he continued. "One night, I did try to sneak out and leave. I was ready to risk it all—but Lucy caught me. The next day, one of the people I'd become close friends with went missing. I think if you broke their rules but didn't leave, they didn't kill you, but they killed someone you were close to as punishment. I genuinely believe that now."

A tear rolled down my cheek as I recalled my rule breaking that ultimately led to Greyson's death.

"The night before they killed Greyson," I began, sniffling, "I was going to sneak out past curfew to see Jackson. I just wanted to talk to him, but when I got to the door, it wasn't completely shut."

Bailey walked over to the edge of the bed and joined me, listening intently as I told him what happened.

"When I pushed the door open, Lucy was in there. She was standing in front of him completely naked, and he was just gawking at her. She saw me, and I ran back to my room in tears. Neither of them came after me to say anything or apologize," I said, looking away. "I don't know if anything happened or if it wasn't the first time, but I've never felt hurt in a relationship like I had that night. Jackson really did a number on me. And for it to be Lucy, of all people"—I laughed sardonically—"that made it even worse."

"He didn't deserve you. I know you care about him and love him, but emotionally and romantically, he doesn't deserve you. I hope we find them both alive, but God, I can't believe he would do that. He seemed like he was head over heels for you that first night you got there. I was so jealous that it made my skin crawl," he admitted.

"I didn't want to go to Opfer. I told them it was a sketchy idea, but they didn't listen. It was like Lucy brainwashed them. On the first day, before we found the motel, I heard a radio broadcast for a sanctuary in Oklahoma City, but they refused to go. I never understood what made Opfer any better. They completely dismissed how I felt."

"Lucy always managed to bring out the worst in people. I never cared for her. I saw right past her fake act, but at the time I needed shelter because I was struggling out there on my own," he said bitterly.

I didn't have a chance to reply, because Ryan ran into the room, looking frantic.

"We've got some trouble, Bailey," he said.

"What's going on?" I asked worriedly.

"Don't worry, I'll be back," Bailey said as he rushed out of the room, following Ryan.

15

A RUDY AWAKENING

I BEGAN TO WORRY about what was going on. Ryan seemed scared and panicked. *Did the remaining group from Opfer find us? Were they here to seek revenge?*

I tried to remain in the hospital bed and let them deal with whatever was going on, but I was never very good at not getting involved in things. I winced as I eased from the bed, my body screaming from pain and stiffness as I shuffled out of my room and down the corridor, toward the entrance of the hospital.

I heard voices as I neared, and not wanting to make my presence known—since I knew Bailey and Ryan would flip if they knew I'd followed them—I poked my head around the corner and watched.

The entrance to the hospital was completely flooded with a community, or army, of people—it was hard to tell which. They were dirty, sweaty, heavily armed, and extremely intense in all aspects: from their stance to their facial expressions, to the atmosphere surrounding them.

Though the group didn't exactly look welcoming, I breathed a sigh of relief as I realized they weren't any of the people that we had been living with at Opfer.

There had to have been around thirty-sum total of them: men and women and one teenage boy. They stood, guns in hand, directly across from

Bailey and Ryan. Each of them held a straight, emotionless expression that seemed serious, maybe even threatened or on edge. We hadn't come across any good people in a while, so who knew if that was going to change now.

"Can we help y'all with something?" Ryan asked, his voice shaking slightly.

After a pause that lingered for what felt like an eternity, someone said, "I think we need to be asking y'all that question."

The voice belonged to a rugged, middle-aged man in the center of the front row. He stepped forward to isolate himself from the crowd.

"I'm sorry?" Ryan asked anxiously, his brow furrowing as he swapped nervous glances with Bailey.

"This is our home. I'm not sure how long y'all have been here, but I think it's time to clear out," he said sternly.

"We've been here for over a week; it was empty when we arrived," Ryan said, managing to sound both confident and confused.

"Didn't you notice that there's solar panels, clean rooms, and a stocked pantry? We did all of that," he said, lifting his arm to give credit to those behind him.

I could see that Ryan and Bailey had started to piece together how this place had been so move-in-ready during an apocalypse.

"I'm sorry. We didn't realize," Ryan apologized.

"We're going to expect y'all to pay us back for all the supplies you took while you were here," the man continued as he casually inched closer. "We worked hard to get this place to this point, and we're not about to let y'all ruin it."

Ryan and Bailey looked at each other, clearly concerned as to how they would manage to replace the water, energy, food, and medical supplies we had taken during the week we'd been here. They knew as well as I did that leaving wasn't an option; Grace and I would jeopardize their safety, and leaving a facility equipped with medical resources would jeopardize ours. They'd never admit that to me though. They didn't think I was mentally stable enough to handle bad news. That's probably why Ryan wouldn't elaborate on the problem at hand when he came to my room to find Bailey.

Tension was high in the lobby of the hospital as the large group of newcomers waited for Bailey and Ryan's next move.

Eventually Bailey spoke, "I'm sorry. We didn't intend to create problems. We—we'd like to stay if we could? We can pull our weight. But if you make us leave, we … well, we've got a newborn that is in critical condition; she'll die if we leave."

"You brought a baby here?" the stranger asked.

"She was delivered here a little over a week ago. She's my daughter," Bailey said calmly. "My girlfriend was shot multiple times, so we had to find somewhere safe to deliver our baby and to save her from bleeding out. She's still healing. She's not ready to go back out there. We will pay you guys back and earn our keep, but please, we have to stay—at least until they are both stable."

"So, you managed to save both of them?" the man asked.

"Ryan here is a doctor. He's done some amazing things. He can help any of you whenever you need it if you let us stay," Bailey said, bargaining for the right to stay here.

The older man looked back at the others surrounding him, and they exchanged looks that I struggled to read. None of them spoke, but it was as if they were silently communicating with each other.

After a lingering pause, the man cleared his throat. "Okay," he said calmly.

"Okay?" Ryan asked, wondering if he'd heard correctly.

"We're just playing hard ass; you never know what kind of people you're going to run into these days. But you can't be too bad if you're caring for a newborn in all of this mess," he said, now sounding a little friendlier.

I saw Bailey's shoulders relax just a little, though I could tell he was still cautious of the situation.

"I'm Rudy, and these are my friends and family," the man said.

The group of people waved, some smiling slightly, and I was relieved that they were now showing some emotion. Maybe these people wouldn't be so bad. I couldn't exactly blame them for being hostile at first; I wouldn't have been thrilled to find several strangers staying in my makeshift home if the situations were reversed. Plus, I could already tell these people had much better energy than those at Opfer.

I wasn't sure how many people survived after everything went down at the temple, and we really didn't know if any of them were trustworthy after the majority turned blind eyes as members "disappeared." I didn't care to ever see any of them again. Besides, I'd never gotten close enough to any of them to form relationships, except with Ryan. Fortunately, he was one of the good ones, and it paid off big time with me and Grace. He'd saved our lives.

Speaking of Ryan, I could also see that he seemed relaxed for the first time in a while as he gave an introduction on behalf of the two of them. "I'm Ryan, and this is Bailey," he said, gesturing toward Bailey, who waved back nervously, pursing his lips into a tiny smile.

"Nice to meet y'all," Rudy said in his strong southern accent.

"How long have you been based here? Were you out on the road just now?" Bailey asked.

"Yeah. We've been out scavenging across the state for a while, but we ran into some trouble. Our bus broke down, and the other vehicles couldn't fit all of us. We had to look all over for another big vehicle and gasoline," Rudy began. "This place is pretty stocked, but we want it to stay that way. With all of us using the supplies, it can run out quickly. And there ain't much left these days. You gotta travel to bigger cities to find places that haven't been raided."

"That's smart," Bailey pitched in.

"Yeah, but it's not smart if you don't go with enough ammunition to kill all of the dead bodies roaming the streets. We lost some good people out there, but that was one of the reasons we went out there in the first place: to get more weapons and ammunition."

"I'm sorry to hear that," Bailey said, and I could tell he was being genuine. "Well, we'll let y'all get settled back in. I'm sure you're probably exhausted and hungry. Please let us know if there's anything at all that we can do. We don't want to intrude, but we really would appreciate it if y'all would let us stay here permanently or at least until our girls are fully healed."

Rudy nodded in approval. "I'm sure we can work something out. We can talk more tomorrow. Y'all just make yourself at home," he said, patting Bailey on the shoulder as he walked past.

Sensing the conversation was almost over, I hurried back to my room and climbed back into the hospital bed.

A few minutes later, Bailey joined me. He let out a huge sigh as he eased down into the bed beside me, placing his arm around my back. The warmth from his body soothed me as I inhaled the scent from his clothing. Somehow, he still smelled the same as the night at the bar, and that fact made me feel at home.

"What happened?" I asked anxiously, turning to face him. I figured it was best to act dumb, not wanting to be scolded for leaving the bed before I was healthy enough to do so.

Bailey raised a sardonic eyebrow and gently brushed a strand of hair behind my ear. "Don't pretend like you didn't follow us down the hall and listen in to the whole conversation."

I blushed a little, lowering my gaze. "How did you know?"

"Because you're predictable," he said with a chuckle.

I laughed too, but grew serious again after a moment. "Do you think we'll actually get to stay?"

"For now, at least. But we're going to talk with Rudy to decide on a permanent deal. It's okay; we're okay," he assured me with a calm smile.

He gently rubbed my cheek with his thumb as our gazes connected. Then I leaned in and kissed him for the first time since that night in Nashville. Our eyes closed, our lips met, and it was the softest, gentlest kiss I'd ever had, much different to our first. I was seeing a slightly different side to him, one that was soft and sweet, and I didn't mind it at all. It was comforting, and a good transition into this new start between us.

For the remainder of the night, the two of us cuddled in the small hospital bed until we both drifted into a restless sleep. I could tell Bailey was anxious about the trustworthiness of Rudy and his community of people. We still weren't in a position to be comfortable or at ease, and our sleep reflected this. A worry-free conscience didn't exist anymore, unfortunately. It would be hard to fully trust anyone and their intentions, especially after Opfer.

The next morning, I woke up to an empty spot beside me where Bailey had been. I couldn't hear anyone or anything, so I wasn't sure what was going on. Then I remembered that Bailey had mentioned talking with Rudy more in depth today about a decision on if we could stay here long-term. I assumed Bailey and the others were downstairs in the hospital's cafeteria, eating breakfast and discussing our situation with Rudy.

I hated that I couldn't be down there with Bailey and Ryan to meet everyone and to plead our case for staying, but after yesterday, I had promised Bailey that I wouldn't keep leaving the room. He said I needed to give myself the chance to heal, and I begrudgingly accepted that he was correct.

But this meant I'd been left alone in this room with nothing to do except burdening myself with the memory of losing Greyson and putting everyone I loved in danger when I made the decision to shoot Gabe. Now I was mentally paying for what I'd done, and I couldn't do anything to take my mind off it.

What I really wanted was to see my daughter. I was prepared to see her, despite Bailey saying it would be better to wait until she was stronger. I'd seen babies in similar conditions throughout my clinicals in labor and delivery, and I'd unfortunately watched babies die. This wasn't foreign territory for me, so I felt like I could handle it.

After mentally drowning in silence for too long, thinking about my baby lying alone in some cold hospital room, I swung the blankets off me and sat up.

The second I moved to stand, I realized that pure adrenaline had fueled my body yesterday when I followed Bailey and Ryan out of the room. Either that or it had depleted my energy so much that my healing process had gone backwards, because today I could barely get the strength to stand. I scooted my feet a few inches, but only managed to take a couple of steps before tripping over a wire hooked to the rolling monitor beside my bed.

I yelped as I collapsed and hit the floor. My abdomen began throbbing, making me regret ever getting out of bed.

I assumed no one was around to hear me, but someone had. A woman, about my age with black hair and dark brown eyes, appeared at the doorway. Once she saw me on the floor, she hurried over and knelt beside me.

"Are you okay?" she asked worriedly as I began to cry.

For several seconds, I couldn't get any words to come out of my mouth. I just cried in pain and embarrassment.

"What can I do?" she asked helplessly.

"I just want to see my baby," I pleaded as I lay hopelessly on the floor in a fetal position.

"I'm going to go get some help. I don't think I can get you up by myself," she said, jumping to her feet and darting down the hallway.

A few minutes later, the woman returned, a panicked-looking Bailey and Ryan in tow. Amid their retrieval, I hadn't moved. I'd just been laying there, crying like a crazy person because I was physically and mentally exhausted. This was hell; I swore it was. I hated feeling this out of touch with myself and those around me. I didn't feel like I was in control of anything, and it was becoming problematic.

"Sammi," Bailey said gently, kneeling on the floor beside me, his hand going to my cheek. "What's going on? Are you hurt?"

"I just want to see Grace," I begged.

He wiped the tear rolling down my cheek and straightened up to look over at Ryan, who gently nodded in approval. For a moment, he waited for me to calm down before encouraging me to move. I used what little strength I had to push myself up enough for Bailey to assist me the rest of the way.

The woman I'd only just met stepped out of the room briefly and soon returned with a wheelchair. She rolled it over to where I stood, holding on to Bailey's shoulder for balance. The wheels creaked every few spins, and the irritating sound was almost enough to distract me from this shit ass world inside my mind.

I turned and lowered myself into the seat, and they wheeled me out of the room. As we moved, I observed the plain paint on the walls and boring tile floor of the hall. It still had that stereotypical hospital scent that I'd never gotten used to, but this time, instead of being a buzzing hub, it had an eerie empty feeling.

I sat with my fingers interlocked, palms sweaty from overthinking. I knew both Bailey and Ryan were worried that I would become discouraged at seeing Grace in such a frail, weak state, and I started to think that maybe they were right. I tried to visualize different scenarios for how seeing her for the first time could go. I was scared, but I also felt comfort in knowing that she had two parents and a doctor to care for her, not to mention I was a nurse myself too.

"Are you ready?" Ryan asked, halting the chair in front of a doorway not too far from mine.

I nodded, a hint of a smile on my tear-swollen and flushed face.

"You've been through a lot and so has Grace. She's still struggling to overcome her problems, but I need you to be strong, okay? Comfort her, let her know you're there for her," he said, looking over to Bailey.

"Okay," I said with a sniffle, wiping my nose with part of the hospital gown I was wearing.

Ryan stayed outside to give us some privacy, and Bailey pushed the wheelchair through the doorway. I took a deep breath as we got closer to the glass surrounding her and I finally got a glimpse of the baby I'd been picturing inside of my head for months. She was so tiny, so fragile, but so perfect.

I'd seen dozens of babies, but when it was one that you created and carried for months, it was so much more special. It made everything worth it.

I knew I probably wouldn't be able to hold her yet, but knowing one day I'd get to touch her tiny fingers and toes gave me a huge sense of relief. I couldn't wait to see what traits she got from me and Bailey.

I looked at her with a smile, admiring every beautiful detail. Her eyes were closed, and she had a thin layer of dark brown hair on her head. Her hands were balled up into tiny fists, and her tiny toes were curled into her feet. She looked peaceful, but it was hard to tell if she was hurting or in pain like me.

They didn't teach you this in nursing school. They didn't teach you how to be calm and fine when your child—your family, your blood—was confined to a glass room due to having premature organs and suffering from the backlash of gunshots. I didn't know how to be there for her if I couldn't hold her and nurture her. I needed her as much as she needed me, but given the circumstances, my voice and company would have to suffice until we were both stable enough to make it on our own.

I couldn't wait for that day.

I looked to my right where Bailey stood, peering over at Grace. I couldn't help but hope that she'd grow up with the qualities of her father that made me love him more every day. He was the perfect example of a gentleman and an honorable human being. There was nothing in the world he'd ever done wrong.

I tried to imagine what my life would've been like if I'd just stuck with him from the start. I wanted to think he and I would've been great together, but I had a bad habit of ruining relationships with my irrational decision-making skills and reckless behavior, whether I was manic or not.

A few weeks ago, I'd seen my future—what little I thought I had—being spent with Jackson. He'd stepped up, and for a while, I'd thought we'd be the ones to make it through an apocalypse strong and in love. Then, Lucy came along. If it hadn't been for her and that shit-ass Opfer, Jackson, Greyson, Grace, and I could've been a family, and Caleb could've been an outstanding uncle; I knew he'd always wanted that.

At one point, I'd believed we could've made it until the world was pieced back together. I'd imagined us having a wedding, where I was dressed in white, Greyson brought us the rings, and Caleb was Jackson's best man. Grace would have been old enough to throw the flower petals down the aisle, and I'd have gone home married to a great man.

I still saw the hope for a white dress and wedding day, just without Greyson and Jackson, and with Bailey instead.

I honestly don't know how things would've turned out between me, Jackson, and Bailey if Opfer was normal. I had a hard time deciphering between the right choice for me and the right choice for everyone else, but it seemed like the two of them did a stellar job helping me make my decision based on their actions. Seeing Jackson with Lucy only clarified my certainty about who I would choose. I just wish it wasn't because of that.

Realizing I'd spaced out for a minute, I leaned closer, trying to get a better look at Grace. Everything about her was the way I felt it should be. She was perfect.

Seeing her had lifted such a weight from my chest. I hadn't been able to trust that she was okay until I'd seen her for myself, and I was glad to finally confirm that this was real—she was here and alive.

I looked up at Bailey, who'd been watching Grace just the same as me, probably hoping that she'd have her mother's eyes or smile, just like I hoped she would have his. He had his hand over his mouth, nervously pulling at his bottom lip.

"Bailey…" I began.

He looked over at me, a soft, watery glaze coating his eyes, as if he were working hard to hold back tears. "Yeah?" he choked out.

"Do you think the world will ever go back to the way it was?"

"I don't think it will ever be the way it was, but I do think it can return to some level of normalcy," he said, smiling slightly.

"Some days I don't feel like I even remember what things were like before. It's like— I feel like this has been my life forever, and I can't imagine how things used to be. I'm actually terrified to lose that part of me," I admitted.

"What helps you hang on to those memories?" he asked, as if wanting advice for himself.

"The night we met," I confessed. "That was the best night of my life."

"Mine too," he said, grabbing my hand and gently pressing his lips to my skin.

"I think that's one memory I will never forget, and that's what's keeping me from forgetting life before all of this," I continued.

He smiled happily as his fingers interlocked with mine. The two of us lingered, looking at Grace for a while, before he wheeled me back to my room. I felt as if a huge weight was lifted from my chest, and the air felt easier to breathe in and out. For the first time in a while, life almost felt normal, or as normal as it could get during an apocalypse. I obviously knew life in this hospital wouldn't be like my life in New York, but it was the safest and happiest I'd felt since the motel.

~

That night, Bailey thought it would be good for me to finally meet Rudy and the rest of his group. He said after meeting me, they'd *have* to agree to let us stay because I was, quote, "Easy to love and have an infectious personality that is worthy of getting to know."

He loved to flatter me, but I never thought those things about myself. However I hoped he was right, because this was where we needed to be right now. It was the safest option for me and Grace during our time of healing, so I was going to make sure I portrayed myself as the person he believed me to be.

I wanted to make a good first impression, so Bailey found me some clothes from the gift shop downstairs: a pair of black leggings and a cream ribbed sweater. The selection in the gift shop was limited because the hospital had been fairly small and didn't need a massive selection, so a pair of fuzzy tan slippers would have to suffice as my footwear of choice. At least they were comfortable.

Bailey helped me to bathe and shampoo my hair, before wrapping it tightly in a towel to dry. Then he helped me get dressed and carefully brushed through the damp strands of my hair. The way this man cared for me was unmatched. I just felt so at ease when I was with him.

I was nervous, but Bailey reassured me that they were such a great community of people. He said everyone he'd met was friendly and eager to finally meet me and Grace. Even so, it was hard to forget the importance of the task weighing on me.

Soon it was officially time for us to go downstairs and plead our case. Ryan was staying behind to keep an eye on Grace, so it would just be the two of us doing the talking tonight.

I still didn't have the strength to walk far, but luckily we had the wheelchair. The solar panels kept the power in the hospital running and the elevators were not far from the room, so that made it easy to get to the floor the cafeteria was on.

Bailey and I stepped into the elevator in silence.

"I love you," Bailey said as the doors slid closed and the elevator began to descend.

Suddenly, I got the worst sense of déjà vu.

I knew I loved Bailey, and normally I would've had no problem saying it back, only now I'd been reminded of the feeling I had that day Jackson told me he loved me in this very hospital. I became overwhelmed all over again, thinking about my brother and Jackson. I missed them so badly, but to tell Bailey that I missed Jackson would only complicate things and make me feel guilty.

The elevator came to a halt, and the doors opened before I had a chance to respond. It opened right into the cafeteria, and voices echoed in every direction. It was a friendly, bustling atmosphere, but I still found it overwhelming. My mind was swamped with worry about Jackson and

Caleb, guilt over Bailey, and fear of being rejected by Rudy and his people. I knew they were understanding, but they didn't owe us protection.

They didn't owe us anything.

Bailey gently rubbed my shoulder to comfort me as we moved closer to the tables full of people eating from plates in front of them.

I tried to scan the room to see which one might be Rudy, and once my eyes landed on one man in particular, I knew it was him. It wasn't because he had a particular appearance; it was because when he and I locked eyes, he froze. It was like he knew something about me that even I didn't know.

Rudy dropped his fork, and it clanked against the table loudly as the room grew quieter. There were still a few conversations going on in the background, but almost everyone seemed to be most interested in me.

I, however, was more interested in Rudy's reaction when he first saw me. We continued to watch each other, even as Bailey pushed me in a different direction.

The woman beside him was trying to speak to him, but it was like he couldn't hear her. She looked confused for a moment until she followed his gaze that was pointing at me. Suddenly she seemed equally as suspicious, as if she knew what he knew. It gave me a seriously unsettled feeling.

Our weird mutual stare finally ended as a woman's voice caught my attention. "You must be the Sammi we've been hearing great things about," she said to me with a welcoming smile.

"That's me," I said, trying to be cheerful in order to convince her I was all of the things Bailey had claimed me to be.

"I'm Josie, Rudy's wife. It's nice to meet you properly. I'll get you two a plate," she offered, before jumping up and walking to the kitchen.

I briefly wondered if this was Rudy's wife, who was the woman sitting next to him who had given me the strange look? A friend or sister, perhaps?

Bailey circled one of the tables, but Rudy beckoned him over. "We've saved you two seats over here," he called from across the room.

Bailey spotted the empty seats across from Rudy and took us in that direction. As we reached the table, Bailey helped me up from the wheelchair and eased me over to the dining chair before taking the seat to my left.

I anxiously looked at Rudy, wondering if he was going to say something about why he'd been so taken aback by my appearance. He didn't, though. Instead, he just acted nonchalant and began making small-talk.

"It's nice to finally meet you, Sammi. I hear you two have been through a lot lately," he said.

Josie returned with two plates of food and sat them in front of me and Bailey, then took a seat next to Rudy.

"Thank you," I said softly. "Yeah, we have," I admitted, rejoining our exchange.

"Bailey told me you were a nurse before all of this."

"I was. I was supposed to start a job at this hospital actually," I said, picking at my plate of food.

"Well, once you're back on your feet, we'd love to see about you helping out in our infirmary."

My eyes widened. "Does that mean we can stay?" I asked.

"I think you guys would be a great addition to our family. I know you are good people; I could tell when I first ran into Ryan and Bailey. Besides, it'll be nice to have a baby around. It's been a while since we've had one of those," he said kindly.

I looked over at Bailey, who appeared ecstatic. I knew this was a relief for him, just as much as it was for me.

"We are so grateful. Thank you so much," I replied.

The rest of dinner went well, and I got to meet almost everyone in the group. I was happy that we didn't have to wonder what was next, or where we could go after leaving here. We could just get comfortable and make this place our home. This was going to be the beginning of a new chapter. I could imagine Grace growing up here and having a chance at a somewhat normal life.

And for several days, everything was great. Grace and I continued to heal, while Ryan and Bailey contributed to Rudy's community.

Though as with everything in this new reality, it didn't last long.

16

DEAD MAN WALKING

ONE NIGHT LATER THAT week, just after I'd gotten readjusted in my bed, screams rang out from somewhere in the hospital. Bailey didn't hesitate to run toward the dense echoing cries without a second thought.

I hated that he was so noble sometimes. I really did.

Yet again, I'd been left alone in this hospital bed to sit and think about every horrible outcome that could happen to Bailey. I was beyond ready to be healed so that I could easily go to see my daughter and be with Bailey, by his side no matter what. I had known that a zombie apocalypse would have its unexpected turns and disasters, but I really wished Bailey's first instinct wouldn't be to run straight toward the threat. I needed him here; I needed him to be safe and to look after our daughter. Without my brother, Bailey was my sole protector, and he was also Grace's.

Caleb and Jackson had initially been everything I needed. I had trusted them unconditionally—until Opfer. I had expected that trust would go both ways, but when it came to Opfer, my feelings weren't validated.

Now Caleb was either dead or lost somewhere in this shithole world, but if I ever saw him again, I had no doubt he'd continue to be what I needed. He'd never let me down again. I was sure of that.

Jackson? I wasn't sure what would happen if we ever reunited. I did care about him, and I certainly didn't want him to die, but he really hurt me. I never imagined in a million years that he would be the kind of guy to cheat, especially after all we'd been through and how he acted when he was with Sophie. There was just no other explanation for what I walked in on with him and Lucy that day. None.

Jackson was once the man I wanted to survive this with, but I think I was always meant to be with Bailey. The universe was trying to tell me something by meeting him at the bar right before the apocalypse, and then somehow finding each other again against all odds, to now escaping Opfer and surviving in this hospital.

And this hospital, God, it was supposed to be my fresh start. I'd had a job waiting for me, a chance to do what I loved and had studied so hard for. It was also where Jackson had told me he loved me. This hospital was supposed to be my future, but now it was a combination of my past and present.

I constantly wondered what my life would look like if none of this zombie shit had ever happened. Jackson would have never met Lucy, and I wouldn't be lying in a hospital bed, worried about Bailey being attacked by a dead man walking.

Several minutes had passed since Bailey ran out of the room, and I could still hear a commotion coming from down the hallway. I couldn't imagine that the threat was from the zombies, because they'd have to hitch a ride on the elevator or climb stairs to even get up here—which, granted, wasn't impossible, but unlikely.

I desperately wanted to investigate. Just peep my head out of the doorway, nothing crazy. Surely, I could handle that?

So, I mustered up the courage to try to get out of bed again. This time, I stepped over the wires and obstacles and didn't faceplant the floor. I still felt aches and pains, but I could tell that I was slowly recovering, which made me happy.

I carefully inched toward the door that Bailey had left open. When I looked down the hallway, I couldn't see anyone. The floor we were located on was divided into two wings: east and west. Everyone slept on this floor, because this had once been the surgical and intensive care unit, and there were many patient rooms tucked away into two perpendicular hallways.

I could still hear the disturbance, but I knew it had to be coming from the east wing, considering I was in the west. I slowly took steps out into the hallway, easing toward the abandoned nurses' station. As I did, the screams turned into sobbing. Loud and hysterical sobbing. Speaking from experience, that usually indicated that the incident was over, and all that would be left was the aftermath.

I continued toward the nurses' station and grabbed onto the counter to rest for a minute. I looked down the other hallway and noticed puddles of blood and splatters on the tiled floor and walls.

My stomach twisted. That much blood indicated that someone was dead.

My heart sank at the thought of losing someone, even someone among Rudy's group that I'd just met. We were all each other had, and strength in numbers meant a lot for our stability and mental states.

A few seconds later, Bailey surfaced from the far left room along the hallway, and I immediately gave a deep sigh of relief. He looked defeated and worried, hurrying over to me as soon as he noticed me standing there, leaning up against the nurses' station. His hands were painted red with blood and his clothes were stained with blood. It was hard to tell if it was his or someone else's.

"Sammi—"

"What happened? What's going on?" I interrupted, worried.

"I-I don't know. Rudy turned into a zombie. But I don't know how this could have happened."

"Are you okay? The blood…" I started.

"It's not mine," he said, trying to comfort me. "Rudy attacked Josie while she was asleep beside him. She tried to escape, but she didn't make it far. I did my best to save her, but she bled out on the floor," he said, swallowing nervously.

"Oh my God," I said quietly, trying to comprehend what had just happened.

"Come on, you need to get back in bed," he said gently, yet I could tell there was no room for debate.

I frowned. *Yes sir,* I thought sarcastically.

He grabbed my arm and helped me walk back toward the room. We'd only made it about halfway there before a woman ran after us. She had true red hair, a full face of freckles, and deep green eyes, and I recognized her as the person who had been sitting beside Rudy in the cafeteria the first day I met everyone.

"Hey, wait up!" she said as she hurried to catch up to us. "Bailey, can I talk to you for a minute?" she asked intensely.

We stopped and turned back in her direction. I could tell something was wrong by the expression on her face and evidence of dried tears, so I was anxious to learn what she wanted to tell Bailey. However it seemed like she was put off by my presence. In fact, the look she gave me was the same one that Rudy gave me the night we first met. I got the sense that she was hoping I'd go on to my room, but I hung back to hear what she had to say.

Looking at her, I realized she must've been in the room after Rudy's attack, because she also had some blood on her. I would have expected her to be more emotional, since she and Rudy were clearly close, but she held herself together.

"What's wrong?" Bailey asked.

She looked at me, then darted her eyes back to Bailey. "I think I know what happened to Rudy," she said carefully.

Bailey raised his eyebrows and swallowed deeply. He moved his hand to mine and squeezed gently. "Okay..." he said with slight confusion in his tone, encouraging her to continue.

"Sammi, you don't know this, but I'm Lola, Rudy's sister. I didn't say much when we met at dinner because I wanted him to have the opportunity to meet with you without me intruding. I've met Bailey a few times, so he knows a little bit about me and my brother. I've been with him since right before everything started going to hell."

I gave her my full attention, surprised at how calm she was. I'd be a train wreck if my brother died out of nowhere in the middle of the night. It was all very odd, and part of me considered whether they'd been preparing for this eventuality.

"I was with him here on the day it happened," she said, then paused and took a deep breath as Bailey and I eagerly waited for her to continue. "Rudy was here in the emergency room. He was a mechanic, and he cut his arm really badly and needed stitches. He called me, and I picked him up and drove him here. They insisted that he get a tetanus shot, but it was strange because he'd just gotten one a year or so ago," she said, furrowing her brow. "I mean, they practically forced him to get the shot, but you only need one shot every ten years. He knew he didn't need another one, but the nurse didn't really give him an option. After he got the shot, the nurse left, and we waited to be discharged."

"What are you saying?" Bailey asked, shaking his head in confusion.

"I think they were giving the virus to people way before they started killing them. I think they made people believe that routine vaccinations and shots were necessary and encouraged, but really they were a ploy to infect people under the radar, even while they were unconscious."

As she said this, my heart sank and chills shot all over my body. I began breathing heavily, on the verge of hyperventilating. Then my head started throbbing and my vision went black. Before I knew it, my legs gave way and I collapsed to the floor.

~

I came around after a couple of minutes, squinting up at Bailey, the lights too bright for my eyes. Ryan and Lola were huddled around, looking concerned.

He brushed my forehead gently, clearly relieved that I was okay after yet another ordeal. "What happened, baby? Did you get dizzy from standing up?"

"Uh, yeah, I think I just got lightheaded," I lied, looking away. I hated lying to him, but I wasn't quite sure what to think right now.

I felt the cold, dusty tile underneath my palms as I worked to sit myself up. Ryan and Bailey grabbed my arms and eased me back up to standing. As they did, Lola gave me an assessing look, and it was like she could read my mind. As if she knew I was hiding something. I tried to act oblivious to her stare, hoping maybe she'd let it go.

Carefully, we'd made it back to my room and I climbed into bed. My heart was racing; I was anxious, and I knew I would continue to be so until I faced what I'd been fearing since Lola had given us her thoughts on Rudy's infection. I couldn't tell Bailey until I knew for sure, but how could I get downstairs without someone noticing that I was gone? It was like I was constantly being monitored, under twenty-four-hour surveillance or something. I needed to go down there. It was the only way I could rule out what I now feared to be my fate.

"I'm going to go check on the others and make sure they're okay. I'll be back, I promise," he said, kissing my forehead.

He left, and Lola and Ryan followed him. I laid there, wondering how long Bailey would be gone to determine if I could sneak off for a few minutes. My finger started to burn, and I looked down to see a patch of blood surfacing around my nail. I'd been picking at my skin as a compulsion. I tried to stop and breathe, but the anxiety was consuming me.

I sat up and placed my feet on the ground. I wasn't quite sure where I was going because I'd only discovered so much about this hospital between my interview and hospitalization here. If I had to guess though, I'd say Medical Records was located on the first floor, probably near Human Resources, where I'd gone for my interview. That's where I'd find my answers.

I quietly made my way over to the doorway and peered out into the hallway. I saw Lola walking back toward the wing that Rudy and his people were in. Quiet so as not to alert her, I slowly moved toward the stairwell. I knew if I took the elevator, someone would likely hear the bell ding and the doors open and shut, so to avoid blowing my cover, I knew the steps were the best option. As I began inching down the stairs, the door shut loudly behind me. I flinched at the sound, hoping no one heard.

Holding on to the railing, I crept down the stairs, occasionally wincing at the pain I felt primarily in my abdominal area. My feet made pathetic smacking sounds as I took the stairs one by one. Eventually I reached the first floor of the hospital. It was quiet, eerie, and almost unfamiliar. In the distance, I could see out of the front doors. It was still daylight outside, but it was almost as scary as the darkness that came with night. It seemed like forever since I'd been able to feel the sun's warmth on my skin.

I longed for that.

I looked around until I saw the marquis hanging on the wall. A dark gray plaque with gold lettering and a gold border hung elegantly, with each room name displayed across it. I scanned down each line until I saw Medical Records: Room 109. I took the hallway toward Human Resources that I'd taken for my interview. I approached numbers posted to the right of each room and watched as they grew with each door: 105, 106, 107, 108, 109—

Fuck, this was overwhelming. Did I even really want to go inside and find out what I'd been fearing? I had to, right? Better to know my fate than be ignorant of it.

Pausing outside the door, I closed my eyes and took a deep breath. Inside this room would be thousands upon thousands of patient charts and information. It'd take me forever to piddle through all of it if it wasn't somewhat organized.

Ugh.

But I needed to know, and this was how I'd find out.

I pushed the door open and was greeted by shelves upon shelves of folders carrying patient files. They each had a couple of letters to help categorize them alphabetically by last name. I took in the overwhelming sight of each folder shoved tightly against the next before finding the section I assumed would have my chart.

Unfortunately, it was on the very top shelf. I looked around for something to stand on, but I didn't see anything particularly useful. Then I noticed an adjoining door which looked to have once belonged to one of the medical record clerks, so I decided to look inside for a chair to stand on.

I turned the metal doorknob and pushed through, only to immediately be met by an extremely hungry and pissed zombie. It was standing in the corner of the office, but quickly came after me as I struggled to pull the door closed. Before I could, the zombie's arms reached through, making it impossible to completely shut the door.

I didn't have the strength to fight this vile creature right now. I just didn't. I also didn't bring a weapon because it never occurred to me that this place hadn't been completely cleared out.

The zombie appeared to be a middle-aged woman who had probably worked in this office before shit hit the fan. She had graying hair and was wearing a blue dress with white birds printed on it. I could tell she'd been dead since near the beginning, based on the decay and the strong stench of death that burned my nose. Still, it seemed she had a surprising wealth of strength.

I was freaking out. I wouldn't be able to hold her off for much longer and I didn't know how I was going to get out of here.

Every push of the zombie against the door widened the gap for it to free itself—to lunge toward me and rip me apart. I looked around for a potential weapon, but my options were limited. I began to groan; it physically pained me to exert this much force against it.

"Damnit," I said in defeat. I was beginning to accept my fate.

A strong push from the zombie resulted in me losing my grip on the doorknob and falling backward. I managed to catch myself with my hands as the zombie came after me like a rabid dog. I tried to scoot further away, toward the door that led back out into the corridor, but I wasn't close enough.

I frantically looked for anything I could use in my defense but there was nothing. My chest became consumed with panic as I imagined an excruciating, bloody death from being ripped apart.

But just as I accepted my fate, the door to the office swung open and Lola quickly shoved a knife into the top of the zombie's skull. It collapsed to the floor immediately, and I exhaled deeply.

"What the hell are you doing?" she asked angrily.

My eyes were wide; I was still shocked from everything that had just happened. How was I still alive?

"Bailey is freaking the hell out looking for you. Come on," she demanded irritably.

"No," I said quietly.

"What?"

"No," I repeated, wiping the sweat from my forehead.

She scoffed. "I don't believe this. I just saved your life, and now you—"

"I think I was given the infection too!" I blurted.

She paused, and what had once been a look of anger changed to one of pity and sadness. "And you wanted to find your chart to see if they documented it," she surmised.

I nodded, and she held out a hand for me to grab so she could help me back onto my feet.

"Thanks for saving me," I said.

"You're welcome. It's nice to properly meet you. I've heard all about you," she joked.

Oh, God. What has she been told? I wondered. *Was that why she gave me those strange looks—because she's heard all my deep, dark secrets?*

"What's your last name, Sammi?"

"Peters," I said, and she headed for the P files. She grabbed a few books from the desk, stacking them on top of each other, using them to stand on so she could reach the top shelf.

As she began searching, I asked, "What have you heard about me?"

"Hmm, well I've heard that you were a badass bipolar nurse that survived a psycho refugee camp while pregnant and then gave birth after being shot. Oh, and Bailey is absolutely in love with you. He worships the ground you walk on, Sammi," she added, while still digging through the files on the shelf.

I smiled silently behind her. The first part was intense, but true. And the second? It illuminated me. I loved Bailey so much it hurt, and hearing that from someone who had only recently met us only solidified my feelings.

"How did you know where I was?" I asked.

"I knew you were lying about something when we were trying to figure out why you passed out. I could hear it in your voice. I was going to keep my eye on you until I knew what was up. Then I heard the stairwell door slam behind me, so I thought I'd see what was going on. I heard the commotion from down the hall, so I tried to hurry and help if you needed it, and you did," she said, pressing her lips together in an annoyed manner.

I rolled my eyes and crossed my arms. So I hadn't been as subtle as I'd hoped.

Finally, she singled out a folder and looked up at me anxiously. "Are you sure you can handle this if it's bad news?"

I nodded, but I was lying again. My palms were sweaty, so I wiped them on the sides of my pants before grabbing the folder. I flipped through the first couple of pages, paying close attention to the sections and headers on each one. I finally came across a page labeled "Visit Summary" with the date of my attack.

I closed my eyes and took a deep breath as Lola placed her hand on my back to try and comfort me. The first few paragraphs included details of my injuries and medical history. I continued to skim down further to find the itemized list of tests, procedures, and treatments administered to me that day.

"X-ray, urinalysis, CT, tramadol 50mg..." I swallowed. "...GPDVA-60 injection."

My heart stopped and tears rushed to my eyes. Lola looked at me with the same pity and sadness as before, not knowing what to say.

Just as I was processing this information, the door opened once again. It was Bailey. He looked genuinely relieved to see me in one piece.

"Oh, thank God. I was so worried," he said as he rushed over to embrace me in his comforting arms, the folder pressed tightly between us.

Once he released me, I lost it. I completely fucking lost it. I began sobbing so deeply that I struggled to catch my breath. I was gasping for air, crying in a way I'd never cried before.

Bailey grew concerned and looked over at Lola, who was at a loss for words.

"What's going on? What happened?" he asked in a panic. He saw the dead zombie on the floor and paled. "Did you get bitten?"

I might as well have been, I thought bitterly.

"No," Lola said quietly.

"What is it? Tell me," he said, longing for someone to reveal what we'd just found out.

I looked over at Lola and nodded. I couldn't face telling him myself.

She stared at him for a few seconds before she choked out, "Sammi was given the injection too."

"What?" Bailey asked, sounding heartbroken. "What is she saying, Sammi?"

"When I was hospitalized—before everything—they gave it to me while I was here," I said, an emptiness filling me. "I didn't know for sure, but I just had a feeling that it was a possibility. I just found my chart from that day, and it was documented."

"Fuck." He began pacing, glancing down at the dead zombie on the floor as he turned anxious circles in the room. "Fuck!" he shouted, punching a hole into the wall behind him.

He was taking this worse than I expected. I wanted to comfort him so badly, but honestly, I needed comforting too. Rudy died—he was dead from this injection, so that meant it was only a matter of time for me, right? I mean, this was like hearing that you have cancer and only have a few months to live.

What should I do?

"You have survived the impossible. You've survived! God, I just— I don't know, Sammi," he pleaded, his eyes wide and slightly unhinged. "Sammi, I can't live without you. I need you here. And Grace … Grace needs you here."

I looked up at him for the first time during this exchange, a tear streaming down my cheek. "I don't want to die," I admitted softly.

His heart was aching. I could feel it, because mine was the same way. I knew exactly what it was like to feel hopeless, useless—like there was absolutely nothing that could be done to fix a situation. But this might be the worst one yet.

It shouldn't have been like this. My life used to look so different. I was a nurse with an apartment in a busy city filled with noise and brightness. I was single and carefree. But now I was a mother living in a hospital room in a ghost town filled with silence and darkness. I was so empty; I wanted to feel again. For once, I wanted to live. I wanted to be healthy. And now that was being taken away from me?

～

After taking a while to try to recover from the news, we decided to go back upstairs to our rooms, where Bailey and I would attempt to figure out how to cope until my clock ran out.

As I lay down in my bed, Bailey went to find Ryan. When they both entered the room again, Ryan looked confused, as if Bailey hadn't given him the news yet.

"What's going on?" he asked, looking between the two of us.

"Rudy died because he was given the injection prior to the apocalypse. His sister thinks that's what killed him," Bailey said.

"Oh wow," Ryan replied.

"He was given that injection when he was a patient here, so Sammi thought they may have given her the same one when she was a patient," Bailey continued.

Ryan's eyes widened, and I could tell his heart had sunk. "They didn't…?"

"They did," I said, frowning in an attempt to hold back any more tears.

Ryan tried to be optimistic. "But we don't know for sure that's what killed him, right?"

"What else could it have been?" Bailey asked.

Ryan frowned. "I wonder if there were any signs. Did he just die, or did he experience any symptoms before? Maybe we could look out for them," he suggested.

"We can talk to Lola after she's had time to grieve and see if she knows anything," Bailey said.

"If she had this theory already, they must've known something," Ryan said, crossing his arms. "I'm so sorry, Sammi."

I lay on my side, looking at the floor, feeling nothing but emptiness. "I just don't know what to think or how to move forward," I admitted. Then I asked, "Do you think I could hold Grace today?"

"I'll go get her," Ryan said with a small smile.

Bailey and Ryan exited the room to collect Grace while I tried to organize the thoughts overcrowding my mind. Despite the crazy world we were living in, I had never really thought about dying much until I was burdened with the knowledge that I was plagued with it coming sooner, rather than seventy years down the road.

It was a scary feeling, especially if you didn't believe in some higher power. And for me, I didn't. I didn't believe that there was a god somewhere up there with a place prepared for me. I think that's what gave peace to so many people riddled with the realization of eventually dying. Their minds wouldn't cease to exist; only their bodies. They'd find themselves in heaven and continue to find comfort in life or eternity. But when I thought of dying, I imagined literally vanishing from existence. I would be no more.

That scared the shit out of me.

But I wasn't scared enough to suddenly have a change of heart to believe that someone died for my manifested sins. Maybe that's what set me apart from Bailey. He was this perfect human that was raised in Sunday school and service at church every week. He was heavily equipped with knowledge for separating right from wrong and thou shalt not do many things to avoid being burnt to smithereens in hell with the very being that felt the same about god as me. Why would the devil kill me for sharing the same beliefs as he did? That never made sense to me.

But—my sweet Bailey—he was pure. His recent outburst of the word "fuck" was about as unholy as he'd ever been aside from our premarital sex in the bathroom that night we met. Still, I think he'd be okay come time for his theoretical judgment day.

He wasn't the right person for me to talk to about my fear of dying though. He'd only give me positive religious affirmations of reuniting with my fallen loved ones and no longer feeling pain or sadness. I found it hard to believe that it would ever be possible for me to feel something *other than* pain and sadness. Sure, I was happy from time to time, but the occurrences were few and far between these days. I just couldn't share those beliefs with him.

Maybe that's what made the connection between Jackson and I so strong; the fact that our knowledge of existence was just not based on believing without seeing, but believing what was logical and realistic. Then again, believing that heaven and hell existed didn't seem so far-fetched in a world now being overrun by dead people. Maybe he wasn't so crazy after all. Maybe I was just destined to be eternally pessimistic.

Maybe, maybe, maybe.

At that moment, Bailey and Ryan returned, interrupting my debate on the eternal life awaiting me. My persistent fears and hopelessness vanished the second I laid eyes on my beautiful daughter, who was cooing her sweet baby noises in Ryan's arms.

For the first time since giving birth, I was given the opportunity to hold my daughter. Suddenly all my doubts and worries were nonexistent, and I basked in the presence of my miracle baby.

17

VACANCY

IT HAD BEEN FIVE or six weeks since we'd found out that I was living with the infection, and things were … different. Bailey was a vacant soul in a functioning body. He seemed lost, but present. Alive, but empty. I could tell he was thinking intently each time I saw him, trying to determine our next move. I knew he was preparing for something, but I wasn't quite sure what.

The good news was that I was finally healed, and so was Grace. I could now walk around easily and hold my beautiful, healthy baby girl. I felt better. Of course, I was still worried that I'd die and thought about it more than your average person—and rightfully so—but I was handling it a lot better than Bailey, especially since I'd been routinely taking my medication for my manic episodes. One of the perks of living in a hospital with a pharmacy.

Today had been a normal day. I was sitting in an old hospital armchair, reading some book that I'd found at the nurses' station a few days ago. I used to love reading books in my apartment back in New York, and since being here I'd picked up that hobby again.

Sometimes it was nice to pretend I was in another world, living life as a fictional character that would inevitably work through their problems by the end of the book. I loved books that romanticized life—living vicariously through the characters living a perfect, cinematic lifestyle. As I read, I imagined that I was the main character who would eventually have a happy ending. It made it hard to put the book down.

Based on the amount of sunlight filtering through the windows and the activity in the hallways it was probably midday when Bailey interrupted. He entered the room abruptly, almost chaotically. I put the book face-down in my lap, curious about what was going on.

"Um, okay, Sammi, we're leaving. We're going up north. Now that you and Grace are healthy, we can get back out there and find a cure. We *have* to find a cure. What do you need to bring? I can get Grace's stuff," he blurted, rustling through our personal belongings.

I furrowed my eyebrows and crossed my arms, concerned at how irrational he was acting. "What? No. We're safe here. Go where, Bailey? What are you talking about?"

"We have to try, Sammi. We have to see if there's anyone else out there—scientists or doctors working on a cure or something. I can't just keep sitting around wondering which day you're going to die."

"I thought we were past this," I began. Was he having a crisis of faith? Jeez, he was losing it. "I'm not going anywhere."

"Sammi, please don't fight me on this," he pleaded.

"The last time I left a safe situation to go somewhere else that was supposedly safer, I nearly died," I said dryly. "Greyson died. And my brother…" I trailed off.

He stopped his hectic fumbling to look over at me with his beautiful, pained eyes. He walked over to the small armchair that I was sitting in and squatted down until he was at eye level. He grabbed my ice-cold hands and held them in his. "I know, I'm sorry. But I will protect you and Grace with my life, I promise you that. I've thought this through."

I closed my eyes and tried to see if the uneasy feeling I'd had about Opfer was the same in regard to heading up north. I didn't get the same sense of dread, so I chose to trust my instinct and agreed to go with Bailey. He smiled, clearly relieved, and left the room to start packing up.

I stood up and walked over to the window, looking out at the vacant world we were prisoners to. Bailey preferred to keep the blinds pulled up so we would always have a clear, bright window to gaze out of. From this floor of the hospital, we could see over the neighboring abandoned businesses and buildings into small, secluded areas of this part of Oklahoma.

It looked dry. We hadn't had rain in weeks, and the plants and trees were withering and shriveling from the minor drought we were experiencing. It was such a different world out there. So unfamiliar.

After Greyson's death and all the other shit, I'd missed my birthday and lost track of the days. I was frozen in time, even though time wasn't frozen with me. Now, it was transitioning from March to April, so I was hoping the showers that were figuratively tied to this month would accompany our troubled ecosystem.

Maybe leaving was the right choice, but the more I thought about it, the more I realized what it would mean: distancing myself further and further from any hope of ever seeing Caleb or Jackson again. I didn't know if I was ready to completely pull the plug on them, but I had to decide, even if that meant leaving what little shred of hope I had behind.

As I contemplated, I started to pack what I thought I would need out on the road. Many of the once busy highways were blocked by abandoned cars, so it was safe to assume that we probably couldn't drive the entire time without car hopping and walking along the way. I'd need to pack lightly but thoroughly.

As I was shoving diapers and bottles inside of a backpack I'd found in the labor and delivery unit, Bailey returned, wearing one of those kangaroo pouch-looking baby body wraps with Grace tightly sitting inside, curiously gazing around the room. He was gently moving his body up and down to keep her entertained while he waited on me to finish packing.

Just for a minute, I tried to imagine a world where we'd just been discharged from the hospital and were returning to a normal life where I was a nurse and Bailey was running his construction company. Several months would go by and I would prepare to return to work after maternity leave. We'd start to interview a list of people, trying to find the perfect fit for a babysitter as we ate some balanced breakfast one Saturday morning. I'd be folding tiny baby clothes with cartoons playing in the background while Bailey mowed the lawn.

Is that what our life would've looked like? Was that too cliché? Maybe. But we could've been so great together. *We could be so great together. Right?*

I got lost in my thoughts for a moment as I looked around at the hospital room I considered home. I thought about all the people I'd met here, some I even considered friends. We were just going to leave it all behind and hit the road.

I was starting to feel like a vagabond; I just wanted some kind of routine normalcy. Was there even anything out there for us? A cure? A home? Caleb or Jackson?

I looked over at the homemade card Lola gave me a few weeks back that she'd made from a spare piece of copy paper left behind in a printer. She wrote, "You are loved. You are resilient. You are enough." At the time, it was a sweet gesture, but now I realized it meant everything. Those were daily affirmations I needed to prosper and move forward with each day.

I realized I couldn't just leave someone who was turning into a great friend without so much as a goodbye. Had Bailey even talked to anyone about this?

"Did you tell the others we were leaving?" I asked, zipping up my bag and slipping it onto my shoulders.

"Yes, I talked to them yesterday. They said we're always welcome to come back if we decide to," he said as Grace began making sweet baby noises.

I half-smiled as I walked closer to them and gently rubbed my fingers across her soft, smooth cheeks. Bailey seemed better, a little less unhinged. I just hoped our leaving wasn't a mistake. I mean, I was all for finding a cure, but I hadn't been exposed to the outside conditions in quite a while. There was no telling what the world—and the surviving people—were now capable of. In a world of no law enforcement, no authority, and no rules, I was sure there was much worse than Opfer going on behind closed doors.

"Are you sure about this?"

He leaned over to kiss me on the cheek before saying, "Yes, it's what's best for us. I promise I'm going to figure this out for you."

I nodded as he put his backpack on and we exited the hospital room, heading for the stairwell. As we reached the first floor and moved toward the main doors, Ryan and Lola approached us.

"Let us come with you," Ryan said.

Bailey stopped and glanced over at me, then turned to his friend. "Really? Are you sure?"

"We've been talking about it since you mentioned it. We want to be a part of this," Ryan said confidently.

"Awesome! How quickly can you pack?"

Lola and Ryan looked at each other before darting back upstairs and toward their rooms.

We remained in the silent lobby as we waited for their return. While I'd started to come around to the idea of leaving, being on the first floor, so close to the outside world and all its unknowns, made me second guess my decision.

Bailey started up his bouncing again to keep Grace occupied, and I felt a flash of annoyance. How dare he be so calm and such a good dad in spite of all of this?

I awkwardly looked around the lobby to avoid conversation, but it didn't work.

"Sammi, are you okay?" Bailey asked, sensing my discomfort.

"Yes, I'm fine." It came out sharper than I'd intended. "Why do you ask?"

"Just checking," he said defensively, and I glared at him.

"Do you have a car? Do you have any weapons? Guns? Ammo?" I interrogated, crossing my arms.

"I do. Do you have your meds?" he asked passive-aggressively.

I narrowed my eyes at him as I reached around to feel the side pouch of my backpack, where I'd stuck the bottle of meds.

Our gazes connected, and a chill shot down my spine. It felt almost like a spark of sexual tension that we had never had the opportunity to release. I tried not to react or show that it affected me, because I wanted him to crave my attention as much as I craved his. I smirked slightly, but forced myself to stop.

Did we just turn aggression and sarcasm into silent sexual flirting? There I went again, smiling like an idiot. *I hope he didn't notice.*

I wandered down one of the hallways to kill time until Ryan and Lola returned, casually looking at pictures on the wall until I heard their voices approaching from the stairwell. We all huddled in the lobby to discuss the plan. This was a spontaneous, abrupt departure—to me, at least—and I felt extremely unprepared. I was hoping they could enlighten me on the journey we were about to take.

Bailey took charge. "Okay, so I have the keys to one of the vans. I put a car seat in yesterday with a few guns and ammo. We can pile all our stuff in the back for now. I don't really know exactly where we're going, but I know that Harvard has a research center where scientists practically lived pre-apocalypse. I'm hoping some of them hung around to try and develop a cure, but we really won't know until we get there. That's our first destination; I just don't know if it's going to be a complete disappointment."

For a second, I felt a hint of hope, but I forced myself to shut out my emotions and humanity to protect myself from disappointment. I needed to forget about everything that was making me sad, and unfortunately, I had the ability to do that; I'd been doing it for years.

I closed my eyes, and a swarm of memories came rushing through my head. I remembered the night Bailey and I shared at the bar, dancing, laughing, and showing each other what it was like to be wanted and happy.

I remembered Greyson being murdered. I remembered the last time I saw Caleb and Jackson. I remembered … everything.

It was so overwhelming; I needed it to stop.

God, now my head was throbbing.

We all stepped outside, following Bailey, who led the way to the van. Ryan and Lola began strategically packing their belongings into the back of the van while Bailey and I fastened Grace into the car seat. Then we all got into the car, Bailey driving, me in the passenger seat, Ryan taking the second row next to Grace, and Lola in the third row. The fourth row had the seats laid down flat with our luggage stacked on top. It wasn't much, but it was all we had.

Everyone was finally settled in, and before I knew it, we were on the road. The ride was silent for a long time; I think Lola and Ryan sensed the tension between me and Bailey, so they kept to themselves for a while. This area of Oklahoma didn't have much going on, so luckily the roads weren't blocked from abandoned cars. Occasionally, we'd have to maneuver around obstacles in the road, but right now we were in a decent position.

I watched the trees pass by until Grace began crying. I looked over at the van radio to see the time, and it was time for her bottle, like clockwork.

"Do you think this is a good spot to pull over for me to feed her?" I asked Bailey.

He nodded before slowly pulling off onto the shoulder of the road. I opened the door and walked around to the back of the van to retrieve my backpack, which carried bottles of premade milk.

Bailey had already unbuckled Grace from her car seat and carried her to the back of the van, talking to her in his adorable baby voice. "Hey, sweet girl. Are you going to smile for daddy? Yes, you are."

I smiled, or at least I did inside. I don't think it resonated with my mouth.

I pulled out one of the bottles from the backpack, then took her from Bailey's arms. She began crying again, so I hurriedly repositioned her before trying to get her to eat.

It was so quiet out here that her cries echoed through the trees and into the distance. It made me nervous. What if it attracted a swarm of zombies? It had been so long since I'd seen one, I was beginning to think they'd been wiped clean from the earth, but being complacent was dangerous.

I tried to hold Grace and bribe her with the bottle, but she continued to cry, louder and louder for several long minutes.

"Here, let me give it a try," Ryan offered, climbing out of the van.

I gently handed Grace over to him, along with the bottle, and walked a few steps away from the van. Tears welled in my eyes, my cheeks feeling warm. I felt so defeated. Caring for Grace seemed so natural for Bailey, and even Ryan, but it was a constant fuss when I tried.

Bailey walked over to join me, trying his best to comfort me by wrapping an arm around my shoulders. I was staring blankly ahead at the forest of trees, trying to distract myself, when the sound of footsteps rustling through the leaves became apparent.

My stomach sank. Grace's cries had summoned a zombie.

Bailey pulled out a handgun from his jeans and pointed it in the direction of the noise, waiting for a possessed body to emerge from the trees. Moments later, a body appeared from the woods. But it wasn't a zombie.

It was Caleb.

I gasped, taking off running toward him. When we met, I threw my arms around my brother, my tears of frustration turning to elation.

"Oh my god, Caleb! You're alive!" I said into his chest. I squeezed him for several seconds, then released him. I looked around behind him, slightly confused and panicked. "Where's Jackson? Did he…"

"Um, actually…" he started, before two more people came from the wooded area.

"No fucking way," I muttered to myself.

Jackson appeared from the woods, but to my surprise, he wasn't alone. Beside him was Sophie, and the two were laughing and holding hands.

As he approached the road, he finally looked up and noticed me. His jaw dropped, and he looked to the side, spotting the crying baby he not all that long ago wanted to play daddy to. His gaze swung back to mine, and he immediately released Sophie's hand. She looked genuinely pissed. Jealous, even.

So, he had reconnected with his slutty, bitchy ex-girlfriend after cheating on his pregnant girlfriend in the middle of an apocalypse. Now I didn't feel guilty about pursuing Bailey, a man who'd never—not once—made me feel the pain I felt the day I saw Jackson with Lucy.

But why was I still oozing with jealousy?

Love is a dangerous thing. It forces us to feel irrational thoughts and emotions, it encourages us to act on certain desires, and it makes us dissociate and become someone we don't recognize.

Just watch.

18

STRANDED

I STOOD THERE IN front of a man I'd presumed dead. We'd been separated for so long that I had forgotten what it felt like to have him in my life. What we'd had was everything to me, despite our differences. But remembering all the bad experiences with Sophie, it made me angry that he could ever rekindle things with her. He'd once told me he'd never go back to her, even if she was the last woman on earth.

How ironic.

Caleb frowned as I looked at Jackson and Sophie, then back to him. I had no doubt the expression on my face showed pain, confusion, and betrayal.

Jackson pursed his lips, and Sophie scoffed. She knew what this was doing to me mentally. All this time I'd been thinking about what happened to Jackson and Caleb, them finding Sophie in the middle of this shit show apocalypse never crossed my mind.

I ignored the two of them and instead chose to appreciate that my brother was alive. This was the antidote to the sadness and fear I'd felt when leaving the hospital community and the hope of finding him again. It was such a surreal moment. What were the odds of bumping into each other? Especially when stopping here to feed Grace was a complete fluke.

This was a good thing, despite Jackson and Sophie. I needed to embrace it.

Where had they been this whole time? Did they jump from place to place, or had they found a community too? I had so many questions.

"I can't believe you're here," I said happily, looking only at Caleb. "Where have you been?"

"We've been stumbling from place to place trying to find somewhere safe and also looking for places you might have gone. We were down by the river resting when we heard a baby cry. I thought, *that can't be—but what if it is?* And it was," Caleb said, smiling from ear to ear.

I couldn't help but share his excitement. "Do you want to meet your niece?"

He grinned. "Oh my God, yes!"

I took his hand, and we hurried toward the van, where Ryan was finishing up Grace's bottle. Bailey was standing close to Ryan, staring blankly past me at Jackson, as if he were waiting on us to hug and dramatically reunite. He'd be waiting a while for that. I guess I expected him to be happier that we'd found my brother, but a part of me felt like he was hoping Jackson wouldn't be with him when the day came.

As the four of us reached the van, I could immediately sense the awkward alpha male shit brewing between Bailey and Jackson. Part of me felt the need to say or do something affectionate to defend his honor or prove something to Jackson, but I stopped myself. Bailey should've known how I felt without fabricating it for the purpose of making Jackson jealous. I didn't need to stoop down to that level of desperation. Not yet, anyways.

Caleb reached for Grace, and Ryan gently handed her over. As he held his niece for the first time, everything about him spoke of love and happiness, from his smile to his glow. He cradled her in his arms and admired every perfect detail about her, softly rubbing her cheeks to keep her calm. This was a moment I'd cherish forever.

"What's her name?" he asked.

"Grace," I replied after a few seconds, trying to avoid tearing up.

He gave me a pitying look, as if he knew I was still a wreck over the loss of Greyson.

"Grace," he quietly repeated, stroking her head. Caleb had this nurturing nature that made it so easy to feel the love he had to offer. Grace had hit the lottery with Caleb as her uncle. There was no doubt about that.

Lola stepped out of the van and joined the rest of us circled around the back door. I saw Sophie and Jackson looking around at the unfamiliar faces.

There was an awkward silence, then Jackson cleared his throat. "I know we talked a few times at Opfer, but I guess I never put two and two together that you were *the* Bailey. Nice to meet you," Jackson said, extending a hand to Bailey.

Bailey shook his hand and gave him the driest smile ever, but I guess it was civil enough. It was weird seeing my two love interests interact. I was almost embarrassed.

I pursed my lips and awkwardly tried to move the conversation along. "I don't think you guys ever got the chance to meet Ryan, but he was the doctor I was seeing at Opfer. Ryan and Bailey saved my life—and Grace's too," I said appreciatively.

Caleb looked over at Ryan and then to Bailey before giving them a nod of approval. "Thank y'all for taking care of her," Caleb said.

Ryan patted Caleb on the shoulder to acknowledge his gratitude.

"This is Lola," I said, walking over to her as she smiled shyly. "We were a part of a bigger group pretty much right after we were separated. Her brother took us in and took care of us."

"What happened? Are y'all still with that group?" Caleb asked.

I exchanged a guilty look with Ryan and Bailey as I thought of what to say to explain why we were traveling north. I wasn't sure if this was the right time to lay this news on my brother, since we'd just been reunited, but when would be the right time? I was sure he'd ask why we were traveling north anyway. Why else would we leave a safe group to venture out on our own?

I side-eyed Bailey to see if I could read his expression, and he gave me a sympathetic head nod.

I took a deep breath, then said, "We have a lot to catch up on, big brother."

"What do you mean? What's wrong?" Caleb asked, his face dropping.

Everyone turned their attention to me, anxiously watching my lips move with each word.

"The injection … Caleb, they were giving it to people way before the soldiers started murdering everyone. Lola's brother was given it before everything went to shit, when he was in the hospital. And a few weeks ago, it killed him."

He scrunched his brow. "What are you saying, Sammi?"

"I'm saying the injection wasn't killing people as fast as they anticipated, so that's when they sent in the soldiers. To activate the infection quicker, they needed to kill everyone to begin the apocalypse, instead of having sporadic zombie transformations. Anyone who got the injection before they sent the soldiers will die from the infection, there's just not a way to know when."

I paused, Caleb looking confused and nervous, waiting for me to explain the significance of the story. I glanced over at Sophie, who seemed annoyed, as if I was wasting their time or seeking attention. Then I looked over at Jackson, who seemed like he wanted to show interest, but couldn't with Sophie present.

"Sammi…" Caleb said worriedly.

"I have the infection too, Caleb."

I saw my brother's heart shatter right then and there. I'm sure all of this was overwhelming, confusing, and fucked up to him, because it was. It was a fucked up situation. Bailey had had a similar look in his eyes when he found out, and even still, it lingered each time I mentioned the infection.

I tried to avoid looking in Jackson's direction, but a piece of me wanted to see if he was affected by the news. I cared if he cared, as much as I hated to admit that.

"What?" Jackson choked out.

"I was given the injection while I was in the hospital after my attack. The group we were with was living in the hospital, so while I was there, I went digging through my medical records, and there it was," I said, hanging my head, watching my feet shuffle from the anxiety consuming me. "So, we left the hospital, and now we're headed up north to see if we can find a cure," I explained.

"Is there room for us to tag along?" Caleb asked, not dwelling on the news of my diagnosis. That was so like my big brother: always focused on the solution rather than the problem.

"Uh, yeah, we can move some stuff around. It'll be a tight squeeze, but we can make it work," Bailey interjected. I could tell he was trying to be supportive through this latest twist, and I half-smiled at him.

We rearranged the car, moving the luggage in the back row to the left side so Sophie and Jackson could squeeze in. Caleb slotted in the third row, next to Lola. After we had settled in and were prepared to continue our journey, Bailey buckled in and started driving again.

I peered out of the windshield as the sun began to set behind the clouds slowly moving across the sky. Everyone was silent—even Grace, who had a pacifier in her mouth to keep her relaxed. We drove in silence for a while, our thoughts keeping us company, and with every minute that passed, the sky grew darker, making it difficult to relax—for me, at least.

We needed somewhere to sleep for the night, since the last thing I wanted was to get caught in some kind of mess in the middle of the night. Unfortunately we weren't in an area with anything more than maybe a gas station here and there. I felt uncomfortable and on edge, and typically that meant my gut was trying to tell me something.

"We should stop soon," I said, turning toward Bailey.

"We will. I just want to drive a little bit further. I think there's a town coming up with some better options," he said.

I pursed my lips because I knew we should stop before it got any later. I knew Bailey thought reaching the next town would be the best option, but I couldn't help but think a bigger town would have way more zombies. But I didn't feel like pressing the issue, so I just sat back as he continued to drive for what felt like another hour or so. The sky was now black with a foggy haze and a few stars scattered around.

We were on a two-lane road surrounded by half dead trees and faded road signs. With each one we passed, my eyes felt heavier. I dozed off for a second, but was quickly woken up when Bailey slammed on the brakes, causing my body to jolt toward the dashboard.

Blinking to clear my sleepy vision, I looked through the windshield, expecting to see abandoned cars blocking the road. Instead, the van's headlights illuminated zombies—hundreds of them, stretching as far as the eye could see.

It only took a few seconds for the zombies to surround the van, banging on the doors and windows, fighting for a way in. The loud hits to the van startled Grace, and she spit out the pacifier and began crying, which only made them want in even more.

My heart raced, anxiety taking over my mind and body. It was like I was in a constant state of panic these days. "What do we do?" I asked, my voice shaking.

"I-I don't know," Bailey responded, seemingly in shock. He turned to look back toward Jackson and Sophie, who were sitting nervously at the very back of the van. I could tell he was thinking intently, as if he regretted his decision to stay on the road. Nothing we could do about it now. We just knew we needed to come up with a plan, and fast. "Jackson, there are guns in a red duffel bag. Do you see it?" Bailey called back to him.

Jackson fumbled around the packed left side of the back row, trying to uncover the red duffel bag that was slightly visible underneath the pile of luggage. After rearranging and moving some items, he was able to access the bag.

I wasn't sure how many guns and bullets Bailey had packed, but I hoped it was enough to save us. The guns and ammo originally intended to protect four people were now being distributed amongst seven of us. It wouldn't take long to blow through all we had. That thought scared me.

Jackson began passing out the guns among everyone in the van, even Sophie, who admitted she had no idea how to use one. There was no time for a crash course; she'd just have to make do. We all checked to see if our gun was loaded, except Sophie of course. I'm sure she was anticipating Jackson and Caleb's protection once we exited the van, but she needed to mentally prepare to not have it.

I knew we'd need to open the doors and make a run for it, but it would probably be difficult for Jackson and Sophie, considering they would need to climb over and escape through the third-row doors.

I imagined scenarios for how this situation could play out, and none ended positively. We were running out of time, and the zombies would only continue to multiply and pile around us, complicating our exit strategy. These were mostly young and middle-aged zombies which meant their speed, stamina, and strength would make things even more difficult for us. We were essentially fucked.

"Caleb?" My voice was panic-filled. As always, I was relying on him to come up with a way to save us.

He looked around in every direction, as if trying to figure out what to do. "Jackson, how many magazines are in the duffel bag?" he asked.

"Um, six. No, seven; there's seven," he said, fumbling around nervously.

"Give one to everyone. Hurry. We'll need as much ammo as possible, but we need to be smart and conserve when we can. After this, we have nothing but knives and creativity."

"Ryan, give me Grace," Bailey said, turning to face his friend.

Ryan nodded and hurriedly began to unbuckle the straps on the car seat. He handed Grace, who was still crying, over to Bailey. He put her back into the kangaroo carrier.

"I'm going to try to kill some with my knife before we make a run for it," Caleb explained. He rolled down his window, pulled a knife from his pocket, and tried to drive it into the skull of as many zombies as he could. But it was a lot harder to stab and remove a blade from a body than it seemed, plus a pile of bodies in front of the door would lead to more problems than solutions.

Though he managed to kill several, the remaining zombies fought harder in return, reaching through the open window and trying to grab onto his arm. He tried rolling the window back up, but their arms prevented it from completely closing. He was able to remove his arm from their grasp, but they grabbed the glass of the window and broke it off, exposing the opening.

"Okay, we're going to have to make a run for it. We need to split up, so the herd does too. Plan to meet back at the van as soon as it's clear. Conserve your bullets as much as you can, but be safe. They're fast," Caleb said.

"Jackson, I'm scared," Sophie admitted.

He placed his hand on her cheek and said, "I know. It's gonna be okay."

It was the first time he'd acted affectionate with Sophie since we'd reunited. It seemed genuine. *Yuck.*

"Okay, let's go," Caleb said, opening his door.

Bailey, Ryan, Lola, and I all followed his lead, running—no, sprinting—as fast as we possibly could through heavily wooded terrain on either side of the road, all of us scattering. Jackson and Sophie exited last. When I glanced back, I could see Jackson, Caleb, Lola, and Bailey, who was carrying Grace, running in the opposite direction to me.

Ryan, Sophie, and I were running in the same direction, but when I turned back for a second time, I noticed they were beginning to get caught in the middle of the zombies. I turned back to help, but before I could reach them, Sophie bumped into Ryan, who lost his balance and fell into the arms of a zombie. I watched him fight and plead for someone to help him.

"Ryan!" I screamed, running toward him, but there was no saving him. I remember his screams so clearly, watching him collapse to the ground as the zombies piled on top of him, ripping his skin and tendons apart.

Sophie caught up to me, grabbing my arm. "Let's go! We can't save him."

My adrenaline was pumping at a rate I'd never felt before. The man who saved mine and my child's life was being eaten alive by dead, infected things. I knew his death would kill me on the inside.

I wanted to blame Sophie; she was the one who essentially placed him in the zombies' hands by carelessly running into him. I felt like she could've helped, but instead, she chose to save only herself. But I couldn't think about that right now; I just knew I needed to survive.

We ran straight through the openings between the trees, not stopping, even with the zombies lingering behind to feast on Ryan. We were safe for now, but that didn't mean it would stay that way. Hyper-vigilance was how I typically operated. If you expected danger, you were less likely to be caught off guard when you encountered it.

A continuous smell of death lingered in the cool air. Twigs snapped and leaves crunched underneath my feet as I ran, adrenaline consuming my body to a capacity that disguised my exhaustion from running for my life, literally.

I ran until I found an old, abandoned house settled in the middle of the woods. I stopped at the concrete steps, observing the evidence of a house fire. The building was severely damaged, with several vulnerable areas for zombies to infiltrate, but I knew my body needed to rest. This was where we'd be seeking shelter tonight, at least until it was safe to return to the van.

I turned to see Sophie, who'd finally caught up. As she panted, trying to catch her breath, I looked at her—like really looked at her—for the first time since she and Jackson had first started dating. I'd never wanted to pay too much attention to her until now. She still had the same green eyes and chestnut hair, and she was wearing a pair of black athletic pants with a light blue jacket zipped up over a tee. Not much had changed about her, especially her selfishness.

"We're not staying here, are we?" she asked, still trying to catch her breath.

"You got any better ideas?"

She didn't respond.

I took the steps into the charred house, desperate to find some part that had survived the fire. I quietly moved from room to room, assessing the situation. The house itself was relatively small, but some parts were salvageable. It wasn't ideal by any means, but there was a halfway decent leather couch positioned in the living room that I could probably sleep on.

The dry, ash, and dust-covered wood floor creaked beneath me with each step, but I didn't suspect that we had company hiding out in this house that would hear me. There wasn't anywhere they could be, except behind the only closed door in the house, at the end of a small hallway.

I walked down the hall, and heard Sophie follow me. I turned to face her, and my facial expression said exactly how I felt about her. She noticed—there's no way she couldn't have. The similar look she gave me in return confirmed that. It made me wonder what Jackson had told her about me during their time together.

"What is your problem?" she asked irritably.

I raised my eyebrows in disbelief. "My problem? God, where do I start?" I asked angrily.

"Please, tell me. I'd love to hear!"

"Don't act like you didn't just get Ryan killed! You could've helped him, and now he's dead—because of you!"

"Because of me? He got himself killed! This is surviving, Sammi! I'm surviving," she yelled.

"He was a doctor! He saved my daughter's life. He saved *my* life! And he could've saved it again," I cried.

Ryan was dead, and he could've played a role in figuring out a way to cure this infection within me. He had been there for me at Opfer, and not once did I ever doubt his intentions. I owed him my life. I owed Sophie nothing. Of all the people left in the world, I had somehow got stranded with her. What were the odds?

"You don't have to like me, but you're going to have to live with me. I'm not going anywhere," she said, crossing her arms.

I rolled my eyes and proceeded to open the bedroom door we'd been standing outside of. To my surprise, the room was intact, despite the fire that had destroyed most of the house. They weren't lying when they said keeping your door shut could save your life in case of a fire; this was evidence that that was true.

Evidently, the room once belonged to a young girl, because it was decorated with white wooden furniture, colorful butterflies and flowers, and lots of pink and bright green throughout. Small picture frames filled with photographs of a girl and her friends and family were settled on top of her dresser and bedside table. I walked over to each one to look at them up close, Sophie remaining silent in the doorway.

"I'm not a bad person," she said after a beat of silence.

"Are you trying to convince me or yourself?" I asked, picking up one of the pictures to admire the happy girl.

"I've loved Jackson forever, but every time we broke up it wasn't because of me," she said calmly.

I turned to face her, putting the frame back down.

She continued, "He was always the one to break it off. When I got with other guys, that was just to keep my mind occupied. Every time I was more heartbroken than the last."

I narrowed my eyes in suspicion, waiting for her to elaborate.

"I love Jackson, but he loves you. It's always been you," she admitted, pain evident in each word.

"Why would you think it was because of me?" I asked curiously.

She walked over to the bed, climbing on top of it, then sat with her back against the wall, crossing her legs. "He told me he was in love with you, every time. But then something would happen. He'd change his mind, or you were with Reece or something. I don't know."

I walked over to the bed, finding a spot next to her. "You said he *loves* me, present tense," I observed.

She swallowed a lump in her throat before admitting the truth behind Jackson's feelings. "When he's sleeping at night, he cries out for you. Every day you were gone, he'd slip away to try and find you. He always lied, saying he was scavenging for food, but he never stopped looking for you. He never stopped loving you."

"Why are you telling me this? You two are together, and Bailey and I are together. What am I supposed to do with that?"

"I'm telling you because we could die. At any moment. And this world is too cruel to not know who truly loves us. We should be with the person we love," she said sadly.

"Do you love Jackson?" I asked.

"I do, but he doesn't love me—not the way he loves you. And he never will."

I frowned. This was the most civil conversation I'd ever had with Sophie. Talking to her like this now, she seemed like a decent human being. She was almost someone I could be friends with. But could I really trust her? Was what she was telling me true?

"When the world started going to shit, I was out kayaking with some friends. We camped out for weeks, hunting for food and drinking from the river. We survived perfectly fine like that for a while until another group killed my friends. I'd been washing off in the water a little way from our tents, and I heard screams and then gunshots—lots of gunshots. I had no choice but to drag the kayak back in and get as far away as I could. I lived alone for a while, moving almost every day, until one day I came across these two guys filling up bottles in the river. When I got closer, I saw that it was Caleb and Jackson. I'd never felt more relieved in my entire life. The three of us have stuck together ever since, looking for you every day."

"I had no idea. I'm sorry that happened to you."

"I don't know what issues you and Jackson have, but it's time you really decide who you want to be with," she said, looking over at me.

I took a deep breath, thinking back to the day I'd walked in on Lucy and Jackson. I was second guessing every thought, decision, and feeling I'd had. Was it even real? It had to be. I wondered if he'd shared that with Sophie or if she'd known about Lucy. I wondered about a lot of things.

"Jackson cheated on me while I was pregnant. I walked in on it," I said.

She furrowed her brows in confusion. "Sammi, Jackson is a lot of things, but a cheater isn't one of them. I swear that to you."

I considered her words. It was true that when I had tried to flirt with him in the past while he was with Sophie, he politely turned me down. Why wouldn't he give me the same respect? Should I have given him the benefit of the doubt? I knew what I had seen, but maybe I should hear him out?

"We should try to get some sleep," I suggested.

She nodded agreeably and we both moved beneath the comforter of the full-sized bed. She turned to face the wall, almost immediately falling asleep.

I shut my eyes and tried to rest, but I struggled to sleep, unable to stop thinking about Bailey and Jackson, hoping that Grace and Caleb were okay, and worrying that a zombie would wander in. But eventually my exhaustion caught up to me, and I fell sound asleep.

19

OUT IN THE OPEN

WHEN MORNING CAME, I could feel someone watching me. You know that feeling—a presence joining you that you are subconsciously aware of? I was almost scared to open my eyes, but when I did, I felt a flood of relief.

"I must be dreaming," Jackson said, staring down at me and Sophie in the bed.

"Oh please," Sophie grumbled as she got up.

I slowly opened my eyes, adjusting to the sunlight beaming in from the bedroom window.

"You two spent the night together, and you didn't kill each other? I'm impressed," Caleb said as he appeared in the doorway.

"The thought did cross my mind," I said, joking. Mostly.

This was embarrassing for me to admit, but for a second—the slightest second—I forgot about Bailey and Grace. It was almost like we were back in the beginning, when it was just us three. But I quickly began to worry when I didn't see anyone else with Caleb and Jackson. Had they lost track of Lola, Bailey, and Grace?

"Where's everyone else?" I asked worriedly, scrambling out of bed.

"Lola and Bailey went to the van. We told them we'd meet them there after we found y'all," Caleb said.

"And Grace?"

"She's fine," Caleb said, reaching over to rub my shoulder. "Come on. We've got some driving to do," he said, smiling.

The four of us exited the house and made our way through the wooded area, following almost our exact trail from last night. Caleb led the way in the direction of the van as Sophie followed behind him, and Jackson and I behind her.

I really wanted to talk to Jackson alone. With everything Sophie laid on me last night, I needed some answers, closure—something. Too bad we couldn't really get any privacy. So instead I continued to walk in silence, so close to Jackson that I could feel his energy.

I repeatedly glanced over at him, noticing how good he looked in a pair of khaki pants and an olive-green tee. He had his hands slightly tucked in his front pockets as he took each step.

At first I worried that he'd catch me looking, but he seemed to be preoccupied with something. It was like he was battling the same demons in his head; it was radiating around us—this absolute need to get things off our chest. I almost reached for his hand out of habit, but I clenched my fist and kept moving forward. It would only complicate matters to let all my deep feelings for him resurface.

God, I almost wished Sophie had never told me anything. I was perfectly content with my life with Bailey. At least, I had thought so? Now I was questioning everything.

The love I had for Jackson and Bailey was the same, yet so different. Bailey was … perfect. He was handsome, kind, gentle, loving, and extremely attractive. He had never once hurt me, and he was the best father Grace could ever have. He'd once been the guy that allowed me to be brave and vulnerable all at once.

He'd created this sexy Prince Charming persona that night at the bar, but unfortunately, it turns out that an apocalypse is the biggest barrier for romance. It was hard to overcome the sense that I was just settling, especially when my options were so limited. I couldn't exactly go to a bar or a nice restaurant; this was what I had to work with now.

Jackson was exciting and adventurous. He was sexy, flirtatious, and still a sweetheart. We had a history that made our relationship seem both easy and complicated, which was confusing. But my heart beat faster just by touching him or feeling his breath on my neck. It sent tingles down my spine, every single time.

We weren't a couple until things went to hell, so I didn't know if he could offer me the same happiness and sense of contentment I'd felt that night with Bailey. But this love I had for Jackson was like the feeling of first love. It was joyful and beautiful—a love I'd never forget, no matter how hard I tried.

I didn't know what to do. My feelings were so conflicted, and I knew as soon as I was in Bailey's presence again that I'd need to make a conscious effort to figure out what was best for me and Grace. What would it mean to choose? Would I lose the guy I didn't pick? This was all too overwhelming.

As I was walking and organizing the jumbled thoughts swarming in my mind like angry hornets, something happened, and I don't know how to explain it without sounding crazy. It was almost like I was dissociating from myself, from reality. For several long minutes I could see myself in a parallel universe. Everything was the same, but duller, colder, and darker.

I was … alone. I couldn't see Jackson, Caleb, or Sophie. I looked around, panicked, turning in circles and trying to figure out where everyone went. Where were they? Where was I?

"Caleb?" I called out in confusion as my vision went blurry for a brief second.

I continued walking for a couple of minutes, trying to see if I could find everyone else. Had I zoned out and somehow fallen behind the rest of the group?

I kept checking my surroundings and eventually spotted someone in the distance. Though my vision was blurry, I knew I didn't recognize them. Once my eyes finally refocused, I could see that it was a young woman wearing jeans and a dirty white tee. She was stumbling and hurrying to me, almost at a run. Her dark hair was messy, and her eyes looked glossy.

I stopped walking as she got closer and closer. Did she need help?

"You need to leave," she begged. "It's not safe here, it's not safe, it's not s—"

"What? Where am I?" I interrupted, but as she started to answer, her voice was drowned out by what sounded like Jackson's.

I looked around, but I couldn't see him. I could only distantly hear his voice echoing around me. It felt like he was close, but I couldn't find him. My head was spinning, and my heart was racing. What the fuck was going on?

I turned in circles, trying to figure out where his voice was coming from, but the only person I could see was the woman who shared the same fear and confusion as me. She just kept repeating the same thing over and over, but I didn't understand what she meant.

Then suddenly, I could make out Jackson's voice again, and it didn't sound drowned out like it had before. It sounded like he was so close I could touch him. "Sammi? Sammi, look out!" he shouted.

And then just like that, I was back with Caleb, Jackson, and Sophie. When I looked over, the woman was still there, but she was a zombie. She was clothed in the same outfit, but instead of telling me to leave, she was dead and growling, inches from my face. I had no clue how she hadn't already bitten me.

Jackson was yelling my name, trying to warn me that the zombie was there. I panicked, reaching for the gun I'd been given the night before. I pointed it at her and pulled the trigger, even though she didn't seem interested in coming any closer, or even harming me, for that matter.

The body collapsed to the ground, and I found myself gasping for air, almost as if I were having a panic attack. My eyes were wide as I put my hands on my chest, reminding myself to inhale and exhale. I needed to calm myself down, but I was so disoriented. I had no idea what had just happened, and I was almost scared to know.

Jackson and Caleb rushed over to me as they expressed their concern, showing the same uncertainty as me.

"Sammi, what's wrong?" Caleb asked.

I looked around, still preoccupied by my mind and the vivid encounter.

"Sammi," Jackson urged, grabbing my arm gently.

The warmth from his palm brought me back completely, helping me reconnect with reality. I looked over at him, Caleb standing close by. Just having him there calmed me down and allowed me to gradually control my breathing.

"I-I'm sorry," was all I managed.

"What happened? Did you not see that zombie?" Jackson asked.

"I … don't know. I-I-I'm dying. We need to get back on the road and find a cure," I said abruptly.

Caleb and Jackson looked at each other with worried expressions, but they couldn't even begin to understand what I'd just experienced.

I broke away from the huddle and continued walking. I needed time to think before I explained this to anyone. So, I began replaying it in my head, considering all possibilities, and knowing that nothing was off the table. Whoever created this virus was intelligent, intentional, and engineered it to kill off humanity—but we already knew it was flawed. It didn't kill at the rate it was intended to, so if it was possible for them to miss perfecting that, it was also possible they left some room for loopholes, ways around death, or the introduction of a cure.

As we made our way further through the trees, I could tell we were getting close to the van. I could vaguely hear Lola and Bailey having a conversation in the distance, but their words were mixed with the wind.

I wasn't sure what to expect once I got up there, but I was worried about how Bailey would react to Ryan being dead. Honestly, in the drama of the morning, I'd kind of forgotten about it, but it didn't make it hurt any less now that I refreshed my mind on his horrific death. With everything we'd survived, I hadn't expected his demise to happen that way, because of Bailey's dumb decision to stay on the road—

Shit. *Bailey.* He was going to blame himself for this.

Now I wanted to turn around and deflect this encounter entirely. Was it too late for that?

With each step, we approached Lola, Bailey, and Grace, who he had lying in his arms, gently rocking her. I smiled when I saw them together. I never imagined the night at the bar leading to this beautiful thing I had with Bailey, and now Grace. It was still one of the best nights ever.

Bailey still looked the same as he did when I'd first met him, with his dark brown hair and beard, both of which were now longer than they once were. He still had piercing blue eyes that drew me in when I looked at him. He also had this attractive country accent that was just so silky and smooth, though sometimes I noticed it more than others. And his presence—it was enough to warm my body for all eternity. To keep my heart beating for as long as I lived.

I slowly moved to Bailey's side, gazing down at Grace and all her beauty. She had her father's eyes and the softest, smoothest skin when I dragged my fingertips across her arms. My shoulder rubbed against Bailey's, and I felt at home again. I felt like I was back at the hospital, safe, playing house while the world continued to die around us.

"Hey! You're okay," he said happily as he leaned over to kiss me.

I gave him my cheek rather than my lips, and it seemed like everyone else noticed the awkward silence we'd found ourselves in. It wasn't that I didn't want to kiss him, I just felt the need to distance myself until I had the chance to talk to Jackson.

Bailey awkwardly withdrew before looking around at the remaining members of our group. He noticed one of us was missing, which was to be expected.

"Where's Ryan?" he asked.

I was surprised Caleb or Jackson hadn't asked prior to this when they'd discovered only me and Sophie in the abandoned house. I was avoiding the topic. I didn't want to blame Sophie because we still had to live with her, but then again, we'd had one good conversation—that didn't make us friends. I didn't owe her loyalty, but I felt like my options for relationships were limited. We were all we had; there was no room for isolating those who were surviving alongside us. So, was I supposed to trust her until she gave me a reason not to? What other choice did I have?

"He didn't make it, Bailey. I'm so sorry. I couldn't save him," I admitted.

His expression dropped. He wasn't a crier, but I could tell that he wanted to. Ryan was his best friend, and he'd saved the two most important girls in his life. Now all he really had was me and Grace.

I took the hand that wasn't cradling Grace, interlocking my fingers with his. I forced a smile, knowing there was nothing I could do except be there for him.

I wanted to let him have his time to grieve, but I needed to talk to someone about what happened in the woods. I didn't necessarily want to share with the group, but I didn't have the option of pulling him to the side without everyone else wondering what we were talking about.

I guess I'll just have to tell everyone and rip the Band-Aid off.

We all quietly loaded into the van, but this time Sophie didn't sit with Jackson; she sat across from Grace, in what had been Ryan's seat. Jackson sat alone in the backseat with a slightly confused look on his face. Was that Sophie's statement that she was done? And was he upset or relieved?

Bailey was busy buckling Grace in when Jackson announced, "Uh, guys, all of our stuff is gone from back here."

"What? The duffel bag and everything?" Bailey asked from where he stood in the open doorway beside Grace's car seat.

"It's all gone," he confirmed.

"Sammi, how much ammo did you use while we were separated?" Caleb asked.

"Just the bullet in the woods, why?"

"Sophie, what about you?"

"I didn't have to use mine," she said.

"Caleb?" I persisted.

"We used up all we had. We got into some pretty deep shit while we were trying to find somewhere to stay for the night. We were kind of relying on reloading from what was left in the duffel bag. So, we're not in a great position if something else goes down. We need to be smart about our next moves until we can stock back up somehow," he said.

Sophie offered up her gun to Caleb, who willingly accepted.

I sat there in deep thought, wondering who would feel the need to steal from an abandoned van when there were stores with unlimited options around us. It was almost like we were being followed.

Then I realized ammo wasn't the only problem. My backpack with all my important items had been in here as well.

My heart dropped. I swung open the passenger door of the van and ran to the back. I opened the two back doors, looking in the small area between the back of Jackson's seat and the doors. There was nothing. Then, I climbed in through the third row doors until I was in the back next to Jackson. I searched under the seat I was sitting on, then leaned over Jackson's lap, fumbling in the emptiness.

I finally stopped and closed my eyes, taking a deep breath. "It's gone. My backpack, it's gone."

"It's okay," Lola said, trying to sound encouraging.

"It's not. They took the last of my medication, diapers, formula, everything," I said, my voice low, slumping down on the seat in defeat.

I saw the look on Jackson's face; he knew what missing my medicine meant. Bailey, on the other hand, had never experienced me in a full-blown manic episode; he'd only ever seen hints of it, probably without realizing that's what it was. He'd surely run for the hills if he got the chance to see that side of me.

Maybe that's what I wanted?

I don't know. Don't listen to me; I'm all messed up right now.

"We'll find a pharmacy or a grocery store while we're on the road. It will be fine," Jackson pitched in, trying to reassure me.

I smiled weakly, but subconsciously, the more I thought about losing the pills, the more I felt a strange sense of relief. Maybe I needed to withdraw from this normal mental state and crazy love triangle. I felt like it might be nice to not feel an obligation toward choosing or acting how people expected me to. Maybe it would help me decide who I wanted to be with.

Anyway, a manic episode scared me a lot less than whatever that episode in the woods was.

I inhaled deeply. "I'm afraid we have bigger problems," I admitted, finally settling beside Jackson in the backseat.

Everyone turned to face me expectantly.

"I'm not sure how much longer I have before the injection kills me. When we were in the woods … I was there, but Caleb, Jackson, Sophie—you guys weren't," I said, gesturing toward me and then to them.

They all had similar confused expressions on their faces and I rubbed my eyes in frustration with the palms of my hands.

"Everything was the same, except I was alone until the woman appeared," I began.

"The zombie?" Sophie asked as if confirming that I saw the same zombie they did.

I nodded. "Yes, but she wasn't a zombie when I saw her; she was a person, like us. She was scared and panicked. She was coming to me to warn me to leave the weird alternate universe I'd found myself in. I asked her where I was, but when I heard Jackson calling my name it was almost like I woke up from a dream or something."

I narrowed my eyes, thinking intently. Then, I found myself making eye contact with Lola, who looked almost guilty. Like she was keeping a secret.

"Lola, you know something," I said.

Her eyes widened as she looked back up at me.

"What is it?" I asked pointedly.

"Um…" she responded as if trying to stall. Then she sighed and admitted the truth. "Well, um, Rudy, he—he told me about that happening to him before he died. He had it happen a few times while we were on the road. The zombies we'd come in contact with during his visions or whatever told him the same thing. It was a lot for him. He felt afraid and alone, especially when we were back at the hospital and there weren't any zombies there. The duration of these visions got longer and longer as his condition progressed. He'd be there for hours. Toward the end, he was there almost an entire day. He was so lonely until…" she trailed off.

"Until what?" Jackson asked.

"Until I showed up. Right?" I added.

She pursed her lips.

"He saw me there with him that day in the cafeteria, right? That's why you two gave me those looks. That's why he let us stay, isn't it?" I asked angrily. "God, you've known this entire time!" I said, hurt and betrayal accompanying each word.

Everyone grew silent, Lola opening and closing her mouth, as if unsure what to say.

"You came to us after Rudy died and gave this big story about when you thought he was given the injection, but you knew from the start that he'd been given the injection in the hospital that day! You told us the story because you knew I'd go searching for answers and figure out that I'd received it too. You just wanted me to be the one to figure it out. Jesus, I can believe you!" I said painfully.

She held a mask of regret over her face and slowly turned back toward the front of the van.

Jackson grabbed my hand and held on to it securely as I tried to wrap my head around this. I noticed Bailey watching Jackson's gesture, and I could tell it pained him more than it made him jealous.

I was already over this day; I was ready to crawl into bed somewhere and just wallow in my self-pity and manifest a manic episode to get me away from all of this.

"Let's just drive, please. I need to feel like there's hope for me somewhere out there," I said.

Bailey nodded and began to drive. We still had a long way to go, so we needed to start covering some ground. In the sunlight, I could see the road in much more detail, and I noticed faded road signs and dry plants. There were maybe two or three straggler zombies roaming in the distance, but nothing compared to last night.

For several hours, I didn't say anything. I sat my elbow on the side of the car and propped my head on my hand, looking out the window. Grace had fallen asleep, and Bailey was driving north. I'd lost track of where we were, but the roads seemed familiar. I knew we had left Oklahoma a while ago, considering Pocola was not too far from Arkansas. I was almost certain we were headed toward Nashville, and that would definitely bring up some feelings and memories.

After a while, Jackson nudged my thigh. I looked over at him as he smiled, a little embarrassed. "Hey," he whispered.

"Hey," I replied with a smile. A part of me felt weird sitting next to Jackson, but maybe this was the perfect opportunity to talk, especially since Bailey had stuck an old CD into the radio, which was now playing soft music in the background.

"What happened with you and Sophie at the house? Why didn't she sit with me?"

"We just talked," I said vaguely, my smile dropping.

"About?"

"You," I admitted.

He raised his eyebrows. "And?"

"We talked about all the times you broke up. She said you were in love with me long before we actually got together," I said, almost as if I wanted him to think I didn't believe it, that I thought it was a joke.

He didn't laugh. "What else did she tell you?"

"Nothing much. It's more so what I told her."

"Sammi," he pleaded.

"Lucy. We've never talked about Lucy. You know, the naked, supermodel-looking blonde you were gawking at while your pregnant girlfriend needed you and while Greyson was being murdered," I hissed angrily, my volume low enough for the rest of the group not to overhear.

His eyes shone with immediate hurt and sadness. "Sammi, I will be sorry for as long as I live for what you saw in that room and for what happened to Greyson. But what you saw was the extent of what happened. I never slept with her," he said.

He seemed convincing, but my heart dropped anyway. "But would you have if I hadn't walked in?"

"I-I thought I was protecting you."

"Protecting me?" I choked out.

∽

Jackson's point of view

My mind was racing. There had never been a single situation that had made me feel so vulnerable, so guilty, and so angry.

The day everything went down, I'd been looking for a quiet space to think. I could tell I was losing Sammi, and that was the one thing I was most afraid of—not the zombies or the soldiers. All I could think was that maybe she had been right about this place. Maybe it was too good to be true.

I was walking down a narrow hallway on the first floor of Opfer when I came across a set of heavy double doors. I could hear Gabe and Lucy's voices, but I couldn't make out what they were saying. One of the doors was open, so I eased up to it, standing right outside, trying to make out what the two of them were saying.

"Yes, the girl needs to go. She is a risk to us all. I can have Peter arrange for her death," Lucy said.

"What about the brother? You're friends, right?" Gabe asked.

"I'll handle it," she said.

Immediately, I understood that they were talking about Sammi and Caleb. I turned, planning to run and warn them, but my arm hit the handle of the door. I winced, fearing what would happen when they found out I knew their plan. I was now a liability.

Lucy swung open the door before I had the chance to flee the scene. But once she saw me, she sighed with relief. "Oh, it's you."

I wasn't quite sure why she seemed so relieved. It was like she thought I would back her decision.

"Are you going to kill Sammi?" I asked.

"Yes. But you have to understand, Jackson, she's a risk to us all. She has the infection, and we aren't sure how this thing spreads. It's only a matter of time," she said.

"What? You think she's infected? That's insane," I said defensively.

"You'll just have to trust that I know she does, Jackson."

"Well if she's infected, why can't you just let her leave? Why does she have to die?" I asked, trying to find a way around this sudden idea that she needed to be killed because she was supposedly infected.

"Because she'll eventually turn. She will be amongst those already killing the people we care about. Sacrifices must be made, Jackson. That's how we survive this thing," she said, grabbing my hands sympathetically, as if I would understand her logic.

Well, her logic was shit. I wanted to get her to elaborate, maybe giving her a slight hint that I was somewhat considering her perspective to temporarily ensure my safety.

"What does that mean for me? For Caleb? Are you going to kill us too?" I asked.

"You two are not the enemy, Jackson. I will not let anything happen to you," she said gently.

"What do I have to do to change your mind? To spare her life," I begged.

She pondered for a minute before smiling devilishly. "Fuck me," she said seductively.

It caught me off guard because they preached about no fornication here; it didn't make sense for her to openly make this suggestion. I'd be lying if I said I wasn't anxious and yet slightly intrigued. My palms were sweaty, and my heart was beating rapidly. It was human nature to have this desire—this lust that consumes you. You forget everything else outside of the moment.

But I can assure you, I didn't agree to it. I took a step back, stumbling almost. I was nervous, and she used that against me.

"If you don't want that option," she began, rubbing her fingers up my arm, "you can sacrifice the boy instead."

I gaped at her, shocked at her suggestion. "Greyson?"

"Those are the terms," she said, her tone now much more serious.

I began playing scenarios in my head. Greyson was a son to me and Sammi. I could never live with myself if he died, knowing my actions were what led to it. But I also couldn't live with myself cheating on Sammi either. Why was she doing this?

"Lucy…" I said, my voice hopeless.

"You must decide. Peter has orders to kill Sammi in thirty minutes. After that, it's out of my control."

"Why are you making me choose between these two things?" I begged.

"Because, no matter what you choose, you'll have lost Sammi forever. She's been a problem since she arrived. Sleeping with me or killing Greyson will make her wish she were dead," she said emotionlessly.

I stood there for what felt like an eternity before inviting her up to my room. I needed her to believe I wanted her. Once we got in the room, I was planning to tie her up and do what needed to be done to escape and rescue Sammi, Greyson, and Caleb from this insane asylum disguised as a safe haven.

As I hatched my plan, I kept thinking about Lucy accusing Sammi of being infected. *Why would she even say that?*

I looked around the room for something I could use as a weapon without causing a commotion. Without seeming too obvious, I had to play along with her mind games. She instructed me to take my clothes off, but I tried to keep what little dignity I had left by keeping my boxers on. Lucy, on the other hand, wasted no time getting completely naked.

She was no doubt overwhelmingly attractive, but I didn't want this. I was so flustered I couldn't help but study every inch of her exposed skin. I tried to stall, but my mind kept wandering. I needed to think of something to say or do to resist the temptation to just take her right here, so I deflected.

"Why do you think Sammi is infected? There must be some mistake," I insisted as she stepped closer. I dug my fingernails into my palms to keep myself from grabbing her. *Fuck, Jackson, what is the matter with you?*

"There's no mistake. I know she's been given the injection," Lucy said calmly.

"How?" I asked.

"Because I'm the nurse that gave it to her," she admitted with a menacing smile.

Chills covered every surface of my body, and suddenly every desire I had vanished, only shock left behind. I felt like a fool. There was no way she was telling the truth. There was no way.

I was sitting on the edge of the bed, my mouth wide open in disbelief, when Sammi opened the door. And that's the moment when I knew I'd lost everything.

I'd royally fucked up, and for what? Greyson still ended up dead.

～

Sammi's point of view

As Jackson told me what happened that day, I didn't know if I was relieved, angry, jealous, or sad. I could see the predicament he'd found himself in, but it didn't make any of it hurt any less. I believed him; I just wished I could erase the image of the two of them from my mind. It was detrimental to my mental health.

"None of this was meant to happen, and it was never something you should've walked in on. Seeing you in that doorway … that hurt me, Sammi. Please believe that. I would never hurt you intentionally, but in that moment I felt like I couldn't save you. I felt hopeless. That's why I didn't come after you."

I looked over at him, trying to avoid getting emotional.

"It still didn't save Greyson, and I will never be able to get past that," he said, his lips quivering.

I could see that he felt terrible. Helpless, even. God, I wanted so badly to hug him and kiss him until he felt better, but how was I supposed to feel this way about two men? I couldn't decide who I loved more. It was an impossible task.

"I didn't want to believe that she'd given you the injection, so when we found you again, I was heartbroken to hear that you'd found what Lucy said to be true."

I squeezed his hand comfortingly, about to say something, when Caleb sat up straight in his seat, turning to look out of the back window. "What the hell?"

Jackson and I turned to see what had caught Caleb's attention, and goosebumps covered every inch of my body. An all-too-familiar green Mustang was trailing us, getting closer and closer as it sped up. I froze for a second before my eyes began watering and I started to hyperventilate.

I knew who was in that Mustang, and I was afraid they'd kill me this time.

Jackson noticed my fear. "Sammi, who's in that car? Sammi?" he asked insistently, shaking my shoulder.

"I need to get out of this van. I need to run," I said, grabbing the back of the seat in front of me.

"Absolutely not. We are not letting you out of this van," Caleb said protectively. "Who's in the car?"

"The guy that nearly killed me at the gas station," I said. The Mustang was now feet away from the back bumper, weaving from the left lane to the right.

"I need to go. He's going to run us off the road and kill all of us if you don't let me out. It's me he wants," I said.

"Just give me a second to think," Caleb pleaded.

In the middle of all of the chaos, a hand holding a gun stretched out of the Mustang's passenger window and sent several bullets spiraling into the back of the van, shattering the window behind me and Jackson. We both ducked down as the bullets kept coming.

Grace started crying, and I knew Bailey was getting worried. "What do I do?" he asked desperately, swerving slightly with each bullet.

"Goddamn it, my baby is in here!" I yelled out, angry and emotional, as if the people in the Mustang could hear me. "You gotta let me out," I said helplessly, begging.

"Sammi, please, no," Caleb argued.

"We collectively have less than twenty bullets, Caleb. We can't exactly afford to waste what little ammo we have left shooting at a moving vehicle," I said. "What are we gonna do when they blow a tire? Die anyways? You have to let me out," I demanded.

Bailey worriedly looked at me through the rear-view mirror before slowing down the van. I climbed up to the third row of seats where Caleb was sitting. He looked angry at my decision, but we all knew this was the safest option for everyone—except me, probably. I gently rubbed his shoulder to try and comfort him, but we were running out of time. I needed to keep everyone else from becoming a victim of my own actions that had angered whoever it was in the Mustang.

"I'll be fine. I have my gun. Just come back for me later, okay?"

"Sammi, please," Jackson begged.

I turned to look at him one last time before preparing to initiate my fight or flight response. "I'm ready," I said to Bailey, who quickly stopped the van.

Caleb sat back in his seat, accepting defeat on my decision to leave.

I opened the door and jumped out, sprinting through the open field to our right. I didn't look back before I heard Bailey gas the van to leave.

As I expected, the Mustang came to a screeching halt before the doors swung open. I didn't want to look at how many people stepped out of the car, so I continued running as fast as I could.

I could hear Caleb trying to shoot at the men from the van as it drove away, but it didn't sound like he made contact, and we were now down to even less ammo. I still had nine bullets in my gun, but there was no way I could shoot them successfully while we were both running at full speed. Plus, the last thing I wanted was to attract another mass of zombies with the noise of flying bullets.

Eventually I came out into a neighborhood filled with houses that all looked eerily similar. I looked around before deciding to run toward the right. It had more houses, which meant more options for me to hide. I was exhausted, but my adrenaline was allowing me to keep fighting.

I ran up to a house that was painted light blue, but after making it up the steps of the porch and reaching for the doorknob, I realized it was dead bolted shut.

Fuck.

I hurried around the side of the wraparound porch to hide while I figured out how to run toward another house without being seen by the people chasing me. I could hear the soles of their shoes smacking against the concrete sidewalk, so I peeped around the corner to see if I could make out who they were.

When I saw who it was, I almost laughed. It was the three stooges from the bar. The three guys that had drugged me before taking me to their apartment to do God knows what. I couldn't believe I'd let some barely twenty-year-old boys not only drug me, but attack me in the gas station parking lot that day.

Now they're back to finish the job, I assumed. This was what I was up against?

Once the three of them stopped, the guy I remembered as Walker instructed them to split up to find me. The blonde sidekick took off to the left-hand houses while the other two split up the right side. I remained in the same spot, now backing up from view.

I tried to watch their movements, but I'd lost track of Walker already. *Which house did he go to?* I looked at each one, searching for any sign of him.

It was only when I felt two hands grab me from behind that I realized he'd found me.

I reached for my gun, but I quickly lost consciousness.

20

NOT SO SOBER MIND

EVERYTHING WAS A BLUR. I didn't know what Walker had done to immobilize me, and I couldn't remember exactly how I'd gotten here, to this room. I was tied to a chair like some stereotypical hostage, though I guess that's what I was. My clothes had been removed, except for my bra and panties.

I felt so uneasy; there was a strange aura surrounding me. I think I was more afraid of being sexually assaulted than being murdered. It was just an uncomfortable feeling to think about the possibilities of being here with these three guys who'd tried it once before.

What was their plan? How would this end for me?

I gently tugged at my arms and looked around at the room. It was unsurprisingly unfamiliar, but I had a feeling we were in one of the houses close to where I'd been attempting to hide from them. The room was painted light pink and there was a dated floral comforter on the bed; the fabric looked thick and itchy. White eyelet curtains lightly covered in dust settled over the windows.

A small opening between the curtains displayed a small glimpse of the street. I squinted, trying to see if I could get a clear view of the building's surroundings. The house across the street had a concrete sidewalk that connected and ran into the other homes in the neighborhood. It looked calm—no sound, no movement, no … one. To be expected, really.

I sat on the chair, uncomfortable and exposed, staring through the curtains for some time—until a person came into view. My heart began racing when I saw that it was Jackson in the street, looking from left to right at the different houses, hoping to find me.

I tried to fight the restraints, but the restraints had very minimal give. I needed to get his attention and let him know that I was here before he got any further away.

"Jackson! Jackson!" I screamed as loud as I could. "Jackson!"

It seemed like no matter how loud I called out, Jackson couldn't hear me. He didn't even budge. I kept trying, hoping he'd come rescue me.

"Jackson! I'm in here!" I cried out, my voice now losing power.

Suddenly the bedroom door swung open, revealing Walker. He laughed maliciously as I tugged as hard as I could at the rope around me, now panicking. This was it. The moment I was certain I would die. The look on his face said it all.

"Jackson isn't out there. You're hallucinating," he said, walking over to the window. He grabbed the edges of the curtains and tugged them completely shut, blocking the only view I had of the outside world.

"What do you want from me?" I groaned helplessly.

"Revenge," he replied almost immediately, as if he'd been waiting for me to ask.

"Just kill me and get it over with," I said in disgust.

"What would be the fun in that, Sammi?" he teased as he turned to face me. "I didn't know I had the ability to be such a … dark person. But you've really brought it out in me."

"You drugged me at the bar. You took me back to your apartment with two other guys to try and take advantage of me. You nearly beat me to death in a gas station parking lot while I was pregnant. You've been a dark person," I said angrily. "I had nothing to do with it."

"And yet, I still don't feel any better," he said, placing his thumb on his chin as if in deep thought. "But don't worry, Sammi, I will soon enough."

He walked around to the back of the chair, where my arms were tied. I couldn't see him, but I could hear him fumbling around with an object in his hands. I closed my eyes and tried to think of some way out of this as I heard Walker thumping whatever was in his hand with his fingers. I recognized that sound from my days in nursing school. That sound mimicked that of someone trying to remove air bubbles from a syringe when drawing up medicine from a vial. I couldn't see him, but I was almost certain that's what he was doing.

"I was in college when I met you, Sammi. I had my future all planned out. I was an honor student with a full ride scholarship. I'd just gotten accepted into med school. But then, the school told me they'd received some calls about me from two different men accusing me of spiking drinks at bars and taking advantage of women. Hmm, I wonder who those two men were?" he said, his voice deceptively soft in a way that I knew meant he was getting increasingly angry.

"I didn't know they did that," I admitted.

"Psshh, you didn't know. Sure," he mocked. "You ruined my life! I lost everything because of you. My professors, my classmates, they all called me a rapist. And then," he chuckled before speaking again, "they paid me a visit at my job, where there they announced to everyone that I was a rapist."

He began pacing in front of me, now revealing the syringe full of a clear substance. I jerked slightly in the chair from fear. What was he planning to give me? I didn't know that these things had happened to him. He deserved it all, but I felt like it should have been my decision as to whether I shared the story and told everyone the truth about him. Me, the victim—not Jackson or Caleb.

"I was fired that day. I lost my scholarship. I was asked to leave campus until the school board decided what to do about me. I had nothing left. So, I went home and put a gun in my mouth, ready to pull the trigger."

He paused. "But then people were turning into zombies, and the authority that was going to control my life was no longer a problem. I was free again." He laughed psychotically. "I thought, what are the odds I'd find you again in a zombie apocalypse? Then, I found this abandoned van in the middle of the road, far from Pocola, and I just had this feeling. You know that feeling," he said, pointing at me with a smirk on his face.

He reached into his pocket with his free hand and revealed the amber bottle containing my medication. It had a white label stuck around it where Ryan had handwritten my name and the name of the medication. Several people back at the hospital had been taking various medications from the pharmacy for illnesses they had prior to the apocalypse or sickness that came after. Ryan had experience as a pharmacy technician before he started medical school, so he helped navigate through refilling medications for those of us taking them. He tried to keep some kind of normalcy to his system by labeling the bottles to prevent any mix ups. I never thought it'd be the thing that helped Walker track me down.

"I took a pharmacology course in my third year in college, and if I'm not mistaken, lithium is indicated for manic bipolar disorder," he said, tapping the bottle into the palm of his hand that was still holding the syringe. "Now, I've met a lot of people, but I've never met two Sammis spelled with an *I* that were batshit crazy."

I looked at him with hatred in my eyes. "Whatever you're going to do, just do it," I began, my voice low. "Just do it before I fucking kill you!" I screamed, fighting the restraints and shuffling the chair, making a scraping noise on the wooden floor.

He raised his eyebrows as if surprised by my reaction. He shoved the pills back into his pocket, now focusing on the syringe again. He removed the plastic cap over the needle and walked back around to my vulnerable, exposed forearms. I grew tense at the thought of him shoving a needle into my arm; my muscles tightened, my body fighting against the ability to stay still.

But before he could inject me, someone else entered the room. It was the blonde friend that was with him that night at the bar. He had a look of ultimate satisfaction once he saw me in the chair.

He took a few steps into the room, watching me closely. "What's the plan, Dillion?"

"Dillion?" I asked.

"Oh, that's right." He laughed. "I forgot I told you my name was Walker."

I yanked my arms as much as I could while he positioned himself behind the chair. But my struggle was futile. A couple of seconds later, he shoved the needle into my vein, injecting the unknown substance. He recapped the needle and walked back toward the blonde.

Walker—Dillion, whatever his name was—put his arm on his friend's shoulder as the two of them exited into the hallway, leaving the door open behind them. "We're going to starve her for a few days, make her weak, and then we'll break her bones one by one before the grand finale," he said enthusiastically.

My heart sank and blood boiled at his words.

I sat there for some time, anxious and worried, before my body began reacting to whatever he had injected me with. I was here, but it was like I wasn't. I felt like my mind wasn't communicating with my body. My hands felt like they weren't even there anymore. I'm pretty sure I was screaming, but nothing came out. My mouth remained closed.

Suddenly, I saw Jackson again. He was in the room with me. I felt so relieved. He was here to rescue me, as always.

Jackson took a few quiet steps over to me and pulled out a pocketknife to cut the ropes around my wrists and ankles. I sighed deeply and checked my wrists to see that there were no marks. They didn't even hurt. Nothing hurt. I felt ... good. Great, even.

I walked over to Jackson and hugged him tightly, appreciating his presence and his warmth that always brought me comfort. I stepped back, and he smiled softly at me, brushing a strand of hair from my forehead and tucking it behind my ear. He cupped the left side of my face and gave me the softest kiss on my cheek.

I blushed. "How did you find me?"

"I walked through the area where you got out of the van and tried to trace your steps. I figured when I came out in this neighborhood that you had to be here somewhere," he explained.

I smiled lovingly, so happy to be here with him right now. This was exactly what I needed. "You're always rescuing me," I said sweetly.

If I could be here with him forever, that'd make me happier than anything in this world.

But, when I turned to look back at the chair I'd been tied to, I was confused to find that I was looking back at myself, still tied up. I looked down to see the body I was in possession of, but everything was suddenly pixelated. I was separating from myself, or what I thought was myself and this room. This room Jackson was in with me.

Where was he?

"Jackson?" I called.

What is going on?

~

I was so cold. I wasn't sure if it was because I was half naked, thirsty, or if it was just another feeling I couldn't resonate with.

I'd slept so much in the day I'd been here, but it was the only thing I could do to pass time and to shelter myself from the fact that I was being drugged and starved. When I was sleeping, I almost felt like I could decipher between what was real and what was yet another convincing hallucination; it was when I was awake that I felt the most vulnerable to my own mind's interpretations.

Dillion and the other two guys were taking shifts to scavenge for food and to listen out for me. He hadn't come back into the room much since the first encounter, but the one time he did, he shot me up with another dose of whatever he'd been giving me. I guess they couldn't sleep or concentrate when I screamed.

I'm sorry guys, am I inconveniencing you?

I'd already been a little hungry yesterday, but today I was really beginning to feel the need to eat something. But after hearing Dillion say his plan was to starve me, I knew I shouldn't get my hopes up. I honestly thought I'd be out of this place by now, but Dillion and his crew were only just getting started, and there was no sign of Caleb, Jackson, Bailey, or any of the others.

Just come back for me.

Why hadn't they yet?

~

I was lying in a field of colorful flowers, holding Jackson's hand. The air smelled so clean and crisp, and the sun felt warm on my face. I could hear the sounds of the wind blowing and birds chirping. The grass was so green and soft under my back as I laid on top of it, appreciating the beauty of Earth. I couldn't think of a better place to be.

"That cloud looks like a bunny," I said, my head resting on Jackson's shoulder as I pointed up at the blue sky.

"Yeah, it does," he said happily. He moved his hand up and down my arm slowly; it was so relaxing.

The clouds drifted across the sky, showing new shapes every minute that passed. After a little while, the two of us sat up, now facing the basket of goodies we'd brought with us. He flipped the wicker lid to one side and pulled out a glass container of strawberries. The plastic lid peeled off easily, and he reached into the container to grab one of the bright red berries. I giggled as he held the strawberry out to me. I took a bite, and it was the sweetest, most refreshing berry I'd ever had.

He smiled back at me, wiping a little bit of the juice from the corner of my mouth. "I love you," he said sweetly.

No matter how many times he said it, it always gave me butterflies—an entire swarm in my stomach.

"I love you," I replied, leaning over to kiss him again.

We were so carefree and happy. I didn't think it could get any better, until I turned to see him down on one knee, an open ring box in his hand.

I gasped, covering my mouth. I was on cloud nine—I'd never been this happy in my life. The thought of spending the rest of my life with him was precious. It was a moment I never knew I was ready for until I saw it happening.

Then, in one quick second, I reappeared in the room, screaming as Dillion began engraving his name into my thigh with a razor blade. Each slice hurt worse than the previous one. The sedative effects of the drug were wearing off, and I was no longer hallucinating. I was very much alert and aware of the torture he was putting me through.

I could tell it pleased him to see me in pain like this. He was practically smiling to himself as he continued trying to split open my quivering leg.

I just wanted to go back to my picnic with Jackson. I didn't want to be here.

I craved the effects of the drug again, since the last round didn't linger as long. The more injections I'd received over the past five days, the lower my tolerance to the drug had become. I knew what that meant, but that didn't stop the feelings that came with the substance he continued to fill into the syringes. Initially, I wondered why he'd pump me full of a drug that took me away from the hurt and suffering, but I now knew what he was doing. It was working.

Being under the influence of the drug was the only thing keeping me sane. It took my pain, depression, and loneliness away by giving me glimpses of Jackson—and it took me far, far away from here. I craved the next dose. I needed it to take me back to him, to Jackson. That's what I longed for.

Instead, Dillion denied me the next dose and left me to suffer from the open wounds left with each letter of his name. I looked down at the bloody mess covering my thigh and cried out for help, wishing someone would come save me.

God, if you're real, please take this pain away, I begged. *Prove me wrong by offering healing and peace when I long doubted you before. Take me away from this hell. Then maybe I'll believe that you might be out there somewhere.*

~

"Drink this," the black headed guy, Alex, said as he shoved a straw between my chapped lips.

My eyes could barely stay open, and my muscles felt weak. The fight I'd been fighting wasn't much of a fight anymore, and it wasn't necessarily because I didn't want to, I just didn't have it in me. I was growing hopeless, realizing I may have made a mistake getting out of the van that day. No, I'd definitely made a mistake.

Every time I looked over at the doorway and saw Jackson, I grew hopeful and relieved. He was finally here to save me! But my conscience would quickly remind me: *He's saved you every day... When are you going to see that you're hallucinating? Jackson isn't here; he hasn't been here, and he's not coming.*

By my count, it had been about eight days since my kidnapping, and they'd been giving me enough water to survive, but still no food. I'd been sitting in urine for days, and I hadn't had a single thought that felt like my own in just as long. The days seemed to be getting shorter, but maybe it was just the combination of thirst, hunger, and the sedative effects of whatever drug Dillion had been giving me. I just slept or hallucinated the days away.

When he'd come in this morning, he looked like he was getting tired of me holding on. But, if he really wanted me to die, he'd quit giving me water. I guess the suffering made it worth it to him. He hadn't given me the drug yet today, which made me more nervous than receiving it.

Dillion and Tanner, the blonde, joined us. They gave each other approving looks before Dillion took out the vial and syringe. He got ready to draw up the substance, but dropped the vial on the floor in the small distance between us. I looked down to try and read the drug name, discovering that he'd been giving me ketamine multiple times a day. I didn't feel like ketamine alone should've been affecting me this deeply, but that's what I had to go off for now.

He slowly bent down to pick it up and continued drawing the dose up into the syringe. He repeated the same routine of injecting the substance into my bruised forearm before grabbing a pocketknife from Alex. I thought he was going to stab me or something, but instead he cut the rope from around my ankles and wrists.

Unfortunately for me, the drug that made my body seemingly useless added to the effects of being withheld food, and I couldn't fight back. Once he'd completely freed me, I just collapsed onto the floor, where I was subjected to the three of them taking turns to kick me over and over again until I vomited and nearly aspirated on it.

Only then did Dillion stop the abuse.

"Alright, that's enough. I think it's time to bring in the grand finale. I'm tired of looking at her," he said emotionlessly as the three of them filtered out of the room.

I'd accepted the fact that I was going to die in the next few minutes, so I laid on the floor helplessly, wishing for another hallucination of Jackson to bring me comfort. But it was no use. My body was rejecting my wishes. I needed a stronger dose to keep giving me the satisfaction, the high, I hoped for. At least the medication somewhat dulled the pain from the kicks.

I stared blankly at the doorway, awaiting their return. I could hear their muffled voices through the house as they made a commotion through the hallway, getting closer to my room again. How strange that I'd come to think of this space as "mine."

Suddenly the growls of several zombies filled the air as Dillion and his friends pushed them into the room with me. Each of the three zombies had their hands tied behind their backs, similar to how I'd been the last week or so. They each freed one by cutting through the rope, then shoving them toward me. They shut the door behind them, leaving me as bait for the starving, dead corpses headed for me.

I moaned in pain as I attempted to push myself away from the bodies approaching me, my aching body covered in vomit, urine, and feces. I was a mess. I didn't want to die this way. Tears filled my eyes as I used up what little fight I had left.

My mind began to drift into that place I'd gone to in the woods that day. It was the first time I'd seen it since that morning we walked back to the van. Like before, the world grew gray and dim and chills from the cool air covered my body.

I looked up at the bodies towering over me, but this time, they weren't just warning me to leave...

They were trying to help me.

The zombies consisted of three red-headed women—sisters maybe? They looked like they had been starved and beaten prior to death, just like me. They were skin and bones, with decaying, purple and blue skin from the bruises covering their bodies. Their hair was matted in several spots and their clothing was ripped and dirty from defecation.

Dillion's name was engraved on the arm of one of the women, the forehead of the second, and the leg of the third. It pained me to think that three, possibly more, women had been through this hell at the hands of Dillion and his friends.

They were monsters.

The women hurried over to me and began speaking. "We don't have much time. We need to get you back into the real world before your brain is permanently damaged," the youngest one said.

I looked back at her, confused but hopeful . "Did they do this to you too?" I asked.

All three of them nodded at once, and my heart ached for them.

"I can't move," I admitted, trying to sit up. The pain was becoming unbearable with each movement.

"They don't have any more ammo. If you can open the door for us, we will do the rest," one of the women said.

"Are you sure it will work?" I asked.

"Trust us, Sammi. We have to save you. It's not safe here."

I began to try and crawl toward the door, but I was moving extremely slow from the wooden floor scraping across my engraved thigh, reopening the wounds that had finally scabbed over. I groaned in pain as I inched closer to the door. The women kept their distance, watching me closely. I tried to stretch up toward the doorknob, but I still wasn't close enough.

I reached one last time before collapsing onto the floor, lying there, wrecked from the realization that I was dying today. I rested my head on the floor, exhaling deeply, then shut my eyes for a moment, trying to rally the strength needed to survive.

I'd all but given up when I heard gunshots in the distance. I quickly opened my eyes, but I was still surrounded by the three zombies.

"Sammi!" one of them said before collapsing to the floor.

I flinched, closing my eyes once more to guard myself from what was happening around me.

I heard a second one hit the ground while the third woman said, "Sammi, wake up! Please, wake up!"

Then, the voice changed to Jackson's. "Sammi, please. I need you. Wake up!" he cried.

I opened my eyes, expecting to see Dillion or one of his cronies towering over me, disappointed that their "grand finale" was a bust. Instead, I found Jackson kneeling beside me, sobbing as he gently stroked my face.

I was struggling to keep my eyes open, but I still managed to give him a glimpse of a smile. Jackson was here to rescue me.

Jackson's been here to save you every day. You're hallucinating again. This isn't real.

Was this real? I felt so discouraged and defeated, yet I still felt comfort in knowing that I could put myself in this place with Jackson when I needed to escape reality.

It was only when Jackson started calling out to my brother, clearly panicked, that I started to realize this was actually happening.

"Caleb! In here. Help!" he shouted, tears streaming down both of his cheeks. "Sammi, I'm here. It's okay, I promise," he said, comforting my near lifeless body.

I opened my eyes once again, looking around at the world that appeared slightly brighter than the zombie realm I'd found myself in twice now. I was back, but I still wondered if this was real. I had a hard time telling the difference now, and that scared me. It scared me to distrust everything. Between the hallucinations, the zombie world, and the real world, I didn't know what to think.

"Oh my God," Caleb said, his heart clearly breaking as he rounded the corner into the room and found me. He knelt beside Jackson as the two of them reacted to the torment I'd undergone over the last week or so. I was still wearing only my undergarments, but I was filthy and disgusting. I was ashamed for anyone to see me this way, but I had no other choice. I was barely alive. For all I knew, I was already dead and this was my hell.

I looked over and saw Dillion, and my body jerked with what little energy I had in fear that he was going to kill me, Caleb, and Jackson. If this really was Caleb and Jackson. Every time I blinked, Dillion would disappear, then reappear, and then disappear on a repeating cycle. Tears rolled down my face as I looked around the room I'd become enemies with.

"This isn't real. You're not real," I said, an unsettled tone in my voice.

Jackson looked over at Caleb with strong concern.

"What did they do to you?" Caleb whispered.

21

RECIPE FOR DISASTER

IT HAD BEEN TWELVE days since I was rescued from Dillion and his friends. I still felt like someone could pinch me and I'd end up back in the room, similarly to how I'd felt when I was seeing Jackson in my hallucinations. Everyone was walking on eggshells around me, and they kept their distance, as if trying to give me time to heal. But honestly, I was in worse shape than anyone thought. I was battling demons in my head that were pulling me further and further away from myself. I needed rescuing from that.

I hadn't spoken a word to anyone since being pulled from that house. I was selectively mute from the traumatic experiences I'd endured, and rightfully so. I was processing each aspect of the abuse and neglect I underwent at the hands of three young men. It would take time.

Bailey especially had been keeping his distance; he wouldn't even bring Grace into the room for me to see her. I could only hear her cries and baby talk from the other end of the house we'd migrated to within the same neighborhood. I guess he thought I could snap or be triggered by something at any moment, so for the time being, he thought it was safer to keep her from me. I understood his intentions, but I think it did more damage to me.

I'd only seen him once since the rescue, and it was only because they carried me into the house, where he'd been waiting on their return. For some reason, I'd expected him to react differently. There was no relief and no happiness at my rescue. It was like he didn't recognize me; like he blamed me and didn't want me to be found.

I could hear the conversations everyone was having about me in the next room. I was mute, but I wasn't deaf.

"It's been almost two weeks. We can't just keep waiting around on something to change. She's broken," Bailey said in frustration.

"She's not broken," Jackson responded angrily. "She's traumatized; not *broken*."

I could hear pain in Jackson's voice every time he talked to Bailey about me. I knew Bailey cared, but he'd been rattled about me and my health since finding out I'd gotten the injection. He was the one so adamant about getting to a cure in the first place; the longer I wasn't mentally stable and ready to get back on the road, the less time I had. That was the only way he could see it. Maybe he'd finally come to terms with the reality that I was a lost cause.

His feelings were valid—I did seem broken. But I'd been broken before. I'd been at rock bottom, and even amid my manic episode and surprise pregnancy, Jackson never once gave up on me or considered me a lost cause. He never called me broken, even when we all knew I was.

"They starved her, abused her, scarred her… How do you expect her to react, Bailey?" Jackson snapped.

As I laid in bed listening to their conversation, all I could think about was how happy I'd been every time I went to that place with Jackson. My hallucinations were mind numbing and filled my body with a joy I'd longed for. I needed to go back. Desperately. I needed to get out of here and find Dillion's stash of ketamine. As scared as I was to expose myself to the world, I was struggling without my daily regimen.

As I contemplated the possibility, my body began showing signs of withdrawal. I was shaking and sweating profusely. It was bad enough I'd been through so much already, but now I was addicted to ketamine.

I removed the covers and sat up, planning to sneak out of the house. But as soon as my feet hit the ground, Jackson entered the room. I flinched, gripping the edge of the mattress tightly.

"I'm sorry. I didn't mean to scare you," he said, holding his hands up defensively. "I'll go."

I didn't speak; I just continued watching him with my empty eyes. I could feel the sweat dripping down my face. It wasn't hot in here; it was actually pretty cool, so it was strange for me to be sweating this heavily given the circumstances. Of course, he picked up on it, especially when I started shivering.

"What's wrong?" he asked worriedly, approaching me slowly. "You look like you're burning up. You must have a fever."

I remained silent but lifted the sleeve from the shirt they'd found me to wear, revealing my bruised arm with the needle holes.

He looked closely, studying my puncture marks. "You're withdrawing from something, aren't you?" he guessed, sounding horrified.

I looked into his eyes blankly. I'd had two black eyes for a while after the beating I'd taken, and they were finally turning a yellow-purple color, rather than a deep black and blue. My body wasn't healing at the rate it once had, due to the substantial loss of nutrients, muscle, and other factors associated with Dillion. I was pale, ghostly, and malnourished, but I was slowly regaining the weight I'd lost while being held hostage. My strength was returning, but I wasn't sure how long it would take for me to recover mentally. I knew that Jackson would probably be the one person to bring me back from this; I just wasn't sure how.

I swallowed the lump in my throat as I began shaking more than I had been. I could tell he was debating how to address the situation. He could either tell Caleb and everyone else and find my next fix, or let me finish withdrawing. I knew what I wanted him to do, but I couldn't quite figure out how he would handle it. I wanted to talk to him, but I couldn't. I don't know how else to explain it.

"What was he giving you?" Jackson asked.

Silence.

"I'm sorry. Can you write it down?"

I nodded ever so slightly, and he gave me a hint of a smile before leaving to grab a pen and paper.

"Did she talk?" I heard Caleb ask as Jackson left the room. It sounded like he was lingering in the hall right outside the room.

There was a beat of silence, during which I assumed Jackson shook his head, because the next thing Caleb asked was, "What happened?"

"She's withdrawing from something. I saw needle marks on her arm, and she's shaking and sweating badly from it. They did a number on her, man."

"What were they giving her?" Caleb asked.

"I don't know. I asked her if she could write it down, so I'm about to find out," he said, keeping his voice low—but not quite low enough that I couldn't hear.

When Jackson entered the room again, carrying a notepad and pen, he smiled so sweetly at me. I always appreciated how patient he was with me in all situations. I was beginning to see that Bailey lacked some of the compassion that Jackson had when it came to this kind of thing. It wasn't his fault he reacted differently than Jackson, but it mattered to me that he did.

"Can I sit beside you?" he asked as he took soft steps toward me.

I scooted over to let him know that he could, and he sat down beside me. This was the closest I'd been to anyone since they'd picked me up and brought me here from the other house. I felt on edge, but I was trying to work through it. Jackson would never hurt me; that's what I kept reminding myself. I just continued to struggle with identifying whether this was all one big hallucination, or if I was safe now.

He held out the pen and notepad, making sure not to touch me. I hesitantly reached for both items before my trembling shakes made a mess of the word I was trying to write down. I managed to get a very sloppy *k* written down before growing frustrated.

Jackson could tell I was getting overwhelmed, so he pitched in another suggestion to take some of the pressure off me. "Here, I have an idea," he said, reaching for the pen and notepad. I gave it back to him, and he used his leg to prop the notepad on while he quickly began writing the alphabet across the page, like you would playing Hangman as a kid. "Can you point to the letters in order?"

I nodded.

He held the notepad out for me again, so I grabbed it, studying each letter nervously as he watched my pale fingers shake. I put my right index finger onto the *k*, holding it steady with my left hand. Then, I moved to the *e*, the *t*, the *a*, and so on, until he quietly said the name aloud.

"Ketamine?"

I avoided eye contact because a part of me was ashamed, even though it was not my intention to become addicted to this drug. The way I was feeling now versus how I'd felt when I was on my high was incomparable. It was night and day … very dark nights and very bright days.

"I'll be back, okay?"

I nodded.

~

Jackson's point of view

I left Sammi in the same position on the edge of the bed as I headed to the kitchen to find Caleb. We shared a concerned look as I entered.

"What did you find out?" Caleb asked.

"They were shooting her up with ketamine," I whispered. Unfortunately Bailey chose this exact moment to enter the kitchen, overhearing the conversation.

"What?" he said angrily. "She's addicted to ketamine?"

"Yeah. She's having withdrawals. I need to go back to that house and see if they left any vials hanging around somewhere," I said.

"Absolutely not. You are not going to get her next fix. She needs to tough out these withdrawals. That's the only way she'll overcome the addiction," Bailey protested.

I sighed. Bailey was really starting to irritate me. "I'm sorry, man, but this isn't your call."

"And what makes you think it's yours?" Bailey said, stepping closer.

"That's enough, both of you," Caleb hissed. "The walls are so thin that she can probably hear everything going on out here. The last thing she needs is you two fighting over what you think is best for her. Only she knows that. Now, I don't know much about addiction and withdrawals, and I can't ask our doctor because we don't have one anymore, but we aren't sure what dose they've been giving her. We should at least try to wean her off rather than forcing her to suffer and stop cold turkey."

"Fine, feed the demon. That's exactly what she needs," Bailey mumbled as he stormed out of the kitchen.

I pursed my lips, having to force myself not to react, while Caleb rubbed his forehead.

"Let's go," I said, wanting to get out of here.

Caleb and I gathered our guns and left the house, walking down the damp, wooden porch onto the sidewalk.

"Are we doing the right thing?" I asked as we walked, seeking reassurance.

"I don't think I've known the answer to that since this apocalypse started. It's not like there's some guidebook that tells us exactly how we're supposed to do any of this," Caleb said, his hands in the front pockets of his khakis.

"I just want what's best for her," I said.

"I know you do."

We continued walking in silence until reaching the house where Sammi had been held hostage. The green mustang was parked outside, which had been the dead giveaway that Sammi was here somewhere. *Smart move from those idiots.*

We were a little hesitant as we walked up the steps, entering through the front door of the house. One of the guy's dead bodies was a few feet from the door, unmoved from where we'd shot him. We stepped around the decaying body, putting our arms to our noses to try and block the horrid scent. We then maneuvered through the narrow entrance into the living room. This was where the blonde's body lay lifelessly from where Caleb had sent a bullet through his head.

We weren't quite sure what to expect as we looked through the house. We hadn't been here long enough that day to explore, more focused on saving Sammi.

Caleb took the kitchen and I headed to the bathroom in search of the vials. I looked around at the blue and white tiled floor, then up to the mirror, where my reflection gazed back at me. My dirty blonde hair and blue eyes stared back at me before I grabbed the mirror's frame, pulling it toward me. The medicine cabinet behind the mirror was nearly empty, except for an opened box of Band-Aids and a lonely pair of tweezers. I immediately went to the other mirror to check it, but found nothing.

I was beginning to grow frustrated, aggressively opening each left-hand side drawer, only to find nothing. But as I opened the top drawer on the right-hand side, I found several vials of drugs, sterile water, and individually wrapped syringes.

I smiled, before realizing that it was wrong to feel so happy about such a discovery. This wasn't a victory—it was compliance.

I tilted my head to the right as I studied the contents of the drawer, noticing a vial that appeared slightly different to the others. "Jesus Christ," I muttered as I realized what it was, my stomach sinking.

"What? What did you find?" Caleb asked, approaching the bathroom door.

"They were giving her more than just ketamine. They were lacing it with fentanyl," I said, picking up the vial and studying each letter printed on the label.

Caleb's eyes widened and he brushed past me to see for himself, grabbing the vial that had the narcotic's name written on the label. "What's in the other vial with the green cap?"

"Naloxone," I said.

"I guess let's just take all of it. We'll figure out the rest later. I'm tired of being in this house; it gives me bad vibes," Caleb said, shivering slightly.

I nodded in agreement, and we grabbed handfuls of supplies and shoved them into our pockets.

After cleaning out the drawer, we traced our steps back to the front door, glad for the breeze of fresh air that greeted us as we stepped outside. The trip home was silent and short. Neither of us knew what to do, and without a doctor or someone with pharmacy experience, we were unprepared for how to proceed.

Sophie, Lola, and Bailey were anxiously waiting in the living room when we returned. I could tell immediately that Bailey had shared the information of Sammi's forced drug use with the two of them while we were gone, so now it was everyone's burden to bear. Part of me wanted to tell him to stay out of it; it wasn't his business. For some reason, I held a grudge against him.

Bailey jumped up to meet us and we walked over to the round wooden dining table where we emptied our pockets, sitting each vial and syringe onto the table. Bailey examined each of them, eventually finding the fentanyl vial.

"What the hell is this?" he asked, looking appalled.

"It looks like they were lacing her ketamine with fentanyl," I said.

Bailey grew enraged, pointing at the two of us before saying, "No. I let you two go ketamine hunting for her because I thought I had no choice, but I refuse to let you play pharmacist with a bunch of drugs when Sammi's body is at stake."

"We can't just let her suffer like this! She needs—" I began, but Bailey interrupted.

"She needs to detox!"

"Let's just take a break from this and regroup after everyone's had time to cool down," Sophie said, stepping into the dining area.

I sighed heavily and exited the room, heading toward the bathroom. I needed a moment to think through this.

~

Sammi's point of view

I was lying in the bed, trying to fight through my aching withdrawal symptoms and listening to everyone talking about me in the other room. Once I heard them mention fentanyl, I grew nervous. We were in a whole new realm of issues now. This was above any of us, even me. We went over pharmacology in nursing school, but we didn't dig that deep into controlled substances like this. I only knew the foundation, and there was so much room for error.

A few minutes after the commotion between all of the guys, I heard Jackson approach the bedroom door. He knocked lightly, then pushed it open.

"Hey, you," he said sweetly.

I was buried under layers of blankets, only my head remaining uncovered. The shakes were still heavily present, consuming my body. I just wanted the pain to stop. I was tired of feeling like a prisoner, physically and mentally. My body was begging me for something. Anything.

Jackson took soft steps toward me. "I need to know I'm doing the right thing, Sammi. Because I drew this up, but if I give it to you, it could really piss off Bailey and maybe even your brother," he said, revealing a syringe in his hands.

My skin began crawling and I twitched in the bed. It was like drowning in the ocean but seeing the surface inches from your face—fresh air to relieve the suffering. That's the feeling I got with ketamine and fentanyl, it seemed. At that point, I didn't care what he put in that syringe; I just wanted to go back to that place where I felt safest. I wanted that high.

"You can't tell them, okay? It will only make things worse," he said.

I moved around, trying to situate myself in a comfortable position. My heart was racing in my chest, feeding into the memory of what it felt like to be under the influence of such drugs. He handed me the syringe, smiling sadly as he exited the room.

The surface was right there; I'd reached it. I could finally breathe again.

~

Two weeks had passed, and I still hadn't made any progress in recovery from the trauma or addiction. I also hadn't seen Bailey since before all this drug nonsense, but he was under the impression that I was continuing to work through this detox. I think the only two people who knew I was still actively receiving the drugs were me and Jackson. Even Caleb was in the dark. I felt horrible deceiving everyone, but none of them had taken the time to even look at me since this all started. In a way, they didn't deserve my honesty.

I looked up as Jackson entered the room with a single red rose. It looked so bright and beautiful. I was surprised he'd found something like this given the dry conditions and hostile creatures among us. Despite everything, Jackson had decided to use his time to pick me a flower, and that was the sweetest thing I'd experienced post-apocalypse. It was rejuvenating. He was really putting in an effort here, and I couldn't say the same for anyone else.

I took the flower, studying it intently.

"I wrote you a poem today when I found that rose. I'm no Edgar Allen Poe, but I tried," he said, smiling to himself. He reached into his pocket and nervously pulled out a crinkled piece of notebook paper, clearing his throat before reading it aloud:

"I found a field of wildflowers almost as beautiful as you, but they don't have your heart or the sweet smile that you do.

I found a yellow marigold, but it doesn't compare to when I have your hand to hold.

I found a yellow daffodil, but it doesn't compare to how you make me feel.

I found a lavender sweet pea, but it doesn't compare to the feelings between you and me.

And in that field, I found a rose. It was perfect like you, so that's the one I chose."

I looked over at him as he blushed all over, his red cheeks giving him away. He stuffed the poem back into his pocket nervously. "I love you, Sammi," he said softly, before turning for the door.

"I love you, Jackson," I said quietly before I realized I'd spoken.

His eyes lit up at the first words I'd said in about a month. He ran over to me, excited but still anxious to trigger me in any way.

I stood up and put my arms around him, hugging him so tightly and never wanting to let go. I put my hand on the back of his head, running my fingers through his hair, finally feeling something real.

"I'm so glad you're okay," he admitted.

I released the hug and looked back up at him, his beautiful eyes staring back into mine.

"Can we go somewhere and talk?" he asked.

I swallowed. "Yes, but where is everyone?"

"They all went to scavenge for food in the neighborhood."

I nodded, following him out of the room and to the front door. I wasn't ready to be bombarded by the entire group, so I was relieved to hear that they'd left for a while.

Once we stepped outside, I took a deep breath. It had been a long time since I'd been able to enjoy the clean air around me. I'd been sitting in that room for what felt like years, feeling trapped; it was time for a change of scenery.

I followed him down the sidewalk until we reached the end of the line of houses that sat right before a set of trees. It was eerily quiet, but with Jackson, I felt safe. I felt like no one could hurt me when I was by his side. That's what I'd needed so desperately when I was being tormented by Dillion—just feeling like Jackson was there to protect me from him and from myself.

Eventually, we found the field of wildflowers he'd been to earlier that day. It took me back to the hallucination I had when Jackson proposed; it had felt so real. I hadn't seen anything like this in such a long time.

Jackson took my hand and guided me to a green patch of grass. I couldn't help but smile at the thought of being here with him. But the more perfect all of this seemed, the more skeptical I was of still being tied up, hallucinating all of this to escape the pain caused by Dillion and his friends.

I jerked my hand out of his and began backing away.

"What's wrong, Sammi?"

"This isn't real. None of this is real," I said, my eyes growing wide.

It took him a second to respond, clearly trying to determine the best way to ease my mind. "I'm real," he said, closing the space I'd created between us. He grabbed my hand and put it on his chest, right above his heart. After a few seconds, I began to feel his heart beating beneath my palm. I closed my eyes and took a deep breath, my eyes tearing up. He always knew just what to do to bring me back down to earth.

I looked up at the clouds that revealed small blurs rather than distinct shapes. I think that minute difference solidified that this was not my hallucination; it was very much real life. I was here. This was truly my own experience, not one that resulted from Dillion's torture. I was relieved that I couldn't see the shape of a bunny in that cloud.

"This is real. You're not in that house anymore. We saved you," he said gently, cupping my cheek with his hand.

I opened my eyes, releasing a tear down my cheek. "What took you so long?" I'd been waiting to ask someone that question.

As Jackson looked at me, I watched his heart break under the surface of his skin. It was like he knew it was a valid question, one he'd been waiting for me to ask.

"Let's sit," he said, and I followed him, sitting down on the soft grass.

He sighed. "A part of me was hoping you'd never ask me that, but you deserve closure," he admitted. "A lot of things happened while you were gone, but when we found you the way we did, it made all of us feel guilty. I'll be honest, Sammi, I almost don't want to tell you the truth because I don't want you to hold a grudge against anyone. But it's time to be honest with you. You deserve that."

I took a deep breath, dreading what he was about to tell me. He began with the moment I stepped out of the van.

~

Jackson's point of view

"Damnit, I can't believe we're letting her do this," Caleb said worriedly as Bailey began speeding off in the van.

"She's a big girl. She can take care of herself," Sophie said. I knew she was trying to sound comforting, but it just came off as bitchy.

"We don't need to go far because Sammi will be waiting for us in this area," I said, trying to remember what the surroundings looked like but getting everything mixed up from the anxiety of it all.

"Well, I can see zombies surfacing from the trees as we speak. All the gunshots attracted them, and we're down to ten bullets. We need to get out of this area before we lose the only ammo we have," Caleb said, sitting up straighter in his seat.

"Okay, I'll keep driving for a minute until we find a place to park while we wait for the chaos to dissipate," Bailey said emotionlessly.

It felt like he didn't care or didn't have any faith in Sammi, which upset and angered me in equal measure.

Grace had finally stopped crying, and the entire van grew quiet. I couldn't help but worry that Sammi hadn't run fast enough or had gotten shot in the process of running from those maniacs. I should've gotten out with her. *Why didn't I go with her?*

I asked myself that question so many times that it began to haunt me.

Eventually, we reached the next town over. We found this nice Victorian-style home perched up on a hill, preceded by a paved, winding driveway. There were solar panels on parts on the roof and in the yard, tucked away beneath some trees. We felt like this place would be a good spot to wait out the zombies and scavenge for weapons and food.

Once we parked, Bailey took Grace from her car seat and put her into the body strap thing. *Sammi would know what it's called,* I thought.

The rest of us cautiously got out. We needed to make sure we were alone, as you never knew for sure until you ran into them. ("Them" being a zombie or an angry survivor.) It wasn't like you'd see them cutting grass or checking the mail. So, we all spread out and circled the house, our only weapons being pocketknives, a hammer, and the one loaded gun in our possession.

We all froze in position when Sophie took it upon herself to press the doorbell and knock on the front door nonchalantly.

"Sophie, what are you doing?" I whispered angrily.

"Relax," she said, shrugging.

When there was no sign of movement inside after a minute, we all let out a sigh of relief, even laughing at her antics, before deciding to enter. The house had two floors and a basement, so we split up into groups to clear each floor. It seemed like every room had a secret closet or addition that made this house seem massive and full of possibilities for hiding spots.

Caleb and I had been searching the first floor for what felt like an hour. Lola and Sophie were checking the basement, and Bailey took the second floor with the company of Grace, who still sat comfortably against his chest. We were wrapping up our search through the house when Sophie and Lola happily cheered from the basement, as if they were celebrating something. The rest of us traveled down to see what the two of them had found.

"Hell yeah, this is exactly what we need," Bailey said, gazing around the room.

It was filled with a pool table, air hockey, a dartboard, and a ping pong table. But the thing that had everyone celebrating was the massive bar stocked with liquor, beer, and wine. Sophie had already begun rustling through the cabinets, trying to find glasses to fill.

It seemed like everyone was genuinely excited about all of this, except me. Had they forgotten Sammi was still out there?

Bailey took a seat on a barstool that was positioned in front of the chestnut counter. "Hey, hand me a beer," he said to Sophie, smiling.

She opened the door to the chilled mini fridge and handed him a bottle. He popped off the cap and took a sip, a drop hitting Grace on the top of her head.

She didn't notice, but I did. I rolled my eyes and approached him, offering to take her for the time being since it seemed like I was the only responsible adult here. He willingly passed her over to me after removing her from the sling thing. I found a seat away from everyone on the couch, perching Grace on my lap.

The solar panels located outside of the house seemed to control all the electricity, which was a luxury. Under different circumstances, I, too, would've been thrilled to see cold drinks, a fully lit house, and games, but I was too worried about Sammi to enjoy it. I anxiously bit my nails while thinking about what to do.

When I turned back to call Caleb over, he was throwing a shot of liquor down his throat while the others excitedly awaited their own shots. It was like the need to let loose and drink themselves into a hole had consumed everyone except me.

While I continued to separate myself, Sophie found a stereo system. She turned it on and began playing music at a moderately loud level, so I took Grace and quietly snuck away upstairs.

"It's just you and me, sweet pea," I said as she stared up at me, giving me a wide, gummy smile.

I could tell she was tired, so I went upstairs, locating a room that had evidently once belonged to a baby boy. There was a white wooden crib still made up with baby blue dinosaur-printed blankets. I laid her down gently before sitting down in the gray fabric glider chair. I don't know how long I sat there, lost inside my head and thoughts, my mind wandering off to think of Sammi. Before I knew it, I'd dozed off, despite the vibrations of the music beneath me.

When I woke up, it was early the next morning. I jumped up from the chair in a panic, knowing Sammi could be out there waiting for us, worried and alone. I peeped over at Grace, who was still sound asleep, then quietly exited the room. I darted down the stairs, heading toward the basement. It was much quieter than yesterday.

When I made it to the bottom of the stairs, there were empty bottles, glasses, chip bags, and other trash laying on every surface. It looked like the aftermath of a frat party.

Caleb was asleep on the couch, and Bailey was asleep in the recliner. Lola and Sophie weren't there, but it wasn't long before I figured out where they were. I could hear one of them vomiting in the bathroom located to the left of the bar, down a short hallway. I followed the painful sounds until I found Sophie on her knees, puking into the toilet, with Lola holding her hair back in support. I pursed my lips in disappointment as I watched her, then turned and left, shaking my head.

It took hours for everyone to eventually wake up, all of them hungover. I was so irritated at their immaturity; it felt like I was the only adult here. Once they'd all gathered around, I took matters into my own hands and decided it was time to get serious again. We didn't come here for this.

"Party's over. Sammi is out there, in case y'all have forgotten. We need to grab whatever we can that's useful and hit the road. We don't know how long it will take to pinpoint where she is," I said sternly.

At that point, everyone went from room to room, looking for weapons, food, and baby gear, since we were back to square one with supplies, thanks to whoever stole our stuff—probably the assholes after Sammi. We managed to find a couple of guns, ammo, knives, and other essentials for Grace and ourselves.

We were loading everything up into the van—Caleb and the girls already seated—when I noticed Bailey nervously fidgeting with his pockets, patting each one over and over again.

"What is it?" I asked.

"I can't find the van key," Bailey admitted.

"What do you mean you can't find the van key?" I said angrily.

"I-I had it last night. I don't know where it could be," he said.

"Jesus Christ," I hissed. "Everyone, get out of the van and help him find the damn key. I'm tired of feeling like I'm running a daycare."

I took the car seat from the van, carrying it inside as the group exited and hurried toward the house. It was a disaster trying to find an object that was lost when everyone involved was under the influence. There was literally no telling where the key was. It could've been flushed down the toilet for all I knew.

After several failed attempts at locating the key, I checked the garage to see if there were any vehicles parked inside of it, but it was empty. We were at least fifteen miles from where we let Sammi out, so without a vehicle, we'd be walking with only the items we could carry until we either found another vehicle or reached Sammi.

This was a fucking nightmare.

By this point the day was progressing, and I couldn't afford for anyone else to die or get separated from the group, so I decided we would flip the house upside down to find the key, to avoid being stranded when the sun set. Come morning, if the key was still lost, we'd be hitchhiking until we found a solution. It would be difficult and dangerous trying to outrun a zombie on foot with supplies in our hands, not to mention I did not want anything to happen to Grace. Sammi could barely get past Greyson; it just wasn't an option for her to lose Grace too.

When the next morning came, there were still no keys. We had to make a choice on what to bring and what to leave behind, since it seemed we'd be going on foot. Bailey was carrying Grace, a handgun, and a backpack full of baby formula and other items. Unfortunately, we had only found two backpacks, so I carried the other one, loaded with bottled water, snacks, and bullets. We found three additional guns, so that allowed everyone except Sophie to have one. But she was useless with a gun anyway, so it was probably for the best.

We walked to the end of the driveway and headed down the street that took us in the direction of where we'd last seen Sammi. Had it just been me, I could've made the trip in a day or two, but traveling with a baby prone to unpredictable crying spells caused issues with attracting the dead and required a lot of stops along the way. It wasn't Grace's fault, obviously; she was just a baby, and that's what babies do, but if Bailey hadn't lost the keys, this could've all been avoided.

Long story short, we experienced many hiccups between every dysfunctional member of the group. Trying to find a car with gas and keys in an area that had virtually no houses or buildings located in proximity was damn near impossible.

Several days later—after walking for miles and miles—we reached the area where we had let Sammi out of the van, but it took us until day eight to finally track down the neighborhood Sammi had likely run to.

Lola, Sophie, Bailey, and Grace took the left side row of houses, and Caleb and I took the right. We went into a couple of empty houses before locating the key piece to this puzzle. Once I saw the green mustang parked outside of one of the houses, I felt confident I'd found her. But I never in a million years expected to find her in the state she was in.

Sammi deserved better.

22

HOME IS WHEREVER YOU ARE

Sammi's point of view

Jackson had finally told me everything that happened during the eight days I'd been waiting for them, wondering if they were ever coming. After hearing the events of that first night, I felt disappointed in my friends, particularly my brother and Bailey. I just couldn't find a way to process all I'd been through while they were living it up in some house, partying and drinking. So many things could have gone wrong, and to me, they did.

"I'm so sorry, Sammi. I truly am. I didn't do enough to protect you," Jackson said as the breeze of the evening air brushed across us.

"You're not the one who should be sorry," I said, trying to reassure him. "Mistakes were made by everyone, but there's nothing we can do about it now."

"When I found you like that, my heart shattered. I thought I'd lost you, and I can't lose you. I can't imagine my life without you," he said desperately, looking deep into my eyes. "I didn't know I could love someone as much as I love you."

I smiled and leaned over to touch my lips to his. It had been a while since I'd felt such a rush of emotions, but it was a feeling I needed.

He kissed me back, and suddenly everything was brighter. Jackson had always been such a delicate yet powerful kisser—the kind of kisser that gave you butterflies, tingles, and made you want more. I wanted more. I'd always wanted more with him. And being with him right now, surrounded by such beautiful wildflowers—wildflowers that were so significant in my hallucinations and brought me comfort—was exactly what I needed.

Jackson and I stayed there for hours, enjoying each other's company until the sun began to set. We stood up and began our walk back to the house, hand in hand. I looked over at him, and he genuinely seemed happy—the happiest I'd seen him in a very long time. I was afraid I'd find a way to ruin it, like it seemed I always did.

"Are you sure you want to do this with me again?" I asked, trying to hide my anxiety.

"Absolutely, yes. I'm all in, Sammi," he said confidently.

"Things are so complicated, all the time. I'm off my meds. I have a baby with Bailey, so that relationship is complicated. I'm just a walking disaster," I explained.

"None of that has ever been an issue with me. You know that," he said.

"I'm addicted to drugs."

"You and I both know that's not your fault. You can get past that," he said reassuringly.

"But what if I can't?"

"You will," he said gently, rubbing my cheek with his other hand.

We continued walking, my mind wandering back to memories of being tormented by Dillion. I swallowed deeply. "It was a long eight days."

"I can't even begin to imagine what you went through," he said, looking down as if ashamed.

"They did a lot of hurtful things to me, but I don't think I would've made it through without the drugs," I admitted.

He looked over at me with a blank expression, as if he wanted to understand but wasn't quite sure what I was implying.

"The drugs … they numbed my pain, they sedated me—and they gave me you. Jackson, every hallucination I had was with you. The hallucinations took me away from that situation I was in and allowed me to find you, even in the darkest times. I can't help but think that those were signs that we belong together. When my mind escaped itself, the safe place it created was with you—not anyone else. Every time," I said.

He gave me a sad smile. "We belong together; we always have. I've just been too afraid to accept it. You have this hold over me, and it makes me scared to ever let you go. With Sophie, I was never afraid, but it's different with you."

I gave him a hint of a smile as we approached the house. Everyone else had returned from scavenging and were all hovering in the living room. Evidently, they'd noticed I was gone and were probably wondering what had happened.

"There you two are," Caleb said, relieved.

Bailey didn't say anything. He just stood off to the side, keeping to himself yet watching me warily. He hadn't seen or spoken to me in weeks, and this was what I got after their fuck up? It was really starting to feel like none of them cared about me at all.

"I thought it might be good to get out of the house," Jackson said casually, releasing his grasp on my hand.

I awkwardly looked around at everyone, eventually making eye contact with Bailey.

"You look good, Sammi. I'm glad we made the decision to let you get sober," he said dryly.

I didn't respond for a few seconds, but then I got the courage to speak. "You mean sober from the drugs that I was being injected with while you guys were getting drunk? I don't need your false praises," I said emotionlessly as I brushed past him, walking toward my room.

He grabbed my arm as I passed him. "Hey, don't just walk away," he said sternly.

"Don't touch me," I yelled, yanking my arm loose from his grip.

"Don't grab her like that again," Jackson said, taking a step toward Bailey.

Bailey released his grip, looking as if his actions surprised him, as if he hadn't known he was capable of reacting that way. I hurried to my room, flustered and upset from feeling ambushed in front of everyone. It seemed like everything I went through required an audience, and I was tired of being the main event.

Caleb followed me into my room, a look of sadness on his face. "Sammi…" he started.

"It's okay," I replied, my voice low.

"No, it's not. I'm supposed to make sure nothing bad ever happens to you, and I keep failing time and time again."

I walked over and gave him a hug because I knew this was killing him inside. He had never let me down, but he made a huge mistake on that night. I knew he'd take longer to forgive himself than I would to forgive him, and with him being the only family I had left, this relationship was important to me.

"Caleb, it's okay. We're living in a time where losing sight of ourselves is inevitable. You messed up, and you realize that. If I held a grudge about it, it wouldn't change anything about what happened. I forgive you, so forgive yourself," I said, releasing the hug.

"I just wish there was something I could do to help you heal from this," he said, frowning.

"Just keep being the big brother I love and look up to, and everything else will fall into place," I said.

"Well, I know this has all been a lot for you, but I think we should consider getting back on the road and looking for someone who could help find a cure. I just got my little sister back, and I'd like to keep you around a lot longer," he said with a half-smile.

I nodded, giving him a small smile back. "There's got to be houses in this neighborhood with vehicles we can use. We may just have to take two if we can't find a van big enough for all of us," I suggested.

"I'll get everyone rounded up," he said as he exited the room.

I followed behind him, walking over to Bailey, who still seemed on edge. "Where's Grace?" I asked softly.

"Uh, she's sleeping right now."

"Can I go see her?"

"I think it's best if you just wait until she wakes up. She hasn't been sleeping well without her mother around, and this is the first time she's slept decently in a while," he said, unable to hide the passive-aggressive note to his voice.

I tried to hold back my tears, but continually being denied seeing my daughter was mentally taking a toll on me. For him to say she hadn't been sleeping well because I was absent was hurtful. Yes, I hadn't been speaking, but he had never been to check on me, nor did he make an effort to let me see Grace.

I knew this heartbreak could easily be masked with a fix of the ketamine and fentanyl hidden somewhere inside of this house. I was fiending for it, and I was too ashamed to admit that to Jackson. He was still the only one who knew I wasn't sober, but I wanted him to believe I could get past this. So, my next dose would remain a secret from everyone, even him.

I walked away from Bailey before I had the chance to burst into tears or react in some other way. I didn't want him to see how his words and actions cut me like a knife. I could feel the heat underneath my cheeks from humiliation, and I could tell I was slipping away from myself again. I'd been off my medication, so it wasn't a matter of *if* but *when* I'd have my next manic episode. I knew this wouldn't end well for me, but I was going to bottle it up as long as I could.

I made my way over to Jackson, trying to contain my tears.

Caleb called the attention of the group. "Okay, we need to split up and look for more weapons, food, and cars. It doesn't have to be a van, but we'll need two vehicles to fit everyone if we can't find another van the size of our last one. Be cautious. It seems clear in this neighborhood, but the houses may still have dead ones roaming around," he announced.

"I think I'm going to stay here with Grace while she sleeps, so we won't have to wake her," I said.

"Okay. We won't be long. Keep a weapon close by just in case," Jackson said, kissing me on the cheek softly.

"Are you sure?" Bailey asked, as if he doubted my ability to care for her.

"Yes." I could tell he didn't want me to stay here alone with her, but keeping Grace here with me rather than bringing her out with the group would be the safest option.

He sighed. "Okay. She should keep sleeping until we get back, so just listen out for her," he instructed.

Everyone gathered their things and exited the house, leaving me and Grace behind.

As ashamed as I am to tell this next part of the story, it happened, and it's something I have to live with.

I walked over to the window and carefully peeked around the side of the curtain, watching as they walked further and further from the house.

Jackson had been giving me a little less with his dosing of the drugs each day, to go along with his original plan of weaning me off, but not receiving the amount my body had been satisfied with only made my cravings worse. The effects were now short lived, and I knew that I needed more to make these anxious feelings go away.

Once they were all out of sight and I figured they wouldn't be returning any time soon, I began looking for the vials they'd brought back from Dillion's stash. I opened every cabinet and drawer, but I couldn't find anything.

I wasn't sure if my behavior was from a manic episode, or if my addiction had possessed my conscious mind and was controlling me, but the longer it took for me to find the vials, the more agitated I grew. I was tearing the house apart, throwing items onto the floor and destroying each room, one by one. I was driving myself crazy, turning in circles and grabbing at my hair like an insane person.

Eventually, I ended up in Jackson's room for the third or fourth time to double check each inch of the room. Eventually I gave up, and feeling defeated, I placed my back up against the wall, sliding my legs forward until I was sitting on the floor. I exhaled deeply before beginning to cry in frustration. I was not in control of my body, and I hadn't been in quite some time.

This was my rock bottom.

Eventually I progressed from sitting up against the wall to lying on the floor, balled up in a fetal position, crying—no, sobbing—from the overwhelming sensation overtaking my body and my mind.

I laid there like that for a while, and when I opened my eyes, I noticed a box hidden beneath Jackson's bed. I sniffled, reaching underneath the mattress until my fingers met the wooden box. I slid it toward myself before opening it to reveal the remaining vials and syringes.

I sat up on the floor, turning to put my back against the bed. I fumbled through the contents of the box with shaking hands, wiping my running nose with my arm before unwrapping the syringe. I removed the plastic cap covering the needle and blindly combined each component.

I struggled finding a vein in the arm I typically received the injection in so I attempted to do it in the other arm, but I couldn't seem to keep my hand still no matter how hard I tried. I looked around the room for something I could use as a tourniquet, but I grew impatient. Luckily, I was finally able to stick the needle in, pushing the contents of the syringe into my vein. I closed my eyes and waited for the release I'd desperately been craving.

Everything that happened next was a blur.

～

Jackson's point of view

"What the fuck happened here?" Caleb exclaimed as we entered the house. The whole place was a chaotic mess; it looked like someone had broken in.

"Sammi?" Bailey called out, stepping through the room behind me and Caleb.

There was no response.

We all stood in the living room, looking around the destroyed house, wondering what had happened. We hadn't been gone for long.

"Sammi?" Bailey called out again. I felt a flash of concern when I heard Grace crying loudly from the bedroom she'd been sleeping in. "What the hell? Where is she?" he said as he hurriedly went to tend to Grace.

I frantically ran to Sammi's room, my heart sinking when I found it empty. I didn't like what my gut was telling me. I took off to my bedroom and, as I suspected, I found Sammi lying unconscious on the floor.

"Oh God!" I cried.

Caleb was the first to run into the room behind me, and Sophie and Lola soon followed.

"Is she breathing?" Sophie asked from the doorway.

"I-I don't know. It doesn't look like it," I cried, noticing the empty syringe slipping from her grasp. "She's turning blue. I think I need to do CPR," I said, voice shaking.

"Here, I got it," Sophie offered, gently nudging me aside. She could probably tell I was in the wrong state of mind, and I was momentarily grateful to my ex-girlfriend for that.

Sophie began to give Sammi chest compressions as Caleb, Lola and I looked on, horror on all our faces.

"Sammi, please don't die," I pleaded quietly, slumping down against the wall in anguish.

"What the hell happened?" Bailey asked as he rounded the corner of the room. He wasn't holding Grace, so he must have settled her down.

"She overdosed," Caleb said emotionlessly as he watched life leave his sister's body yet again.

"You told me you threw the drugs out," Bailey said angrily, directing his words toward me.

Sophie was still administering mouth to mouth and chest compressions, but I could tell she was beginning to tire. Lola offered to take over to give her a chance to recuperate, and they switched positions.

Sophie got to her feet, signaling for Caleb and Bailey to leave the room. "Let's go. None of this is helping right now," she said, rubbing her forehead.

They stepped out of the room and into the hall, though their voices were still loud enough for me to hear every word of their tense conversation.

"I thought she was sober," Bailey said angrily.

"People relapse all of the time," Caleb said. I glanced into the hall and watched him pace back and forth, thinking intently.

"Come on, she hasn't been sober. She has new needle marks on her arm, and she still has bruises from sticking herself. No one just drops drugs cold turkey and goes back to normal, especially after what she went through. She's working through some deep shit; we can't expect her to just go back to normal after all of that," Sophie reasoned.

I buried my head in my hands. This was my worst nightmare.

"You said Jackson threw the drugs out," Bailey said to Caleb, tone accusatory.

"That's what he told me!" he said defensively.

"So, you had no idea she was still using?"

"No, this is news to me too," he said.

Tears streamed down my face. Had I done the wrong thing by still providing Sammi with the drugs? I thought by slowly lowering her dose she could safely become less dependent, but I never accounted for the fact that she might take it upon herself to find them.

I'm not surprised nobody else in the house noticed she'd still been using. Everyone had been avoiding her like the plague since her rescue, mostly because they felt guilty over their behavior on the night she was kidnapped.

"If she overdosed on fentanyl, she needs naloxone," Sophie said nervously.

"We grabbed some. When we went to the house it was in the drawer with the other stuff. I wasn't sure what it was at first so I just took everything," Caleb said.

"We need that," she said, pushing into the room.

I beat them to it, scrambling over to the box of vials open beside Sammi's lifeless body, digging through until I found the naloxone. Sophie grabbed a syringe and took the vial from me before drawing up the amount needed to reverse the effects of the overdose. She injected Sammi with the medication, and everyone grew a little more hopeful.

When Sammi took her first breath of air, I felt instant relief. She was going to be okay.

"Oh, thank God," I said, sniffling as I gently cupped the side of her face.

"Sammi, hey, you're okay," Lola said reassuringly.

Sophie, Caleb, and Bailey hovered over her, letting out matching sighs of relief. It was apparent that Caleb and Bailey wanted to have it out with me for hiding Sammi's ongoing drug use from them, but Sophie stepped in, wanting to prevent that from happening, at least for the time being.

"Whatever negative thing you want to say, save it. This isn't about either of you. Okay?" she said in a stern whisper.

Bailey rolled his eyes, but nodded agreeably, as did Caleb.

After a few shallow, stuttering breaths, Sammi began breathing normally again. Her skin slowly gained somewhat normal coloring, though her eyes were closed for a while as she fully regained consciousness.

It took her another ten minutes to fully recover and sit up, by which point everyone else had filtered out of the room. We sat in silence, aside from Sammi's occasional sobs, both of us understanding the pain we'd experienced with this incident.

Then it seemed to finally hit her; she just lost it, crying so hard that she was hyperventilating. I tried my best to comfort her, and once she calmed down, I offered to grab her a glass of water. She nodded, and I climbed to my feet.

As I entered the kitchen to retrieve the water, I was met by Caleb and Bailey.

"How long?" Bailey asked, crossing his arms. They stood shoulder to shoulder, blocking my way.

"What?"

"How long has she been using again?"

"She never stopped," I admitted, trying to brush past them.

Bailey grabbed my arm tightly, yanking me back to face him. "You had no right," he hissed.

"Don't you think I know that?" I said from behind my grinding teeth, yanking his arm back from his grip and walking over to the sink in defeat. "I thought I was helping," I choked out once I'd filled the glass, propping my elbows on the counter and dropping my head into my hands.

I think Caleb could tell I was aware of my mistake, because he took pity on me, herding Bailey out of the room. He probably knew I didn't need any more guilt added to the mix.

After collecting myself, I grabbed the glass of water and took it to Sammi, who was now tucked into my bed. I smiled softly at her, climbing in beside her and snuggling up. We both fell into dreamless sleeps, getting some much-needed rest.

$\sim$

Sammi's point of view

The next day, we both hesitated to exit Jackson's room. I was ashamed to face Bailey because I'd done this while being the only adult here to watch over Grace. I don't think I could've lived with myself if something had happened to her. Jackson told me she'd been crying out for someone while I was unconscious on the floor, and the thought of that made me feel sick with shame. I was sure Bailey would keep her from me now.

And Jackson? He'd lied to his best friend about giving his sister drugs after they'd all seemingly agreed to discard them upon discovering the fentanyl. He'd also lied to the father of my child, who hadn't been on board with it in the first place.

So yeah, we were hesitating. In fact, we were still in bed.

"I'm sorry," I said, rolling over to face Jackson.

"I know," he said sweetly, reaching over to kiss me. "Me too."

"This wasn't your fault," I said. I was trying my best to reassure him, but I knew he still felt guilty.

"It kind of was."

"What am I going to do? I don't know if I can handle the withdrawals," I admitted with a frown.

"We'll figure it out, I promise."

I paused for a moment, looking over at him. "Have you talked to Caleb?"

"Not really, but I can tell he's pissed at me. And Bailey is for sure. I've given him plenty of reasons to hate me."

"Caleb will forgive you. You're his best friend."

"I hope so," he said softly.

Eventually we dragged ourselves out of bed. Jackson went to the bathroom, and I decided it was finally time to face everyone else. I stepped out of Jackson's room and passed through the hall, heading toward the living room. I stopped when I noticed Sophie settled on the couch in silence. She seemed to be in deep thought following the events of my overdose, troubled by her swarming thoughts.

I was about to announce my presence, but paused when Bailey entered the living room from the kitchen and took a seat next to her.

"How did you know what to do to save her from the overdose?" he asked.

Sophie took a deep breath. "Jackson and I were off and on for a very long time. During one of our breaks, I met this guy, Nathan. We were friends at first, but over time, we became more than that. He was special to me, and we grew very close. One night, I told him I loved him. His response was, 'Don't fall for me. I hurt everyone I love,'" she admitted with a wistful smile.

I held my breath, wondering where this story was going. It seemed like Bailey was doing the same, as he stayed quiet while she continued her story.

"I later found out that he was addicted to fentanyl and some other drugs. He started using after a traumatic experience he had. One night I showed up at his house, and he'd overdosed. I called for paramedics, but I felt useless waiting, not knowing what to do except CPR. He died in my arms. I felt him take his last breath," she said, her voice unsteady.

"Oh, Sophie. I'm so sorry. I can't imagine how that felt for you," Bailey said, his tone laced with sympathy.

"After that day, I wanted to make sure I never lost anyone else the way I did with him. If I'd had naloxone that day, I could've saved him too," she said sadly.

Bailey gently grabbed her hand and tried to comfort her. "You did that yesterday. You saved Sammi's life, and you should be proud of that."

She half-smiled. "Yeah. Sammi and I haven't always been civil, but I see how much she means to everyone in this group."

Bailey sighed. "I just haven't really seen this side of her. When I met her, she was so full of life and carefree in the best way possible. Now she's just reckless," he said, frowning.

"Look, I don't know how hung up on Sammi you are, but Jackson is down bad for that girl. Trust me, it was an issue in our relationship for years."

"I love Sammi, I do, but I think as long as Jackson is in the picture, I don't stand a chance. He seems more well equipped to handle the shit she has going on with her bipolar disorder and this drug addiction. She and I had this exciting and fun night, one I will never forget, but I don't think I can compete with him," he lamented.

"Well, if you want to be with her, you need to make more of an effort. You have every capability to be equipped like Jackson, but you're finding reasons not to be. Stop making excuses. If you love her and want to be with her, fight back, because I've seen the way she's loved both of you. You're not completely out of the question, Bailey," Sophie said supportively.

He blinked in surprise, then nodded as if processing everything she'd just said.

"You have a fighting chance," she added.

He gave a small smile before standing up and walking back into the kitchen. I took that as my cue to enter, and announced my presence, moving over to Sophie and giving her a well-deserved hug. At first, she seemed caught off guard, but she quickly realized what the hug was for and put her arms around me gently.

"Thank you," I whispered into her ear.

She rubbed my back soothingly without saying a word.

Before I had a chance to say anything else, everyone else filtered into the room, and we began to discuss our plans for the day, all agreeing that we would pack up and start heading north again. No one said anything about the incident that occurred yesterday, instead clearly deciding to put that behind us for now and focus on the day ahead.

The guys began carrying the items we had in the house outside onto the sidewalk. Most of the supplies they'd found while scavenging the neighborhood were already packed into the two new cars they'd managed to acquire: a blue Nissan Sentra and a white Ford Fiesta.

Bailey sat a few things down into the back seat of the white car while carrying Grace. I thought about asking him if I could hold her for a few minutes before we left, but I didn't have to; he walked over and offered to let me hold her. I was caught by surprise, but happily reached out for her.

"Hey, pretty girl," I said in my sickly-sweet baby voice. I had missed her smell and her little baby noises so much.

Bailey smiled at me for the first time in a while, and I stood there appreciating this moment with my daughter until Caleb called all our attention, announcing today's plan. It felt like forever since we'd been on the road, but I had a promising feeling about this journey. I was optimistic that we would get to where we needed and that everything was going to be okay for once.

"Lola, Sophie, and Bailey are taking the Fiesta with Grace. We've already set up the car seat for her. Jackson, Sammi, and I will take the Sentra," Caleb said as he closed the trunk of the blue car.

"I'm going to lead the way. We're going to stop by my house in Nashville because I have some guns and stuff that we can use that are hopefully still there," Bailey said. I detected a slight nervousness in his tone.

I'd always wondered what Bailey's house looked like. I felt like it would give me a glimpse into his life and his personality that I hadn't gotten the chance to explore yet. He was a pretty private person, and we'd never really gotten the chance to know each other deeply. Maybe it would help me see who he really was.

We all slowly migrated toward the cars. I decided to let Grace ride with Bailey so that I could talk to Caleb and Jackson. Plus Sophie had been begging to see and play with her. I buckled Grace into the car seat beside Sophie in the backseat of the Fiesta, then gave her seatbelt a firm tug to ensure that it was properly connected before shutting the door. Jackson had taken the driver's seat of the car we'd be riding in, so I took the front passenger seat. Caleb sat behind Jackson, who promptly started the car. We waited for Bailey to pull out of the driveway and followed him around the neighborhood and back out onto the main road.

I was anxious for a couple of reasons, one being that it seemed like every time we were back on the road, something bad happened. The second being that I'd used up the rest of the ketamine and fentanyl in our possession. Right now I was fine, but I'd set myself up for failure by injecting myself with such a large amount yesterday. It would only make my tolerance— which had been slowly declining with Jackson's regime—higher, as well as my cravings. But what other options did I have?

Oh look, it's the consequences of your own actions.

I looked out of the window, watching everything pass us by. No one was saying a word, but I could tell Caleb was holding on to his feelings. He clearly wanted to get some things off his chest.

"We have a long ride ahead of us, so we might as well address the elephant in the room," he said from behind us.

"Okay," Jackson said plainly before giving Caleb a glance through the rear-view mirror.

"I thought you two trusted me. I thought you could tell me anything and not worry about what I'd think. Had I known you were struggling this bad, Sammi, I could have tried to help—or at least been there for you while you got through this."

"I do trust you, Caleb, but you weren't there. None of you were. You were out partying at some house while I was being withheld food, tied to a chair, and hallucinating that Jackson was saving me over and over again, only to wake up and find that I was still in that chair. I'd start to feel hungry and numb from my arms being pulled tightly behind my back, and then I'd feel nothing—no pain at all—because I was receiving this drug that allowed me to be okay," I began, gesturing erratically with my hands as I tried to express my feelings.

Caleb sighed. "Sammi, I lost sight of myself. It was the first time we'd been in a house that felt normal for such a long time. I was so certain that you'd get away and find us, and I never thought those hours of fun would lead to an eight-day struggle of getting back to you," he said sadly.

"I was convinced I could get away from them too, but Dillion found me before I had the chance."

"I feel responsible for the pain you've been through, and I feel like this drug addiction you're suffering with is my fault. I feel responsible for helping you get past this."

"It's not drugs that make you become addicted; it's the neutralization of pain and trauma that the drugs are able to offer. I'm sorry, but I don't know what you can offer that would give me that relief," I admitted painfully.

A moment passed before I continued. "I was sitting in my own waste, filthy and ashamed. And then he untied me, and I was so weak that I just collapsed from the chair. They kicked me until I vomited on the floor." I watched through the rear-view mirror as Caleb flinched at this information. "It was traumatic, Caleb. I could've died. I *should've* died," I continued, staring straight ahead, barely blinking.

Jackson's hands tightened on the steering wheel. He hadn't said anything since the start of mine and Caleb's discussion, but I knew he was taking every moment in.

"While I was lying on that floor, I prayed the lingering effects of the drugs would get me through it. When they sent the zombies in, I was fully convinced that I was going to die, and there was nothing I could do." I paused. "But zombies don't want to attack me. It's … strange," I said, narrowing my eyes in thought as I considered the incident in the woods and the three zombies Dillion had sent to kill me. "It's like they know I'm on the verge of becoming one of them, and that makes them feel the need to protect me, rather than attack me."

"We shot them," Caleb said with slight confusion.

"They were in the room long before you arrived. I'd found myself back in that weird parallel universe where the zombies were people. The three zombies in that room with me were regular women in my visions … or whatever they are. They were trying to help me escape." I paused. "You both probably think I'm crazy. I sound crazy," I admitted.

"No, it's not crazy because we saw it firsthand in the woods that day. We saw that zombie get inches from you without attacking. I think maybe you're right about that," Jackson said.

"I don't know if that makes me feel worse or better."

"Yeah, me either," Caleb said, as if he was in deep thought.

"Do you really think someone is working on a cure?" I asked.

"I honestly don't know, Sammi. I hope so," Caleb said softly.

23

BLEED

THE CONVERSATION CAME TO a natural end and we continued our drive, occasionally talking or looking out of the window—doing whatever we could to pass the time.

I could tell when we made the transition from Arkansas to Tennessee, and specifically when we reached Nashville. The city was familiar to me from the night I'd stayed here, and despite all that had happened since, it seemed like it was just yesterday.

There was something about Nashville that made it feel hospitable and welcoming, even as a ghost town. Wide streets and old brick buildings that were once occupied by lively businesses and ambitious musicians were all that was left of this city. But even with it being practically vacant and stripped of most of its previous character, it still gave me a peace of mind I hadn't felt in quite some time.

Right outside of the city there were several neighborhoods similar to the one I stayed in previously. There were more abandoned cars here than we'd seen throughout Arkansas and Oklahoma, but we found ways around them. It was doable now, but I feared the further north we drove, the less passable the roads would be. It felt like the idea of a cure was getting more out of reach the closer we got, but I was trying not to lose faith.

We continued following behind the white car Bailey was driving, entering a particularly idyllic neighborhood. It almost appeared untouched, other than the evident empty homes surrounding us. There was no blood pooled in dry patches on the road—a rarity these days—and it was so quiet. I was so used to hearing some kind of distant noise from zombies in the area, but here, it was silent. Where were all the zombies?

Eventually we arrived at a beautiful off-white modern farmhouse settled on the greenest lot of grass. Everything about it was perfect. My mind wandered, imagining the two of us living here together, raising Grace, laughing as we ran around in the yard with her. That would've been the perfect life.

Bailey pulled his car onto the concrete driveway, and we parked right behind them.

"Well, it looks like this is it," Caleb said, looking out of the front window between the headrests of our seats.

We simultaneously exited the car, assembling on the driveway.

"I thought maybe we could stay here for the night. I know there's still a little daylight left, but at least here we know there's some sense of familiarity and safety," Bailey said.

With the rest of the group agreeing to his plan, he bent over to dig out a key from the mulch in his flowerbeds. He unlocked one of the double doors, and we all followed him inside, still prepared to meet unwanted guests. After carefully searching his house, we were able to let out matching sighs of relief that we had all made it here safely. Most people collapsed onto the sectional sofa, excited to finally be able to rest after the long drive here.

Everyone was busy doing their own thing, so I decided to slip away and give myself a tour. I wanted to see what Bailey's life was like prior to dropping everything to come to me. I quietly took the stairs up to the second floor, where I was greeted by several different doors.

The first room I entered was his office. It had tall white bookcases in both corners and a brown wooden desk settled in the center of the room.

I walked over to the desk, dragging my fingers across the surface as I studied the many papers scattered over it. There were bank statements for his business, postcards from friends, and a book that looked like a photo album.

I tilted my head to the side and curiously slid it toward me. The cover was a beige color with a linen texture. I was curious to see what kind of photos he would keep in an album on his desk, so I grabbed the corner to pull it open.

I flipped through the first few pages to see pictures of him and his friends posing with bottles of beer in the summertime. Once I was about halfway through, a certain group of photographs caught my eye. They were of the two of us at the bar that night, laughing and dancing. It looked like the bar staff had taken pictures of everyone line dancing. I smiled to myself. It meant something to me that he felt the need to have these printed off and put into a photo album he kept close to him in his office.

The last photos were of us after the dancing. They looked like they'd been taken from a cellphone, probably by his friends who had been watching us. We were so happy and carefree.

God, I wished I could relive that night.

I was still admiring the pictures when I heard the floor creak. I looked up and saw Bailey watching me from the doorway. I quickly shut the album, blushing from the embarrassment of being caught plundering through his belongings.

"I'm sorry," I apologized as he entered the room.

"It's okay," he said softly, smiling. "The owner of the bar is one of my good friends—or *was*, not sure if he made it through the soldiers at the beginning. He usually took pictures every time they did line dancing to help advertise and bring people in. I told him about meeting you there, and when he was going through the photos, he sent me those of me and you."

"That's so sweet," I said.

"My buddies who were there that night, they told me the next day that they could tell you were special. They took a few pictures with their cellphones because they were convinced that I'd need them to display at my wedding one day, when I told the story of how I met you," he said, blushing slightly.

I smiled shyly, my cheeks also flushing.

"Look, I'm sorry I haven't been the man you deserve lately, but I don't want you to count me out as being the man you do deserve."

I looked at him with wonder, because it had seemed like he was counting himself out with his behavior. But in all honesty, I was to blame too. I was reckless with our daughter when I overdosed, and I had continuously put myself and others in danger. I was a ticking time bomb, and it wasn't fair to blame him one bit for how he chose to react. So, I decided to cut him some slack.

"Noted," I said sweetly. He stood quietly for a second as I gazed around the room once more. "Well, you have a beautiful home."

"At one point, yes, I had a beautiful home, but this isn't home now. Home is wherever you are. And that's where I want to be," he said gently.

I smiled in response, and we left the office together, heading back downstairs to find the others.

Bailey's home ran off well water, so one positive that came from being here was the ability to use the shower—a cold shower, but a shower, nonetheless. Once we'd all gotten cleaned up, Bailey gave some fresh clothes to Caleb and Jackson, and the guys searched a few houses nearby to find us girls some clean clothes as well. We felt much better and were all in a much more positive mindset.

Later that night, we played board games, ate some slightly stale s'mores over a fire, and told stories from before the apocalypse. We had a genuinely pleasant and fun time. It was a much-needed night, considering what we'd been through lately. For a little while, things almost felt normal.

~

The next morning, I felt the first signs of withdrawal.

I'd been trying to keep my mind busy, because that was the only way I'd be able to brave through it. I was worried that no matter how hard I tried, I wouldn't be able to quit cold turkey, but there weren't many options for me at this point. It wasn't like I could find fentanyl and ketamine just lying around these days.

My skin was already crawling, as if to preface my looming downward spiral. I was uncomfortable just from the beginning of this detox, but I tried to mask any evidence from the others.

"Before everything went to hell, I had a friend of mine take an internship at the University of Missouri. He raved about how they had one of the best laboratories for infectious diseases. We're about six or so hours from there, I believe. Might be worth looking into," Lola said as we sat at the dining room table eating stale, dry cereal.

I looked around to see what the others thought about her idea, and it seemed like they were on board. Our initial plan had been Harvard, but this other place seemed like it would be more equipped to focus on this pandemic. Bailey had what seemed like a hopeful expression for the first time in a while. I didn't want to get my hopes up, but it was almost within reach. It wasn't completely out of the scope of realistic solutions and possibilities.

"Does that sound good, Sammi?" Caleb asked.

They all turned to me for my response, but as I prepared to answer, I went back to that dark, cold place where only me and the zombies resided. This was now my third time falling into this alternate headspace, and it still didn't get any easier. I always ended up feeling scared and alone. I wondered how I looked to the others when I did this.

The first two times I'd transitioned to what I refer to as *dark reality*, I'd been in the presence of zombies, so I was never really alone. I was accompanied by others who'd ultimately succumbed to the fate I'd soon share. I was never here long enough to get answers; there was always an unsettling sense of urgency, with them pleading for me to leave and get back to reality.

This time, however, I was all alone, because at the breakfast table it was just me and the people in my group who weren't part of this secret society. The seats at the dining room table once filled by those I loved were now empty. The natural light beaming in through the windows was dimmer and eerie.

I didn't like being alone—never have—so I stood up from the table and walked out of the front door, eager to find a zombie nearby for me to question. I knew just getting up and leaving would probably startle the others, but by now they had to have known where my mind was. I just hoped they trusted my instincts.

When I stepped outside, I looked in both directions, hoping I'd see someone or something wandering around, but it was still just an empty neighborhood. I turned in circles, trying to manifest an encounter, but it was useless; there was obviously nothing here.

I decided to call out, thinking maybe I could attract one by making noise. It was reckless, but I was desperate.

"Hello? Is anyone out there? I need help!" I yelled.

Several minutes passed, and I began walking away from Bailey's house and toward the sidewalk.

"Anyone, please, help me!"

Still, nothing.

I took a left onto the road that separated more houses and began running, not toward anything in particular, just hoping to encounter a zombie. I wasn't sure how long I would stay in this dark reality, and I needed to find someone quickly before I found myself back with the others. I needed answers, and I was determined to get some.

"Hello?" I called out once more, cupping my hands around my mouth to amplify my voice.

Suddenly something startled the small group of birds settled in a nearby tree, sending them fluttering into the sky.

"You're going to wake up the entire city if you keep that up," an unfamiliar voice said from behind me.

"I'm sorry, I didn't know what else to do," I said, turning around. A younger guy, around my age, was walking over to me.

"So, what's up?" he asked casually.

"Aren't you going to tell me to leave, that it's not safe or something?" I asked, crossing my arms.

"Ah, I could, but I'm sure you know that by now," he said, now only a few feet away from me.

I know this is going to sound bizarre, since he was a zombie, after all, but he made me feel comfortable. The way he spoke and carried himself was warm and honest. He had blonde hair with piercing blue eyes and a demeanor that housed a calmness that I needed—a nice change from the previous exchanges I'd had here. I think the panicked aura of the women I'd spoken to the first two times gave me an uneasy feeling, but this guy made it a lot less haunting. I needed that right now.

"How can you tell?" I asked.

"You're looking for one of us. You have questions—it's normal," he said, shrugging his shoulders.

"Are there others like me?"

"Not many, but there have been a few here and there."

"So, what can you tell me? How long do I have left before I turn? How do I go back to reality?"

"Woah, slow down; we've got time," he said nonchalantly.

I furrowed my brows in confusion. "Time? You know how long I'll be here?"

"I mean there's not necessarily a clock counting down, but I can tell that you'll be here longer than you probably have been before."

"Okay, so what is this? Is this the other side?" I said jokingly.

He chuckled. "I guess you could call it something like that. It's only where zombies are, not all dead people. This isn't heaven or hell. As long as the zombie version of yourself is alive, you have the ability to be here," he said.

"So, how do I get here?"

"It's not really up to you. It just kind of happens."

"I'm going to need you to elaborate," I said calmly, raising my eyebrows.

"Well, the infection is affecting the parts of your brain that have the ability to temporarily shut down your real, conscious mind. You're essentially brain dead while you're here. It's slowly killing you. That's why we tell you to leave—the longer you're here, the more damage is being done to your brain and organs."

"What causes my body to start doing this? Is there a trigger?"

"I don't really know. I think it's almost like a seizure, a really long seizure…" he said, his words drifting with his thoughts.

"Did you get murdered by the soldiers giving the injection, or did you die from the injection after the fact?" I asked curiously.

"I was murdered, but not by the soldiers."

I looked at him worriedly. "Who murdered you?"

"I lived in this neighborhood with my wife and son. We did everything we could to survive, and I did everything I could to protect them, but there was a group of these psychopathic people prowling around the area, looking for others to steal from and torment. They showed up to my home and killed me and my wife, even after we did everything that they asked of us," he said, frowning.

"That's terrible. I'm so sorry," I said sympathetically.

"The apocalypse made people crazy. Or maybe they were crazy before and now there's no one to stop them from acting on their malicious desires," he said, staring ahead as if in deep thought.

"Did you know you had the injection before you died?"

"I had a suspicion. I was always one of those people who believed the government was conspiring against us. When I first found out about the zombies, I just had this gut feeling that they'd done something to us. After I died, it took me a while to figure out what this was, who I was, where I was. It took finding people like you and others like me to put all of the pieces together."

"It's a big puzzle to try and solve. This is all so confusing. I didn't know what this was either, until recently. I've only been here three times, but I know the more I come, the less time I have with my family."

"Yeah, I think the worst part of all of this is not having my wife here with me. She didn't have the injection. She just … died," he said sadly. "Now I feel so alone, roaming the streets with strangers just like me."

My mind wandered to many different places. I still had questions for him, but I didn't even know where to start. I'd already been in this dark reality for longer than ever before, so I was worried I was running out of time.

"Can you tell me if there's a cure? Can I survive this?"

"It's not that simple. Nothing nowadays is," he said calmly.

"I have a daughter. I need to survive for her. Can I survive this?" I said, a little more intense this time.

"Well, they said cancer was incurable for a long time, but there were loopholes. Chemotherapy and radiation. They've done miraculous things to people with incurable illnesses. Everything has a loophole, you just have to get creative, Sammi," he began.

"What is my loophole?" I asked, begging for an answer to take back with me.

"You've already got—" he began, but suddenly collapsed to the ground before he could finish his thought.

"No!" I screamed, dropping down to my knees, tears streaming down my face. "Please, no," I repeated as the world around me grew brighter.

I'd returned to my conscious mind, carrying the sadness of losing my connection to the other side. When I turned to look behind me, Bailey was standing there with his gun. He dropped it down by his side as I yelled, "Why did you do that?"

He looked confused, as if he thought he'd been doing me a favor; saving me somehow. "That thing could've killed you, Sammi," he began.

"That thing was about to save me! You just fucked it all up," I said angrily before standing up and storming past him, back toward the house.

Bailey hadn't been in the car that day when I shared with Caleb and Jackson that zombies wouldn't hurt me, so to him, he didn't know any better. He saw a perceived threat and acted on it. I couldn't blame him for that, but now the answers I needed were worlds away. I didn't know what to do anymore, but had I just found out that there was a cure—a loophole, or something? I didn't know what it was.

I approached Jackson and Caleb, who had run outside toward the commotion. I brushed past them, and they turned to look at me in confusion as Bailey trailed behind me. All they knew was a gun had been fired and a dead zombie was left behind in the street.

"What happened?" Caleb asked Bailey as they followed me back to the house, me hurrying ahead of them.

"I thought I was helping," he said sadly.

I knew Bailey thought he was helping, but really he'd just alerted every zombie around us that we were out in the open and vulnerable, because here they came, ready to eliminate each of us until there was no sign we had ever existed. His single gunshot had echoed through the streets and trees, and the zombies were following it like a bunch of brainwashed puppets. You could actually hear them making their way down each surrounding street like a marching band, or a riot—definitely a riot.

"Sammi, come back," Caleb called out.

I stopped in my tracks as I came face to face with dozens of hungry zombies. I slowly began backing up toward Bailey, Caleb, and Jackson, realizing we were about to be in deep shit.

It was quickly becoming evident that when I wasn't in the dark reality, I was not safe from the dead bodies starving for flesh and guts. They wanted to kill and eat me just like any other person they'd encountered, drooling and growling at the thought of tasting my bright red blood and fresh pink skin.

I continued taking steps backwards as my mind momentarily jerked back to the gray world I'd been in when Bailey found me. Zombie growls turned to panicked voices telling me to leave, that it wasn't safe here. But which "here" were they referring to? Because it seemed like the "here" with immunity from being torn apart was safer than the "here" where the zombies wanted to feast on me.

Every few seconds I flipped from one world to the other. I felt schizophrenic. Hearing all of these voices in my head and seeing things that weren't really there outlined part of that diagnosis—to the average person anyways.

It's the infection. You're not *crazy.*

Entering and exiting both realities—back and forth, back and forth—was making me dizzy, and before I knew it, I was collapsing to the ground.

What is happening to me?

∼

Jackson's point of view

"Sammi!" I cried out, sprinting toward where she was laying, not far from the zombies closing in around us. Caleb and Bailey were not far behind.

To my horror, she started to convulse, her head slamming against the concrete. I knelt down next to her, carefully rolling her to her side as foamy saliva poured out of her mouth. We were running out of time. The only option we had was to find an unlocked house close by that we could hide in until the swarm dissipated.

"We need to get out of the street and find protection," Caleb suggested. He sounded out of breath; from the sprint to Sammi or the anxiety that came with this many zombies, I couldn't tell.

I placed my arms underneath Sammi's body—which had thankfully stopped convulsing—before lifting her up and following Caleb and Bailey. The two of them had taken off toward a sage green home settled to our left. The home had overgrown grass and a playground set in the front yard where a young child probably once spent most of their days before all the complexities and dangers the world had taken over.

Caleb grabbed the doorknob, thankfully finding it to be unlocked. He signaled for me to hurry, immediately locking the deadbolt behind us once we were all inside. I laid Sammi down on a sofa in the next room before helping Caleb and Bailey stack furniture against the door to keep the zombies from breaking it off the hinges. We were in the clear for now, but zombies were smart; they'd seen us come into this house, and they would be coming for us.

~

Sammi's point of view

I panicked as I regained consciousness, realizing I was in a house I didn't recognize. Had Dillion found me again?

I shook my head. *Dillion is dead,* I reminded myself.

I looked around at my surroundings, hoping to see a familiar face, but I was alone. I forced myself to stay calm, and was soon flooded with relief when I heard Jackson and Caleb talking at the front of the house. I mustered the energy to stand before walking toward the front door. Both of them were peeking through the blinds, keeping tabs on the zombies wreaking havoc in the neighborhood.

Jackson ran over to me with his arms stretched out wide. "I'm glad you're okay," he whispered as we hugged tightly.

"Is Bailey here?" I asked, realizing I'd been unfair to him earlier in the street. I wanted to tell him I was sorry for yelling at him for shooting the zombie.

"I think he went into the kitchen," Jackson said.

"I'm going to go find him."

He nodded.

I eased down the entryway, looking at the photographs hanging on the walls. They all showed a happy family: dad, mom and son. I was surprised to recognize the dad in each one; it was the zombie I'd encountered earlier, who Bailey had killed.

I replayed our conversation while I continued walking through the house. Thinking about how they were brutally murdered was an eerie feeling while being inside the very home where it happened. I could see trails of dried blood on the floor, leading to the kitchen. I'd never had the chance to ask him what happened to his son. Was he murdered too?

As I approached the kitchen, I heard Bailey talking to someone.

"Hey, we're not here to hurt you," he said calmly.

I could see Bailey, but I couldn't see who he was talking to. Before I had the chance to step into the kitchen, the sound of a gunshot echoed in my ears.

It went straight through his head.

I flinched in shock before screaming bloody murder as the killer dropped the gun and ran off.

The father of my child was dead.

I heard Caleb and Jackson sprinting in my direction as I fell to the floor, hysterically screaming and crying. The sense of helplessness and my failure to save Bailey from this would leave me broken for a very long time.

Caleb and Jackson froze as they ran into the kitchen and found me with Bailey's body. They had no idea what to make of the situation or how it even happened. I laid my head on his chest, not feeling any heartbeat or sign of life. The blood from his head pooled on the laminate kitchen floor, soaking me. I was distraught and heartbroken beyond belief.

Once again, the gunshot attracted every zombie within the neighborhood, their hands pounding on the side of the house and on the doors and windows. We were no longer safe here.

Apparently, we weren't safe here to begin with.

Caleb came to my side, gently rubbing my shoulder to try and convince me to leave Bailey's side, but I didn't think I could physically leave him. I needed to stay and comfort what parts of him were left, even if he wasn't alive to feel it.

"Sammi, we've got to go. We can't stay here," Caleb pleaded.

I continued crying as I looked up to see the outline of someone peeking from behind the far kitchen door frame. I couldn't make out who it was, but they caught Jackson's eye, sending him to investigate. He took careful steps toward the door frame as he tried to gain their trust. They no longer had their murder weapon—that lay feet from me—so it was safe to pursue Bailey's killer.

"Hey, it's okay," he said calmly.

"Is he dead?" a young boy asked as he revealed himself from behind the wall.

"Yes. We aren't going to hurt you. It's okay," Jackson said calmly.

I rubbed the tears from my eyes and found the strength to stand before walking over to the gun the boy left behind after he murdered Bailey. I was angry. I was hurt. I was seeing nothing but shades of red. I'd never felt this type of rage and grief—it consumed me.

Jackson had finally convinced the boy to come back into the kitchen, where he assured him it was safe. But he hurt me, and he hurt Bailey, so I took the gun and, without hesitation, shot into the young boy's body— legs, chest, head, anything, until the gun was out of bullets.

I'll never forget the look he gave me after the first bullet entered his body. Now he lay lifelessly in a pool of blood, like Bailey. It was almost symbolic.

I threw the gun down on the ground as Jackson and Caleb stood wide-eyed and traumatized by my actions. They had no idea what to say or do. I had murdered a young boy who was probably scared the people who killed his parents were back to finish the job.

But he killed Bailey. That was the only explanation I owed anyone.

As petrified as the two of them were, our time was up. The zombies were breaking through the doors and windows, knocking over the furniture stacked against the front door. We needed to get the hell out of here.

Caleb grabbed a set of car keys hanging on a hook in the kitchen before signaling us to follow him into the garage.

I took one final look at Bailey before hurrying out of the kitchen and into the garage. Zombies were now inside of the house and only feet from me as I lingered behind. I heard Caleb crank up a car, so I snapped back into a world that was spinning to find the strength to move at their pace. I shut the door leading to the garage right before an older male zombie reached for me.

I was stomping down the stairs toward the silver sedan when a Spider-Man backpack hanging up in the garage caught my eye. It stopped me in my tracks, consuming me with aggressive guilt for murdering a boy no older than Greyson was.

Was I turning into a monster after all? I didn't even need the help of the infection.

Caleb was in the driver's seat, and Jackson was in the passenger side, staring out of the window with an emptiness that radiated throughout the garage. We were all rattled, not knowing what to say or do. Unfortunately, the only thing I knew that would completely take my pain away was in a vial tucked away in a hospital or pharmacy somewhere. I just didn't know how to cognitively function when a piece of my heart was left behind. I needed something to take me away from this.

Zombies were beginning to push through the door from the kitchen out into the garage. Caleb put the car in drive and floored the gas until we drove right through the big white door. There weren't as many surrounding the garage as there were on the other side of the house, so after hitting a few of them as speed bumps we were on the road toward Bailey's house.

Oh God. Were Lola, Sophie, and Grace okay? Had the swarm come through that area?

I was having the most difficult time concentrating and thinking rationally. I was like a robot going through the motions but unable to process thoughts as my own. Someone needed to pull the hard drive out of me and completely shut me off—to protect myself and keep those around me safe from my impulsive actions.

For the first time in a while, I could say wholeheartedly that I wanted to die.

I wanted to slit my wrists and bleed out poetically in a bathtub while listening to a depressing song and enjoying the warmth of the bath water.

I wanted to leave a note addressed to my brother and Jackson, apologizing for all I continued to put them through, and adding my suicide to that list.

I wanted the adrenaline of knowing it was too late to turn back; the deed was done, and I would be dead soon.

Do you know how much blood is in the human body? So much blood. I witnessed it firsthand as Bailey's body emptied out in the floor of that house.

I was afraid to think about whether Grace was okay. I couldn't stomach the thought of losing the one piece of me that was still pure, loving, and kind. Lately it seemed like everyone I cared about was dying. First Greyson, then Ryan, and now Bailey. It felt so unfair.

Caleb hurriedly maneuvered us through the streets, and we were eventually able to find Bailey's house amid the straggler zombies that had wandered off from the larger group. The flower beds around the house were torn apart as if the herd trampled through on their way to the gunshots. It made my stomach turn in knots, thinking about what we might find inside.

Caleb parked the car, and the two of them began stabbing the handful of straggler zombies until none remained. I watched with an empty expression as each one fell to the ground, dulled knives protruding into each decaying brain.

Taking a deep breath, I found the courage to follow them toward the door with slow, heavy footsteps. I could feel the weight of the world on my shoulders, dragging me down with it. It was suffocating me. I hated feeling so *woe is me*, but that's all the world had to offer me lately.

But as my brother would gracefully say, *Life goes on*. I just didn't believe it was that easy.

As we approached the front doors, I noticed the glass from the windows and double doors were broken through. Then Caleb and Jackson eased inside, and I saw splatters of blood in a trail leading toward the kitchen. They looked back at me in fear of what we'd discover.

Would I be able to handle it?

Probably not. *I haven't been handling much of anything these days.*

After reaching the end of the blood drops, we found Lola with her back up against the chestnut cabinets, holding onto her side to try and stop the blood gushing from her wounds. She was barely alive; her eyes bloodshot red, and her skin pale. She was trying to tell us something, but she began coughing up an excessive amount of blood instead.

So much blood.

The three of us stood frozen for several moments, unsure of what to do. Eventually Jackson knelt down beside her, lifting up the bottom of her shirt to reveal at least three gaping wounds from where the zombies had removed chunks of her abdomen.

The strength she had to hold pressure on her wounds had vanished. She was dead, just like almost everyone else.

Jackson took one last look at her, feeling for a pulse in her neck before looking back at us in defeat. "She's gone," he said, easing her body down onto the floor.

"Damnit," Caleb said angrily, kicking a bar stool.

"Where are Sophie and Grace?" Jackson asked, standing up.

"Check everywhere," Caleb said, and they split up to search different areas of the house.

I remained in the kitchen, staring at Lola's dead body and subconsciously preparing for the worst. Jackson looked upstairs, and Caleb looked downstairs. But the two of them returned to the kitchen with hopeless expressions on their faces.

My heart sank.

"They're not here," Caleb said worriedly.

"They're dead too, aren't they? Everyone is dead," I said as my eyes glossed over.

"We don't know that, Sammi," Jackson said, trying to remain optimistic.

"Yeah, there wasn't any blood or bodies anywhere except the kitchen. They're out there somewhere," Caleb said as he walked over to me, trying his best to provide what little comfort he could.

My lips began to quiver as I slipped into labored breathing—the makings of a panic attack. I was housing every urge to shoot up the first drug I laid my hands on; I needed it badly. There wasn't anything I could do to manage this. I had all the components and qualities to turn myself into a complete psychopath.

I needed to keep fighting, but right now, I didn't know what I would be fighting for.

24

BURN

I SHOULD'VE DIED. I had every reason to. I deserved to. But somehow, I still managed to live, even when Bailey was denied that chance.

Honestly, fuck this world. Is this all you've got?

~

After failing to find Sophie and Grace, the three of us left Bailey's house and found a new home in a nearby neighborhood. We wanted to be close by so we could continue our search for them. The house was in good shape and would provide the needed security if another army of zombies came through.

Jackson and I claimed a queen-sized bed in a room decorated in outdated furniture and floral wallpaper, while Caleb took the next room over.

Once Jackson fell into a deep sleep, I slipped out of bed. I was wearing a black tee, along with a pair of hot pink boy short-style underwear that I found while plundering through the dresser drawers inside this vacant house. The jeans I'd been wearing were lying on the floor beside the bed, so I slowly grabbed them before sneaking downstairs as quietly as possible.

It was now the second week of May, so the days were beginning to radiate the early summer heat, yet the nights remained cool. I'd been contemplating this excursion since we got to this house, strategically planning every aspect so I could be in and out and back in bed before the sun even rose. I knew it would become an ordeal if either of them woke up to me missing, so I was planning to sneak out like a rebellious teen without them ever knowing. That was the goal, at least.

Once I was downstairs, I squeezed into my wrinkled, ripped skinny jeans before browsing through one of the closets. I found an old olive-green jacket hanging up in a coat closet and threw it on to keep the late night breeze off of me.

I glanced around the almost pitch black downstairs area before spotting the keys to the sedan we'd taken from the house where Bailey died. I took gentle steps toward the round stone kitchen table to retrieve them, and then I moved to the front door. I took one last look around me to ensure that Jackson or Caleb hadn't woken up. Fortunately for me, they were still tucked neatly in bed as I snuck off to find something that would take my mind off of Bailey's death and Grace's disappearance.

I drove the car out of the neighborhood and onto the main highway in the direction of the blue hospital signs I'd seen when we first arrived in Nashville. It was eerily dark and quiet, with nothing to illuminate the road or my surroundings except the dim headlights of the car. Everything in the area had finally simmered down following the chaotic terrorization of the dead corpses. I hadn't seen a single zombie since then.

I continued following the street signs until I saw the huge glass hospital growing closer. I quickly turned into the massive parking lot, finding a spot near the entrance, and shut off the headlights and engine.

My stomach turned in knots from the strange, unsettling feeling I got from being here. I should've taken my ass straight back home, but there was something about addiction that made me irrational and blinded me to my subconscious fears, especially when a manic episode was thrown into the mix. So, I chose to ignore that gut feeling and instead satisfy my inner demon's cravings.

Taking hesitant steps toward the entrance, I approached the once automatic doors. I attempted to pull them apart, but it was difficult to get a good grasp on them. I groaned in annoyance as I struggled, then eventually gave up, walking around to the side of the hospital where I found a lonely door. I turned the handle and sighed a breath of relief when I discovered that it was unlocked.

The old door creaked open, revealing a dark room where the fire escape stairwell was located. There was a faint smell of mildew, and I could vaguely hear water dripping from several floors above me. Every few seconds, *drip, drip, drip* into a small puddle in the corner of the room.

I took hold of the cold, paint-flaked handrail and climbed the stairs. Chill bumps covered my body as I navigated through the alternating diagonal steps, finally reaching a metal door with a bright red sign to the right of it that read "Floor Two."

I opened the door and found myself in an empty hallway. I didn't see anything or hear anyone, so I inched down the hall until I found a sign with room and floor numbers for each area of the hospital.

Strangely, I felt like I was back at the hospital with Rudy's group, experiencing the same uncertainties as I had back then. I also had this lingering feeling that I wasn't alone here.

I avoided my persistent worries and studied the sign until I saw "Pharmacy" etched out in black lettering. It was located on the third floor.

Before I headed back to the stairwell, I turned to look behind me, just to make sure I wasn't being watched. I couldn't see anyone, so I continued my journey through the stairwell and up to the third floor.

There hadn't been any evidence of power on the second floor or in the ground floor stairwell, but when I stepped out onto the third floor, I saw a single light flickering down one of the hallways, accompanied by a low buzzing noise. Right behind that light there was a sign hanging from the ceiling with an arrow pointing to the left and the words "Psychiatric Unit" and "Pharmacy" labeled on it.

I carefully walked toward the sign, following the arrow by taking the adjacent dimly-lit hallway. At the very far end, I noticed two double doors with "Authorized Personnel Only" written across the front of them. The way it seemed so closed off and secluded from the rest of the hospital gave me the creeps, but before I got too far down the hall, I found the entrance to the pharmacy.

I heaved a sigh of relief.

It was fully lit within the moderately-sized room housing tons of medications. I peeped through the small window on the door, and once I saw it was empty, I entered. I immediately began rummaging around, trying to locate either of the two drugs I desperately craved. I tirelessly fumbled through shelves, cabinets, and drawers, becoming frustrated with myself when I found nothing.

But then I located the cabinet I'd been looking for, my eyes locking on the hospital's stash of ketamine and fentanyl. I took all the stock, along with several syringes, and laid them on top of the large counter located in the center of the room. I studied each component, picturing how it would feel to be high right now.

It would've been stupid and reckless for me to shoot up while in an unfamiliar, sketchy environment, so that's exactly what I did—because as we've established, I made shit decisions, and I needed the cravings to stop.

I needed all of this to stop.

I drew up small amounts of both drugs into the syringe before finding a vein to insert the needle into. Even though the impact of the drugs themselves wasn't exactly immediate, it still gave me a sense of relief and comfort, knowing I would soon find that place I wanted to be in.

I stood in the pharmacy for a short period of time, waiting for the effects of the injection to kick in. I looked at the white cabinets and shelves I'd looted and then up at the ceiling, where there was one small stain from the evidence of a leak. As I found the lights scattered throughout the ceiling, they turned to blurs, and I felt myself drifting into that high that I so desperately longed for.

Only this time I had the strangest hallucination.

"Sammi?" Sophie said in a confused tone. Grace rested gently in her arms.

My legs didn't even feel like they were attached to my body; I was weak and numb. Everything I looked at was black or splotchy, including Sophie and Grace. The sedative effects of the drugs were kicking in, and before I knew it, everything went black, and Grace and Sophie were gone.

I have no clue how much time passed, but when I woke up, I could hear Sophie's voice.

"Sammi, wake up. We need to get out of here," she said in a worried whisper.

I blinked several times to clear my vision before realizing this wasn't a hallucination. Sophie was really here, and so was Grace. They were alive. The three of us were on the floor, hidden behind the counter in the center of the room.

"You're both here. How?" was all I managed to slur.

"There's no time to explain. We need to get out of here before they find us," she whispered.

It was then we heard the door open. She quickly held her finger up to her mouth, signaling for me to keep quiet while the person investigated the pharmacy. Unfortunately, there was plenty of evidence that I'd been here—from the vials and syringes left on the countertop, to the ransacked shelves. It wouldn't take them long to figure out that we were hiding here.

I feared what Sophie knew about this place, and I dreaded what would happen if we were found.

I'd find out soon enough, because Grace made some of her sweet baby noises, which gave the person the green light that someone was hiding out in here.

I closed my eyes anxiously, reopening them once the person revealed themselves. I'd never in my life seen anyone that looked so far gone and completely mad. I felt like I was in a house of horrors.

I screamed as I made eye contact with this … thing. I wasn't even sure it was still a person.

They had a perfectly bald head with the darkest veins I'd ever seen pulsing on their scalp and around their face. Their eyes were almost black, like there wasn't a soul behind them. They had dark circles around their eyes, and their teeth had been filed into sharp, pointed shapes that became known when they gave me a sinister smile.

I continued screaming as Sophie and I scrambled to stand and ran. Only I didn't. It was like I froze; I thought I was moving quickly, but in reality I was functioning in slow motion.

Sophie managed to run quick enough to escape the pharmacy, and part of me was relieved that she made it away with Grace, but the other part of me was terrified of what this place was.

The thing grabbed my arm, dragging me across the pharmacy as I continued to scream. They laughed psychotically before sinking their teeth into my arm like a fucking vampire, only this was its way of inflicting pain, not supernatural feeding.

My skin crawled at the thought of this horrific person biting me like some kind of rabid animal. And it did it over and over, leaving bloody holes all over while I kicked and fought against it.

They dragged me down the hall and through the double doors of the psychiatric unit, where I was thrown into a room with several others who seemed either as afraid as me, or who were almost too far gone, like the thing I'd just encountered.

The door slammed shut behind me, and I slunk into the far corner. The bloody bites on my arms stung so badly, but I had a feeling that wouldn't be the worst thing that would happen to me here.

To distract myself from the reality of my new surroundings, I gazed around the room, observing the space. I noticed one group of women on the left side sobbing hysterically against the wall.

In the very back, there were a few women eating something, but I couldn't quite make out what it was—until I saw one of them cleaning off a human humerus.

My eyes widened, and I turned toward the right side of the room, where another set of women had their eyes and mouths sewed shut. No joke, their fucking lips were completely stitched closed, and you could see no part of their eyes, only their eyelids sealed together. They were propped up against the wall like puppets, not moving, and possibly not even alive.

I pulled my knees up to my chest, shaking from the beginnings of a full-blown panic attack, thinking of all that could happen to me while I was trapped here.

Jesus fucking Christ. I'm going to die here. I was certain of it.

~

Sophie's point of view

"Hang in there, Grace. We're getting out of here," I said, struggling to catch my breath as I carried her down the stairs toward the exit. My adrenaline was in full force, immediately sending me into fight or flight mode.

I sincerely hated the thought of leaving Sammi behind, but I was banking on the chance that she'd survive long enough for me to find Caleb, Jackson, and Bailey. They were the only chance we had of winning this fight and saving Sammi—or anyone—from this insane asylum. I had to find them.

I *had* to.

I rushed to the exit door and raced toward a gray sedan parked conveniently by the main entrance. I turned to look behind me, and thankfully it appeared no one had seen my escape.

I wished I could've elaborated more about that hellhole to Sammi or given her insight on the weak points within the hospital—like how there were only maybe eight of the psychopaths living there. Everyone else was an unfortunate victim. It was a huge hospital, and the people living there never explored the majority of the building; they tended to stay tucked away in their hallway unless they were in need of new victims or heard someone creeping around. There were opportunities to get out. I managed to.

I was on my way out when I saw Sammi in the pharmacy. It caught me off guard to see her, but I immediately knew what she was doing there—finding her next fix, probably behind everyone's back. I couldn't leave her high and unconscious in that place. She'd proudly displayed evidence of her presence with vials and syringes chaotically tossed on the counter, and I knew they'd find her if I left her there to linger. I needed to show her that Grace and I were alive, and I'd truly hoped I could get all three of us out together safely.

It just didn't work out that way.

I approached the vehicle and I swung open the door, sighing a breath of relief upon discovering the keys in the ignition. There was no car seat, so I kept Grace in one arm, started the engine, and raced away from the hospital of horrors, leaving Sammi to fend for herself for the time being.

I knew it would be risky to drive toward the neighborhood where the giant herd of zombies bulldozed through yesterday, but that's where I'd last seen any of my friends. It would be my best chance at finding any of the guys.

I drove in that direction for a few miles as the sun slowly began to rise in the distance. It was still mostly dark, but you could see hints of the sun's glow behind the foggy sky. I held my foot on the gas, my heart racing from everything I'd experienced over the past twelve hours. The roads were clear, giving me ease to speed down each stretch, until I saw a set of headlights approaching me.

I worried that any person I encountered would be the psycho that picked me and Grace up not too far from Bailey's neighborhood when I made a run for it from the zombies. I didn't know too much about the freaks from the hospital, but I did know that they had one designated individual that drove around the area to find victims to bring back. Probably because not too many people wandered around anymore, and they were running low on innocent victims to force cannibalism upon, or who they could stitch up like rag dolls for some disturbing maniacal reason.

I was afraid—no, *terrified* of who might be in the car heading in my direction. I thought about turning my headlights off and swerving down the street I was passing, but it was too late; I knew I'd already been seen. The only thing I could do was stay strong and see what came of this.

I continued driving until the headlights began to blind me as they grew closer. My heart began to race and my palms grew sweaty. I looked down at Grace worriedly. She was still cradled in my arm, the other steering us away from potential danger.

I glanced up at the rear-view mirror and noticed the car behind flashing their high beams at me, off and on, off and on. It was strange; it almost seemed like they were trying to get my attention, rather than harm me. They could've easily run me off the road or chased me belligerently, but they kept a safe distance between us, still flashing their lights.

I finally decided to pull over, realizing whoever was in the car probably wasn't a psychotic killer. I couldn't know for sure, but I did know that I had no weapons and would only continue to be followed the entire ride to Bailey's neighborhood, and it wasn't safe to drive so erratically, especially while I was carrying Grace. I figured I could die now or die in a few minutes; that's just how this new world worked.

I shut my eyes briefly, nervously waiting for the car to come to a stop at my rear bumper. When it did, the driver exited the car, leaving their door wide open. They approached my window, and I hesitantly rolled it down, revealing the person who'd been following me.

I let out the biggest sigh of relief when I discovered it was Caleb.

"Sam— *Sophie?*"

"Hey," I said. I gave him a watery smile, tears of joy streaming down my face.

He returned the same warm smile, peering down at Grace in my arms, but his expression turned to one of concern upon realizing it was only the two of us in the car.

"Sammi … she took this car while me and Jackson were sleeping. How did you—"

I interrupted. "We don't have much time. Sammi is in trouble. I was trying to find you guys because I need your help; I can't save her on my own. Do you have any weapons on you?" I asked.

He looked at me in despair, but before he could say anything, Jackson exited the other vehicle. When he found a spot beside Caleb, he shared the same worry when he realized it wasn't Sammi in the car.

It was a painful reminder that he chose her, always. For several years I'd desperately wished he'd look at me the way he looked at Sammi. It solidified the constant feeling of rejection and jealousy I housed every time we'd been a couple, and even the months between when I'd sit in my bed and cry all day, wishing I could offer him the same level of comfort and love that she did. No matter how hard I tried, I never gave those feelings to him, or anyone.

I wanted them to be happy I was alive. I wanted reassurance that I wasn't a burden to them. I wanted them to accept me as a part of their family. I wanted them to drop everything and risk their lives without debating if I was in danger or missing, like I had been for some twelve hours.

A part of me felt like if Grace hadn't been missing with me, they never would've considered pursuing a search to see if I made it out somehow. I would've been another name on a long list of people lost along the way. But instead, I was dead weight, dragging them down every step of the way, no matter what.

I desperately needed to find my place in this world, and no matter how bad I wanted it to be with Sammi and the others, I didn't think I'd ever fit into their bubble. I strongly considered going my own way after reuniting everyone. Maybe I could find another group. Or maybe I could just live alone for weeks, or months, or years to come, until I was bitten or murdered by one of the few people left in this shit world.

I just needed Sammi to survive, because if she didn't, I feared Caleb, Jackson, and Bailey would blame me for leaving her behind in the first place. I didn't think they would see it how I did. It would simply be my fault.

I frowned when Jackson gave me that look, asking, "Where's Sammi?"

"She's at the hospital in town. We need to hurry back," I said insistently.

"What kind of trouble is she in, Sophie?" Caleb asked in a concerned manner.

"Just get any weapons you have and get in. I'll explain on the way."

The two of them ran back to the car they'd been driving and grabbed a few knives and a single handgun they explained they'd found hidden within the newly acquired vehicle. Once they retrieved all that they could, they shut the doors and hopped into the car with me. Caleb took the front passenger seat, and Jackson took the back.

I turned to look at Jackson, then over to Caleb, before realizing that Bailey hadn't been in the car with them. "Where's Bailey?"

Caleb pursed his lips as he shook his head.

I frowned and gently handed Grace to Caleb, then U-turned back in the direction of the hospital as the three of us caught up on the most recent events.

"When the big herd came through, the four of us ran into one of the houses nearby until it blew over. While we were there, some kid with a gun came out and killed Bailey right in front of Sammi. Shot him right in the head. It was awful," Caleb said sadly.

"That explains a lot," I replied. My heart sank as I thought about Sammi witnessing the father of her child being taken away from her in a matter of seconds, based on one small decision and one wrong house.

"What do you mean?" Jackson asked.

I continued driving, speaking to him through the rear-view mirror. "While y'all were hiding from the herd, Lola and I were trying to do the same. Only Grace started crying, and it rang the dinner bell for dozens of them to break through the door of Bailey's house. When I saw them surrounding Lola, I grabbed Grace and took off running . I kept running until this car pulled up. It was this normal-looking man who was wearing a white coat, like a doctor. He told me he could help me find you guys, so I got in and tried to tell him which direction I thought you'd gone. He sped away from the neighborhood, and I knew then that he never intended on helping me. He told me there was no point in trying to escape; that I couldn't jump out of a moving vehicle with a baby," I began.

They hung on to every word I said.

"Where did he take you?" Caleb asked.

"The hospital in town," I told him, and they both grew looks of concern.

"And that's where Sammi is now?" Caleb said.

I nodded sadly.

"I don't understand," Jackson said.

"I escaped with Grace. I was on my way out of that place when I saw Sammi shooting up some fucking drugs in the pharmacy. I wasn't going to leave her there while she was high, but right after she sobered up just enough, one of the freaks found us. I got away, but she didn't."

"She left in the middle of the night to go find ketamine?" Jackson asked helplessly.

I nodded once again.

"So, what kind of people are we dealing with? You called them freaks," Caleb asked, gently rocking Grace in his arms as we grew closer to the parking lot.

I began to explain what I'd learned from one of the long-term hostages I met while trapped in the Hospital of Horrors: "When the world went to shit, the hospital employees abandoned the place. Most of the patients were killed by the soldiers or got away somehow, but the employees had locked the psychiatric patients inside the department's hallway, leaving them to die. They lived amongst each other, thriving off of each other's delusions and desires, until the power shut off for around thirty seconds before the backup generator came on. The security measures in place to keep the automatic doors locked were no longer effective without someone there to re-initiate it, and they were able to escape. But while they were isolated from everything, they turned to cannibalism and human torture tactics. They're not people anymore, Caleb. They experiment on innocent women, sewing their eyes and mouths shut, attempting lobotomy procedures, and whisking away every sane bone in their hostages' bodies."

"Is there anything you can tell me that will make me freak out less?" he asked.

"There are only eight of them left. If we can find them while they're spread out, we can kill them and save Sammi and the others they have held up inside."

"Do you think she has the capability to survive there until we can save her?" Jackson asked.

"I wouldn't have left her behind if I didn't," I said. "Grace and I did it for twelve hours," I added, thinking back to the grueling memories of watching women tear each other apart and wishing I could help those who had no quality of life without a way to eat or see from having thread stitched through their skin.

The two of them remained silent as I turned into the hospital parking lot.

I grew alarmed when I noticed a cloud of smoke rising from the building. I sat up straighter in my seat as I watched angry flames fill the windows of the hospital floor Sammi was being held on.

My heart dropped for Caleb and Jackson, and I immediately felt like I'd failed them. I knew I would be chastised for this.

When I pulled up to the front entrance, no one moved for several seconds. Caleb pursed his lips and looked away as if he were holding back tears. I placed my hands over my eyes and drew a deep breath.

Suddenly Jackson opened his door and took off running. Caleb and I looked up to see where he was going. Surely running into that burning building to save Sammi was a lost cause?

But then something miraculous happened. Sammi pushed through the stairwell door, running toward the car. Jackson met her with the biggest hug, squeezing her tightly.

I'd never felt so relieved in my life.

But then another thought hit me. Now that she'd been found safely, I would need to start thinking about where I would go next. I needed to find my role within another group.

At least, that was my thought—until Caleb grabbed my face and pulled it toward his. He kissed me gently on the lips before pressing his forehead against mine and whispering, "Thank you, Sophie."

I wanted to smile like an idiot, and I did, because I couldn't hold it back. I'd honestly never thought about pursuing anything with Caleb, mainly because he was Jackson's best friend and Sammi's brother, but he'd just opened up a whole new world for me—a world where I belonged, and a world I wanted to be in.

~

Sammi's point of view

"Are you okay?" Jackson asked as he held me tightly in his arms.

"I am now," I said, sighing a breath of relief, grateful to finally be back together and safe.

I was beginning to think that everyone left in this world was batshit crazy. The zombie apocalypse had brought out the true reality of what people were capable of.

I'd sat in that room for what seemed like forever, planning a way to escape. I'd be lying if I said that plan included saving the other innocent people there, but it didn't. It was solely about my wellbeing and getting back to my family.

And it worked. It fucking worked.

But I'll never forget the screams and pleas for help from the victims locked behind the doors.

Once he and I released our hug, we found our way into the backseat of the car. Seeing Sophie, Caleb, and Grace made me sob with relief, and I reached over to hug my daughter and brother.

Then I looked at Sophie, full of appreciation that, in the midst of the herd attack that killed Lola, Sophie found it in her heart to risk everything to save Grace too. She'd earned my trust a million times over. I'd never forget that.

"Sammi, are you okay?" Caleb asked, turning to look at me.

"I'm okay," I said, forcing a smile.

Once the car was back on the road, Sophie glanced up at me through the rear-view mirror as she said, "Sammi, I'm so sorry I left you. I thought I was doing the right thing. I was going to find Caleb and Jackson."

"I know. You did exactly what I would've done," I said gently.

"What happened in there?" she asked, fear in her eyes.

I explained my short but horrific time in the psychiatric unit, and how they'd taken me to the room with the others.

I'd sat there for a while, watching them cry and eat each other and scream. I soon noticed that a man dressed like a doctor was standing outside of the door, smoking a cigarette in the hallway. I kept watching him, realizing the cannibalistic girls were eyeing me from across the room. For some reason, they'd marked me as their next meal, and I was not going out that way.

So I knocked on the door of the room to get the doctor's attention. He cracked open the door, and I asked him if I could have one of his cigarettes. He'd looked confused at first, but he took one out of the pack to light it.

Before he could react, I took the pocketknife from his lab coat and slit his throat, right as the girls took off running after me. I grabbed the lighter before pushing his body into the room and locking the door, leaving him as their next meal.

Knowing I couldn't leave them to continue their torture and worried they would come after me, I headed back to the pharmacy and found tons of isopropyl alcohol. I dumped the containers down the entire hallway behind the psychiatric unit double doors and set it on fire with the lighter.

Then I ran as fast as I could to the control panel on the floor and locked the doors. Everyone inside was trapped, burning with the hospital. I felt sick with guilt, but I had to save myself.

"Oh my God," Sophie said as I finished my story.

"I put you all in danger, again. I'm sorry. One of these days it'll just be best for you guys to leave me behind," I added, looking down at my bleeding fingers that I'd been picking as I told them what happened.

"We'd never leave you behind—or anyone in this group. We're a family." Caleb glanced at Sophie as he said this.

Weird. I got the feeling that there was something going on there, and while it should have been strange for my brother to date my boyfriend's ex, it made me happy. For the first time in a while, it seemed like everything might be okay.

"So, what's next?" I asked, feeling more positive.

"We need to get the fuck out of Nashville," Caleb said.

25

HOPE ON THE HORIZON

AFTER EVERYTHING THAT HAPPENED in Nashville—Bailey and Lola's deaths, the freaks at the hospital, and the fatalities I was responsible for—we decided we shouldn't waste any more time lingering in that godforsaken place. We headed north once again toward the infectious disease research laboratory in Missouri that Lola had talked about.

I was nervous. I couldn't deny it. I was hoping I would swoop back into the dark reality at least one more time before we arrived so that I could have something to go off of if we did find a researcher or scientist, but it seemed like for now all I had was the small glimmer of the idea of a cure being possible—I just didn't know how.

I didn't know how I would explain that to a doctor either.

"Yeah, every now and then I fall into this parallel universe where the zombies aren't zombies, even though you see them as zombies. I talk to them, and they talk to me—and they told me there's a loophole for a cure."

It sounded insane. They would literally think I was mental, but it was the truth. And if zombies were possible, shouldn't that be proof enough that this was within the realm of possibility?

So, still hopeful of finding this mystery loophole cure, we drove straight to the University of Missouri without any detours.

Once in the parking lot, we stared up at the huge buildings anxiously. There were scattered zombies roaming around; probably students just starting their independent lives when the soldiers started killing people. Most of the lingering zombies were still wearing fraternity and sorority tees or collegiate gear that once defined their place on this campus.

Being here brought back memories of my time in college. I'd spent four years working so hard for a degree I would probably never get the opportunity to use. But in those four years, I dealt with some of the biggest heartaches I'd ever encountered that played a role in defining who I was today and the relationships I had, especially with Jackson and Caleb.

The biggest shift in my life occurred when I was at the end of my freshman year of nursing school. I was attending New York University, which was about three hours away from Schoharie, the city I grew up in. My parents had been raving on and on about how they missed me and wanted to meet my nonexistent friends and see my dorm I'd decorated in all of my favorite pastel colors. I was their baby, so they were still adjusting to an empty nest back at home while I was away.

I hadn't really made any friends, but I was too embarrassed to admit that to them. They had been confident that I would be flooded with friends once I started school, and that gave them peace in knowing I would never be alone. But the truth of the matter was that I was alone more than not. My roommate was never around, and we rarely spoke when she was.

I was lonely and missing home, so when my parents texted to see if it would be a good weekend for them to drive down, I was ecstatic.

They were on the road within minutes, and I sat by the clock all morning, waiting for them to arrive. I'd framed a collage of pictures of me and Caleb to gift to them once they got here, and I smiled to myself, knowing they would love it. I held on to it for hours and hours, eager to show them and be filled with the happiness they always delivered in their presence.

When the afternoon came and I hadn't heard from them, a pit developed in my stomach. That feeling when your heart seems like it's beating through your fingertips; when you feel pale from your blood pressure bottoming out; or when you're on the edge of a cliff, looking down at the long drop to the dark hole below.

I just knew something was wrong.

I called their phones and left messages over and over until it finally stopped ringing when their voicemails were full. I laid down in my bed in a panic, trying to figure out what to do. I eventually picked up my phone and called Caleb, who answered after two rings.

"Hello?" he answered casually.

"Caleb, have you heard from Mom and Dad? They were coming to visit me, but they should've been here hours ago. I can't get them to pick up," I said nervously.

"No, I haven't. I can try to call them if you want me to?" he suggested.

My reply was halted by a knock on my dorm door.

"Hold on, Caleb, I think that's them," I said.

I ran quickly to open it, smiling because I thought it would be my sweet parents waiting to surprise me. Instead, I was greeted by two police officers with glum expressions on their faces. I knew they weren't here for any good reasons.

My phone slipped out of my grasp. I could distinctly hear Caleb still talking, asking if it was our parents. His tone became concerned once he heard me begin to sob helplessly and uncontrollably.

The police officers tried to console me as they began explaining that a car accident had taken the lives of both of my parents. They said a tractor trailer's brakes went out while going through a traffic light at about eighty miles per hour. My parents, who were driving across the intersection, didn't have time to react to the horn of the massive truck hauling down the hill, straight toward their vehicle.

They both died on impact. And it happened one mile away from campus.

One.

Fucking.

Mile.

My heart shattered into a million pieces, and I had never fully recovered. I blamed myself for a long time, constantly thinking that if I hadn't been so incapable of finding friends, my parents wouldn't have been on their way to me that day. They would've encouraged me to go out and make memories.

But I didn't want that. I'd just wanted my parents to be here to hold me and see all I'd accomplished in my first year of college.

I'd bawled my eyes out for hours while Caleb hopped on the first plane he could to New York. We were both extremely close to our parents, so it was a detrimental loss to me and him. It was a detrimental loss to the world.

Caleb found me curled up in my bed with red, swollen eyes. He climbed in to hold me, trying to be strong for the both of us. Neither of us spoke a word; we just stayed in each other's company until we found the strength to stand.

A part of me hoped that Caleb would finally give up on the idea of Oklahoma and come back to New York, but he just couldn't move past the life he'd built down there. He stayed around long enough to help me plan a funeral, and after the headstones were laid on their graves, he went back to Pocola. I tried to understand why he felt like Oklahoma was home for him, but I'd never comprehended the connection he had with it.

The night of their funeral, I found myself sitting on the wet asphalt of the dark parking lot behind the funeral home, wearing a silky black dress symbolizing death and grief.

I was startled when someone walked up behind me, gently rubbing my shoulder before joining me on the ground. I turned to my right to see who it was, and it was Jackson. He'd flown all the way to New York to attend my parents' funeral. Even though subconsciously I knew he was here in support of Caleb, it still meant something to me that he'd come at all.

Jackson and I weren't super close at that point, but we had shared a few conversations from time to time during previous encounters. He always made me feel comfortable in his presence; his careful, gentle demeanor taking me to places no one else could.

He wrapped his arm around me before giving me a gentle kiss on my cheek. I rested my head on his shoulder, taking in everything that had happened. It didn't feel real.

After my parents' funeral, I really shifted as a person. I'd known about my bipolar disorder for several years, but it had been controlled until that point. I stopped taking my medication and spiraled during a manic episode on campus, and that's when I was hospitalized for a period of time while I recovered mentally. I wasn't there against my will, but I didn't feel like I could leave because I wasn't ready to be on my own again.

Caleb came and visited regularly whenever he could get time off at work, and I held out hope that one day I'd see Jackson walking through the door with him.

I always felt like Jackson saw me when no one else did. Or maybe I was just being delusional about his gestures. Besides, he was with Sophie at that time. Was he just comforting me because I was his best friend's sister? Did he genuinely care? I battled with that for several days while I was in the inpatient facility.

Then, one day, Jackson did walk through that door.

I was lying in bed, facing away from the door, when I heard it open. I assumed it was a nurse or Caleb, so I continued to sulk and ponder my thoughts—until I saw his face.

He looked sad. Broken, even.

I furrowed my brows in confusion while quickly sitting up in bed. It made me nauseous, seeing him distraught like this, and I wanted nothing more than to make his pain go away.

I watched as he sat down in the chair beside my bed and buried his face in his hands.

"Jackson?"

"My mom died last night," he choked out, tears rolling down his puffy cheeks.

My heart sank. "Oh, Jackson. I'm so sorry. What happened?"

"She had a heart attack," he said, crying into his palms.

I picked at the skin around my fingernails as I tried to think of ways to make him feel better, like he had done for me when I was in his position not all that long ago. I knew from experience that there was nothing anyone could say to make it better or to make the sadness magically go away somehow. All I could offer was moral support, because I knew it was not easy going through that kind of loss alone.

So, we sat there in silence, taking comfort in each other's company the entire night. Nothing happened between us—it seemed like it never would—but I was okay with that.

The bond we had after that day was more important than any romantic relationship we could have had. But now that I'd had the opportunity to experience what it was like to be loved by Jackson, I never wanted to lose him.

He was the strength I needed to carry on each day.

He was the air I needed to breathe.

He was my beginning and my ending.

He was my everything.

As I later learned, to be loved by Jackson was consummate, remarkable, and incomparable to anything else in this ordinary world.

And now we were sitting in front of our last hope of a cure.

I looked down and took a deep breath as Jackson grabbed my hand, squeezing it gently. Caleb smiled up at me through the rear-view mirror, and we all simultaneously exited the car.

The heat from the sun beaming onto my skin felt so rejuvenating.

I looked over at Sophie, smiling at the sight of her and Grace, who she'd been holding for the last hour of the car ride. Sophie was so good with her. She kept Grace calm and happy, and it made me see Sophie in a different light. She was becoming worthy of my trust and love, and part of this small family I had now. I could see potential for her and my brother, which seemed so weird, but it was true. I knew he would bring out the best in her, like he did with everyone he met.

I gazed up at the big sign displaying the name of the school, before slowly walking toward the entrance. The campus was huge and filled with tons of buildings. None of us had ever been here before, so I knew we'd have to do a little exploring before we found the research laboratory. I figured the best place to start would be at the registrar and admission offices.

I was the first one to walk through the doors. We were greeted by a musty smell which wasn't unusual nowadays. There was no power, but luckily the natural light shining through the windows and doors helped illuminate most of the inside.

The first thing I noticed was a huge glass trophy case positioned straight ahead, filled with dozens of awards, metals, trophies, and team pictures. To the left I saw a financial aid office as well as a few other small offices, and to the right was a longer hallway full of more offices and a door at the end that presumably led back outside.

I began taking careful steps in that direction before stopping in front of a door that said "Karen Hayes, Admissions Counselor" in white letters across the frosted glass. The room appeared dark behind the window positioned in the center of the door.

I turned the knob and entered, immediately met by a lone zombie dressed in a light pink sundress, blood oozing through the fabric. It was a heavy-set woman with brown hair and brassy highlights surrounding her graying skin. On her dress there was a name tag with the name "Karen Hayes" embedded on it.

She lunged after me, her body seemingly unsteady over the two feet beneath her. Her jaw extended open and shut like an angry snapping turtle, her teeth clanking together each time.

I didn't have a weapon on me, so I kept both of my hands pressed against the decaying body to protect myself from being bitten. I gazed around the room for something to kill it with as Caleb and the others nervously watched from the doorway. Apparently we'd now encountered enough zombies that finding one alone wasn't too much cause for concern.

Eventually, Jackson stepped up behind me, reaching over and stabbing his knife straight into her head.

For a second I felt weak, entranced by the feeling of his body pressed up against mine and the sensation of his breath on my neck when he whispered, "I know you could've handled it, but I just wanted an excuse to get close to you."

God, it sent chills down my spine.

I smiled, hoping he wouldn't notice, but he knew what he was doing. He always did.

I watched the zombie collapse to the floor. There were small traces of blood underneath my fingernails from my hands sinking into its softened flesh.

Jackson stuck the knife back down into its holster. His eyes met mine, and I gave him a devilish smile before brushing past him to continue exploring the office.

Caleb, Sophie, and Grace hung back in the hallway while the two of us rooted around in the room. It wasn't long before I found a brochure with the layout of campus bunched up in a clear plastic bin attached to the wall. I unfolded it and stepped back out into the hallway to get a better look at it with the light beaming in from the nearby door.

Studying the paper, Caleb pointed at the right-hand corner, recognizing the laboratory labeled on the page.

"Okay, so the lab is on the back side of campus, and this is where we are now," he said, moving his finger to the building we were currently in.

"Lead the way," I suggested, and Caleb nodded, taking the map. He took off toward the door at the end of the hallway, with Sophie and Grace right behind him, and Jackson and I lingering in the back.

We stepped outside onto the concrete sidewalk and I watched as my brother eagerly took us in the direction of the laboratory. He was using the brochure as if it were a map that led to buried treasure with an X marked on top. Finding the laboratory with a doctor or scientist in it would be like finding treasure. I knew it would feel that way for me, at least.

I guess I was drowning in my own thoughts while we walked in silence, because I jumped slightly when Jackson called my name.

"Sammi," he repeated.

"What? I'm sorry," I said, blinking and turning to face him.

"Are you okay?"

"Yeah, I'm fine," I said, rubbing my arms and staring blankly at him. "No, actually, I'm not. Uh, I'm nervous, and I'm fiending," I admitted as I battled with feeling uncomfortable, unable to keep my hands and arms still.

"Is there anything I can do?" he asked helplessly.

I frowned and shook my head, refraining from elaborating further.

It was a particularly warm day, with summer beginning to heat up, and I could feel sweat rolling down my back with each step we took across campus.

We were approaching an open courtyard filled with a dozen or so zombies walking in confused circles—until the wind carried our scent to them. Then their aimless wandering turned to beelines toward the five of us. My first thought was protecting Grace, so I instructed Sophie to keep her distance and stay back.

Caleb and Jackson both had knives on them to use as weapons, but I had nothing. I scanned the area in hopes of finding something, anything, when Sophie got my attention, pointing to an abandoned tool bag by a nearby maintenance shed. I ran over to it while Caleb and Jackson distracted the group of zombies, killing them one by one while trying to avoid being bitten in the process.

I dug around in the bag until I pulled out a hammer. But as I turned back to join them, I realized one of the zombies had snuck up behind me, grabbing onto my shoulder. I panicked, trying to push it away until I was able to get a proper grip on the hammer. I finally found the opportunity to drive the curved end of the hammer into its head.

But I barely had a chance to collect myself, because a second zombie was coming after me. The first zombie collapsed, and I tried to remove the hammer from its skull. I struggled for several seconds, becoming overwhelmed with defeat.

"Seriously?" I grumbled to myself in annoyance before giving up my efforts to salvage the weapon.

Caleb and Jackson had almost cleared the rest of the zombies. Only three remained, including the one currently trying to kill me. I was running out of options, so I decided to see if the maintenance shed door was unlocked.

I grabbed the handle, discovering that it was open, and the zombie and I found our way into the dark, damp shed. I could no longer see the zombie because the door had shut behind it, eliminating any light from the sun. I knew it would still be able to find me despite the darkness, because I was tripping and falling over numerous objects, basically waving a red flag in front of an angry bull.

I continued to stumble over equipment and tools, blindly feeling for anything I could until I got my hands on what felt like a power drill. At that point I was banking on good faith and a charged battery to kill this zombie, so I plunged the drill bit toward its temple, holding down the button and hoping for the best.

To my surprise, the battery had a little bit of juice left and drilled straight into the zombie's brain. It fell to the ground and I was just about to relax when I felt something crawl across my hand. I screamed bloody murder, frantically shaking and wiping off the spider.

Caleb and Jackson swung open the door, and I tried to catch my breath as the two of them hurried over to me.

"Did you get bitten? Are you hurt?" Caleb asked frantically.

"Uh, no," I said, shivering from disgust at the sensation of such an intricate, tiny creature crawling over my skin.

"Why did you scream?" Jackson asked, concerned.

"It's nothing," I said, brushing them off.

"Sammi," Jackson insisted.

"It was a spider, okay?" I said, displaying my disgust once more.

Jackson looked at Caleb and the two of them spouted out into laughter while I rolled my eyes irritably.

"It was gross," I said, storming back into the courtyard where Sophie and Grace awaited us.

"Do you even know where you're going?" Caleb asked playfully. They were following behind me, still chuckling to themselves.

"Ugh, just get me away from that shed," I said, stopping to wait until they caught back up to me, crossing my arms.

They continued to laugh and mock my girly antics, and even Sophie snickered once she saw that I was okay.

Caleb took another look at the brochure, and we began walking again. I knew we were getting close. My stomach was turning knots, thinking about each possible scenario upon entering this laboratory.

There could be nothing and no one left. Or there could be more psychopaths waiting to kill us. But maybe, just maybe, there were still people here formulating some kind of cure for those like me. I didn't want to get my hopes up, but I couldn't help but feel optimistic for once.

I looked up to see a big brick and metal building ahead of us. This was the university's laboratory for infectious diseases and research. My last chance to see if there was a future for me.

I stared up at it, intimidated by the power it held, just hoping we hadn't lost Ryan, Lola, and Bailey along this journey for nothing. I hoped the people I sacrificed and killed along the way at the expense of my own selfish protection weren't in vain.

I sighed deeply, walking ahead, continuing to close the gap between me and the answers I hoped I'd be given.

Once we reached the front of the laboratory building, I glanced at everyone in the group before finding the courage to enter. As we stepped inside, I got a whiff of clean, refreshing air for the first time in a while. Inside there was a narrow hallway that led to a big, secluded research area to the right, with a space to the left that led to supply closets, a conference room, and computer rooms.

Before I could even begin making my way down the hallway, I was met by a man who had just exited the room on the right. He was middle aged with graying brown hair and glasses. He looked well kept, and I couldn't help but become overwhelmed with excitement when I noticed he was wearing a white coat.

His eyes grew wide when he realized he wasn't alone. He stopped and looked at each of us before speaking. "Um, hello. I don't believe I've met any of you before."

"No, you haven't," I choked out.

"I suppose you've come here looking for something in particular. Is that right?" he asked, placing his hands in his coat pockets.

"Actually, yes. This is going to sound far-fetched, but I'm hoping there is someone here who has started working on a cure for…" I paused, looking around before shrugging my shoulders. "…this."

He looked down before smacking his lips together. "You wouldn't be the first person," he said with a hint of disdain.

"So, you know how it ends, right?" I asked, fishing for an ounce of sympathy.

He remained quiet while Caleb stepped up to speak. "My sister was given the infection somewhere around a year ago. She doesn't have much time to waste. If there is anything—" he began, but the man interrupted.

"I'm sorry. I can't help you," he said, before turning to walk away.

"That's it? You don't have anything?" Caleb asked angrily.

"I've tried hundreds upon hundreds of combinations of formulas in treating this disease, every single person in the same predicament as your sister. I'm afraid my research is nearing the conclusion of being incurable."

My heart dropped thousands of feet beneath the earth's surface as I tried to let this prognosis sink in. As I stood there, the world crashing down around me, Grace began crying. I turned toward Sophie as she tried gently rocking her, but she only continued crying.

Me too, Grace. Me too, I thought.

I held out my arms to grab her as the man started to walk away. "Come here, sweet pea. Mommy's got you," I said quietly, trying my best to hold back tears.

The man pivoted. "Is this your daughter?"

"Yes," I said with slight confusion. Grace's cries slowed down slightly.

"How old is she?"

"About three months," I said, rubbing her head softly.

"You were given the injection while you were pregnant?"

"Yes," I answered, watching as his demeanor changed drastically.

"Come on," he said, waving for us to follow him.

I turned to look at Jackson, who seemed optimistic. We followed the man back toward the research area. He took hurried steps toward the entrance of his big lab while we tried to keep up, then opened the door, holding it for all of us to enter.

Once we were inside, I saw another man who looked to be around my age with jet black hair, bright green eyes, sleeve tattoos, and a septum piercing. I'm not going to lie, he was very good looking, but there was something about him that was off-putting. I couldn't figure out why though.

I watched his body language once he saw me, and he seemed intrigued by my presence. I felt myself blush as he smiled at me with his perfect, white teeth.

Is he off-putting or am I trying to find a reason to avoid thinking about how attractive he is?

The man in the white coat made his way over to the attractive guy, introducing him to us.

"This is Gage. He's my assistant," he said, and Gage raised his hand to wave at us. "Gage, this is our next trial patient…"

"Sammi," I filled in.

"Sammi, I've never had anyone come here who received the injection while they were pregnant. This is incredible."

"So, what does that mean?" Caleb asked.

"I think Sammi's daughter could be the key factor in creating a cure for her infection. Think about it, we give pregnant mothers vaccinations all the time to help protect them and their babies from potential diseases. The babies can respond in a variety of ways, one of those being producing antibodies to protect against the active diseases incorporated in the vaccination. I can take antibodies from her child to create a cure for this disease, but it would be specific to her. It wouldn't work for anyone else," he explained. "But, if this works, it could open up a new world for my research."

I was ecstatic. I'd never even thought that Grace could be the loophole to this infection in my body, but it made so much sense. This was exactly what I'd hoped would come out of this journey. For once, something was going according to plan. For once, I felt like I was being given a second chance.

Or third.

Or fiftieth.

"It's going to take a bit of time to gather my thoughts and really understand the steps I need to take, but I can at least start doing some preliminary studies and learn about you and your daughter's immune systems and how you are each responding to the injection," he said, grabbing a clipboard.

"Can I get a blood sample from you?" Gage asked.

I nodded before taking a seat in the gray chair positioned beside him. He put a pair of gloves on before preparing to wrap a tourniquet around my arm. Once he got closer, I saw him staring at the needle marks on my arm.

"What happened there?" he asked.

"Um, I-I have an addiction to ketamine and fentanyl."

He laid the tourniquet down before turning to face the scientist, whose name I still didn't know.

"We'll need to wait until it's completely out of your system for the bloodwork portion of my research. That can take up to a month, but it's usually only a couple of weeks," the man said.

I looked down in embarrassment as Gage rubbed my shoulder, trying to comfort me. "It's not a big deal. We have a little bit of time to start planning out our next steps for curating this before we can accomplish anything anyways."

I forced a smile, but was still humiliated that this addiction continued to wreak havoc in my life.

"So, what should we do in the meantime?" Sophie asked.

"Well, Keith and I have been living in the dorms on the right side of campus since basically the beginning. We never stopped working after everything went down. People from all the world have come here after disappointment from other research facilities, and unfortunately, we've been another dead end on their list of destinations. Some of them moved on, others stuck around in hopes that we'd have a breakthrough, and others have died while battling the infection. There's a set of dorms right up the sidewalk that no one is staying in. You all are welcome to stay there until we can get this thing going. How's that sound?" Gage said warmly.

I looked at Caleb and Jackson, who nodded agreeably.

"You said others have stuck around. Are they still here?" Sophie asked.

"Some of them, yes. There's an apartment complex on the other side of campus where most of them live. Over time we've kind of become a little community," the scientist—Keith—said.

"What does your stock of food look like?" Caleb asked.

"Well, there's a dining hall in the middle of campus with leftovers from before, and the people that live here help keep the pantry stocked. You are welcome to anything, we just ask that you help whenever you can," he said.

"Of course," Caleb said politely.

"Oh, and I forgot to mention that this campus runs off of solar panels and wind turbines, so you will have hot water and power in most areas, except for a few buildings."

We all smiled at that, eager to relax for once.

"Let's plan to try and get blood work again in two weeks, once the drugs are out of your system. I am eager to begin this process," Keith said confidently.

I nodded, and we all dismissed ourselves to find our next home within the dorms.

~

We all found rooms close to each other on the second floor of the dormitory. Jackson and I were staying with Grace, and Caleb and Sophie had their own separate rooms, although something told me that it may not stay that way for long with the vibes I was picking up on between the two of them.

While Jackson was checking out our room, I met Caleb in the hallway.

"So, I have a favor to ask," I said hesitantly, holding Grace.

"Yes, I'll take her," he said.

"You don't even know what I was going to ask!" I protested, narrowing my eyes in annoyance.

"You want me to watch Grace because you want some alone time with Jackson," he said, raising his eyebrows and folding his arms, a smug expression on his face.

I rolled my eyes. He knew me too well. "Actually, yes."

He held out his arms, taking Grace from me.

"You're the best," I said, hurrying back to my room.

The dorm Jackson and I found had two twin beds on opposite sides of the room. We pushed them together to make one big bed, and I plopped on top of it, desperate to relax.

Jackson climbed on top of me playfully, and I smiled up at him. He looked genuinely happy for the first time in quite a while. It was infectious.

"I love you," he said, kissing me all over.

I giggled and jerked around, feeling ticklish. "I love you, too."

"You heard him say hot water too, right?" Jackson asked, raising a brow.

"Oh yeah," I said, and he pulled me up off the bed, carrying me to the bathroom.

He sat my feet down on the cold tile floor before the two of us quickly undressed. Then he reached into the shower to turn the water on, and soon enough we were both inside, letting the warm water embrace our bodies.

It had been a long time since I'd felt entirely clean and comfortable in my own skin, but that would change with this newly acquired living situation. I was hoping we'd be here for a while because I was getting tired of being a vagabond. I wanted so badly to settle down with Jackson and the others and finally feel a sense of security.

Once we'd freshened up in the shower, we began drying off with two soft towels. I wrapped mine around my body, my damp hair resting over my shoulders. Jackson dried off with his and dropped it to the floor before walking up behind me.

God, I was like a dog in heat. I simply melted when he was close to me, touching me, kissing me.

Standing behind me, he gently kissed my neck, sending shivers up my spine and tingles through my stomach when he whispered in my ear, "Get on the bed."

He could cast a spell on me with his words and touch. Everything about him consumed me in a way that made me susceptible to do anything he wanted. He could say jump, and I'd ask how high.

I made my way to the bed, dropping my towel to the floor, and he followed quickly behind me. I couldn't tell you how long we were at it, but we migrated from the bed to the bathroom counter, to the desk, and finally to the floor.

I'm weak in the knees just thinking about it.

I could get used to this.

26

LIES AND LIES

FOR A LITTLE OVER two weeks, we all lived a semi-normal life in the dormitory. We had food, shelter, water, and most importantly we had a researcher dedicating his time to finding a cure for me. For once, I had hope for my future.

Things between Jackson and I were also exciting and perfect.

I will say though that regardless of how great my life was in this small window of a moment, I still had demons I was battling. I could not seem to shake my cravings for the drugs. Yet again, I was lying to myself and my family about being sober, when in reality, I'd made a pit stop before leaving the hospital after I sent it up in flames that day. I walked back through the pharmacy and filled my jacket pockets up completely with vials and syringes, keeping them a secret from the others this entire time.

So typical, Sammi.

Each night when Jackson fell asleep, I injected myself with more and more of the drugs, even though doing so meant prolonging the time until research for the cure could begin—and also being subjected to wearing long sleeves in the summer to disguise my bruised arms.

I needed to be clean for them to do the blood work, and with today being the day that it was expected all the drugs would have left my system,

I knew the cards would be put face-up on the table for everyone to see. But I couldn't let that happen, so I went in search of Gage to seek advice. I'd started to feel comfortable with him, and I hoped he could give me insight on how to proceed.

I found him in the research laboratory early that morning. As usual, he was sitting in his chair, wearing black converse and ripped skinny jeans that he wore cuffed at the bottom. He smiled once he saw me, but it quickly changed to a worried expression as he noticed that I had been crying. He sat up straighter in his seat, watching as I took slow steps toward him.

"Sammi, what's wrong?"

"I know we're planning on getting blood work today, but I've got to be honest with you, I'm not clean," I said with a sniffle.

"Did you find drugs on campus?" he asked, slightly confused.

"No, I had a stash from before that they didn't know about," I confessed.

He gave me a saddened smile.

"I don't know how to move past this. I've tried getting sober before, but I always relapse. The detoxification is excruciating."

"I can try to come up with a reason to wait a little bit longer if you're afraid of how your friends will react," he suggested.

"I hate making this your burden to bear," I said, feeling guilty for dragging him into this.

"It's okay, I promise," he said, patting my hand sympathetically and gesturing for me to take a seat next to him.

After a lingering pause, I decided to confide in him about how my addiction began—that ketamine and fentanyl were what I'd prescribed myself with as the only way to cope after Dillion's torture.

"Just under two months ago, I was kidnapped. They tortured me and injected me with a ketamine and fentanyl mixture, sometimes multiple times a day. It was the only thing that allowed me to cope and move forward each day I was there because it gave me hallucinations of what I needed to carry on. Now it seems like it's the only thing that makes life manageable, especially when I keep losing people I care about."

"I had no idea. I am so sorry, Sammi."

"It's okay. I just—" I began, but was cut off when the laboratory door opened, revealing Caleb and Jackson.

I stood up quickly, giving Gage a worried look before trying to act as if nothing was wrong. "Hey, I didn't expect you guys to be here this early," I said, my voice slightly higher in pitch than usual.

"We're just excited to get this thing going. I figured this was where you'd be," Caleb said happily.

"Just follow my lead," Gage whispered behind me as he got up from his seat. Then he turned to Caleb and Jackson. "I was just getting ready to take some blood from Sammi now, so you had perfect timing."

"Is Sophie with Grace?" I asked.

"Yeah, she is. They will be by in a little bit," Caleb said.

Gage slid his hands into a pair of blue latex gloves and grabbed a tourniquet. I was nervous, but I trusted that he had a plan in mind. I walked over to the gray chair and smiled nervously at Jackson, who had the sweetest sense of hope in his beautiful eyes. I pulled up my sleeve while Gage tied the tourniquet tightly around my upper arm to prepare for the blood draw.

While I sat there in fear of them seeing fresh needle marks, Gage tried to keep them engaged in conversation as a distraction, saying, "Keith ran out about an hour ago to look for a book in the library, so he should be back soon to fill you guys in on his plan."

"That's great," Caleb said cheerfully.

"Oh, I also forgot that I need a blood sample from Grace's father as well," he said.

The three of us looked at each other nervously, then back to Gage.

"He's dead," I said.

"Oh, I'm sorry; I didn't realize. Um. This, uh, just got complicated," Gage said, holding the needle in his hand.

"What does that mean?" Jackson asked worriedly.

"I'm not quite sure yet. I'll have to talk with Keith about alternatives, but for now, we'll just start with Sammi's lab tests."

I wasn't worried, because I thought this was just a diversion. I figured Gage would get the samples today and discard them, or find a way to tell Keith he didn't obtain them. I didn't exactly know the plan because it was pretty improvised. I was just rolling with it.

Gage wiped my inner arm with an alcohol pad and then proceeded to draw blood. Jackson and Caleb were facing each other as they whispered amongst themselves about something. I narrowed my eyes in suspicion, trying to figure out what they were discussing. At one point, I caught a glimpse from Jackson, who smiled sweetly at me—a smile that could illuminate any room. I returned the smile while still investigating their secrecy.

A minute or two later, Gage had completed his blood draw, placing a cotton ball over the mark and wrapping it tightly with a bandage. I grabbed my sleeve, pulling it back down over my arm before taking a deep breath.

"That's all I need from Sammi right now, but I will try to find Keith to talk to him about our options," Gage said.

Caleb and Jackson stepped outside to continue their conversation while I hung back to talk with Gage.

"Hey, thanks for having my back. It would've broken their hearts if they knew I prolonged this entire thing we've worked so hard to find," I said with a sense of relief. "Good improvisation on needing Grace's father's input."

His body stiffened as he gave me a saddened expression, brushing his hair with his fingertips. He took a deep breath, and suddenly I felt uneasy.

"Actually, Sammi, that wasn't a lie. We need both parents involved in this process. Just you and Grace alone will leave her as the sole donator of everything we need. She likely wouldn't survive that process, and it still may not result in enough for the cure. We will have to make hundreds of trial doses before reaching the ideal injection. It would medically drain her," he said.

I looked at him in defeat, trying to hold back frustrated tears. I just wanted to yell "*Fuck!*" over and over until the world wasn't pinned against me for once. Could anything ever just fucking work out?

Gage could tell I was struggling. Something about death terrified me more than literally anything else. As reckless as I'd been, I felt like I had something to live for now. I wanted a future with Jackson. I wanted him forever.

Would it make me the worst person in the world if I thought, just for a tiny moment, that if Grace were my only loophole for a cure, I'd still do it, even if it meant she might die? God, it was inhumane for me to even think that, but I guess I was just an inhumane person.

I have a chemical imbalance. Sue me.

My intrusive thoughts withered away once Gage spoke again. "Don't think of this as the end. Keith will be able to think of another way. I've seen him do miraculous things," he said, leaning in to give me a hug.

"Okay," I said with a sniffle before releasing the hug and walking away with my head down to find Jackson and Caleb.

I guess it had never dawned on me that Gage didn't know Jackson wasn't the father of my child. It should've clicked when he genuinely seemed surprised when I said her father was dead, but I was too worried about being exposed as an active addict that I wasn't paying attention to the details of the world around me.

I was terrified. Not only was I unable to provide him with clean blood work, but I was unable to provide him with the father. I couldn't imagine that there was the possibility of an alternative solution.

God, why was this my life? I didn't understand it.

Outside, I found Sophie and Grace with my brother and Jackson. Caleb was playing peek-a-boo with Grace while Sophie held her. At times it felt like Sophie and Caleb were more like her parents than me.

What would it be like if they adopted her? I wasn't sure if it would make me sad or relieved to not be responsible for another tiny human being. To think I could just wake up and function without fearing that I wasn't providing adequate care to such a delicate individual was refreshing.

I knew I sounded like the worst person ever, but I was in a dark place. Unfortunately, I had too much on my mind that didn't involve being a mother. And a single mother at that, as I hadn't really given Jackson the chance to act as a father figure to Grace, since I typically pawned her off on Sophie and Caleb. Maybe if I'd given him the opportunity to show me that I wasn't in this alone, I would feel differently about everything.

I had this sense of imposter syndrome when it came to being a mother. I felt like a teen mom on one of those MTV shows that had a baby but still wanted to party and hang out with boys, because they weren't ready to be a parent.

I had to sort this shit out.

"What else did he say?" Caleb asked eagerly as I approached them.

"He said he's confident that Keith could find another way, but for now we're just waiting again," I said, frowning.

The walk back to the dormitory was silent. Once we reached the dorms, Caleb took Grace from Sophie, and she and I went to her room to talk. We'd been spending a lot of time together throughout our long days here on campus, and I'd really found a friend in her. I felt like I could talk to her about things I kept hidden from everyone else. She never radiated judgmental or negative energy toward me, and I think that's why I felt so comfortable confiding in her.

We both laid down on her bed, heads propped on our hands as we talked.

"Sammi, we're friends right?" Sophie asked me.

"Yeah…" I answered in a slightly confused tone.

"Would you be okay with me and Caleb dating?"

"Do you think you need my permission?" I asked jokingly.

"No, I just don't want to cause any problems. I know it's a little weird for me to be dating your brother, especially because he's Jackson's best friend," she said awkwardly.

"Do you see him as a long-term thing?"

"Yeah, I do. He's great; you know that," she said with a radiating grin.

"He is," I agreed, returning her smile. "Would you want to have kids with him?"

She frowned.

"I'm sorry. I shouldn't have asked that."

"No, it's okay. Um, sorry, I feel weird talking to you about this, but when I was dating Jackson, I … got pregnant."

My eyes widened. This was news to me.

"We weren't planning on it. At least, I wasn't," she said, gesturing to herself. "I was on birth control, but evidently it wasn't foolproof. It happened while I was in nursing school, and I just couldn't afford to drop out and take care of a baby. I made the decision to get an abortion, and it crushed Jackson. He's got this pure heart that sees the world in bright colors, not black and white. He was devastated, and it was definitely a factor in our breakups. I knew he could never look at me the same way. I saw it in his eyes every time we were together. It still gives me a lot of insecurity, even though he seems to have finally moved past it," she said sadly.

"Are you afraid of what Caleb will think? Because he won't hold it against you, and it wouldn't change the way he feels about you," I said.

"I know. I see the way he looks at Grace, and I know that kids are something he's probably always wanted. I think I might finally be at that point where it could be an option for me to have a baby. That's the only way you can really start a family now anyways. It's not like we can just adopt."

Briefly, my mind wandered. It's terrible to admit, but I kept thinking, *Would Grace be better off with Caleb and Sophie as her parents?* Or was I just in my own head about being an unfit mother again?

Recently it seemed like there was more going on inside my brain than I was willing to accept. I felt like my humanity was deteriorating. Was it the infection eating away at my body? Or the seizures depriving my brain of oxygen for too long? Was it the non-adherence to my medication for my manic bipolar disorder? Or was it the effects of continued drug use?

Maybe it was everything. Maybe it was nothing.

"Do you think I'm a bad person for having an abortion?" she asked.

"No, I don't. I considered it with Grace. Mentally I wasn't anywhere close to being a fit mother, and some days I still don't think I am. It's a human reaction to consider your options, and you did what you thought was best for you. Sometimes that's not what's best for everyone else, but you come first, not them," I said supportively.

"What made you change your mind?" she asked softly.

"Bailey," I said, smiling at the memory of the day I made that call. "He was so excited when I told him. I guess there was a part of me that thought he would hang up the phone and block my number, but he immediately began planning this future that included us and our baby. It made me feel like I wouldn't have to go through it alone."

"Bailey was a great guy. I'm so sorry you had to experience his death. I can't imagine what that was like for you," she said sympathetically.

My arms were covered with chills as my mind took me back to the day that I watched a bullet race through his skull. I felt guilty for what I'd done to that boy. Really guilty.

I stared at her blankly for a moment before admitting, "I killed a little boy that day. I didn't even hesitate. I just grabbed the gun and killed him."

"You reacted to a tragedy. You watched your child's father cease to exist; you watched him die," she said.

I gazed at her, feeling a sense of relief from finally saying these things out loud to someone. It was therapeutic. So, we kept talking, really opening up to each other about some of our past traumas and stories.

We talked for a couple of hours until we were interrupted by a knock on her door. I jumped up from the bed and opened it, where I was greeted by Gage. He had a look on his face that I was having a hard time reading. I couldn't tell if it was happy, sad, relieved, or something else.

"Hey Gage, what's up?" I asked.

"Keith is back at the laboratory, and we have some things to talk about. Do you want to grab your brother, Jackson, and Sophie, and meet me there?"

"Yeah, sure. We'll be right over," I said, turning back to look at Sophie, who held a promising expression on her face.

She stood from the bed and followed me out into the hallway, where the two of us split up. She went to find Caleb and Grace, and I went to find Jackson.

I walked into our dorm to find him sitting at the desk, doodling on a piece of paper. He perked up when he saw that it was me and stood up from the chair, meeting me halfway across the room.

"Hey. Gage just came by. He wants all of us to meet him and Keith at the laboratory," I explained.

"Did he say if it was good news?"

"It was hard to tell," I said softly, temporarily spacing out at the thought of bad news.

"Let me put my shoes on, and we can head that way," he said eagerly.

A minute or two passed before he and I met the rest of the group to walk back down to the building that could make or break any hope of my future. As we walked, the wind blew, and I caught the scent of fresh gardenias and lilies. It reminded me of the smell that singed my nostrils while I tethered back and forth between mania and decaying mentally in the funeral home after my parents died.

I never understood why everyone religiously drowned mourning people with such bulky acts of sympathy. People sent so many floral arrangements. They flooded the small room we'd been given to display my parents, who were hidden beneath closed caskets. The mortician had said they didn't even look recognizable, which made me feel even more dissociated from the reality of their deaths. All I had were photographs.

And what the fuck was I going to do with fifty baskets and bouquets of flowers? Not only had I just buried my parents, but now I'd have to wrestle all these clunky plants into the back of my car. Then what? Pile them randomly around my apartment so I could constantly be reminded that my soul and heart were dying each day, along with each falling petal?

It wasn't what grieving families wanted or needed.

Lost in thought, I was surprised when we reached the laboratory without even noticing.

"Hey guys. Come on in," Gage said warmly while looking down at a clipboard settled in his hands.

Keith was writing something on a piece of paper, but he looked up at me as we entered, his reading glasses resting on the end of his nose. He clicked his pen and removed the glasses, folding them and laying them on the table.

"So, we've got a couple of things to go over," he said.

"Okay," I replied nervously, finding my way to a chair.

"Without the father's blood, antibodies, and other components, it's close to impossible to formulate with just Grace. Now, I don't know if you're familiar with savior babies, but they're often conceived for the purpose of donating bone marrow, cell transplants, or organs to a sibling in need, usually if they have cancer or another threatening condition. The way we do this is by in vitro fertilization. We have to do genetic compatibility tests to ensure that it matches Grace before implantation, otherwise it wouldn't be successful."

"So, you're saying I need to have another baby?" I asked, shocked.

"Yes. It's the only way to fully protect Grace in this process."

"Would the other baby survive?" I asked, my voice shaking slightly.

Jackson and the others stood silently across the room, listening to every word.

"I'm confident they would. They will likely have to donate blood, stem cells, or even organs if Grace's body can't handle the stress of everything, but I don't think it will come to that," he said, giving me a little hint of a smile.

"And that's how you can create the cure?" Jackson asked, as if he needed reassurance that I could survive this.

"That's how I would create the cure," he said confidently.

Jackson smiled at me, and I returned it.

"There is one problem," Keith added.

"What is it?" I asked as my heart palpitated in my chest.

"Well, Gage ran a few tests on your blood work, and it showed that you are already pregnant."

Suddenly I felt like I was on a merry-go-round at one hundred miles per hour. I felt déjà vu from when the doctor had told me I was pregnant with Grace. It was humiliating having Caleb and Jackson witness yet another unexpected pregnancy announcement.

But more importantly, what did this mean?

I was going to ask Keith, but then he was gone. *Everyone* was gone. At least I knew what was happening this time as I watched the room grow darker. I was becoming more and more aware each time I fell into this hole of dark reality.

But then my unease returned, because I was mistaken the first time. Not everyone was gone...

Gage was here.

He was here, but he couldn't see me, because he wasn't in that headspace like I was. His body was there, but his mind wasn't.

Gage was infected, and he'd never mentioned it. Not once.

Why didn't he tell me?

I wanted to walk over and shake him to somehow bring him into this reality, but I didn't have to. He found his way here not long after me. Now we were looking at each other, bewildered—or at least I was.

"Gage?"

"Hey, Sammi."

"W-what? You're infected too?"

"Yes. I'm sorry you're finding out this way," he admitted.

"I don't understand?"

"I got the infection when I started graduate school here studying under Keith. They required everyone to be up to date on their vaccinations, and my hepatitis titer wasn't what it needed to be. I went to a clinic off campus to get the first vaccine, but I've come to realize that isn't what they gave me," he said, looking down at the ground.

"Keith has been working on a cure for you?" I asked.

"He was, but we hit a wall several months ago. He's tried thinking of ways to modify his technique, but we were left with nothing—until you arrived."

"And now?"

"And now I get to help him make a cure for you," he said, smiling. I could tell he was trying to disguise a hint of envy, though.

"You don't think he could do the same for you?" I asked, furrowing my brow.

"There wasn't a baby involved when I got injected. I'm afraid you had a very, very rare situation. You're probably the only person in the entire world to be that lucky."

I looked down at the ground shamefully. "This isn't fair."

"It's okay, Sammi. I promise," he said.

I stared at him until my vision went black.

27

SKIN AND BONES

I DIDN'T KNOW IF I'd fainted or had another seizure, but sometime later, I woke up in my dorm.

"Hey," Jackson said once he noticed my eyes had opened.

"What happened?" I asked.

"You and Gage both had an episode of that zombie vision stuff. It was weird. After you were gone for ten minutes or so, you fell out of the chair and started seizing. Gage didn't, though. He stayed in that place for a few minutes longer. Keith and Caleb helped me get you back to bed, and I've just been waiting on you to wake up."

"I-I don't know where we left off. I'm pregnant?" I asked in dismay.

"Yeah, you are," he said, looking away momentarily.

"What else did Keith say?" I asked.

"He said we'd have to terminate the baby because it isn't a match for Grace."

My eyes became glassy, and I could tell it broke his heart to say those words out loud. A baby with Jackson just seemed like the perfect outlet to this crazy mess of a world we were in. Oh, and Sophie—Jesus, she'd literally just told me she terminated what would've been Jackson's first baby. It was a sensitive subject for him, so I felt terrible that this was the solution Keith gave us. It had to have brought back the suppressed feelings he had about Sophie. It made me wonder if he'd feel the same had it been me in that position.

"He wants me to have an abortion?"

He nodded.

"We can still have a baby together. They'll need sperm to create the donor baby," I said.

"I know. I just wish we didn't have to kill this baby—our baby that we created when we were happy, without having to scientifically test genetics and take pieces of it for Grace."

I sighed, watching the light leave his eyes.

"I know. If I knew I had another eighteen months in me I could carry this baby to full term and then make a donor baby, but I'm not sure I would survive with my episodes and going through two deliveries. That's a lot," I said, thinking of the possibility of going that route.

"So, we just make a fertilized egg that matches Grace, give birth to the child, and immediately start taking pieces of it? That just sounds callous. It doesn't seem fair, killing a baby to make another and using it for spare parts. I just… This is hard for me," he said sadly.

"I know," I said, running my fingers through his hair. "But every day that goes by, I'm withering away. I need this cure, Jackson. I'm going to die soon without it."

He frowned, giving me a look of defeat. "Do you want me to be there when they do the procedure?" he asked, sounding heartbroken.

"I don't think it will help the way you're feeling," I admitted.

When I was in nursing school, I shadowed at a women's health clinic and unfortunately learned about the gruesome procedures that were done for women having abortions or that miscarried and needed the procedure to remove the unborn baby. Witnessing it would only make Jackson feel guilty and distraught.

I didn't want to do it alone, but I felt terrible aborting a healthy baby when Jackson had already experienced that pain before. I also didn't want to drag my brother into it, and I didn't think it would be a good idea to bring Sophie to hold my hand while another child was taken from Jackson. It almost felt like a betrayal to him.

I left Jackson to ponder his thoughts while I slipped away to find Gage and Keith. When I re-entered the laboratory building, I didn't see any sign of the two of them. I thought about waiting around for one of them to return, but instead, I decided to go to their dormitory to find them so we could get this over with.

I'd never gone to the building they lived in before, so I knew it might take a while to narrow down exactly where they were staying.

I entered the clean building and headed for the elevator, pressing the up arrow. After several short moments, the elevator doors opened, and I stepped inside. I decided to go up to the top floor and work my way down in search of Keith and Gage, so I pressed the fourth-floor button and waited for the elevator to take me up.

I looked at my reflection in the metallic sheen. Even that seemed broken—a messy blur that reminded me of my misconfigured mind and my weak, dissipating body.

I looked down at my flat stomach that held a developing baby Jackson and I had unintentionally conceived. I pictured the two of us living this wonderful life, and Grace being a big sister to a little boy or girl.

There had to be another way. But did I have time for us to find one?

Once the elevator doors opened, I hesitantly took a step out into the hallway. The floor looked vacant, with no signs of either of them, but I still went from door to door, knocking to make sure I didn't miss them.

After no response to any of my knocks, I stepped back into the elevator and went down to the third floor.

As soon as I got out of the elevator on the third floor, I had an unsettling feeling. Dust particles floated around in the light of the sun beaming in from the window, and everything seemed normal on the surface, but there was an eerie aura that made me feel like I did at the hospital that night—like I should turn around and run.

But I didn't.

I repeated the same movements of walking, knocking, walking, knocking, until I heard a faint whimper from behind one of the doors. I placed my ear against it, and it wasn't long until I heard it again.

"Hello?" I called.

Again, I heard another whimper. It sounded as if there was a girl trapped inside with tape over her mouth.

I had just reached for the doorknob when I heard the elevator begin moving. Something was going on here, and I was afraid I was about to get caught in the middle of whatever it was.

I quickly tiptoed down to the first room on the left side of the hallway and slipped inside, right as the elevator stopped on the floor I was on, letting out the person inside.

I quietly locked the door to the room I was hiding in before pressing my eye against the peephole to investigate what was happening.

I saw Gage exit into the hallway carrying a tray with a large assortment of food on it, which seemed odd.

Maybe he stayed in a room on this floor, and he was really hungry? At least, I was hoping that was the case. Unfortunately, I had a feeling that food was to feed whoever was hidden behind that door.

Things were about to get a lot more complicated for me.

I continued scoping out the activity in the hallway to try and make sense of everything when I heard movement from behind me. I jerked around in a panic, suddenly afraid that I was not alone.

Leaving the room wasn't an option, so I took careful steps in the direction of the noise until I found a teenage girl. She was visibly distraught, shaking in fear, and more scared of me than I was of her.

She was sitting on the bathroom floor, knees to her chest and breathing heavily and anxiously. I put my index finger to my mouth, instructing her to keep quiet while I inched closer.

Once I was beside her, I could see that she was seemingly healthy. She wasn't underweight or bruised, so why was she here? Was she hiding from Gage?

I squatted down next to her and whispered, "Are you okay?"

She shook her head while biting her nails.

"I can help you, but you have to tell me what's going on. Are you hiding from someone?" I asked quietly.

She nodded.

"Who is it? Do you know their name?"

"K-Keith," she said.

The name pained me, and I swallowed the lump in my throat, wondering what to do. Why was this girl so terrified of the man who was my last hope of survival?

Suddenly, the doorknob rattled behind me. My eyes grew wide, and the girl shut her eyes, rocking back and forth fearfully.

"Shit," I whispered.

I hurried back to the peephole to find Keith angrily fidgeting with the locked door.

Gage appeared behind him, and I heard Keith say, "She's got to be in there. This door's never been locked. Go get the master key from the closet." He was speaking calmly and low enough to think he was being discreet, but I heard the intention behind his words.

I refused to be involved in another human centipede lab experiment type shit with some deranged doctor. I needed to think of a way to get me and this girl out of this room before Gage returned with the key. If they found me here, I would basically flush my chances at a cure down the toilet. That wasn't an option.

But for once I needed to think about someone other than myself. This wasn't the hospital; I wasn't going to abandon the girl here like I had several others before. I had a choice to make, and I was finally making the right one.

So please, Universe, can you be on my side this time?

I rushed to the window and looked down at the distance to the ground. There was a window directly below us that had a small ledge resting above it. After that, it was a drop from the second floor to the ground. It wasn't ideal, but it was the only option I had at such short notice.

I quickly ran back to the girl and anxiously told her to follow me. She stood and rushed over to the window, looking down at the same intimidating jump. As I unlocked the window, I tried to explain the plan to her.

"Okay, right below us, there's a tiny ledge above the second story window. If you can climb out of this one and reach your feet down, you can stand on it and jump from there. Can you do that?" I asked in a whisper.

She nodded.

I pushed the screen out of the window and helped ease her out. The ledge was still a little way from the bottom of her feet, but after she pointed her toes down and trusted that she could land on it, she released my hand and successfully found the ledge. It took her a second to get the courage to jump the rest of the way down, but she was able to land safely on the ground.

I could hear Gage racing down the hallway with the keys jingling in his hands, so I knew I needed to get out quickly. I climbed over the windowsill and dangled above the ledge, but my hands slipped.

I completely missed the ledge and fell three stories to the ground.

I landed on my leg, hearing one of my bones snap before the instant rush of agonizing pain.

The young girl covered my mouth with her hand to prevent Keith and Gage from hearing my pained cries. She grabbed my body, encouraging me to scoot out of sight from the dorm window. Luckily, we were at the corner of the dormitory, so we managed to ease to the side of the building, behind several thick bushes and greenery, giving us a short minute to breathe before they no doubt hopped into the elevator and came after us.

I wanted to scream so badly from my broken leg, but I knew we'd be discovered if they heard me. I just had to cry as quietly as possible into her hand until I found the strength to move.

The girl looked at me admirably before trying to help me stand. I could tell she felt a sense of safety with me, and I was proud that I could offer that to someone for once.

We began carefully hobbling in the direction of the dormitory I lived in, but it was taking too long. We were too exposed, and I was paranoid that they'd catch up to us and see that I was involved. We needed to hide in another building until I was sure they weren't on our trail.

I'm not going to make it. They're going to find me, and then I'll never get the cure.

I took a deep breath as metaphorical knives stabbed every inch of my broken leg. "I need to stop for a minute, I'm going to throw up if I keep moving on this leg."

I saw appreciation in her brown eyes as she studied me, continuing to support my shaking body as she brushed her brown hair out of her face with her free hand. "Are you sure? We're not far."

"They're going to catch us before we make it to my dorm. Just leave me and find my brother," I pleaded.

"I'm not leaving you," she said sternly.

"I'll be fine."

"No. You didn't leave me behind in that room, so I'm not leaving you behind out here on that leg," she said, nodding at my injured limb.

"Fine. Let's hide in the library for a minute," I said, wincing in pain. The library was right ahead—a damp brick building settled beneath a circle of thick oak trees.

The girl helped me up the short steps to the library entrance, and the two of us tried navigating through the dark interior. I assumed this was one of the buildings that wasn't included in the power package that Keith mentioned when we first arrived. It gave me a sense of comfort knowing at least we had darkness to aid in our disguise if they did end up in here with us.

The girl helped me into a chair close to the front door before she ran across to look out of the side windows.

After several seconds, she perked up. "They're headed toward the dining hall. I think we can make it to your dorm if we go now," she said anxiously.

"Are you sure?" I asked.

"I'm positive," she said confidently, hurrying back over to where I was sitting.

She helped me walk once again as we headed back down the steps and continued toward my dorm. After several long minutes of slow, struggling movements, I could finally see the front of the building.

We were so close to the building when one of the straggler zombies that continually roamed campus darted toward us. Before she could even react, the zombie latched onto her left arm, nearly detaching it from her body in one bite.

She screamed at the top of her lungs and I cried out in pain as I felt her body—which I had been leaning on for support—fall to the ground. The zombie tore into her limb by limb, covering most of my body in her blood as it gushed from her extremities.

Then she stopped screaming, because it tore into her vocal cords.

I stood in shock for a second before I managed to limp the rest of the way to the entrance of the building. The preoccupied zombie wasn't focused on me, but the girl's dying screams had to have set off alarms for Keith, Gage, and the other lingering zombies on campus.

I needed to get help. I needed Jackson.

As soon as I was safely inside the building, I fell to the floor. I couldn't stand on my leg any longer, so I tried crawling toward the elevator, hoping I could get to the second floor before either being caught or passing out.

I was mentally and physically exhausted, sobbing from the flood of emotions hitting me, and hopelessly seeking saving from this situation I'd unintentionally found myself in.

Suddenly, the elevator beside me opened, revealing Caleb and Jackson.

"Oh my God, Sammi!" Jackson cried out.

"We need to get Keith," Caleb suggested in a worried tone.

"No! You have to take me to my room!" I almost shouted, voice cracking.

"Sammi, you're hurt," Jackson pleaded sweetly.

"He can't find me like this. He can't find me!" I repeated as they exchanged fearful looks.

"Okay, okay. We'll take you to your room," Caleb said, trying to calm me down.

Jackson carefully scooped me up into his arms. As he began to move, I looked at the blood I'd smeared across the wooden floor, realizing they might put two and two together if they saw it.

"You can't let them see the blood," I choked out.

"You take her upstairs, and I'll clean this up," Caleb said to Jackson.

He held me in his arms as we entered the elevator and found our way up to the second floor. My heart was pounding harder than it ever had before, even though I wasn't exactly sure what the girl had been so afraid of.

There was no doubt in my mind that Keith was up to no good, I just needed more time to figure it out.

Sophie met us at the elevator in complete disbelief as she saw me covered in blood. There was a metallic taste on my tongue, and the splatters on my skin were now drying, my body stiffening beneath the patches of the girl's blood.

I couldn't help but feel responsible for her death too.

"Grab the door for me, Sophie," Jackson instructed, following closely behind her into our room. Caleb joined us seconds later, having quickly cleaned the blood from the lobby floor.

Jackson laid me down on the bed and used his pocketknife to cut the fabric from around my injury, exposing the bruised skin and protruding bone in my lower leg. They all gasped at the gruesome sight, each simultaneously asking questions.

"What happened?" Jackson asked helplessly.

"What can I do?" Caleb added.

I dragged my hands across my swollen, wet eyes as I tried to speak through my nauseating pain. "I went to go find Keith and Gage at the lab building, but they weren't there," I began, taking in a gasp of air. "So, I walked to their dorms to see if that's where they were, but before I found them, I found a teenage girl hidden in an empty room. She said she was hiding from Keith."

"Did she say why?" Sophie asked anxiously.

"I never got the chance to ask her. He found the door was locked to the room we were hiding in and tried to unlock it. I knew my chances of getting the cure would be ruined if he caught me there, so we jumped from the third-floor window. I landed on my leg, and she helped me get back here," I said as more tears flooded down my warm, rosy cheeks.

"What happened to her?" Caleb asked.

"A zombie got her right outside the building. It ripped her out of my arms," I said, still in shock.

"Is that who screamed? Is this her blood?" Jackson asked worriedly.

I nodded before rolling over and sobbing into the sheets. "He can't know I was with her. He can't know I helped her escape," I mumbled into the mattress.

The pain was overwhelming; it was too much to bear. I knew the drugs I had would be the fastest way for me to find relief, but I had a baby to consider now, even if Keith had suggested I terminate. I didn't want to harm this baby any more than I probably had the last two weeks I had been routinely injecting myself, unaware that I was pregnant. If there was anything that could get me sober, this just might be it.

I cried and cried until there were no more tears left in me. I was a cold body lying in the bed that Jackson and I were once so happy in. I was nothing more than a deteriorating corpse, no different to the others roaming around campus. I was the epitome of sadness; just skin and bones cradling an already dead soul.

28

NEVER BE LIKE YOU

WHEN I WAS YOUNGER, I had nightmares quite often. I'd wake myself up, gasping for air, my heart pounding against my chest. The nightmares would be about three teachers chasing after me in the dark. I knew their names, and I saw their faces in these dreams, but I never actually met them or even knew they existed in real life; I just saw them as characters I'd dreamt up to torture my mind as it slept.

Then one day at school, I found an old yearbook on a shelf in my classroom with each teacher pictured and the names and faces I'd given them in my bad dreams. They were actual people, and oddly enough, they were all dead in real life.

Isn't that strange?

My mind had these capabilities that scared even myself. How do you dream about real people without ever seeing them?

It happened multiple times, with the same teachers tormenting me in my sleep for an entire year. I started a journal to document each creepy, intrusive nightmare I had, adding to it immediately after waking up because it was easy to forget them.

For some reason, they motivated me to remember them. And now, I was living the life of the girl in my nightmares—running from symbolic, foreshadowing death, with those who were already dead chasing me. It's funny how that works.

Maybe I deserved this. Maybe this was my fault; my choices had led to this. Now I had found myself with a broken bone in the middle of an apocalypse, when a hindrance in my ability to walk or run could mean the difference between life and death.

I was not looking forward to feeling like a burden and a prisoner to my bed. That was when I really got inside of my own head. I was already laying here, thinking about how depressed and unattractive I felt when I was pregnant with Grace. I remembered the way it created this disconnect between me and Jackson. We had this weird hiatus in our relationship that I was afraid would happen again.

Not to mention, Jackson found himself alone in a room with Lucy when I was pregnant. A part of me still subconsciously thought he'd wished something had happened between them. Maybe he was curious about what else was still out there.

Did he feel trapped? Was he staying with me because he was worried that I'd get myself killed? Didn't he know that it was so easy to feel alone in a world where there were more dead than there were living?

We could try to escape the overwhelming sense of isolation in this world, or we could continue societal norms and repopulate and create families. But was that realistic? Was it morally ethical to continue bringing lives into a world that possibly could never be rebuilt? Or was it just me looking for an excuse to feel detached from this pregnancy, so when it came time to terminate, I could let my sad emotions dissipate into the harrowing air?

Pregnancy just had this sort of negative connotation attached to it for me. I didn't see it as this nurturing, organic experience that had picturesque moments radiating maternal love and the celebration of a new life. Maybe because being pregnant in an apocalypse was much different than being pregnant when the world wasn't shit, but I wouldn't know. I'd only ever experienced it one way.

An abortion with this baby wasn't what I wanted. Terminating this baby only meant there would be another one—one we'd pluck pieces from like the operation game. I found no comfort whatsoever in any of this, and I didn't think I would until I had the cure in my body with no more visions or seizures. None of this mattered until then, but even so, I could terminate this healthy and pure baby that Jackson and I created, only to produce a donor baby for a cure that still may or may not work.

Oh, and let's not forget about the sketchy ass doctor and lab assistant that were holding who knew how many girls hostage in their dormitory building. That could cause many problems in our fight for a cure.

I felt like, at one point, I could talk to Gage about mostly anything, even though I'd initially had a weird off-putting vibe from him. I just didn't understand why a guy that looked like him would need to kidnap girls.

I wanted to talk to him about it, but I wasn't sure how loyal he was to Keith. Once I told him I knew, my fate was in his hands. He could either tell Keith and they could try to kill us, or he could give me some sort of logical explanation. Unfortunately, I found it difficult to believe that there was any reason he could give me that excused this.

The longer I laid in bed, the worse I felt about everything. I was so anxious that Keith would come by to snoop on us and pick up on us acting suspicious. I hoped he would take time to reassess his current problem at hand and assume we had no involvement, but that was optimistic of me.

Jackson had been lying beside me in the bed, and luckily with Sophie once being a nurse, she was able to somewhat doctor me up with makeshift supplies and bandages they found in various rooms. While I was grateful and appreciative of their gestures, I knew I needed surgery for my leg to properly heal. And I was afraid that wasn't going to happen.

An hour or so after the nerves had simmered down between everyone, Gage showed up at my dorm room. We were on edge, but honestly, I felt better knowing it was Gage and not Keith. For some reason, I still trusted him. So, when Caleb opened the door and saw him, he played along as if nothing in our lives had changed.

"Hey, Caleb; I was looking for Sammi. I was hoping I could talk to her for a minute," he said.

Caleb turned to look back at me, and I gave him a nod of approval.

Jackson stood up from the bed before kissing me on the cheek and following Sophie and Caleb out into the hallway.

Gage entered the room and shut the door behind him. He took slow steps toward me, as if he was more nervous than I was, then sat on the edge of the bed beside me. He took a deep breath before releasing it anxiously.

"I know that you know about the dorms," he said, looking over at me.

I swallowed deeply, wondering if I should even try to lie. "Gage—"

He interrupted. "Keith doesn't know, but I saw you when I looked out of the dorm window. You're lucky I was the one who got there first, because I was able to divert him toward the dining hall by telling him I'd seen her running that way."

I stayed silent.

"Look, I don't know what she told you…" he started.

"She didn't tell me anything," I said quickly.

He took a deep breath. "Keith keeps girls in the dormitory. Some of them are students from the class he was teaching when the military came in and tore the place apart. He managed to get some of them to the dormitory, and once he realized the laws didn't apply to us anymore, he let his inner desires consume him. He keeps those girls there for pleasure. He has sex with them," he admitted.

"You mean he rapes them? Because it didn't seem like they had much choice," I said sternly.

"If I say something to him, it could ruin any chance I have at a cure, just like you. We have the same stakes in this, Sammi," he said, his green eyes piercing right through me.

"So, you what, feed them for him?"

"Essentially, yes. I feed them, let them bathe, and talk amongst each other—but only when he or I are around to supervise them, because as you've come to realize, they could call out for help or escape."

"So how did that girl get out of the dorm away from the others?" I asked, wanting to keep my exact involvement in her escape a secret.

"I still haven't figured that out," he admitted.

"She's dead," I said.

"I know."

"I wasn't trying to find the skeletons in his closet. I stumbled upon them when I came looking for you. I was just ready to get the procedure over with," I said emotionlessly.

"I don't know if I should tell you this, but Sophie came to me privately after everything in the lab. She asked me a question about the process and the options we had," he began.

I gave him a confused look. I'd had no idea Sophie had gone to him.

"What do you mean?" I asked.

"She asked about the survival rate and other details about the donor baby. She asked me if it would be possible for her to be a surrogate," he said anxiously.

"A surrogate? She asked you that?"

"Yes. She told me she hadn't gotten the chance to talk with everyone about it, but I think she saw it as a way for you to keep this baby while still getting a donor baby to help with the cure."

I furrowed my brows in confusion as I considered this as a realistic option. "Would that be an option?"

"I don't see why not. I mean, ideally a surrogate would be someone who's already successfully delivered one baby, but she's healthy and young. It could be an option, if you wanted it to be," he said, looking at me sympathetically.

I was going to respond, but suddenly my leg began throbbing again, way worse than before. I winced in pain before grinding my teeth together and scrunching my eyes closed, hoping it would shut out the pain, but it didn't. It definitely didn't.

"Fuck," I groaned.

"What is it, Sammi?" he asked, concerned.

I pulled back the blanket covering my leg to reveal the purple, swollen, and broken bone I had hidden beneath a homemade wrap. "I helped the girl jump out of the window when I found her. I came down after her, but I slipped. I landed on my leg, and it snapped. It hurts so bad," I whined.

Gage brushed the hair from my face and examined my leg. "Let me take you to the clinic on campus. It has casts and bandages, pain killers, and an X-ray machine."

"Do you think Keith will suspect anything when he sees my leg?"

"I don't think so. We just need to make up a believable story, like you fell down some stairs or something. We'll figure it out, I promise," he said sweetly.

His level of concern and his touch hypnotized me. It seemed like had cast a spell on me. He could tell me to do anything, and I'd do it. I didn't know why I felt so brainwashed by him, but I did.

Looking back, I think I wanted to go with him because we'd be alone. Maybe I wanted something to happen, maybe I wanted to fill a void, or maybe I wanted to ruin my life a little bit more. So when he mentioned the clinic, I took him up on his offer, curious to see where it would go.

Sophie, Jackson, and Caleb hung back with Grace while I went with Gage to the clinic. I assured my brother and Jackson that I would be okay and not to worry, because we could trust him. I think they were still skeptical, but they complied because I was insistent and convincing when trying to tell them I could take care of myself.

When we arrived at the clinic, I couldn't deny that this persistent impulsive and reckless behavior was at the forefront of my mind. I couldn't help but feel like, for once, someone understood me. There was someone going through everything I was. There was someone witnessing the cruel, deviant aftermath of the human species, like I had been. He was seeing the dark desires of Keith being executed like I'd seen with Dillion and the freaks at the hospital. He didn't see the world like Jackson. He saw it for what it was—fucked up. That made me intrigued by him. And attracted to him.

When we made our way inside, he helped me up onto the patient bench covered in crinkling paper as I kept my legs dangling off the side. When I looked up, I saw Gage was reading the names on a few stock bottles of medication. I watched him intently, assessing the details of each of his tattoos.

I could see that he had good intentions, despite all that Keith was doing in his free time.

I closed my eyes, trying to relax, but the pants I had forced over the bandage were making me feel claustrophobic and trapped. I was feeling anxious and constricted, and I wanted to get out of them before I had a panic attack.

I rubbed my sweaty palms on my thighs, catching the attention of Gage.

"You nervous?" he asked as he poured a couple of pills into his hand.

"I just want to put something more comfortable on," I said, picking at the skin around my fingernail.

"Oh, okay. Here, take these and let me see if I can find something. The bookstore is right next door; it has some t-shirts and sweatpants. I'll grab you a pair," he said as he dropped the pills and a cup of water into my hand before quickly stepping out of the door.

I threw the pills into my mouth and took a sip of water, tossing the cup into a trash can across the room. I looked around at each detail of the clinic examination room, trying to forget about the pain in my leg and hoping the pills he gave me would kick in soon.

A few short minutes later, Gage walked back through the door with a yellow collegiate tee and a pair of black sweatpants that had the school logo embroidered on the side. He sat them down on the end of the bench as I began unbuttoning my pants. He held out his hand for me as I carefully eased down onto the floor, then turned away as I tried to pull them down, my broken leg slightly lifted off the floor.

"Do you need some help?" he asked, able to tell I was struggling.

"Yeah, I think I do," I said helplessly.

He walked up behind me and helped me pull the jeans down my legs. It seemed so effortless with him, and at some point, his body became pressed against mine. I felt his hands slide underneath my shirt and across my smooth skin.

I could've stopped it from going any further, but I didn't have any desire to. I wanted it to happen, as awful as it sounded. It felt great not giving a single fuck about the consequences of my actions.

He wasn't Jackson. He would never be Jackson. But at that moment, I had tunnel vision. I had no comprehension whatsoever between right and wrong. Something was wrong with me; I was experiencing mania like I never had before. Was it from being unmedicated for such a long period of time? Or was the infection deteriorating my mind at an exponentially high rate? I didn't know. I just knew this felt wrong in all the right ways.

My eyes rolled into the back of my head as his hands wandered to other parts of my body. He had this sensual, charismatic touch that trailed from my breasts to between my legs. I bit my lip as he gently pushed me forward onto the bench in front of me.

I'd forgotten all about my leg. Maybe the medicine had finally kicked in, or maybe it was the euphoric high I was on. In the long hour we shared being reckless with each other, I forgot about Jackson.

How could I have forgotten about Jackson? I mean this sincerely when I tell you that something was seriously wrong with me. I'm not trying to make excuses for my behavior, but it was like the conscious decision-making part of my brain was shut off completely.

After the sex with Gage was finished, I got dressed in the tee and sweatpants and quietly sat on the bench. I watched him as he finished casting my leg, wishing he'd say something—anything. Instead, he remained silent as he pulled the pants leg over the cast.

"So can we agree that we will never do that again?" I asked, finally realizing what I'd done to Jackson.

"You didn't like it?" he asked, leaning against the counter.

"No, I really liked it," I admitted painfully.

He grinned devilishly as I pursed my lips in embarrassment. "I really liked it too, but it doesn't have to happen again—unless you want it to," he said slyly.

I blushed shamefully as Sophie appeared in the doorway. For some reason I felt like I'd been caught, even though the cheating part was over. I had this guilty and anxious feeling now that she was here, but at the same time, I was glad she was. Maybe she was my buffer to stop me from repeating what happened earlier with Gage.

"Hey, did Gage get you fixed up?" she asked.

"What?" I asked worriedly.

"Your leg, did he get it taken care of?" she asked, giving me a suspicious look.

"Oh, yes, he did. I'm good to go," I said as he handed me a pair of crutches from the corner of the room.

Gage didn't say anything as the two of us exited the clinic; he just held the door open while I made my way out.

Once we got back to Sophie's room, she gave me this look as if to say *something's up*, and I had this all-consuming urge to tell her what happened. I needed to get it off my chest. I don't know what I thought it would do for me.

"I fucked Gage," I blurted.

She gave me this empty stare and just nonchalantly said, "I know."

My eyes widened. "How?"

"Well, for one, I saw you when I came to check on you. The door has a window, and the two of you weren't exactly being discreet. What the hell were you thinking?" she asked sternly.

"I don't think I was," I replied.

"You're manic right now, aren't you?"

"Would that make it okay?" I asked glumly.

"Fuck, Sammi, I don't know. I don't have the rule book for your manic bipolar fucking zombie-infected brain," she said angrily.

I wanted to react, I did, but my brain told me not to care. It told me not to take this situation seriously. I just gave her a surprised look, waiting on her to say something else.

"That cannot happen again. You've got to promise me that. Because if you're going to continue to fuck around on Jackson, I'm not just going to stand back and watch you drive him into the ground. You know he doesn't deserve that."

I rubbed my face with my hands and groaned.

"You love Jackson, right?" she asked.

"You know I love Jackson," I said irritably.

"Then act like it. Act like you care if you lose him."

God, the stress of this situation was really making me need a fix of my ketamine mixture. I stood up on my crutches to withdraw myself from this situation.

"Where are you going?" Sophie called out to me.

"To shoot up some drugs," I said openly.

"No, you're not! You're pregnant," she yelled before standing up to come after me.

"Don't follow me," I said angrily.

"I'm not going to let you do drugs while you're carrying that baby, Sammi!" she protested.

"I'm going to have to kill it anyways, why do you care so much?"

"Because I was willing to let you keep it! I was willing to be a surrogate so that you could keep the baby you have now!"

"Well, I don't need your help!"

At that point Sophie and I were screaming at each other from across the room as I inched closer to the door. We continued our argument until Caleb intervened, bolting into the room.

"What the hell is going on in here?" he asked.

"I was just leaving," I said in an annoyed tone.

"Sammi, stop," she said as she hurried after me. She attempted to grab my shoulder, and as I turned around to take a swing at her, I lost my balance and fell to the floor.

"Goddamnit," I screamed as I hit my hip on the hard tile of the hallway.

Jackson happened to be exiting the elevator, and rushed over to me in a panic. "Are you okay?"

"Caleb, I didn't mean to," Sophie began.

"I know. I know," he said, wrapping an arm around her.

Jackson helped me up back onto my crutches as I cut my eyes at Sophie.

"She's manic," she announced to Jackson and my brother.

I was so mad at everything. I was angry and fuming from feeling so overwhelmed and consumed by all that I'd done. My face was probably as red as a tomato from the anger I held toward myself and Sophie, even though she had every right to say everything she had to me.

Realizing my current state, Jackson and Caleb tried to convince me to go back to my room and calm down, but I didn't want to. I wanted to get far away from this place. Unfortunately, it was hard for me to go much of anywhere, considering I was at the mercy of painkillers and crutches. I would be a prisoner to my mind and my bed yet again.

And so, for a couple of long weeks, I was.

~

The manic episode had come to an end, for now at least. It was by far one of the longest episodes I'd experienced since finding out I had manic bipolar disorder. Now it was time for the smothering guilt that came with every incident that occurred during one of my manic episodes.

I had a lot of amends to make for my behavior, but I just couldn't risk losing Jackson by telling him the truth about Gage. Even I was well aware that cheating was close to unforgivable. No, I was going to take it with me to my grave.

At least, that was my plan.

It seemed like Sophie was keeping my secret, even though I'd given her every reason to tell. She and I hadn't spoken since I blew up at her that day, so I figured I'd ruined our friendship. That was something I'd always been good at.

I hated using my disorder as an excuse for all the bad things I'd done, but I refuse to believe I was just that shitty of a person naturally.

In the two weeks that had passed, we hadn't done anything as far as aborting my baby or progressed at all with the cure. I didn't know if Gage was avoiding me as much as I was avoiding him, but I was also trying to keep my distance from Keith for the time being until I felt confident enough to lie about my injury.

I could tell Caleb and Jackson were getting antsy about our stationary progress, and I wasn't sure if Sophie had mentioned the surrogacy route to either of them. Hell, she probably wasn't interested in the idea anymore after the way I treated her. And at this point, I wasn't sure if Jackson would want this baby with me if he found out I slept with Gage.

I was just a lost cause. All I did was cause stress and sadness to everyone I loved.

If I were dead, I wouldn't be able to go batshit crazy, cheat on Jackson, blow up at Sophie, shoot up drugs, break my leg by finding myself in the middle of something I had no business in, or constantly waste everyone's time looking for a cure.

I knew I wasn't worth saving. I wasn't worth consuming the time and effort of everyone around me. Let's face it, it would be better if I were dead. I mean, I was already as good as dead anyways. It was only a matter of time. This was just me speeding up the process to prevent hurting my brother, Jackson, Sophie, and Grace over and over again until it finally happened.

Jackson had gone with Caleb to the dining hall to grab something to eat, so I found a seat at the desk next to the paper he'd been drawing on. I was at least going to leave a note. They deserved that much. So, I picked up the pen and began writing.

Dear Jackson, Caleb, Sophie, and Grace,

I'm sorry. I'm sorry for everything I've put you all through. I'm sorry that you've dedicated your lives to finding a way to save me when you need to be enjoying the lives you saved for yourselves. It's not fair of me to keep letting you guys waste the time you have left on the little time I have left. I'm not worth the trouble—I'm realizing that now.

You guys deserve so much better than what I'm giving. I only ever hurt you over and over again. It's not fair.

I wish I could apologize to your faces for all that I've done, but I'm a coward. I would rather hide behind this note like I've been hiding from my doomed diagnosis for nearly a year. I'm sorry I couldn't be what you needed me to be. I'm sorry I couldn't just be normal. I could never be like you, any of you.

Please take care of Grace. Tell her the good parts of me. Tell her everything happy about me, but please, please don't tell her it was because I didn't love her enough. I loved all of you. I loved you so much. That's why I needed to withdraw myself from hurting you anymore than I already have. I'm not worth the trouble. I'm not. I never will be.

Sincerely, Sammi ♥

The ink smeared from the teardrops that fell onto the paper as I wrote my last words. I sniffled and cried while realizing my death would be a relief for them. They didn't know it now, but they would. They would finally know what it was like to live and be free, even in a world that had completely gone to shit.

I laid the pen beside the paper and stood with my crutches. Then I exited the room and made my way to the elevator. My heart was beating faster the further I got away from the room, and I felt this sense of relief knowing I couldn't hurt anyone else after today.

I hobbled toward the clinic, where I knew there was a stash of medications I could take enough of to overdose. As I reached the entrance, a black-haired zombie with an all-too-familiar face plunged itself at the door.

It was Gage.

He was dead.

My heart sank. I should've left, but I thought there was something poetic about letting Gage be the thing that killed me. He was what would have killed my relationship, anyway.

So I pushed through the door.

"Sammi!" I heard Sophie scream, running after me as Gage's possessed body bolted for the two of us.

"Sophie just go—please! I don't want you here," I sobbed, trying to balance on my crutches. This wasn't her fight.

"I'm not letting you get yourself killed," she said, pushing back at his body as hard as she could, his mouth hungry for her flesh.

"Just let me die," I said, the words causing physical pain.

She gave me a heartbroken look, and it was in that moment that I realized Sophie was willing to get herself killed in an effort to protect me. I couldn't let that happen. I couldn't risk her getting bitten while I survived to tell the story.

I grabbed a pair of scissors from the counter and stabbed them into Gage's skull.

That was right after he bit me.

29

EARTH WOULD STOP SPINNING

I REMEMBER ONE DAY at my brother's house I was sitting outside on his porch, watching the sun rise over the trees, when the sliding glass door opened behind me.

It was Jackson. He said he wanted to make sure I was okay, because if I wasn't, he said the sun wouldn't rise until I was.

I asked him why, and his response was, *"Because you are the sun, Sammi. Without you, the sun wouldn't rise, and the earth would stop spinning."*

If I had known that those days would be simultaneously the most normal and most special moments of our lives, I would've appreciated them and held on to them for as long as possible. I would have lived my life much differently and cherished the love of my life. Now, I was grasping for even the possibility of one more chance.

I changed my mind, okay? Please, give me one more chance.

"Sammi, you can't keep doing this shit," Sophie said as Gage's body collapsed to the floor.

It was when she looked up at me that she realized I had been bitten. The two of us stood in shock, unsure how to react for what felt like an eternity. We'd never experienced anyone being bitten without being brutally attacked to the point of death, so did just being bit mean death too? Would it transmit something else into my body?

Seconds later, Jackson and Caleb rushed in. I could tell from their severely panicked expressions that they'd discovered my letter in the room. Jackson had red, swollen eyes from crying and ruffled hair from running his hands through it.

They both seemed relieved to see me still alive, until Jackson looked down and noticed the bite. He looked as if his heart was ripping from his chest as his unborn child, his girlfriend, and his future were stripped from him in an instant. I'd never seen him look so defeated and empty inside. I was going to ruin this man. I was truly going to send him into the darkest hole to ever consume someone.

That's when I realized he needed me almost as much as I needed him. I couldn't abandon him now. I had to find a way to live.

Caleb froze in the doorway before carefully walking over to me and grabbing my wrist to turn my arm and assess the deep, bloody bite mark. I could feel his hand shaking as he held on to me.

The imprint on my arm stung and throbbed as it sent my mind back and forth between the real and dark worlds that I'd been playing limbo with for months. It was like a fuzzy television screen trying to find a channel in range. One minute I was there; the next I wasn't.

"Sammi," he said, his voice cracking.

"I'm sorry. I'm so sorry," I cried as I buried my face into his shoulder. He wrapped his arms around me tightly, a sense of forgiveness in his touch.

"W-we've got to find Keith. We've got to fix this," Jackson said, eyes wild with panic. He was a complete mess.

"Let's see if we can find him," Caleb said, rubbing his shoulder.

The two of them left to track down Keith while I hung back with Sophie, who just gave me a broken stare.

"Did you come here to die?" she asked, unaware of the letter I'd left behind.

"Yes," I said honestly as I turned around to find my way to a chair.

She sighed as she paced around the clinic room. "Don't you get it? Jackson needs you. Caleb needs you. Grace needs you. Fuck, Sammi, even *I* need you."

I looked up at her with guilty, glassy eyes. "There's something wrong with me," I cried.

"It's not your fault, Sammi. We're living in a deserted world. We have scraps for food and scarce medical supplies. We know you're going untreated. No one is disappointed or upset with you; we just want you to be okay—because after all that you've been through, you deserve to finally be okay. Don't you see that?"

"I've done horrible things. Unforgivable things," I said.

"We all have. That doesn't mean you should have to die because of it. Look, Jackson doesn't know what happened, and I wasn't planning on telling him."

As she said this, Caleb and Jackson returned with Keith. My heart sank, knowing he'd overheard us.

"Tell me what, Sophie? What happened?" Jackson asked, a confused look on his face.

"Nothing. It's not important," she said, hoping he would move on, but he was persistent.

"I want to know." His voice had gone from confused to stern.

"Later," Sophie said insistently.

"Sophie—" he started, but I interrupted.

"I slept with Gage," I admitted shamefully.

"What?" he asked in a broken tone. I watched the light leave his eyes.

"I'm so sorry, Jackson," I cried as he stormed out of the clinic room.

Caleb looked as if he wasn't sure what to do. On one hand, his best friend had just found out he'd been cheated on, and on the other hand, his sister—who did the cheating—had been bitten by a zombie; the zombie of the man she'd cheated with. Did he go after Jackson, or did he beg Keith to somehow fix this? And was there anything to fix?

Keith just stood there shocked, especially after noticing Gage's lifeless body on the floor near me. He seemed saddened by the discovery, but I couldn't help but think he was only upset because his lock and key were no longer of service to him. The secrets Gage kept for him were unmatched.

There was still so much to uncover about Keith, but for now, he was the prize pony at the fair. He was my red slippers to click together. He was my one chance to undo my tragic fate. He could find a cure. I needed him to.

I stood up from the chair to go after Jackson, but Caleb stopped me.

"I have to go after him," I begged, heavy tears rolling down my flushed cheeks.

"Not now. For once can you just do what I'm asking you to do?" he said in frustration.

My heart was beating at a rapid rate as I panicked about losing Jackson forever. He meant so much to me it hurt. I couldn't just stand by and let him walk away without giving him an explanation or begging for his forgiveness.

"Caleb, please," I pleaded.

"Sophie, can you make sure Jackson's okay?" he asked, clearly hoping that would be sufficient for me to let it go for now.

She nodded and slipped out of the room to find Jackson while Caleb and I stood with Keith in silence.

"He-he was dead when I came by the clinic. He'd turned. He bit me before I killed him," I said.

"What does this mean?" Caleb asked Keith, who stepped over to me to take a closer look.

I held out my arm for him to examine. It looked noticeably worse than it had several minutes prior, which made me extremely nervous. There were so many unknowns with this virus, and I was afraid to be a guinea pig for some experimental treatment, but what other options did I have?

Suddenly my mind fell into the zombie world again, Keith and Caleb vanishing, just like that.

I couldn't help but feel like I was dead for good this time. I felt like I'd used up my last chance at living, and now I was another thoughtless body roaming around.

I didn't get the chance to say goodbye. Jackson's last memory of me was finding out I'd cheated on him. I knew he'd be destroyed indefinitely.

~

Jackson's point of view

"Jackson!" Sophie called out, hurrying behind me as I was walking up the stairs toward the dormitory.

"I just want to be alone right now," I shouted, my back still turned to her.

"Just listen to me," she begged.

I spun around angrily, tears forming in my eyes. "There's nothing you can say that will make this okay."

"Jackson, s-she was in the middle of a manic episode. You know she's not fully aware of her decisions when she's like that. And you know this infection is only making it worse. I don't think she fully understood what she was getting into," she explained.

"I don't know what to do, Sophie. She cheated on me. My heart is broken," I said, voice shaking.

I couldn't believe she had slept with Gage, a guy I'd been intimidated by since we arrived here. I saw the way he looked at her, and I just had this feeling in my gut that I was right in being threatened by him. I'd hoped it was all in my head, but it wasn't.

Maybe I didn't do enough? Maybe I wasn't there for her? Did I push her to do it? Or was all this inevitable? Maybe the common denominator in all her downfalls was me. Maybe I was bad for her.

It was as if Sophie read my mind. "She's not me, Jackson. She didn't cheat for the same selfish reasons I did, and it wasn't anything you did. You're perfect, Jackson. She knows that, and she's going to punish herself forever for what she's done to you."

"Do you think that's why she wanted to die? Is that why she got bitten?" I asked, losing my ability to control the heartbreak I was feeling.

"I think that was her initial plan. I saw her leave the dorm, so I followed her. She was trying to go into the clinic. I realized Gage was in there as a zombie, so I tried to stop her. I went in hoping I could keep her from doing something she would regret. While we were in there, I think she realized dying wasn't the answer, so she stabbed him in the head. It was when she was trying to kill him that he bit her. I don't think she meant for it to happen."

"None of this was meant to happen," I cried, slumping down on the steps outside our building.

"I know," Sophie said as she joined me.

We sat in silence for a few moments until I saw Keith and Caleb leaving the clinic with Sammi lying lifelessly in Caleb's arms. I stood up and ran as fast as I could toward them.

Behind me, Sophie called out, "Jackson wait!" I think she was afraid of how I would react if Sammi were dead. She probably should've been.

"Sophie, go get Grace and meet us at the lab," Caleb yelled worriedly.

She didn't ask any questions; she just sprinted for the dorms, where they'd left Grace asleep in her crib.

When I reached them, Caleb gave me this saddened look that made me fear that I'd lost her forever, never even getting the chance to say goodbye. If Sammi died, it wouldn't just be a loss to me; it would be a loss to the world.

No one said anything as we all hurried back into the laboratory building. I just repeatedly kept asking, "Is she okay? Is she alive?" but no one was responding.

Once we got to the lab, they laid her down on the hospital bed. Caleb checked her pulse, which was weak, and noted her shallow breaths.

My mind was turning circles as the room spun around me. I felt like I was suffocating. Was this what it would feel like to live without Sammi every day?

I never wanted to find out.

A few minutes later, Sophie burst through the door with Grace as Keith fumbled around with test tubes and vials on the counters around him. He was mixing ingredients and erratically gathering materials. Once Sophie made her way over with Grace, he prepared to take blood from her to create a Hail Mary cure that would somehow exempt Sammi from the fate of a bite which was still unknown to us.

We'd encountered that man at Walmart with a bite to the leg at the beginning of it all, but he didn't live long enough for us to actually see how it affected his body. Maybe had he not been eaten alive he could've survived the bite. Maybe it wasn't lethal.

I watched Sophie as she held Grace while Keith drew blood from her tiny veins. I don't think she realized I was listening to the words exchanged between the two of them, but I was.

"You better do everything you can to save her. I've paid her dues. I've given you everything you've asked for. So fucking save her," she hissed from behind grinding teeth.

I couldn't help but wonder what she was implying. She seemed angry, resentful even, toward Keith. I didn't think they'd had too many encounters with each other, unless there was something going on that none of us knew about.

He gave her a guilty look before taking a deep breath. "I'm working on it," he mumbled nervously.

I finally got the courage to find a spot beside Sammi's body, watching her lie there, somewhere far from here. I watched her chest rise and fall with each tiny breath she took—

Until it stopped.

At that moment, I think my breathing stopped with hers. It felt like an eternity before I was able to choke out the words, "She's not breathing anymore. S-she stopped breathing."

Caleb jumped up from where he'd been sitting and hurried over to us.

"Give her CPR," Keith instructed as he began drawing his concoction into a syringe.

I climbed on top of the bed, straddling her body while I began doing chest compressions. I couldn't let her die. I couldn't lose the one thing that had ever truly made me happy in this world.

After a minute, Keith ran over, holding a syringe. He advised me to stop the compressions while he injected the substance into her body. After he'd emptied the syringe and removed the needle from her arm, I resumed CPR until, slowly, I saw the color return to Sammi's body.

I heard her gasp for air as she crawled out of the dark place she'd been held. I smiled, tears streaming down my face like an idiot as I sighed a breath of relief.

I climbed down and stood beside the bed, waiting for her to wake up.

It took several long, anxious hours for her to return to us. But she did, and when she opened those beautiful golden-brown eyes, I felt like the pieces of my world had come back together. I could breathe again.

My sweet Sammi, you don't understand how much I adore you.

Sammi's point of view

I was almost certain I was dead, especially when I'd gone to the dark reality for a moment and suddenly saw everyone in the lab there with me. I'd never been able to see anyone who wasn't infected or a zombie until, for a split second, I too was a zombie.

That's when I realized I'd died—when suddenly the thought of warm human flesh and blood sounded familiar, replenishing, ungodly.

And then, in another instant, I was nauseated at the thought of being a decomposing cannibalistic corpse. My mind now belonged to me again. I felt life return to my body, air filling my lungs, my heart fully beating, and it was rejuvenating.

The only thing that made it better was seeing Jackson's face when I opened my eyes. There he stood, towering over me with his gorgeous smile and warm tears trailing his cheeks.

"Oh my God. Hey," he said with the biggest smile, grabbing my hand.

I tried to sit up on the bed, my stomach and ribs aching from the stress inflicted by the chest compressions, but I was alive. I was actually alive. I didn't know how, but I was.

I looked around at everyone in the room, then down at my arm, which still held minor evidence of a bite. I was confused.

Keith rushed to my side once he saw Jackson talking to me, realizing I'd woken up. His eyes were wide, like he was surprised I was even alive at all. He stumbled over his tongue as he tried to spit out the words in his mouth. "I-I just… Wow. You are a remarkable woman, Sammi. I have never seen anyone that was bitten survive. They normally die within the hour, but you, you've made a miraculous recovery. I-I took some blood from Grace and made a trial dose of the cure, but I didn't expect it to bring you back from this. I hoped it would, but normally it takes me several months to develop an exact formula for anything like this. I would like to take the credit and say that I'm the reason you're alive, but I think it has more to do with you," he said, full of wonder.

"What do you mean?" I asked.

"I think it all goes back to receiving the injection while you were pregnant with Grace. I think it allowed your body and your immune system to become introduced to the infection, while also having the ability to adapt and create responses to it. It's incredible," he said.

During this exchange with Keith, I couldn't help but notice that Sophie was staring at him lifelessly, as if she were angry with him. It was strange.

Caleb gave Keith a different look, one that seemed hopeful and appreciative. "Do you think she's out of the woods?" he asked, his arms folded in front of him.

"I can't know for certain, but this is a great sign."

Jackson shut his eyes and took a deep breath before happily releasing it.

"I'd like to take a new sample of your blood and compare it to the first one," Keith said.

Fortunately for me, my isolation in the dorm during my manic episode was like rehab for me. I couldn't shoot up with Jackson and Caleb breathing down my neck, and after several days of reflecting and recovering, I didn't feel the need to.

I lost myself today. Dozens of suicidal thoughts were trying to persuade me to give in and give up, but I had realized that wouldn't solve anything. It wouldn't change a single thing going on in the world; it would only bring despair and sadness to those I loved.

I had a real chance to live now. I wanted a family with Jackson—one that included Grace and this new baby, if it had somehow survived today. I was going to fight for our relationship, no matter what it took. I'd now been given a millionth chance, and I was determined to make the most of it, even if we weren't certain of the extent of my miraculous healing.

After Keith drew more samples of blood, we returned to our dorms to breathe—Sophie and Caleb together in her room, and Jackson, Grace and I in ours.

Grace soon fell asleep in her crib, and silence descended on the room. Neither of us knew what to say; it was like we were both nervous of the other.

I was still ashamed of everything that happened between me and Gage, and especially embarrassed that Jackson had found out in front of everyone. I can't imagine how he must've felt. It was humiliating for both of us, but I deserved it; he didn't.

He finally mustered up the courage to speak, looking down at his shaking hands. "Sammi, when I saw Caleb carrying your body to the lab, I felt the world collapse around me. Worse than any collapse from an apocalypse. I'd learned what it felt like to lose the last bit of hope and sanity a person could have. I wasn't sure if you were okay or if you ever would be okay, and in that moment, the earth did stop spinning."

"I'm so sorry for everything I've put you through," I cried.

But when my eyes met his, I could see that the light in his eyes had returned. It was something I never wanted him to lose again. He was such a kind, beautiful soul that deserved every ounce of grace and love in this shithole world.

I halfway expected him to say something mean or hurtful about what happened with Gage, but he never mentioned it. He just stared at me with his sweet, forgiving eyes, and simply said, "It's okay," even though I knew it wasn't.

He had every reason not to forgive me or show me any sympathy, yet he'd done both of those things endlessly in our relationship and in this life with me. He'd shown me the grace I needed to show myself. I felt as if a weight had been lifted off my shoulders, my chest, my heart. That moment freed me.

I gave him a smile, and he took a deep breath. "Can I read you something?" he asked.

I nodded, and he pulled a crumpled piece of paper from his pocket. He unfolded it before nervously rubbing his sweaty palm on his thigh.

"My whole life I thought my eyes were what let me see.
I thought every lock required a key.
I thought every day needed night, and every star had to be bright.
But lately I've realized that none of that is true.
At the end of the day, all I need is you.
It doesn't matter if the winter brings snow, or if spring flowers grow.
I just know that my whole life I thought my eyes were what let me see,
But then I met you, and you changed "me" to "we."
With you by my side, happy is all I'll ever be.
So, Samantha Jane Peters, will you marry me?"

He pulled a small velvet box from his back pocket before revealing the most beautiful ring I'd ever seen.

I smiled like an idiot before giving him an intimate kiss on the lips, feeling his warm cheeks under the palms of my hands. I pressed my forehead against his before saying, "I love you more than anything, Jackson. Yes, I will marry you."

Together we laughed and smiled between a dozen more kisses, then I held my hand out for him to slip the ring onto my finger, at which point I finally got to admire how intricate and stunning the ring was. It was silver with a round halo, and in the center there was a red rose protected by a clear coat of resin. It was handcrafted with nothing but pure love.

It was perfect.

"I got Caleb to help me make it." He blushed. "I preserved the rose I brought you from the field of wildflowers the day I read you my first poem. I knew there was a reason it stuck out; it brought you back to me when you told me you loved me. So, I held on to it. I knew exactly what I needed to do with it," he said sweetly.

"It's gorgeous, Jackson. I love everything about it," I said, admiring its beauty.

He brushed the hair from my face, and we cherished this happy moment all evening.

❧

The next morning, Keith invited us all back to the lab to discuss his findings and to reevaluate my condition. Sophie volunteered to stay back and watch Grace, which magnified my suspicion that something was going on.

I was almost afraid to find out what. I wouldn't be able to fully accept this victory until I made sure everything was okay with her. She played a huge part in all of this, and that would never go unnoticed. So it was important that she was safe and okay too.

Once we reached the lab, Jackson helped me to my seat, grabbing the crutches from me and leaving a soft kiss on my cheek. Caleb smiled once he noticed the ring was on my hand.

Keith grabbed his clipboard and stood before us with an eager expression. "It truly is amazing that Sammi survived everything," he began. "When I compared the blood samples, it was remarkable. Sammi had a part of her brain that was wired like a zombie from the infection mutating inside of her body. It gave her seizures; it gave her sight into the world they control. When she died, it gave her body a taste of becoming a zombie before fully taking over. We gave her the substance, and in the process, we also brought her back to life. All of those moving parts allowed us to trick her mind into believing the zombie portion of her brain was what died, while bringing her human mind completely back to life."

"So I don't have the infection anymore?"

He grinned devilishly. "You control the infection."

I looked over at Jackson and then back to Keith in a confused manner. "What do you mean?"

"My formula, mixed with Grace's blood and added to your blood, reinvented the infection. Meaning not only are you immune to the bite of a zombie and the infection, but your blood is toxic to them and can cure others who have been bitten."

"Oh my God," I whispered. "How do you know for sure?"

"I gave a small portion of your blood to a zombie. It wasn't immediate, but it eventually died. It's almost like when a honey bee dies after stinging someone. The zombie bites, it dies."

"And as far as it being a cure?" I asked, narrowing my eyes.

"I gave it to someone staying on campus who was bitten. I went back to check on them several hours later when they theoretically should've died, but they were as good as new."

I swallowed the lump in my throat, thinking of the girls he had trapped in his dormitory. Were they his test subjects?

For the sake of the moment, I decided not to instigate any issues until I'd gotten the chance to talk to Sophie. I kept my mouth shut, looking down at my flat stomach as I worried about whether or not the baby had survived my brief visit with death.

For now, I chose to appreciate this win, and the three of us returned to the dorms, celebratory with the news Keith had given us.

I hung around the room with Jackson for quite a while before I decided to go talk to Sophie. But when I stepped into the hallway, I could hear her crying and talking to Caleb. I listened carefully from right outside the door.

"I had to sell my soul to the devil to get this cure for Sammi. I wanted her to live. I wanted Grace to have a mother. I wanted you to have your sister. I wanted Jackson to have the love of his life, and I wanted to have my best friend. I need you to understand that," she pleaded from inside their room.

"I'm going to kill him. I'm going to fucking kill him," Caleb said angrily. It sounded like he was pacing back and forth. "We could've found another way, Sophie. We could've handled this."

"We were running out of time," she cried in frustration.

At that point, Caleb had swung the door open, revealing me eavesdropping in the hallway.

"What's going on?" I asked worriedly.

"Keith! H-he preyed on Sophie. He raped her like he's been raping those poor girls in his dormitory for God knows how long! We don't need him anymore. We've got to end this, right now," Caleb said as Jackson joined in on the commotion, hearing all that was said.

"What are you going to do? Shoot him?" I asked as the two of them prepared to leave.

"No, he doesn't deserve to get off that easy," Caleb seethed. They began walking toward the elevator.

"Caleb!" I yelled, and he turned to look at me. "When you make the decision to kill someone, it changes you. Once you do it, you can't take it back."

"People like Keith don't deserve to live in this world. Dillion and his friends didn't deserve to live in this world. The world became a better place after we killed them, and it will continue to become a better place without Keith in it."

I didn't argue, I just begged them to be careful. Once they'd gone, I entered Sophie's room to check on her. She was lying in bed, buried underneath her covers while she sobbed into the sheets. I climbed in beside her, offering her a shoulder to cry on and brushing her hair back gently with my hands as she wept.

I couldn't help but continuously feel responsible for the cruel presents given to us by this world.

As they later told us, Caleb and Jackson found Keith in his dormitory room before dragging him to a nearby closet, where they trapped him inside with a zombie they captured from the courtyard. They listened as it ripped the skin from his bones, exposing his insides for the zombie to feast on.

There was some sort of poetry in killing the man who saved your life.

Keith was one of those people that were made for this new world. Someone dark, twisted, and diabolical that fit right into the narrative of this ungoverned, dystopian shithole.

Those people were what would keep us from rebuilding society, so they needed to die with the apocalyptic world—because we held the ability to change everything.

30

EPILOGUE

One year later

"Dada. Dada!" Grace babbled from her highchair.

Jackson took a seat beside her with a bowl of applesauce. He playfully gave her tiny bites, accompanied by silly airplane noises.

I smiled to myself, appreciating the precious moments I'd gotten to experience the last several months with this little family of mine, especially after I gave birth to a beautiful baby boy that we named Jacob. Jackson and I were the happiest we'd ever been.

We'd found a quaint, tucked away town—Ash Grove, Missouri—relatively untouched from the dead of the world. There was a beautiful townhome within one of the neighborhoods that we decided to move into, sharing the other side with Caleb and Sophie. We wanted to find something with a more authentic normalcy that reminded us of the pre-apocalyptic world, and this was definitely it.

It was just the six of us in this little neighborhood, navigating through our past traumas and finding a way to cope and move forward in a positive way. We all finally felt like we could breathe again.

After Keith's death at the lab, Caleb and Jackson went to the dorm to release the girls he'd kept locked up. But it became evident that after using them for sexual pleasure for months, he started using them as test subjects. It appeared that he knew he was about to be outed as a sociopathic pedophile, so he'd killed anyone who could've exposed him for what he was—except Sophie.

Still, there was justice in his death. He'd never be able to hurt anyone again. But he'd also never be able to share his formula for the cure. I guess it didn't really matter, since he'd turned me into a hypothetical blood bank for anyone in need.

I was going to keep that a secret from anyone outside of our home for now, though. I had a life of my own to live. I was happy. I finally felt like I had a place in this world.

Jackson and I had an unofficial wedding ceremony after my leg healed, and it was everything I'd ever wanted. He was a great husband and an even better father to both Jacob and Grace, who was now calling him "Dada."

I found peace in knowing Bailey would have approved of who I was today, and the man filling the shoes of a father figure for Grace. One day I'll be able to tell her all about her father and how he loved her. She'll be able to imagine what it was like to know and love him.

I couldn't wait to watch my children grow up. I could imagine Grace with my attitude and Jacob with his daddy's kind heart. I could see Grace growing up to be a beautiful butterfly, not afraid of the world around her. I could see Jacob copying everything Jackson did, because he'd want to be just like him. I could see it in all colors—I could finally see the world how Jackson did.

If you'd told me two years ago that I'd be married with two kids in the middle of a zombie apocalypse, I would've called you insane a million times over. But here I was, embracing it.

Two summers ago, the world went to shit—and it changed me in more ways than one. But if it hadn't gone to shit, I don't think I'd be anywhere close to the woman I am today.

So, fuck you, world—I'm doing the damn thing.

www.ingramcontent.com/pod-product-compliance
Lightning Source LLC
Chambersburg PA
CBHW030627310726
48979CB00003B/916